THE RANKS

V. ASHTHORN

MILTON & HUGO L.L.C.
1001 3rd Avenue West, Suite 430
Bradenton, FL 34205, USA

Website: *www. miltonandhugo.com*
Hotline: *1- 888-778-0033*
Email: *info@miltonandhugo.com*

Ordering Information:
Quantity sales. Special discounts are granted to corporations, associations, and other organizations. For more information on these discounts, please reach out to the publisher using the contact information provided above.

Library of Congress Control Number:		2026901797
ISBN-13:	979-8-89285-789-5	[Paperback Edition]
	979-8-89285-783-3	[Digital Edition]

Rev. date: 01/05/2026

This book is dedicated to my late grandparents.
Also a huge thanks to my friends for reading through
this mess of a story.

Please enjoy this book that I dedicated nearly four years to.

Prologue

In a faraway land only existing to the frame of imagination is the home to three magical kingdoms. The kingdoms each have their own rulers specified to their needs. The first kingdom is the Mycologia kingdom, these mushrooms live underwater and are a very stable kingdom. The mushrooms of the Mycologia kingdom are all assigned jobs to keep the peace within their kingdom, which they don't fight against.

The second kingdom is the Pyromania kingdom. This kingdom is constantly under fire quite literally. The people of the pyromania kingdom are practically slaves to their king's and queen's, abiding to everything they ordered no matter what. It doesn't help that their royalty tends to be *quiet* the needy as well.

The third kingdom is the kingdom this story is about, the kingdom of Equilibrium. The mushrooms within Equilibrium all have ranks depending on the colour of their mushrooms. Most are ranked by their talents that are associated with their colour. Others are unknown but those who aren't known for a talent are ranked lower. The kingdom isn't in a horrible condition, but in the areas that aren't taxed correctly it's very unfair and dangerous. Many things go on within the kingdom but they keep it under wraps and concealed. They are also very closed off, they have nothing to do with the Pyromaine or Mycolgian kingdoms.

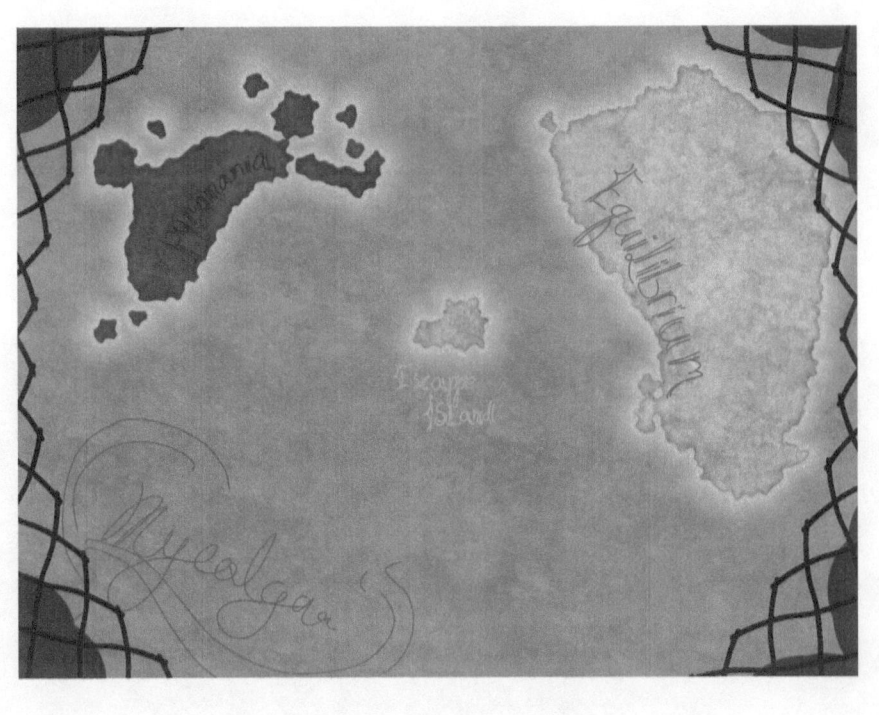

The Equilibrium Mushroom

The Female Mushroom

The Male mushroom

Chapter 1. The Daughter

I sat there silently, poking at my food with my fork, not interested in eating at the moment. I picked up a piece of the vegetables with my fork and examined it closely before taking a bite.

"Oh for god's sake Magdolin stop acting like it's poison." My father's voice rang through the huge dining room of the castle.

"Sorry father," I said, returning to my food and eating what was left on my plate and kept my gaze down waiting to be excused.

I was sick of living in this castle stuck here all day every day of my life. Father said it was too dangerous for me to roam the kingdom, so I was stuck here.

As my mother finished eating my father excused her, leaving just him and I in the large room alone.

"Magdolin, we need to speak." My father spoke in a low demeanor. In the kind of tone that would make a small child concerned.

"Yes father?" I mumbled under my breath.

"You are nineteen. It is time, you must marry someone. I have two young mushrooms you are going to choose from, they are wealthy, will keep you happy and the kingdom at peace. Even though they are not purple they are still fine young men." My father spoke to me dimly.

"But..., but father we can not mix colours. It is against your own word, my child wouldn't have a good start to li-" I spoke, but my father cut me off.

"You think I don't know that Magdolin? This kingdom is at stake though," My father shouted at me in a strong tone echoing through the huge room. "You will do as I say and choose one of them. Be grateful I'm even giving you a choice because I know which of them I want you to marry." He growled again as I composed myself from speaking back to him.

"Yes father." I said as I stood and pulled the skirt of my dress out from under the table and held it in front of me as I walked out of the dining room.

I didn't like how the dress drug the ground as I walked. I couldn't wait until I returned to my room to change into my evening wear.

As I entered my room I saw Natalia, my maid and bestfriend, sitting on the seat of my chest that sat at the end of my bed. I then went behind the curtain drapery and changed out of my dress, requesting Natalia's help to undo my corset. I then slid on my knee length nightgown. I especially loved this nightgown. It was pure white silk and not dyed purple like all of our other clothing. I wanted to have other colours of clothes, rather than just white and purple. I saw Natalia's long floor length dress that matched her navy blue mushroom head. I envied her having that freedom and she knew it.

"Oh Maggie, how do you do it everyday, just being stuck here?" Natalia said as she gently ran water through my hair and followed it with soap and then more water. I didn't stand it here, i was about to lose my mind. I didn't want to marry anyone, this was the most idiotic thing ever, im only nineteen and I definitely don't want a husband anytime soon. At least a husband I can't decide on, I know whoever I end up with will be some stick up there ass prick.

"Oh Nat, you know I can barely stand it, I'd much rather be in your shoes." I spoke in a moderate tone with no forward feelings to the statement.

"Well I spoke to a fellow about our age I think you would've liked." Natalia spoke in a sly tone almost as if she was mocking me.

"Oh really, thank you for reminding me of my crippling loneliness." I groaned

"Well I mean I may be able to let you meet him, maybe..." She paused for a moment before speaking again. "...Maybe finally get you out of this palace."

I stopped braiding my hair for a moment and quickly turned to face Natalia. "What did you say?" I asked quickly.

Natalia quickly ran to my side putting her mouth to my ear whispering. "Listen, there is a mushroom who is willing to help you escape. It is his profession, to get mushrooms out of their homes and run away. They will take you to an island off the coast of the mainland. You will be free of your duties there, you just need to move fast and you cannot come back if you do this." She spoke this all at a tone I barely heard.

I looked at Natalia with a wide eyed stare. "Are you serious Nat?" I asked breathlessly. A chance at freedom would be something I'd grasp at a moment's break.

Natalia looked at me with a serious face not moving an inch, I understood she was serious. Her deep navy eyes were all that I could see in her stern look.

I didn't like my life in the palace at all. I was trapped and I wasn't allowed to do anything. But did I really want to leave forever? My mother didn't care that much for me and my father only saw me as his own blood. Natalia picked up my hair and finished braiding it the rest of the way.

"...You are a very messy braider Maggie." Natalia spoke in a bright upbeat tone before leaning back down towards my ear. "The mushroom will be here tonight after dusk. It is your choice."

I pondered for a few moments, still shocked from all of this. Then a thought slammed into me like a wall

"Nat, what will you do? You're the princess's maid, you are only here for me. They will instantly accuse you of my disappearance!" I whispered, peering up at her.

Natalia cut me off. "No they won't, we have this completely covered up. I'll stay here and make sure it stays covered up so you can be free."

"But you're my best friend. I can't leave you behind here. I don't want to leave you. You're the only one who ever heard me out and listened to me." I started to sob.

3

"I'll be fine, I want you to be free of this place." Natalia spoke with a calm gentle voice.

I wrapped Natalia in a tight embrace. I could never ask for a better companion. "I will go, but I will do my best to come back for you, I promise." I rasped, starting to cry into Natalia's shoulder.

"No. No, that's the one thing you can not do. You can't return here." Natalia said in a stern voice. I looked at Natalia's stricken face and knew her seriousness. I nodded my head and held her even closer to me. "We need to get you prepared ok, I made you something specifically for this but you can't take much with you." Natalia spoke in a lighter tone and then walked over to the large wood dresser in my room. She pulled out a short knee length dress that had a purple bodice and white skirt with designs on it. She then followed the dress with what almost looked like an apron but was meant to be a waistcoat and a pair of knee high boots.

I was surprised by this. My dress code was always a floor length dress besides night time apparel.

She handed me the dress and accessories to try on. I put the dress on swiftly because it had no corset and Natalia tied the waist coat around me as I slid on the boots.

As I looked in the large mirror I felt a sense of confidence, I felt like I was ready to go, I was ready to be free. Natalia then picked up my dagger and sheath, the dagger has been passed down for hundreds of generations and it is fit for only the toughest of fighters. Natalia slipped it into a small pocket on the side of the waist coat.

I wrapped Natalia in a tight embrace once more as she spoke. "You can't take much more than what you have on now ok, this man has almost anything you'll need."

I nodded my head yes in agreement before turning to the small desk in the corner of the room.

"We must hurry Maggie, so choose wisely and quickly." Natalia spoke as she watched the sun set.

I looked over my cabinet and grabbed a tube of luxury lipstick my mother had given me. If I was leaving I wanted to take something that reminded me of my home.

Natalia, without hesitation, grabbed my wrist and pulled the door of my room open, gently and silently. We then quickly made our way through the corridors and rooms, passing through empty halls that hadn't been opened in years. We made it to the north wing of the palace, this wing was normally always empty, besides the guards that watched the hollow halls and such.

As we passed through the corridors all of the guards looked away from us and down at their feet. I looked at Natalia as she whispered. "I have paid them off to see nothing".

I couldn't believe how she had planned all of this out, by now it was night and we had reached the end of the north wing and ended up in a huge empty room.

Chapter 2. The Escape

I stood in the open room full of dust and old furniture that hadn't been cleaned in ages. Natalia slowly opened one of the large doors that has a small terrace on it with lots of vines and other plants dangling down. As she waved me over and pointed down at the small cart at the bottom of the palace I felt my eyes start to tear up. I looked at Natalia and embraced her again once more. She pulled away and nodded gently, crying a little bit as she walked me over to the window. Outside were some sturdy looking vines that had engraved themselves into the brick wall of the palace. We were many stories up at this point, maybe one hundred feet off the ground. As I started scaling down the palace wall I felt the gentle breeze of the cool night air.

I continued down the side of the wall, curious to who was going to be guiding me to this safe land. As I reached about thirty feet from the ground I felt the vines in my feet and hands start to crumble. I felt my body weight start to plummet for the ground.

This is it. This is how the princess dies, trying to escape and falls to her death! I thought to myself, wishing I had just stayed in my room. I felt the ground nearing closer and closer and felt myself give up. But before I reached the ground I felt a pair of arms wrap around my torso, I felt my body crash into another body right before I hit the ground.

"Are you alright?" I heard a male's voice say. He looked to be close to my age. I felt him as he picked me up more and onto my feet. "Are you alright ma'am?"

"Huh… oh yes I'm fine." I said as the mushroom held me up by my arms and then gently let go and backed away.

"Are you Magdolin?" he said gently and turned to the cart. I was just now readjusting my eyes in the dark as I felt a warm glow and saw a dim green glow coming from the cap of the males mushroom. I looked up in astonishment, this was a poison mushroom.

I looked at him silent with my mouth slightly agape. "Y-yes." I stuttered out.

"Great, I'm assuming you're named after the princess?" he said quickly as he let down the tail gate of the small trailer that was pulled behind the horses.

"You could say that." I said quietly before he picked me up and set me in the bed of hay in his cart.

He then gently threw a blanket over me and covered the blanket with hay. "Ok, try and just sleep through this and don't get out from under there. I have to hide you till we get out of town, I'm sure the palace will be looking for one of their workers." The male said as he hopped in the front of the cart and took off.

Workers? I thought to myself. *This guy is a bit weird.*

·• ⊰≓⊱• •·

I felt myself dozing off laying in the hay and I slept through most of the night, waking up occasionally to rough roads and what not. After about a four hour trip by horse I felt the cart come to a halt, jerking everything in it forward. I heard the back of the tail gate open and the male's voice again. "You can come out now. I'm sure we're out of their searching perimeters."

"Thank the lords above." I said quietly as I dug my hands through the hay around me and cleared it out of my way.

I poked my head out finally getting a breath of fresh air, and finally getting a good look at the mushroom. I was correct this was a poison mushroom, he had longer dark brown hair that rested halfway between his shoulder and chin in waves. Green eyes, and a slightly darker skin complexion to match. His face had a boxy shape and a little bit of an unshaven stubble here and there. He had a tall stance and a wide frame.

I took note of his ragged looking undershirt and small aristocrat vest that was unbuttoned and barely reached his waist. Along with some black slacks and a small waist satchel. He was handsome nonetheless, but I presumed it just helped him get away with things.

After I took note of his appearance I asked politely. "May I know your name?"

"Alexander, my name is Alexander, it's a pleasure to meet you. I do have to admit I have a question for you though, why was a maid wanting out of the palace this bad?" He spoke, cocking his head in curiosity.

"Why do you presume I'm a maid?" I asked again, sitting me up in the hay as the blanket still covered my head and most of my body.

"I'm assuming that's what you are right? A maid?" He said, slightly more agitated sounding because of his curiosity.

I looked at Alexander with a blank face and slowly shook my head no. I watched his face fill with confusion. He then noticed the purple bodice on my dress and his face slowly went pale. He reached up and pulled at the blanket, revealing the light lavender hue of my mushroom.

Alexander pieced it together right at that moment.

"Oh my lord no yo- your, no no. Absolutely not. This is some joke right? You are not the princess. You can't be." He said, rushed and slightly panicked with a hysterical laugh coating his voice.

"I-I am." I said quietly, not wanting to make it a big deal.

Alexander looked at me with a wide eyed expression and began walking in circles murmuring to himself.

"Oh my god I'm gonna die they'll look for you forever. They're going to hang me!" He said as he grabbed his neck. I stood up off the cart and hopped down and approached Alexander.

I laid my hand on his shoulder. "Alexander everything's going to be alright-"

He cut me off. "Everything will be alright for YOU, not me. I will be hung and tortured. I'm going to be blamed for this. You would go back to your pampered little castle life." He said harshly

I felt my heart sink at Alexander's cruel demeanour towards me. I slowly backed away and sat back down on the tail gate of the cart and looked at my hands. Alexander turned his head around quickly and ran over to me on his knees.

"My lady -er- uh I mean, your majesty, please forgive me I didn't mean to be rude I'm just very lost in what to do."

"Don't call me that. My name is Magdolin," I said quietly and calmly. "I understand if you don't want to continue this. I'm sure I can find my own way. I can already see what a burden I am." I said, giving Alexander the chance to not have to do this.

"You'll die or get captured, one or the other. I can't let you go alone," He said, burying his face in his hands. He stood in front of me and sighed deeply. "We have about twelve hours of light to make it out of this area. We need to keep moving, you can either sit up front in the front of the cart or in the back. I don't care which one you choose." He said as he started walking towards a box and pulling out some carrots for his horses.

I walked towards the two large horses and gently ran my hand through the white mare's hair. The mare's hair was braided back in an intricate way. It was beautiful. I examined the horses carefully, I had never been this close to one before. I petted the white mare's soft nose and watched as she calmly closed her eyes. "That's serenity. She's a big love bug." Alexander said aloud as I continued petting on the horse.

Once the horses were fed we jumped in the front of the cart on the little bench-like seat. Alexander turned his head to me and sighed as he stood up again. He pulled out a large bonnet looking hat and handed it to me.

"You wish for me to wear this?" I said to him to see if he was serious.

"Yes. We are going to be going through a few different towns today. The last thing I need is for some mushroom to recognize you."

I slid the bonnet on and tied the two ribbons under my chin. I felt stupid with it on but I knew it was for the best. When the cart took off I felt the jerk of the reins tighten as the horses trotted forward. I watched the trees as we rode by them in all the different colours of the fall. The feeling was calming, the wind and cool air filling my lungs. This was the first time I had been outside like this in years.

Chapter 3. Alexander Malencoy

I felt my hands grip around the reigns of my horse as they slowly trotted along. I had special personnel in the cart now and I knew if I did or said anything wrong she'd order to have my head chopped off. Everything is tense in my head. I can barely think straight to remember where the first safe house is. I was so stressed yet she is so calm sitting there watching all the trees and wildlife. How is she so calm?

We rode until the sun was setting by that time we were close to my safe house. When we arrived I pulled the cart around the house and tied the horses to a post for the night and gave them food and water. I then walked to the side of the cart where the princess sat on the bench still.

"Your majesty," I said as I held out my hand to help her down.

"Please just call me Magdolin. I'm not as uptight as my parents." She said gently as she took my hand and stepped down.

Her hand was soft and small, her nails were filed down nicely as well. She must've been used like a baby doll back in the palace; it appeared as if she had never even been outside. She had her hair nicely brushed out and her skin was perfect and smooth. She had a dainty walk and long pretty legs. I didn't let my eyes wander too long though fearing she'd notice.

I opened the door to the small two room cottage, as the door creaked open a smell of dust and such hit the both of us.

"I'm sorry it's not the best out of the safe houses, but it was the only one we could make it to tonight." I said fearing it wouldn't be good enough for her.

She then brushed past me and walked over to the small cots in the corner of the room. She started brushing off dust and picked up the mattresses off them and took them outside to get the nasty off of them.

"No Princess, let me do that." I said as I ran to her trying to take the small thin mattresses from her. All I got in return was a small smack on my wrist.

"I have this, don't worry, you are doing me a favour, it is the least I can do." She said in a quiet but audible voice as she shook out the mattresses and took them back inside.

She neatly put the mattresses back down and then walked around the small kitchenette and into the small back room, it was full of old junk that hasn't been touched in years. "Is there not a washroom?" Magdolin asked quietly.

"No, I'm sorry princess. I don't have one in this house." I said in a quiet disposition back to her. "There is a creek bay out back if you are wanting to rinse off."

What the hell is a washroom? Somewhere to bathe?

"I'm sure I could find you something else to wear somewhere around here" I said in reply to that.

"A bath in a dirty creek?" She said, slightly confused.

"It's not really dirty, actually creeks are clean, there all moving water, and look!" I walked over to Magdolin and held up my arms. "I don't smell bad at all!" I said trying to bring light into my situation. I felt an extreme amount of embarrassment as she just looked up at me blankly.

Magdolin looked up at me with a slightly confused face before cracking a small smile. "I assume it wouldn't hurt to try it?" she said in agreement.

I felt a sigh of relief exit my body before I turned to look outside. The sun was still setting so we had time. I walked to the small back room and pulled out a small bottle that had hair wash etched into the glass bottle. I then pulled out the bar of body soap and handed them to Magdolin. She looked at me with the same small smile and kind of emotionless. I looked over at a large crate that was locked shut, before I had even though I grabbed my keys and began trying all of them to unlock it.

The lock then popped open and the lid swung up. A few pictures fell out of the crate as it opened. I then saw what I wanted to grab, a dim gold and black dress folded up nicely on the top of the other items in the crate. I pulled out the dress and quickly grabbed all the other pictures that had fallen out and stuffed them in the crate, hoping Magdolin hadn't looked at many of them.

I hate this entire crate, I need to get rid of it.

I stood up and held the dress up and compared it to Magdolin. "Will this work for you?" I asked as she took the dress from my hands. Her eyes were full of amazement at the dress. I watched her smile grow as she examined the dress.

"Yes, it's beautiful," she said looking up from the dress.

"I'm glad you like it, Your Highness." She looked at me as I said that.

"Please just call me Magdolin, or Maggie. Don't call me something that I'm not anymore." I was slightly shocked at her saying that. I'd think she'd want to be known as a princess.

But she was running away after all, so I agreed. "Yes Magdolin I'll try my hardest."

"Thank you." she spoke in her quiet tone of voice. I looked out the window again checking the suns set.

"Welp, we better get you down to the creek before it gets too dark," I said, leading Magdolin out of the house and behind it towards the creek.

⋯•◁ ᕤ ᕤ ▷•⋯

"Ok, look out into the entrance, do you see that set of rocks?" I said pointing at a small circle or rocks.

"Yes, I do," She said in reply, looking around, gently turning her head in every direction.

"Ok, that's the bath ring. Set your dress on the shore so it doesn't get soaked. Then you undress on the shore. I'll take your dress you have on and wash it, then you go out in the circle, bathe, then wrap the towel around you and come back to shore and put your dress on okay?" I said trying not to sound weird but failed. I mean she's a full grown mushroom who's never bathed on her own, of course it's weird.

12

"Ok, thank you." she said quietly as she walked down the grass and into the sandy shore of the small creek.

I headed back towards the house as she bathed I laid down on one of the small cots and silently dozed off

Chapter 4. Magdolin Poni

As I stepped into the cold creek I felt the presence of being completely alone, just me and the woods. The water was cold but not frigid yet. I sank down to my chin, the more I walked into the circle of rocks, I could still stand but barely. I quickly got done and out of there I washed my hair fast and body.

I felt my skin fill with needles when my body left the water. I wrapped the towel around me fast and dried off and slid the dress on.

I started walking towards the house with my other dress in my hand. The floorboards creaked as I stepped onto the covered porch. I gently opened the door to the house and walked in. It was getting cold outside and the house was colder. I looked around and saw the fireplace and some small stacks of wood. I walked over and prepared myself to light the fire.

I sat crouched down for some minutes struggling to get a spark or anything. I felt a pair of warm hands take the two small pieces of flint from my hands. I saw them clash together and make the wood burst into flames.

"There you go princes-err Magdolin I mean." A soft, groggy voice said in reply to the actions.

"Thank you." I said, taking in the warmth of the flames. Soon the whole room was warm and had a calming dim light. Alexander had already fallen back asleep before I headed off to bed. I laid down on the small cot and tried to drift asleep.

Alexander seemed very nice. Maybe just a little anxious, hopefully his nerves would calm more. Even if he has settled after a few hours, that first outburst when we first met stuck with me.

It would make it much easier and better if we both would agree to not be nervous and get this whole trip over with then we would split ways and never have to speak again.

·• ⪦⪥ •··

I shot awake a few hours later. It was pitch black outside, nothing but the moon shown. There was a high pitched scream coming from outside. Alexander shot up soon after I did. I jerked my head around to look at him. His face was full of worry and concern, he jumped up and grabbed a large pipe that was on a small table and ran out the front door.

I got a shot of adrenaline, something told me this was bad, horrible. I needed to act, I'm the one with magic. All Alexander has to defend us is… well, he's a poison mushroom. *So poison?*

I stood up and grabbed my dagger and ran outside to see what was happening. When I stepped outside a warm wretched odor hit me, it smelled as if death had a child. Alexander was standing at the edge of the porch with a look of horror.

"What is-" I was cut off. Alexander threw his hand over my mouth.

A creature with long hair was standing in front of the house smelling the ground like a dog. But the creature was huge; it had to be at least eight feet tall. It had long limbs and was acting almost like a wild animal. It let out a loud ear piercing screech that caused Alexander and I to both tumble to our knees grabbing our ears. At the sound of us hitting the ground the beast ran towards us. I felt it's nasty breath run over my whole body.

I stayed motionless as Alexander grabbed my wrist so tight I thought I'd lose my hand. The beast moved its head from me to Alexander next. The beast was inches from Alexander's face. His eyes were wide with panic and fear. That's when I took charge.

I slowly crept up to my feet while the beast was on top of Alexander. I ran across the porch and off to a tree in the yard. I watched the creature as it closely examined Alexander. The beast's mouth then slowly started to crack its mouth open and I heard a small but audible noise of worry come from Alexander. I pulled my dagger out and started beating on the tree next to me trying to make as much noise as possible.

The creature turned fast and started running towards me. In the few moments I had I remembered what my father had shown me. I focused all my blood into my wrists and made the dagger grow.

The dagger shot from a small seven inch blade to a full length sword. I jumped and took a few steps up the tree. I rotated my body around and met the beast mid air. Right now I was so happy that I paid attention in those stupid aerobic classes I had to attend for my flexibility.

I hurled the sword around my body gaining momentum and swung hard at the beast.

I felt the blade of my sword dig into the side of the beast. Its cry was ear piercing as it ran off into the dark of the night.

My sword then returned to its small dagger form as I turned to see Alexander on the porch his mouth still agape.

"What was that creature?" I asked, cocking my head to the side out of curiosity.

"Better question, how does the princess know how to do things like THAT!" Alexander said, throwing his hands up in the air dramatically.

"My whole family is a span of great fighters." I said with a small smile. I was secretly proud of how I fought, even though I don't amount to my father.

"So you don't know what that creature was?" I added to Alexander as I walked toward the house. "Why didn't you use your poison though? That would've been much easier," I added looking up at him.

"No you- Magdolin I don't." he said, correcting himself and locking the door. "And that's all just a folk tale, it's not true," he added with a grimace.

"Alright then," I said slightly ashamed. As I sat back down on the cot resting my head gently against the thin mattress once again. It was rude of me to say, poison mushrooms aren't favoured for their abilities.

But what if he was right, what if he wasn't deadly? What if I was deadlier than him?!

It was true that my skin didn't melt when he touched me.

Shit, why must I feel like this?

As I slept I could hear Alexander rummaging throughout the house digging through boxes and such. But it stopped eventually and it fell silent again.

·• ⧼≡≡⧽ •·

As the sun started to rise I began to wake up, I sat up in the cot and looked about the room. Alexander had fallen asleep sitting upright in his bed crouched over a small book. My curiosity got the best of me as I leaned over to look at the small black book in his lap. The book had a very detailed drawing of the beast screaming in pain and what appeared to be me next to it as I gauged it with my dagger. There was very little writing underneath it, it had to be at least a paragraph.

Before I could begin reading he started to wake up. I looked away awkwardly as Alexander looked at me drowsily.

"What are you looking at…" he said in a tiered voice.

"Nothing, I'm sorry."

He looked down at the book in his lap and quickly closed it and shoved it into his side satchel.

"I didn't see anything I promise." I said quickly to his fast response.

"No no it's fine I just don't want anyone seeing that book." He said with urgency in his voice. I was curious now to what was in the book, recipes? A family pass down book? It all sparked my curiosity.

"I understand," I said while scooting towards my small cot.

I settled down and gently brushed through my hair with my fingers to get it slightly straightened out. I then braided my hair into a janky loose braid.

Darnnit natalia always used to do my hair. I thought to myself.

"You're not very good at that," Alexander said, standing up and situating his belt on his waist.

"Oh hush it." I said with a smile as I slid on my boots and folded my dress next to me.

"You should let me do your hair some time. I'm surprisingly good at it, Miss Magdolin." He said as he held out a hand to help me off the ground.

"Charming, but playful banter isn't how you win me over sir Alexander." I said as I stood up on my own with a sly smile. Many of many males had tried such things like that in the castle.

"Oh but who said I was trying to win you over Miss? Who said I'm not married?" He said, stepping back.

"The absence of a ring on your marital hand tells me." I said as I walked past him.

Chapter 5. Escaping the Trenches

I watched as she walked straight out the door to the wagon. *She didn't even let me help her up!* I thought to myself. Not that it matters I guess, it's not like I was making *advances* on her. Or was I?!

Oh god that is what it sounded like.

I quickly grabbed all my stuff and headed for the wagon. As I sat down on the wagon and began turning the horses around to face the path, there was an awkward silence. I turned to look at Magdolin and she was gazing up at the sky through the thick woods. I noticed then that she didn't have the bonnet on, and as a wave of fear ran over me, I halted the horses in a tight jerky motion.

"I'll be right back." I said as I took off running back into the house. I grabbed the bonnet and ran quickly back to the wagon, not noticing that Magdolin had scooted over to look around the wagon, I ran into her.

I grabbed her upper arms to prevent her from falling. "Oh my lord I'm so sorry Princess- Magdolin I'm so sorry." I said as I looked down at her only to see her break a smile then a laugh.

Is she... laughing? I thought to myself, I couldn't help but smile at the sight as I stood her back up.

"No no, It's quite alright I should've stayed where I was, Alexander." she said as she stopped laughing.

"Well I went and grabbed your bonnet. We're going through some towns so you'll want it." I said, handing her the bonnet as we loaded back into the wagon.

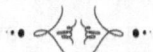

We drove for hours through the day only stopping for food and water and using the lavatory. Magdolin seemed to like the road anytime we'd cross an animal or something new she hadn't seen before. She'd jump and practically lean over the wagon front to get closer.

"That is a very odd cat." she said, pointing at a street cat.

"That's a street cat and that one's been in a few fights. See, it's missing an ear and a leg, they aren't taken care of out here." I said in response to her.

She looked up at me with a look of surprise and worry. "What? Why aren't they?"

"They don't have owners and they're mean cruel animals they fight and scratch and hiss at you." I said looking at her with a look of disappointment, she hadn't even been out to see a cat on the streets.

She looked at me with a look of stubbornness as she stood up in the wagon and darted off.

"Hey! Come back here!" I said with worry I didn't know where she was going. I watched as she slowly approached the disabled cat and as she got closer it hissed but it didn't seem to phase her.

I felt fear rush over me, she has basically never been hurt before she has no scars and flawless skin and this cat will tear her to shreds.

But suddenly my fear faded as the cat walked to her and into her arms. She then walked back to the wagon with the cat.

"Magdolin! You can't just run out like that and what if that cat just attacked you!" I said as she hushed me.

"Shh she's asleep." Magdolin said as she sat crisscrossed in the seat next to me with the cat in her lap.

I sighed and motioned the horses forward. It was impressive she could calm that cat that fast though I was very surprised. It actually wasn't very shocking that a cat isn't scared of her. Isn't that what fairytale states? The princess always is kind and attracts anything mean or cruel and can make it harmless?

"She's so mean and cruel and just wants to attack me for sure Alexander". She added, looking up at me with a small smile, rubbing in the fact I was wrong. I rolled my eyes and sighed looking at the grey cat in her arms. Besides the missing ear and leg it was a pretty thing I suppose.

The cat turned and fought in Magdolins arms after a while of her holding it. The cat darted off her lap and off the cart and I could see the disappointment in Magdolins eyes as she tried to stand up.

"Hey hey no that isn't your cat you can't keep it forever." I said, grabbing her shoulder to keep her from jumping off the wagon again.

She looked up at me with a sad expression as she sat back down. "Why are the cats left alone? Why does no one take care of them?"

I looked at her worried face and then spoke. "This isn't the best town Magdolin, the people here can barely keep their families alive, nevertheless a cat."

She cut me off then "lies you're lying, my father lived his life to keep the whole kingdom happy unlike the Pyromena people, he wouldn't tax this city if they were having hardships."

I looked at her with a sorrowful face. "Magdolin, your father is not a good king. I'm sorry to tell you that."

Her face was full of surprise, disgust, and a bit of confusion. "You're lying, all the servants and he himself told me all the great things he's done for everyone."

"Magdolin open your eyes please, he kept you locked in that palace your whole life and if he was so good, would I be sneaking people out illegally?" I said in a loud whisper.

"Well you're just getting them out because they don't want to work or… or pay taxes…t-the only reason I left was because I didn't want to be queen!" she stuttered out trying to find excuses.

"Are you really sure about that Magdolin" I said looking at her in her deep purple amethyst like eyes, I could see the weariness in them as she searched for an answer.

"I-… I don't know." she said, looking back at me. I brushed my hand across her face to push her gaze towards the other side of the road. There sat a family.

The family was clothed in flea-bitten rags and matted hair. They had not clearly showered in weeks. Her face dropped as she noticed them, and it got worse when she noticed their colour, reds, they were townsmen and merchants.

"What have they done? I'm sure they've done something horrible to deserve that type of punishment, their crooks, vandalists, something along that line!" She said looking back up at me.

"They've done nothing, they can't afford your father's ridiculous taxes and they barely make ends meet." I could see the tears start to well in her eyes

I felt sorry as soon as I started to see the tears drop from her eyes. I wrapped my right arm around her, pulling her close as she cried. She cried as I led the wagon outside of the town.

"So have I just been living a lie thinking my father was the good mushroom here?" She spoke in a crackled tone from crying. I looked down at her letting go of her and back onto the reign.

"I'm sorry Magdolin but you're right your father is not a good person at all."

She looked down at her lap for a few moments and a few more tears proceeded to fall to her hands. A few seconds later she wiped her face and looked up ahead of the wagon. "I should've known from how he treated me, his own daughter." She spoke with a more confident tone.

"May I ask what all he did to you besides leaving you in a palace forever?" I spoke, slightly curious to what she had seen and been through.

"He's always treated me as an object, like I'm something to be kept on a shelf. I may sound spoiled because I got anything I asked for but it had no meaning. It was nothing to my father to give it to me. He only looked at me as his predecessor to his crown, a predecessor that couldn't fit the role. The closest I've ever got to even going into town square was my practice fields." she spoke somberly as she told the small story.

"I think you could fit the role Magdolin you're stro-" She cut me off.

"To him I wasn't and he had to find someone better than me, someone better than his own blood. He had two men for me to choose between. I didn't want to marry them; they were most likely mean and cruel." She got more outraged as she spoke. "He never cared about my feelings, nevertheless the kingdoms, I told him I didn't want to marry because it's not allowed." I paused and looked at her a bit puzzled.

"Not allowed?" I asked, confused

"I don't have a love, I don't have a soulmate like how you do somewhere, you know why? because I'm going to be the last ever purple mushroom. The rest have all been killed off. I have no one waiting for me because of the rules made for the kingdom." She spoke in a somber tone. I looked at her with a shocked face and started to laugh slightly. She looked up at me with a scowl. "You don't seriously believe that's right Magdolin, right?" I said as her scowl faded to a confused look of anger. "Your soulmate is out there everyone has one you've just gotta find them, and honestly I call poppycock on your dads no mixing rule, so your soulmate could be out there with a white a pink a gold coloured mushroom who knows!"

"Alexander I could never, it's wrong and your kids could be very messed up and it's not allowed!" she spoke in a loud tone as we were now entering the woods.

"Oh psh please I'm sure you'll find him Maggie, hm I like that, Maggie, wait no, Mags," she looked at me with an annoyed look. "Oh c'mon you know I'm your best friend now." I said as I nudged her and she let out a small laugh.

She stopped and looked up again. "How will I know he's my soulmate Alexander"

"They say you'll just know, that's what I was told." I said bringing my focus back to the road.

The conversation went quiet for a while maybe ten minutes before Magdolin's voice was heard again. "Who's your soulmate Alexander?" That question felt like a sword to the heart for someone like me who has been over the entire kingdom and still hadn't found a wife.

"I- I don't know, I thought I'd found her but it just didn't work out ya know?" I said ending it with a nervous chuckle.

She looked at me with a sad face. "I'm so sorry, that's so sad."

"No no no it's okay, I'm glad I haven't found her yet. I mean I'd rather spend my life finding THE one than A one, you know?" I exclaimed with another nervous laugh following it before turning my attention to the road again.

I could still feel her gaze on me. It was one of confusion. As I continued down the road we neared the next safe house. I could feel the sun's warm rays beam through the trees, it reminded me of being home.

"This house is a bit nicer Magdolin I can promise you that." I said as we rounded another path revealing a beautiful cottage tucked away near a small river bed. There were vines growing around it but it fit the look of the house's grey brick and the pink flowers sprouting helped a lot too.

"There's a lot more here than the other house," I spoke as I parked the wagon and horses.

Chapter 6. Magdolin Poni

As the wagon halted I removed my bonnet. The small cottage was beautiful, the scenery was immaculate with the river bed and tall trees surrounding it. "It's gorgeous here!" I said in an excited tone.

"I'm glad you think so," Alexander said as he unhooked the horses into a small pasture for them to roam. "There's some things inside you might like my mother left them there before she had left the kingdom".

"Oh Alexander, I could care less about the things inside, look at all of this, it's beautiful! I feel free here." I said as I grabbed my things out of the wagon and quickly ran inside to change out of the black floor length dress and back into the one Natalia had made me.

I ran back outside laughing and running through the shallow part of the river and into the small field where the horses resided. When I ran across the small sand bar the mist clung to my legs. The cool mist from the rushing water was calming.

The light wind that brushed my skirt made me laugh to myself.

I'm free, I'm actually free, I thought to myself. "There's nothing more I have to do.. No more requirements to reach, no more having to be perfect, no more being a princess and having princess duties!" I said, getting more excited as I spoke.

I ran through the field dancing and feeling the wind through my hair, serenity walked over to me brushing her head against my shoulder. I laughed and asked where her sister was knowing she couldn't understand me.

I looked around and saw Alexander grooming the brown and white horse by the small stable area.

I remembered reading stories with my mother about how people rode on the backs of horses and guided them with their hair. I just believed there were old wives tales but now looking at the horse I was curious.

I led Serenity over to the side of the small wooden fence as I climbed up the side of it. My conscience then got to me. I started to wonder if this was the right thing to do, what if I got hurt? I would be such a burden for Alexander.

I noticed that if I was going to be free and out of the kingdom and making my own decisions I had to not be afraid. I swallowed my fears and jumped onto serenity's back. I was expecting her to take off running or kicking and try to hurt me but she just stood calmly. I gently sat up from my crouched down position and steadied myself on her back. I reached forward grabbing two strands of her hair, when I would pull the left hand of hair she would move her head to the left and same to the right side.

I moved forward some on her back to get more comfortable and she started walking. I fell forward on her again as she took off in a trot *oh my god oh my god oh my god!*

I lifted myself up and took hold of her hair again and guided her around a bit. I started to get used to the feeling of her fast walking as I would move side to side with her. Out of nowhere a loud hissing and a fearful neigh could be heard from right in front of me. I looked around, holding onto Serenity's neck praying I wouldn't fall off. There was a large snake laying on the ground in front of Serenity's right foot.

In the blink of an eye Serenity was darting off away from the snake. I was holding on for dear life as she galloped at full speed back towards the stable. I felt her slow down as we got up to the stable where Alexander was.

"Wow, serenity slow down, " Alexander said as he calmed the horse down from her frightened state. "You could have asked me for a saddle Magdolin, riding bareback isn't the safest option for a princess." He said as he picked me off the horse like a flea on a dog.

"Oh please I didn't even know you could ride horses like that. I thought it was a fairytale." I said in proclamation.

"Well you're certainly wrong Mags, people do it as a sport, sometimes others use it for transportation like me," he said as he finished putting the last braid in the brown and white horse's hair.

"What's her name?" I said curiously.

He paused for a moment before answering "her name? Hope." He said it in a somber tone which felt like a weight on my shoulders, pressuring me to say the right thing back.

"That's a beautiful name" I said quickly trying to make up for the silence prior to him talking.

He didn't respond so I took that as my cue to drop that conversation. "Should I go start something for dinner?" I said in a quieter voice, I knew I didn't have a clue on how to cook what-so-ever but how hard could it be?

"If you'd like to, go right ahead," he said, flashing a small smile. I smiled right back as I crossed the yard and into the cottage.

I was in the small kitchenette of the house, I started opening up cabinets trying to find where to start. I found a cookbook in one of the cabinets full of recipes, this is where I'd start. I opened it up and began flipping through the pages trying to find something easy looking.

I found a recipe for a simple egg washed steak. I thought it couldn't be that hard. I stepped down into the cellar of the cottage and began searching around the walls full of canned goods. A few cured steaks hung on the wall and I grabbed them down along with a beef broth. I could only imagine I could use it too.

I climbed back out of the cellar and started out towards a group of chickens in the front lawn. There I found a few eggs in a small dirt dug out nest. I snatched them and ran inside to begin preparing the dish.

I was doing my best to try and follow the instructions written in the book but I was completely lost. The words written down made no sense to me and I didn't know if I could use the things I had to make this. Alexander walked into the kitchen then walking in on me curled over the book trying to make sense of it.

"What are you making?" He said looking at the ingredients I had laid out and then down at the book. He had a look of amusement as he saw what I was doing and realised I was completely lost. "Here let me do it, Mags," he said, taking the book into his hands and then pulling out a skillet. I watched him as he prepared it all, watching how he did it and taking a mental note of all of it.

Within about twenty minutes the steaks were done and done perfectly on top of that. I felt slightly embarrassed that a male could cook with such ease but I had so much trouble. In my excuse I was never taught.

The steaks were amazing; they were just as good as what the castle chef could prepare. "These are amazing Alexander." I said, practically drooling over them.

"I'm glad you like it," he said as he sat down on the ledge of the counter with his dish.

After he was done I grabbed his dish from him, that's one thing I knew how to do. I used to help the maids do it sometimes after meals.

Chapter 7. Alexander Malencoy

Dinner was nice but I wasn't surprised she didn't know how to cook. She had been raised and pampered her whole life. It's a wonder how she isn't a spoiled brat like I would have expected. She's smart when she needs to be and she's not as uptight as other higher ranked people. I guess that explains why she wanted to leave then. I thought to myself.

"Y'know Magdolin it's really great that you aren't a brat." I said as she picked the dishes up off the table.

"Excuse me?" she said, frowning at me.

Oh crap that sounded really wrong.

"Sorry sorry that's my fault, I didn't mean for that to sound like that. I mean I'm glad you aren't a spoiled rotten princess like the other people in the palace." I said awkwardly as I took the dishes from her hands.

DAMNIT that didn't sound better.

She paused for a moment and unfurrowed her brow. "Oh I see, you'd be surprised though the people I was around in the palace weren't that way, you knew Natalia and she was the most humble female I knew." she said, leaning against the counter as I set the dishes down into the sink. I thought to myself for a moment trying to come up with a Natalia in my memory.

"You said her name was Natalia?" I said, raising an eyebrow.

"Yes, the one who got you to get me out of there." She said calmly.

"I don't know any Natalia, I got my smuggling request through a long line of people." I said with a more neutral face.

"Ah I see, that's a very smart way of going about it, I wouldn't have expected something that smart to come from a ruffian like you." She said in an almost playful tone of voice. *And was that sarcasm?*

"Hey woah sister don't make me take back the brat statement." I said with a smile as I dried my hands off from the sink.

·•· ⟨≡⟩ ·•·

We then stepped outside looking outside as the sun set. I leaned against the post on the porch as Magdolin set down on the step of the porch. It was a calming mood as the birds chirped and the animals called throughout the forest. It was slightly humid and the air felt sticky but it felt nice. As the sun set and the sky got dim and all around the cottage was dim, the horses were laying down for rest in the stable area and the animals in the forest started to go quiet and the cricket and tree frogs took over the noise. I felt so comfortable standing there just listening to the wildlife I let my mind wander off. Eventually my thoughts slowed and I felt myself almost nod off to sleep.

I looked back up fast, why am I so tired all of the sudden? I thought to myself. I looked down at Magdolin who had fallen asleep herself, something is majorly off. She was literally toppled over on her side sleeping, like she'd fainted.

A light mist covered the ground, it wasn't fog though it was a dark navy colour and it smelled pleasant like baked goods. I leaned down and tried to wake Magdolin up but she wouldn't wake up, I felt myself getting drowsier as I breathed in the mist.

I quickly picked Magdolin up off the porch and quickly took her inside the cottage, away from what was out there.

I set Magdolin down on the guest bedroom bed and hurried back into the main room of the cottage. The mist was starting to seep through the crack under the doors and windows making its way into the house. This was not natural. Someone was behind this whatever it was.

I grabbed a bunch of clothes lying on the counter and the huntsman's axe from the door and ran back to the room where Magdolin laid. I closed the door and jammed the clothes under the door and up in the window seal to prevent the mist from getting in.

Magdolin started to stir awake and I could tell she was dazed. "What's happening, what are you doing?" she said, looking up at me as I was holding the axe up defensively.

"I, uhm the mist knocks you out and now it's enclosed the cottage and something's going on." I said awkwardly trying to not sound crazy, and Magdolin still looked at me like I'd lost my sanity.

All of the sudden the clothes from the window were knocked out of the window seal. A black with red tint tentacle looking arm slithered through the crack of the window seal.

Magdolin jumped up from the bed with a shriek and we both froze staring at it for a moment before it started to try and crawl into the room.

I swung the axe hard hitting it at the base of the tentacle and a loud deep screech was heard from outside of the house, loud thuds that shook the ground echoed as it stomped around the house. The axe was caught in the side of the wall and I knew we needed to move. I flung the door open and dragged Magdolin down into the back bedroom and opened the cellar hatch door.

"Come on now." I said in a whisper as I led her down and closed the door behind us.

We both hurried into the small cellar and I found a small carry candle and lit it. The cellar was now slightly illuminated from the dim light of the candle. The cellar was dark and cold, all you could hear was the sounds of us breathing down here. The sounds of the creature outside were still audible except now it was paired with a voice.

"Do you think they're here to help?" Magdolin whispered to me. I threw my hand over her mouth and quickly put her over in the corner of the cellar with the candle. It hit me what was going on now

"Bounty hunters" I whispered in a worried tone.

They were here looking for Magdolin I'd be willing to bet. Who else would they be looking for, the princess went missing two days ago. My mind was racing. I didn't know what to do. I blew out the candle and huddled in the corner along with Magdolin. All you could hear was both of our rushed, worried breathing. The warmth of our bodies filled the air around us from the cool climate of the cellar

We sat in the corner shoulder to shoulder as the creature still thumped its feet around outside. There was a loud crash, something thudded across the floor of the main room of the cottage. I felt both of us flinch at the sound. I could tell it was the front door getting knocked off of its hinges.

A set of footsteps could be heard going throughout the cottage. They sounded commanding and almost angry, the footsteps trailed through the layout of the house until it reached the room above us. I could hear the bed being shoved across the room and hitting the wall. I heard the dresser being pushed next, Magdolin was breathing hard and I could hear it, and if I could hear it so could the bounty hunter.

I gently slid my hand over her mouth again to try and quiet her, I felt warm tears on her cheeks. I couldn't say anything and I couldn't do much to try and comfort her. I felt useless. I looked around the cracks of the cellar seeing moonlight spill in. It was still too dark to make things out. All of the sudden the gaps of moonlight slowly started to disappear.

I felt something crawl up the side of my back and Magdolin clinging onto me now. It was warm and sticky and it felt like a snake, it had to be the tentacles again. I grabbed Magdolin around her waist firmly and kicked away from the walls.

We slid to the middle of the cellar and now that the tentacles were enclosing around us from the sounds I could hear.

I felt the slime covered tentacles slowly crawl up my leg, not allowing me to move at all. I felt squeamish as multiple tentacles began to cover us, keeping us held, not being able to move. I looked down at Magdolin not being able to make out any details, I could tell from her breathing she was crying still. Her body trembled ever so lightly against my own as she silently sobbed. My arms were stuck around her from how the tentacles held us.

Just as soon as they had come into the cellar the tentacles had us tethered together in the middle of the cellar, the only thing exposed was our shoulders and heads. I couldn't move at all as I tried to fight my way out of this.

Then out of the darkness a flash of light showed through the darkness, the cellar door was flung open. It exposed Magdolin and I stuck in the middle or the cellar, caught up in the mangled tentacle mess. I heard footsteps above us and then saw a pair of black and gold boots walking down the steps of the cellar. They clinked and stomped as they took the steps down and then another pair followed almost matching except heavier footsteps.

"Look at the scum, tied up with the princess," one of the voices said. It was clearly a female but she had a very rough voice, almost threatening.

"Is he holding you captive, your majesty?" The other voice said, this one clearly a male except he had an almost teasing tone and a gravely but higher pitched voice.

I stayed quiet glaring up at the figures as my eyes adjusted to the dim lighting and at how the light was directed at us. All of the sudden the tentacles tightened squeezing us so hard I could barely breathe.

"We expect an answer!" The female voice said in a harsh tone.

"No!" Magdolin yelled with a squeeze in her voice as the tentacles tightened.

"Well that's wonderful, then why'd you leave princess? Daddy issues get too much to bear?" The male voice with a laugh.

"Do you find that funny?" I said as my eyes adjusted and I could finally see the figures. The female had on a loose set of armour and a spear in her right hand. She had long black hair braided down her back and appeared to have a sage mushroom, same as for the male except he carried a mace and had brown shorter hair.

"Well clearly you don't have a sense of humour poison shroom," the male said laughing again.

"Stop it August, we have business to get to. Why did you leave princess?" The female said, cutting in.

"Hey! Don't use my nickname while we are intimidating, it sounds dumb." The male said in an almost whine.

"Fine, Augustus," the female said, rolling her eyes and then focused back on Magdolin.

"Why should I tell you, you're a bounty hunter, all you want to do is return me and kill him." Magdolin said with a hiss in her voice.

"Actually princess, it's five thousand shillings to give a tip on where you may be at and that's all I'm looking to do, I want to let you two go and take the five thousand, but if you're going to talk in that tone to me I guess I could just return you to the palace, I'm sure the reward would be much greater." The female said in a hiss right back at Magdolin. I felt a chill go up my spine as she spoke.

Magdolin paused for a moment before speaking again. "I just wanted to escape. I was sick of being treated like I was a doll, who had to be kept locked up." Magdolin spoke in a much lower tone, almost accepting defeat from what I could hear.

"Wonderful darling, I'm glad the princess knows how to handle herself, well I mean sort of because you have to have a poison mushroom tour you away, you aren't fully capable of being on your own obviously." she said with a smirk and a small laugh and tapping Magdolin's nose with the end of her pen as she took out a notebook and jotted some things down.

"And where may this address be, I need it to report it to the town officers." The female spoke again as Augustus approached me.

"Hey poison mushroom-" He said before I cut him off.

"Alexander." I said, rolling my eyes.

"Yeah whatever, how is the princess not burning at your touch, is it because she's magic or something."

"That's an old wives tale it's not true, I'm not really poisonous," I said annoyed.

"Uh huh like I'd believe that, I've read the stories of your kind, killing mushrooms off by their poisonous spores and melting their skin off by touching them, I have to say it sounds wicked cool." Augustus said with a laugh.

"I can touch anything, and it won't melt and I don't have poisonous spores, those are lies that some cruel person made up to ruin my kind." I said, getting slightly agitated.

"For sure Allen or whatever your name is." Augustus said, stepping back behind the female again as she finished writing and put her book back in her satchel.

"Thank you for your cooperation." she said, closing her satchel and the tentacles moved off of us, it left a nasty slime that had an awful odour to it.

"Wait! You cannot just barge in and leave like that." Magdolin said standing up to her feet.

"Yes we can, and I'd shut your mouth girly," Augustus said, starting to go up the stairs.

This Augustus really pissed me off, he acted like he owned it all. Clearly she was more capable of more than him.

"I would get moving, we are going straight to town in the morning and turning this address in. So they'll be here ASAP, so a tip of advice is to not keep running your mouth and get a move on princess." she said leaving the cellar.

Me and Magdolin ran out as well after the two as they left the house. "Wait!" Magodlin said, running out into the yard to the female's horse, and Augustus was seated on the tentacle creature. It looked utterly disgusting. It had the body of a huge bear and long tentacles that spewed over its entire body. It was indescribable. And the smell was even worse.

"What's your name?" she asked, holding the stirrups off the horse, not letting her leave.

"Amarila, your majesty," she said, looking down at Magdolin.

"Thank you Amarilla, for not fully turning us in." Magdolin said, stepping back from the horse.

"Don't stay here long your majesty and please get somewhere where the other bounty hunters won't find you, the others aren't as kind." Amarilla said, taking off.

"Byeee Anthony." Augustus said, saying my name wrong again, and taking off behind Amarilla.

I walked out to where Magdolin was in the yard as she watched the two leave. I knew we needed to leave as soon as possible because the officers would be here by dawn.

"We need to leave now, I can't take the risk of not getting out of here in time." I said, placing my hand on her shoulder.

"That's probably the best option we have," she said in agreement and turned to gather things from inside.

I ran out to the creek in the back and dove into a deep part, I couldn't stand that awful reeking smell of that slime the tentacles left on me. I was soaking wet, and my hair curled up from the water but I didn't care. I hated my natural curls but it was better than the stench.

In the dark I made my way to the stables, getting the horses saddled in the cart, and hooking the horses up to the wagon.

I pulled the wagon up to the front of the house where the door was still knocked to the ground. I jumped out and saw Magdolin had changed back into the dress I gave her and a bag of stuff to take.

I decided I was going to attach the door back on before we left so it didn't look as if we had run, and so animals wouldn't get inside.

"I'm going to put the door on again." I said as I ran to get some nails and a hammer.

"Okay," she said, putting the bag in the wagon.

I slammed the nails back in the door with a hammer and I made sure to leave it unlocked so they wouldn't knock it down again. I made my way back up to the wagon and sat down on the bench seat along with Magdolin. As I sat down I noticed her hair soaking wet.

"Those tentacles were awful weren't they?" I said with a laugh as I sat down.

"Oh they were awful, I can't believe how they could reek like that, phew." she said, waving across her nose. "I see you had the same idea of getting in the creek," she said following her past sentence.

"Oh I had to, that was horrid, I couldn't stand it," I said, whipping the stirrups and the horses took off.

I felt Magdolin's eyes on me still, I turned my head looking at her with my eyebrow raised.

"Your hair, it's curly?" She said, touching my hair.

"Yeah I usually press it after I get it wet, I don't like it curly." I said, feeling my own hair.

"Why, I think it looks nice," she said with a smile. I liked her smile. It was a soft smile and she had pretty teeth and pretty lips. She had a pretty face over all with an upturned button nose, how could it not be pretty.

"Well thank you, but I don't. My mother has the same hair and I think I look girly with it." I said, shrugging my shoulders.

She scoffed "oh you're kidding me right, curly hair is not girly, it suits you, I like it!" She said smiling and let out a yawn. It was pretty late and it was pitch black now.

"Thank you Mags." I said with a smile looking down at her as she looked up at me while still observing the tight curls in my hair. It felt like there was a tension at that moment as we just looked at each other.

It was a calming tension and it was nice but it was something I hadn't felt in years.

I looked away back at the road clearing my throat. "Sorry, if you're tired you can always crawl in the back and go to sleep." I said slightly embarrassed.

She just shook her head and grabbed her bonnet and put it over her head

"Nope I won't let you just sit here alone, that's not polite." She said with a royal accent to it.

"I was just offering it." I said with a small laugh.

For the next few hours we passed through a few small towns and occasionally would make small talk. Eventually I noticed her nodding off to sleep, she would wake herself up though and she was clearly exhausted.

I was somewhat used to long days and all nighters. I gently patted the entrance to the wagon, gesturing for her to go back there.

"No, I'm fine, I'm just resting my head," she said, yawning still. I just shook my head as she was almost asleep sitting upright.

I kept leading the horses down the roads and eventually in my peripheral I saw her falter. She fell forward, almost hitting her head on the rail but I grabbed her in time. She was dead asleep now and I leaned her back upright but she just fell to the side this time. I left her laying on her side across the bench, she looked so innocent like that. Her body draped elegantly across the bench of the wagon and then her head just centimeters from my thigh. I wondered to myself if I should pull her up to rest on my leg, that way her head would be elevated, but that sounds creepy.

I had to admit she looked beautiful like this. I pulled her legs up on the bench too so she would sleep easier and wouldn't be sore.

Chapter 8. Magdolin Poni

I woke up with the sun shining in my eyes and Alexander's hand on my shoulder holding me on the bench so I wouldn't fall out. I sat up on the bench of the wagon and stretched my arms out.

"Good Morning Sleeping Beauty, you can just sleep anywhere can't you?" Alexander's voice cut through the air with a hint of sarcasm.

"Well thank you for the compliment, and good morning to you too." I said back with a teasing tone.

Alexander rolled his eyes and went back to looking at the road. I could see eye bags on his face, I felt bad. I slept through the night while he stayed awake to make sure the horses went the right way.

"We're coming up through a town here so be ready for that, we have to stop as well. My next safe house didn't have much supplies there last time so it's due for a restock." Alexander said with a small smile.

As the wagon pulled through the town we got mean stares from the people on foot. They were all dressed prestigiously and had walked with a sway to their step. The men wore suits tapered perfectly to their fit and had top hats to boat along with it. The women wore long elegant dresses, like what I'd wear to a ball when I lived in the palace. To add to it they had big, frilly hats and umbrellas that matched perfectly with their dresses.

The kids didn't run through the street like the other town, they stood with their parents and walked properly like they were professionals at this. The little boys had on dress shirts and nice slacks and the girls had nice Sunday dresses on. It was an odd sight, but the rude stares made it even worse.

Alexander then pulled the wagon around a few streets and then stopped the horses in front of an alley. He tied the horses to a post and then gave me a hand getting out of the wagon.

"You're about to meet a very good friend of mine, Mags, I'm sure you'll love her,'" Alexander said with a smirk. I didn't know if he was being serious or sarcastic.

"Okay?" I said as he led us both through the alley. It was dim and trash was all over the ground, I stepped in puddles every few seconds. I didn't even look down to see what I was stepping in, then a small door was at the end of the alley.

Alexander ducked as he entered through the door, I followed behind him as we entered what appeared to be a store. But it was like we entered through the back door. The store was filled with tons of glass ornaments and other little things that just purely sparkled. It was beautiful and as I stood inside looking around Alexander grabbed my shoulders. "Do not break anything Mags, my friends a bit... touchy about her glass."

"O- ok." I said awkwardly, smiling as he led me through the crowded cluster of glass in the store. The glass shimmered against the walls and it was such a beautiful sight. As we rounded a few corners there was another door and Alexander slowly opened the door.

As the door slowly opened up a female with long bouncy orange hair stood at a table. She had a torch lit ablaze and she had drops of glass melting over it. It was a new sight for me and I was truly dragged in by it.

"Charlie! So good to see you! Ah ha ha." Alexander said with a loud happy cheerful tone.

She dropped the glass and it melted into the metal table as she jumped from surprise.

"ανάθεμα! θα σε κρεμάσω Αλέξανδρε" she said with anger in her voice. I didn't know what language she was speaking in, it was an odd accent and I didn't understand any of it.

"Uhm I think you're forgetting I don't know Greek sweetie." Alexander said flipping up Charlie's mask, a beautiful freckled face with dark brown eyes appeared and she turned a lever which lightened up the room.

I could see now she had on a fitted blouse, an apron and trousers! I've never seen a female in trousers before. She was beautiful in them though, she was an orange mushroom so I didn't know much about them. I'd read about them before but couldn't really recall much.

"You made me ruin my new piece, and I am NOT your sweetie" Charlie said pointing angrily at the ruined glass and then at Alexander. He just smirked down at her with his hand resting on the work table.

"Okay darlin', well you have company, I'd like you to meet the one and only princesses… Magdolin," Alexander said as he grabbed me by the shoulder and pulled me closer to Charlie, he pulled off my bonnet to show my lavender mushroom as well. She was very tall like a beauty model, I just gazed up at her.

I had to admit I was very confused at this point. Darlin'? Sweetie? Was this his wife? Where is his ring if it is?

"I AM NOT YOUR DARL- … .oh my lords, your majesty." Charlie said, going down on one knee bowing. I was surprised at her reaction to me.

"You are beautiful, please don't bow before me." I said, holding my hand out to her. I helped her stand back up and we both just made eye contact.

"Ah look at that, two of my girls are getting along." Alexander said with a big dumb smirk across his face.

"I thought you said you did not have a mate, or a wife?" I said looking up at Alexander confused.

"He doesn't have a wife, no one would want to marry someone like him princess." Charlie said with a sigh.

"Just call me Magdolin please." I said with a soft smile.

"What she means to say Mags is that I was just too good for her to give her a shot at me." Alexander said with a smirk as he put a finger up as he talked.

I rolled my eyes and so did Charlie. I'd never seen Alexander act like this but I suppose it was because we were around someone else. And it was someone he probably knew a lot better than me so he was more comfortable with her.

Chapter 9. Charlie Diginton

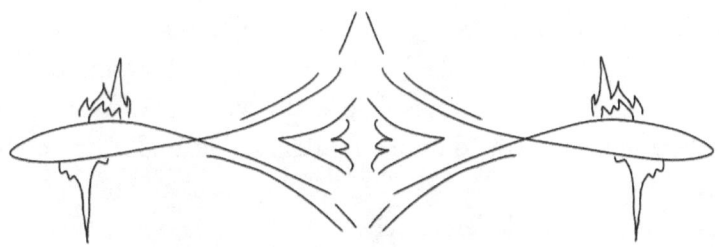

I rolled my eyes at Alexander's dumb comments, and I looked back down at the princess then back at Alexander and how he held her around the shoulder.

Alexander and I were childhood friends, my parents didn't like me growing up with him because of his mushroom. I always felt bad for him because he was set up for a hard time in life, but I was proud he made his way through life even if he was a smuggler.

"What do you need Alexander?" I said with a serious tone and face as I set my glass mask down on the work table.

"Oh just the usual if you would." Alexander said, still smirking dumbly

"Wipe that smirk off your face if you want anything from me." I said as I walked past them and out into the main room. I went over to my work fridge and grabbed out a bag of fruits, bread, and other articles of food for the two of them. I walked over towards the exit where the two were standing and threw the bag at Alexander. "There are you happy now?" I said as the princess did a slight courtesy.

"Yes thank you mam." She said with a soft tone.

"It's no issue your majesty, it's just your friend here owes me." I said pointing at Alexander.

"Oh come on, you know I'll pay you back, just give me a bit of time." Alexander said, shrugging his shoulders. The princess frowned up at Alexander and he just awkwardly smiled down at her.

"It doesn't matter, but you really shouldn't fool around with this important of smuggle, Alexander." I said in a stern tone and crossed my arms.

"I know I know, we travelled through the night to make it here now!" Alexander said, crossing his arms mimicking me.

I rolled my eyes and looked at the two again, observing them both, they stuck out like sore thumbs. Especially with her wearing a bonnet.

"Alexander, are you dumb?" I said as Alexander's face slightly dropped.

"No!" He said back defensively.

"Then tell me why you have the princess walking around in the most outlandish outfit" I said, crossing my arms again.

"W-well …I let her choose what she wears" Alexander said, turning his nose up.

"Come here your majesty, have you ever sewn?" I said taking her arm and leading her through the store to the front.

"Magdolin, please, and I have once or twice." She said softly.

"Well take these, and I want you to make yourself a good dress but don't make yourself stick out," I said, setting a few yards of pale pink and white fabric in her arms. "Oh and here, this is a sewing pattern for a colour cap, it will cover the purple, use the pink fabric and paint on white and you'll be able to do whatever with no one questioning you." I said, setting the sewing pattern on the fabric and a dress pattern as well.

"Thank you Charlie, really you are such a help." Magdolin said smiling.

"Yeah yeah whatever, come on Magdolin." Alexander said, holding her shoulder again.

"He is right, you two better get back on the road." I said with a soft smile. I walked the two back to the back door again.

Magdolin then ran and wrapped her arms around my waist.

"Thank you truly." she said as she pulled away. A smile spread across my face, something about the princess truly did just bring light into the room. Something about her was special.

"Of course Magdolin, if you ever need anything my shop is always here." I said with a smile. As Alexander opened the door for her and she walked out to the wagon. "Alex, you really need to be careful with her, she's a real gem." I said as Alexander was about to leave the door frame.

"What are you crazy, I won't, I'm always careful with my clients." Alexander said cockily.

"That's not what I mean dumbass, wait here." I said, propping open the door with a small rock. I grabbed one of the rings I made a glass gemstone for.

"Here, I think you may need it later," I said, handing him the small black box. When he opened it his eyes widened at the small white stone with the wire wrapped intricately around it. The ring was one of the many engagement rings I made.

"Thank me later buddy" I said as I started to close the door. Alex grabbed the door and looked at me.

Alexander needed every opportunity to be quite honest. I want him to have those opportunities. And from what I've heard when the princess was still in the castle they wanted her to get married, meaning she's not taken.

Maybe just maybe by some chance, she'll look to Alexander if he plays his cards right, and maybe by some other odd chance his stubborn ass will take this ring and get an idea to look at her.

"Thank you, for everything." He said with a small smile and closed the door.

The look on his face was all I needed to see. Alexander deserved happiness, do I think he will ever have the balls to do it? No, absolutely not. But if I was him, I wouldn't care how that Magdolin looked at me. I'd jump at her, she seemed so perfect, perfect for him. He was broken and saughtened, she would be a fresh canvas for him. Something to heal him, only if he'd allow it of course.

Chapter 10. Alexander Malencoy

I quickly threw the small box into my satchell. As I ran back to the wagon, we needed to get a move on now.

I can't believe Charlie would believe such a thing like that, me and Magdolin? Psh, if ever. I thought to myself as I got the reins and moved the horses back on track on the road.

I couldn't easily get my mind back off of the idea though. I'd glance over at Magdolin as she was looking all around the wagon as we went down the dirt roads. There was this feeling in my chest, I didn't know what to really make of it. I was confused on what it was, but didn't want to jump to conclusions. I couldn't help but feel my face get hot as well, it felt like I wasn't really breathing.

"Hey Alexander." She said out of nowhere and turned to look at me with that big pretty smile. I turned quickly so she wouldn't see me looking at her. I cleared my throat before turning and flashing her a smile too.

"Yes Mags?"

"If you're right about being able to mix colours, I think if I was you, I'd be going for that Charlie girl." She said, leaning over to me with her eyebrow raised as if she was teasing me. I rolled my eyes and sighed.

"Oh please, Charlie is not my type of female. She's rude, and she's my childhood friend." I said with a scoff.

"Hm, okay," She said, shrugging her shoulders and looking back around. "Do you think that there are other purple mushrooms on the island?" She asked in a bit more somber tone.

"I- um I don't know, there wasn't any beforehand at least, but please, listen to me when I say the colour of your mushroom doesn't affect anything, it just depends on how they treat you ok?" I said, giving her a soft smile trying to make it not as tense.

She looked down at her hands that were neatly folded in her lap. "It still feels weird, going against the law like that. I don't know if I could." She said, frowning and looking to the side of the wagon.

"Well just remember the law doesn't control you anymore, and as I already said your person may be a pink mushroom, tan or gold.. Or blue,..green ….black and green." I said looking over at her making eye contact. Then it felt like I snapped out of it.

Damnit Charlie's got in my head, as always.

"B- because I have a lot of my cousins and they're really cool, like I think you'd love them." I said awkwardly.

That was the biggest lie I've ever told, I don't even have a single cousin to my knowledge.

I felt my face going red as I looked back at the road.

"I don't think I want your cousin, Alexander." She said laughing.

"Yeah that's fair." I said, laughing as well trying to get my mind off of it.

·•· ⟨ᢩᢛᢩ⟩ ·•·

We crossed a few more towns before it started to get dark. I really started to feel the sleepiness hit me then from not sleeping the night prior. Eventually we pulled into the next safe house.

This safe house was a small cabin in the woods. Trees surrounded everything around us and it was on top of a hill. I hooked the horses up and unlocked the door for us. It started to get cold as it got darker outside. I lit the fire in the chimney as it brought warmth into the house.

"Magdolin, there's a nice bed in that room there for you." I said, smiling and pointing to the room's door. I felt exhausted and I could feel my eye bags were very prominent.

"Well then where are you going to sleep?" She said, turning and looking at me as her eyebrows furrowed together.

"Well I was going to stay by the fire, if that's ok." I said with a tired smile.

"No, that's not good. You can't sleep on the floor, you're ridiculously tired," She said, putting her foot down and crossing her arms.

"Really Magdolin, it's ok." I said, smiling and grabbing a small throw pillow, laying down beside the fireplace.

"You really are stubborn." She said, shrugging her shoulders and I heard her boots click across the ground and into the other room.

I felt my eyes get heavy incredibly fast and I fell asleep in no time. It was as if when I laid down my body gave out from exhaustion.

Chapter 11. Magdolin Poni

I walked into the bedroom. It was a nice small bedroom but I couldn't just let him sleep out there like that on the ground. I pulled the comforter quilt off the bed and carried it into the small living room. I saw that he was asleep already with the pillow and nothing else. I threw the blanket over him and made sure he was fully covered by it. I walked away and grabbed the fabric and sat beside him next to the fire. I started sewing the dress together with the beautiful fabric.

I couldn't help but look over at Alexander a few times as he slept so peacefully. I could tell he was exhausted for two days with no sleep. I was glad he was getting sleep now though. As I stitched across the seams of the fabric the dress started to come together and it was beautiful. I had the fabric draped over my lap as I kept sewing it together. I finished the dress and looked at my work, smiling.

The way the pink and white flowed together was perfect, and the dress's angles looked right when I held it up. I picked up the pattern for the colour cap. I laid it over the pink fabric that was left over and started to cut it out. I sewed a few seams and it was done. I couldn't believe how little effort it took to make. I hung it up with the dress on a hook that stuck out of the wall. I looked at the fire as it started to die down, I gazed out the window and through the trees at the night sky. The moon was nearly full and it shone brightly.

Whenever the full moon came around I'd get strange dreams. My whole family did, they were hyper realistic and sometimes scary to sleep through. So I wasn't looking forward to that.

I yawned quietly as I realised how late it was getting now. I felt my head get heavier as I laid down beside the fire on the stone laid around it. It wasn't comfortable, but I wasn't going to sleep in a comfortable bed while Alexander slept on the stone. It was a challenge to fall asleep on the hard stone but I did eventually, the rock was slightly heated from the fire that was now dying out in the fireplace.

About an hour passed and the fire was now completely out, I could hear the sounds of the animals outside as we slept in the living room. It started to get colder as the fire was now gone and it sent chills down my spine, and made me shiver slightly as I curled into a ball.

I felt two arms wrap around me, under my legs and behind my back. I didn't want to open my eyes but I did, only to see Alexander picking me up. I started to murmur something under my breath and he cut me off. "Shh " he said as he carried me into the bedroom and set me on the bed and threw a blanket off the shelf over me.

"No, Alexander, I'm not letting you sleep on the floor alone " I said groggily as I sat up in the bed before he gently pushed me back down by my shoulders.

It felt like my heart got lurched into the ball in my throat. The sight of him hovering over me with his hands on my shoulder was immersive. Impressive? Exhilarating? I couldn't say the right word if I searched for years. No male dared to touch me like that.

Maybe it's because of his sleep deprivation?

"I won't go back out there then" He said with a tired smile.

He then laid on the other side of the bed beside me and turned away from me. I felt my cheeks flush a shade of red slightly as I laid there opposite to him.

The image of him holding my shoulders like that flashing through my head as I tried to fall back asleep.

Alexander is my friend. What am I thinking?! Plus, he's a poison mushroom, remember your morals Magdolin! I thought to myself with a straight face as I fell back asleep.

The next morning the sun was shining into the room and I started to stir awake, then remembered that he was asleep next to me. I looked over to see that he was gone and already awake.

I walked out of the room and looked around the cabin. Alexander was nowhere to be found. I stepped outside on the small porch, he wasn't there either. I walked out to the horses and petted them before seeing a beautiful sight in my peripheral vision.

I turned my head quickly, through the trees there was a gorgeous view of a lake with fog. The fog draped over the calm still water and the deer and rabbits ran around it so peacefully. All just living in harmony. I walked closer to the edge of the hill to get a better view of the sight. I saw Alexander sitting on the edge of the hill looking out over the mountains and hills and most of all the lake.

"Good Morning." I said, interrupting the dense silence.

Alexander jumped slightly and shoved something back in the satchel bag, but I ignored it. "Good Morning Mags," He said, flipping around with a smile. "I hope you slept well, at least more than the floor." He said, following up his previous statement.

"I did and I'd hope the same for you my friend." I said sitting down looking over the mountains with him. I could feel Alexander's eyes looking at me, I turned my head quickly to him.

"Can I help you?" I said with a smile and a teasing tone.

"Oh shush it," he said looking away back at the lake. "I'm hoping to have you to the island in about a week." He said as he picked at the grass next to him. I looked over at him shocked, only a week?

"Once I'm there, what is it like, what will I do, where will you go?" I said, looking at him curiously.

"Well that's for you to decide, you'll have to get a job but there's no taxes there, and you're free, so you can do whatever you want Mags." He said, leaning back on his elbows as he laid in the grass. "No princess treatment there, anyone there has to contribute somehow." He said, shooting me a small smirk.

"You didn't answer the whole question, what are you going to do?" I said, looking over at him.

He hesitated for a moment looking over the hill and then sat back upright.

49

"I… I don't know for sure. I don't want to just stay there for good because other people need to be helped out of situations, like you, but it's just getting old." He said, hugging his knees loosely.

"Well, I know you'll make the right decision for yourself," I said with a small smile on my face. He just smiled back while standing up.

"Well we better hit the road, Mags." he said offering me a hand, I took his hand and stood to my feet.

"I agree," I said, walking towards the house.

I grabbed the dress I made the night prior and changed into it. I loved how it fit me so perfectly, it was as if the fabric was draped across me. And when I put the colour cap on you would've never known I wasn't a pink mushroom. I decided to finish the look off with the lipstick I took from the palace. I looked in the mirror at myself, I was astonished at how different I looked.

The dress fell just below my ankle and the bodice was simple but elegant and the sleeves were puffy but not too loose. I couldn't believe I had made it myself without any help.

The colour cap was on fleek. You could tell nothing was off about it; it was almost flawless.

The lipstick topped it off because the pink and red clashed wonderfully, I looked mature and grown into myself. I slid on my tights and boots and headed out the door to where Alexander was untying the horses.

Alexander got the horses up to the front of the road and then hopped off and walked towards the house. When he looked up and met my eyes he looked surprised as he got to the porch where I was standing.

"Well hello there miss, have you seen my friend Magdolin? I've left her somewhere." He said with a smirk as he put his hands on his hips.

"Oh shush your mouth you big chump." I said, rolling my eyes and stepping off the porch towards the wagon as he locked the door. He then followed me over to the wagon.

"Oh so I'm a chump now? I see Mags, so you're just trying to mess with me". He said teasingly as he sat on the bench.

"And how exactly am I tricking you?" I said as I crawled onto the wagon as well.

"Oh never mind," he said as he whipped the reins and the horses started their journey.

.•⋈⋈•.

We travelled for a few more days, we didn't go through many towns and occasionally Alexander would let me hold the reins of the horses. Soon we were going to be coming up on a big city though, one with a powerful barron ruling it. This was the time that we needed to be very careful because the chances of me being recognized was high.

We stopped in a small village on the way, Alexander then halted the wagon. "Hey, this village has a nice little market with cool things there, do you want to go check it out?" He said, looking over at me.

"Is it safe do you think?" I said, slightly antsy, I did want to go see the market.

"Of course it is, this village is nice and calm, plus most of them are pinks so you'll fit right in." He said with a smile and tapped my nose before hopping off the wagon and tying the horses to a pole.

"Okay!" I said, getting off the wagon and following behind Alexander closely through the street.

Just over the hill I could see a town circle with booths and stands where vendors were selling their products. "It's an art fair Mags, you'll love this!" He said quietly.

"Call me Mary while we're here, I don't want to risk being noticed." I said in a whisper.

"Alright Mary." He said, rolling his eyes and smiling.

"A- and you're my husband while we're here ok?" I worried that someone would try to mess with me.

"W- what, fine," he said as we walked along and into the crowd of people. "Go look at whatever you want, Mary." He said as he separated himself and went to the booth and struck up a conversation with another mushroom.

I grunted slightly and then looked around, I saw a stand with stained glass and walked over to it. They were beautiful and caught my attention quickly. I walked over, swerving my way through the crowd of people and then to the stand. I was surprised to see none other than Charlie standing behind the front of the booth.

"Charlie!" I said with a smile.

"Mag- pri- …hey you!" She said with a smile and waved for me to come behind the stand with her. I walked to her side gratefully with a smile. "Why are you here?" She hissed quietly with almost urgency in her voice.

"Alexander wanted me to see the market and so did I. Everything here is so interesting," I said, still looking around at the different booths.

"Please be careful out here, I don't want anything happening to you while you're out here. Remember you're a pretty precious prize to a bounty hunter." She said with a serious tone. "Where's Alexander? Why isn't he with you?" she said again looking around and then spotted him talking to the other mushroom.

"Oh he's fine im letting him talk to other people right now, I can handle myself!" I said, crossing my arms with a smile.

"If you say so Mag-"

I cut her off. "Mary,"

"Okay Mary, well the dress suits you well and I think you'll be fine as well, he just needs to be more responsible." She said glaring at Alexander.

"Okay well you go have fun Mary, be safe." she said, holding my hands and giving them a squeeze before I smiled and left her booth to look around. I moved my way through the crowd of people and to the center of the circle. I peered around.

There was a flower booth and another one with jewellery, and one with lots of little knick knacks. One caught my interest though, it was a weapons dealer in the very western side of the market.

I decided to make my way over there but then stopped myself. Weapons? There's probably some kind of royal guard over there. And plus that would make me stand out as a female looking at weapons. They'd call me a witch or worse.

I turned around to make my way over to the jewellery booth instead, but I was rudely interrupted by a tall mushroom. He wore a heavily detailed suit with amazing embroidery on it, he'd clearly spent his pretty penny on it for sure.

It had a pink and white theme and he was a pink mushroom. His face was fairly long with a roman nose and light pink eyes. His hair was long and black, pulled into a ponytail.

The male grabbed my left hand and observed it. "No husband I see?" He said with a chuckle before taking my hand and gently planting a kiss on it. I cringed and gently pulled my hand back.

"Ehh… I'm sorry, I am married. I just forgot my ring today." I said with a fake smile.

"Oh please, and who may be your husband? I'm sure I beat his looks in every way." He said, slicking his hair back with his hand and looking around.

The arrogance emanating off this mushroom is choking me out.

"No thank you." I said again pulling away and turning around, starting to walk away.

"Now, now you're going to wait. I want to see my competition, even though I'm sure it's not competition, I'm sure I could … satisfy you more than him." the male said, grabbing my shoulders so I couldn't walk away.

"Let go of me! Who do you think you are?" I said in a loud tone. People started to look as we started to make a scene as I threw his hands off of me.

"Feisty, I like it. I am the great Lapel Sanchez. It is truly an honour for you to be in my presence." He said, throwing a hand in the air. I rolled my eyes

"Please, you mean merely nothing to me." I said turning away from him. Some people audibly gasped as the moment unfolded. Lapel visibly was getting angrier by the moment.

I let out a small gasp as I felt him grab me again. I pushed against his grapes and was at the point of physically trying to escape him.

The audacity!

Chapter 12. Alexander Malencoy

I was over by one of an old pal of mine's booth as I heard a big commotion from the other side of the circle. I started to worry about Magdolin and went to look for her. I searched around for her through the crowds only to see a mushroom grabbing her by the wrists and yelling at her. I jumped into the large circle of people surrounding the two of them.

"What do you you think you're doing!" I said with a loud, assertive voice.

Magdolin looked up at me with a smile and let out a sigh. I heard gasps and nasty whispers from around us. I was used to it by now for being a poison mushroom.

"I'm clearly trying to get this female to calm down. Your kind wouldn't understand!" The mushroom said with a large amount of pride in his voice.

"You're going to let my wife go right now." I said, marching towards him angrily.

"Wife! You expect me to believe a beauty like this could even live with a monstrous male like you," Lapel said, laughing out loud. I glared at him with pure hatred as I filled with fury.

Even more exasperated gasps rung out from the people surrounding us. This was horrible, I don't think anything could've gone worse.

"Well he's much more distinguished and a gentleman than you Lapel. I'm glad he is my husband!" Magdolin said, squirming as the mushroom held her restrained.

More gasps and whispers came from the crowd around us. I knew if I didn't do anything now that this could end up really bad. And I think I'd pay for everyone to just shut up and leave.

I walked over to the two of them but Lapel grabbed Magdolin again and held her behind him away from me. "Give me her" I said, gritting my teeth and clenching my fists.

"No, now keep getting more angry. Why don't you show everyone how much of a beast your kind is?" He said quietly and I felt my blood boil.

I felt my fists unclench and I put a calm face on and a smile. Lapel looked confused at first but then my arm shot up grabbing his pony tail and I yanked at it. The whole ponytail ripped from his head. He let go of Magdolin and grabbed his head as his hair was now gone. He growled under his breath as he felt the now bald spot on the back of his head where his hairline meets his mushroom.

I threw the hair on the ground and motioned for Magdolin to get behind me. She ran behind me as the male got visibly more angry by the second.

"You monster! Oh you... You ... I'm going to kill you!" He said, throwing his hands in the air.

"You can try," I said, standing calmly as he ran at me. I put my arm out moving Magdolin out of the way so he wouldn't hit her. He ran past me and rolled in a somersault on the ground as he missed us.

"You piece of worthless scum!" He screamed as he got to his feet. He ran at me again, grabbing my shoulders, pushing me around, trying to get me on the ground, but I wouldn't budge. I used my upper arms to push against me, digging my heels into the ground.

God right now was the time I missed not working out more. All I really do anymore is split wood occasionally.

As we spun in circles fighting over who was going to go to the ground first, I caught a glimpse of Magdolin. She had her hands clamped over her mouth watching the whole fight go down.

The innocence.

The pure. Absolute. Undiluted. Innocence.

This needed to end now, I don't want her being exposed to this. *Exposed to me.* I don't want her to think I'm the monster everyone makes my kind out to be.

I have to handle this civilly, if lapel wants to kill me, so be it.

Three hits, that's it. That's all I am allowing myself. I've already used one technically, so two left.

I swung hard, not even watching where I was hitting. I was able to land a punch in his face.

Hit two.

He screamed again and mumbled to himself as he held his face. I felt sorry for the male. His pride and confidence were clearly key to him. And I did not help him out whatsoever. He was making a fool of himself in front of his audience. I circled around him in an almost taunting way.

"So how do you plan on *killing* me?" I asked with a snicker in my voice. Lapel swung around again looking at me, glaring and breathing hard.

He lunged at me again, but this time I grabbed him by his wrists and jumped behind him, restraining him like an animal. "Well that certainly didn't work." I said, laughing. He let out a low growl.

"I'm done with this shit" He said, squirming out of my grip and ran for Magdolin, grabbing her and throwing her over his shoulder. She let out a small scream and he turned laughing and smiling. His smile was sick and sinister. It was ugly and disgusting.

I ran over, quickly grabbing Magdolin as well. I had her arms and he had her legs. She had a face of worry as I held onto her and he pulled at her.

It irked me to see her scared like that. *He irked me.*

"You have no manners. Didn't your parents tell you not to take what's not yours?" I said with a small smirk to hide my horrified feelings that were growing in my chest as the seconds ticked by.

"Uh no.. Well, aren't you taught how to share." Lapel said with the same gross smile.

"That's not how marriage works," I said, raising an eyebrow. But before anything else happened the sound of glass shattering made everyone go silent.

Lapel fell backward with his eyes rolled back in his head. I quickly helped Magdolin to her feet and brushed off the dirt on her back. My eyes met with hers just for a moment before she wrapped her arms around my waist holding on tightly.

I looked up to see Charlie holding a now broken glass table ornament. She looked very mad and looked down at Lapel on the ground unconscious. I didn't even realize one of my arms had snaked around Magdolin's back.

"That'll be ten shillings, Dirtbag." She said, dropping the rest of the ornament on his torso as she walked back to her stand. The crowd slowly went back to doing their thing and shopping around.

"I believe that's our sign, it's time to go." I said, looking down at Magdolin.

"I agree. " She said, catching her breath and fixing a few strands of her hair as she let go of me.

Lapel started groaning and began to sit up, brushing the glass off of him. I grabbed Magdolin's hand and we began running up the street towards the wagon. Her hand was small and delicate. It was soft to the touch. But I was focused on getting her out of harm's way right now.

As we got back to the wagon I quickly untied the horses and jumped in the wagon on the bench. I leaned over and offered Magdolin a hand but that took too long. I grabbed her under her arms and lifted her up into the wagon.

I had adrenaline pumping through my blood so she felt extremely light at this second. I pulled the reins and the horses took off. I was out of breath and so was she. As I steadied my breathing I felt myself calming down. I turned to Magdolin, looking at her.

"Are you hurt! Are you alright? I'm so so sorry about that I shouldn't have left you alo-" She cut me off. "It's okay. I'm fine, people are just crude sometimes, and some men can't take no as an answer." She said, shaking her head.

"I know and I'm sorry Mags, I shouldn't have let that happen, I- I'm just-"

I got cut off again by her, except this time she grabbed my face with one of her hands and I felt her lips press against the side of my face.

I felt myself freeze. *Physically freeze.* Her lips were soft and calming. I felt euphoric at that second.

She pulled away after a moment. "Thank you Alexander." She said, smiling. Her thumb subconsciously rubbed my cheeks before she pulled her hand from my cheek.

I felt a tint of red form across my face as I looked at the road ahead of us with a serious look on my face. "O- of course Mags, it was no problem." I said not being able to make eye contact at the moment.

The feeling that ran straight from my heart to my face that felt like my whole body was on fire, ran through me rapidly. I seriously haven't felt this way in years. Even down to my fingertips I felt it.

I heard her snicker slightly to herself. That only made me more embarrassed about this. I turned to look at her. "What's so funny!" I said awkwardly, smiling.

"You're blushing!" She said, laughing now. I rolled my eyes dramatically.

"Oh please, this is just from that lipstick you've got on Mags, if you think you could make me blush you're very wrong my friend." I said, smiling and waving my hand looking back at the road. I could still feel her eyes on me but I just kept my eyes forward to stay calm.

Lapel had got my blood boiling, and the way she had just calmed me down so fast was surprising nonetheless. I kept my eyes on the road and as the sun started to set we barely had made it out of the village

"I don't believe we're going to make it to the next safe house Mags." I said with a frown, knowing we'd have to just stick it through the night with the wagon.

"We can just find a clearing in the woods, I'm sure we'll be fine." She said with a small smile.

I looked around the road and saw a small off trail. I directed the horses down towards it. The path was rough and rutted up but after a few minutes we made it into a small clearing. There is nothing exceptional about the spot other than that it was grassy and a small creek was running nearby.

I staked the wagon down and let the horses roam around the patch. Magdolin was running her fingers through her hair as she sat in the grass. Her hair looked dry and tangled from not being washed for a few days.

"Hey Mags if you want to go wash your hair there's a small creek. I'm sure you could find a deep spot," I said, crawling in the wagon and pulling out a soap bar.

"Oh thank goodness, my hair feels awful," She said with a sigh as she stood up and took the bar from me.

"Yeah the creek's right over there." I said, pointing through a few trees.

"Thank you." she said, walking off with the soap and her purple dress in hand.

Chapter 13. Magdoin Poni

I made my way down towards the bank of the creek, there were roots and rocks sticking out on the bank of the creek. I set my dress on one of the larger roots of the tree, and I walked into the deep part of the creek. It came up to my shoulder height, so this creek certainly wasn't large compared to the other one.

I felt a needle-like sensation in my skin as the cold water flowed around my body. I leaned forward and dipped my hair in the water, washing it thoroughly, getting every strand of hair wet. I took the soap and frothed it in my hands, making suds and bubbles out of it. I ran the soap through my hair and scrubbed my scalp making sure I got every inch of my head with the bar. I dipped my hair back in the water, rinsing out the bubbles into the flowing water.

My hair smelled like petals of lavender from the soap. My hair wasn't as soft as it normally was, like when Natalia would put oils and regimens in my hair to massage it.

I then used the soap on the rest of my body, I rinsed off again and then stood up squeezing the water out of my hair. I could see the moon rising in the sky brightly as I dried off.

It was the full moon and I knew that tonight was the night I'd get the dream.

I threw on my dress and pulled myself out of the creek. I walked over to the wagon where Alexander was standing and looking up at the stars.

"Alexander?" I said, interrupting the silence. He jumped as if I was startling him.

"Oh, hey Mags, the stars are beautiful tonight." He said as he looked down at me for a moment before looking up at the sky again

I had to admit, he looked cute looking up at the sky like that. The moonlight flashed across his tan skin beautifully. He complimented the night sky, not the other way around.

"I know, a- and about the stars, I need to warn you of something." I said looking up at the sky as well.

"Of course, anything Mags." He said calmly.

"Well, I don't want to seem like a lunatic or a mad mushroom, but my whole family has had these weird dreams whenever there's a full moon out" I said as Alexander looked at me with an eyebrow raised.

"Okay? It sounds interesting actually." He said, shrugging his shoulders.

"Well it is interesting..." I paused for a moment. "Natalia said that I try to get up and walk around and I sometimes talk when these dreams come around." I said nervously. Alexander looked at me again with a bit of a curious look on his face. "My whole family was gifted the ability, it dates back to when the ancient rulers of equilibrium had to face against pyromania and mycologia in the war. The dreams hint to what may come in the future. It helped so they could predict attacks." I said quietly.

"Ok, that should be no problem Mags, I've dealt with worse, trust me." He said, tying it off with a smile. "Plus I think that's a pretty interesting thing, is it just an extension of your magic?" He added, looking at me more intently.

I sighed, relieved he didn't think I was crazy. "Lovely, I just wanted to tell you so you didn't get scared if I did get up in the night" I said with a small laugh. "And yes, kind of. My magic is just with weapons, that's how my dagger works. And it gives me crazy aim and other tactics like that." I said acting out like I'd shot something with a bow.

"Yeah I would have been heavily confused if I woke up to you just gone." He said laughing as well. Inside it felt reassuring that he didn't mind it, but part of me still feared I might scare him? I don't know how I act during these, I'm asleep so how would I know?

"But the magic sounds very cool. It'd be cool if it extended to the whole kingdom." He said, knocking his hip to my side playfully.

I just shook my head and let out a small snort. I threw my hand over my mouth.

Ugh I hate when I do that! I sound like a pig.

Alexander let out a small laugh and I felt his gaze stay on me. I threw a glare up at him, how could he laugh at me?

He grabbed my hand and pulled it from my face. "I like your real laugh… it's cute." He said smiling down at me as he let my wrist fall to my side

I looked away from him, denying the heating feeling in my face. I stared up at the endless night sky, the darkness filled my eyes with the small speckles or light forming stars. The sky was encapsulating. It just sucked me in how it was so beautiful.

"I wish that you find a wife as divine as the night sky Alexander." I said looking up into the night sky with a small grin.

"I know I h- will." He said quietly, staring up at the stars as well. "Well I prepped the back of the wagon with hay and blankets for you Mags, so you can sleep under the stars if you'd like." He said smiling. Also subtly changing the subject.

"Why thank you." I said, looking at him and then walking to the side of the wagon and jumping up into the back. I laid on the blanket on top of the small pile of hay in the wagon. I pulled the end of the blanket over me as well.

"Well Mags, I'm gonna head down to the creek as well, I'll be right back. Don't worry, I'll be back before you can even start dreaming so don't worry about falling asleep. I'll be back to keep an eye on you." He said, smirking and walking off into the tree line. I rolled my eyes and nodded my head as I leaned back into the hay looking at the stars.

I felt my eyes get heavy after a few minutes, and I started to drift off under the stars.

As soon as I closed my eyes I felt myself wake up again. This time I was in a white void, it seemed as if it never ended in every direction I looked.

I stood up knowing this was my dream. I flipped around, looking for anything, I flipped around once more and there was a horrifying creature. I gasped and fell backwards. The creature looked like a monstrous version of my father. His skin looked as if it was melting off and he'd been rotting for years. I swear I could smell the horrific scent of flesh rotting.

As soon as my body hit the ground I was back in the castle, in the main hall before my parent's thrones.

I started to panic and hyperventilate. I knew it was a dream but it was all so real I couldn't comprehend it. It was the palace, every single bland white detail was the palaces. I heard fighting from the ballroom, so I rushed over to the door to see who it was. I walked in and my parents were normal again and screaming at each other.

As I walked in they both turned to me. "Magdolin!" they both said in union, running up to me.

"You've been gone so long, it's been years since we've seen you!" My mother said, wrapping her arms around me. I embraced her back tightly. I longed to feel my mother's hug once more and now I was. Even if she hadn't ever paid attention to me I couldn't deny her affection. Especially since it was so rare when I got it, even in dreams.

"You've grown so much, and don't worry about anything. We're just glad you've returned!" My father said, joining the hug. I was wide eyed staring up at his glowing form in my dream. I accepted his embrace as well, seeing him normal was better than the monstrous form previously. I held him as well, but it was an odd feeling after learning everything he had done to our kingdom. I just took in the moment though, knowing it was all fake.

After a moment I tried pulling away, they wouldn't let go though they just held me tighter. Their fingers dug into my skin aggressively. I gasped and tried to pull away again. "You're never leaving us again." My father said quietly.

"You simply aren't." My mother keyed in. She held my hand tightly as they let go of me. They both shoved me forward and I landed on my face, this time I reappeared in a hall. Natalia was handcuffed to the wall and two maids were adjusting my sleeves.

Natalia's whole person was disheveled. Her hair looked chopped and bruises were visible from the ripped gown she was wearing.

"Natalia!" I yelled trying to walk towards her but the maids yanked me back, I saw then what I was wearing. I had on a full wedding gown, a big puffy white dress with a lace and silk train. "What's going on!" I screamed and the double doors opened up and light showed in, it was a wedding hall and the maids started to drag me down the aisle as I tried to fight back from walking. I dug my heels into the ruby red carpet of the aisle. I tried to stop it, it needed to stop.

My father stood at the end of the aisle smiling as he held the kingdom's rule book. A male mushroom stood there, a gold and white mushroom, he was tall with a strong stature. Clearly the groom that my father had chosen.

As I was forced up to the altar, I scanned the room. A maid held Natalia still with her hand over her mouth. A guard stood next to the two and restrained Alexander who had a cloth tied over his mouth and a muzzle as well. He had chains holding him down, they had him restrained like an animal. I started to dart towards the two but a guard grabbed me and held me still with a hand over my mouth.

I cried and screamed against the guard, this was breaking my heart. Alexander looked like he'd been halfway beaten to death, as goes for Natalia. Alexander did not fight against the restraints as Natalia was, he looked *dead*. I started to fight against the guard even more. They were all going to pay, I had to prevent this somehow.

"I now pronounce you husband and wife." My father spoke loudly with a smile. Before anything else happened I broke myself free from the guard and hit the ground with my side.

I woke up in a dark room, I was sitting on a bed and I could barely see my own hands, a spotlight hit down on me and about a foot around me. The cover on the bed looked like a handmade quilt and I looked around for anything in sight. Another spotlight shone about three feet from me.

Two little girls were standing hand in hand, one looked about nine and the other couldn't have been more than two years old. I stood up from the bed, shocked to see the two girls. I didn't recognize either of them but the smaller, younger girl looked reminiscent of something. I couldn't put my finger on it but it synced a feeling of nostalgia or deja vu that I couldn't ignore.

The littlest girl had long, brown hair with a wave to it. She had a black based mushroom and white spots. And the older girl was a pink mushroom with white spots and she wore a knee length plaid skirt and a white blouse. They both just stared up at me as I did back down at them.

"Who are you?" I asked in a worried voice. I tried to mask my slight fear with a bit of command but it failed to appeal.

"It's us, Momma, don't you recognize us?" the bigger girl replied, looking a little hurt. It felt like my heart dropped through the floor.

"I- I'm not your mother." I said, scooting back on the bed, there's no way these could be my daughters with their colour variation.

The smaller girl started to let out a whine which turned into little sobs, crying. "No Momma, you made Elizabeth cry." The older girl said, holding her little sister.

"No stop saying that! I'm not your mother!" I said, getting more frightened as the girl cried into her sister's arms. The other little girl looked up at me and tears ran down her face as well. I didn't know what to do now. I was trapped in this dream state and I was stuck with these two little girls who were clearly demented!

I started to panic slightly as the two cried, I looked around but still couldn't see anything, just the two girls.

I crouched down to their level on my knees. "No, now …don't cry please, I'll help you find your mom I promise." I said trying to help comfort them but it only made it worse.

The older sister started wailing which put the little one into more distress. "You're our momma!" She said, crying as she held her little sister, her little voice was cracked and separated from crying. I was completely lost on what to do, I just held my arms out to the two hoping it may help somehow.

The two girls collapsed into my arms as they cried. The little one was sitting on my leg as she cried and the other one held around my torso. I held them up to my chest and just felt lost on what to do. I don't know how to comfort children, nevertheless two girls who think I'm their mother.

Eventually they stopped crying and just stayed there holding onto me. I stayed there holding them as well, it felt like the smaller one had fallen asleep. She laid limp in my right arm as I held her against me.

I felt a weird sensation come over me and it felt like gravity had lifted off of me. My body felt weightless as I looked at my hands and it looked like they were fading. I was coming out of the dream state. It felt like relief as I was able to open my eyes again.

I felt something hard in my hand, I gripped it tightly and recognized my dagger handle.

Chapter 14. Alexander Malencoy

I was walking back up to the wagon, my shirt and vest in hand. It was hot and humid out tonight, probably about seventy five degrees out. The bugs and animals sang through the night sky and the full moon lit over the entire forest. I threw my shirt over the side of the wagon and saw that Magdolin was lying in the hay still. It was weird though. I heard her murmuring to herself and she would squirm around every few seconds. I walked over so I could see her better. Her eyes were wide open. They weren't her eyes though, they were stark white and had no pupils. It freaked me out a little but I didn't let it affect me.

It grabbed my curiosity. I analysed her face and eyes specifically. Her eyes looked like they were glowing almost. I crawled up into the wagon and sat in the hay a few feet from her. I could hear what all she was murmuring. It was something about her parents now. I listened as I looked up into the night.

I felt her sit up and she started to move off of the wagon. I sat up quickly and watched her as she walked around in the clearing barefoot. I wanted to go and pick her up and put her back, but I remembered my mother telling me that you should never wake a sleepwalker.

But it's not sleepwalking right? It's something else because it's almost scheduled. So surely it should be fine if I just moved her back. I jumped up from the wagon and picked her up. She went almost limp and still had her eyes wide open.

I put my arm under her legs and one holding her torso up, in a bridal style. I started walking her back over and I heard footsteps, I thought possibly might be an animal of some sort. I flipped around, looking, and almost dropped Magdolin when I saw a mushroom's figure. I jumped back as I held Magdolin close to my chest. The mushroom was approaching us fast through the wooded tree line.

I started to run towards the wagon, holding Magdolin close. I set her down on the hay and ran around the wagon to grab a metal bar. I ran at the mushroom and swung and the mushroom dodged it. As he entered the moonlight, I recognized the stranger as Lapel.

"What the hell!" I yelled as he ran at me.

"Where is she? I'm sick of this!" He screamed as he shoved me to the ground, pinning me down.

"Get off of me!" I yelled back, throwing him off me and he came back at me, wrestling me on the ground. His nails dug at the bare skin that was exposed from me not having my shirt on.

Everytime he shows up it's at the worst possible moments! I don't even have a belt on!

"I'm tired of this game! Just tell me where she is!" He screamed at the top of his lungs, as his nails dug into my shoulder. I yelled in pain as he gripped me tight.

I heard footsteps running up to us, and what sounded like giggles approaching us fast. I looked up as I was still pinned down and saw Magdolin running at us. She had her dagger in hand with a grin across her face. Her eyes were still white with that little glow to them.

Lapel pulled away as she ran at us. Lapel rolled off of me and Magdolin tripped over us on the ground. I felt my heart jump. What if she landed on her dagger!?

He had a look of astonishment. "Why is she purple now? What did you do to her, you monster!" He yelled as Magdolin picked herself up off the ground. It felt like a building just got lifted off of me as she stood.

"I didn't do shit!" I said as Magdolin lunged at Lapel. He rolled on the ground, trying to dodge her dagger, but failed. She got a good hit on his left arm and he screamed out.

"BLOODY HELL" He screamed, standing up and backing away.

I didn't know what to do as Magolin stood there, breathing hard with the dagger. She looked like she was panting and sweating. She looked down at me as I was still on the ground and just observed me closely. She froze there as I stood up. Her fingers gently flexed on the handle of her dagger as the dagger shot out to a full length battle sword. It gently glowed in the dim moonlight. Part of me was slightly scared considering she was staring right at me as she did it.

Lapel looked shocked and amazed.

"What the hell is happening to her?" He asked, holding his arm and speaking in an infuriated tone.

"It's none of your business" I said, snapping back at him as I watched him hold his arm, hunched over. It was pathetic.

"Wait… is she the… princess?" He said with his eyes growing wider and looked fearful.

"I won't be answering that, but think of it this way. If she is, and you go spreading it that she's here, you'll be decapitated and tortured for doing what you did to her. If I were you, I'd make the right choice of keeping your mouth shut." I said with a slight growl to my voice, Lapel infuriated me. He had a look of worry across his face as he looked at Magdolin, who was still in her dream state.

"Poison mushroom." Magdolin barely whispered. I turned to look back at her. She was still frozen there with her sword over her shoulder defensively.

I watched as he stood there hunched over and grunted as he breathed. He was clearly in pain from the gash that dug probably about two inches into his skin. It cut the sleeve of his shirt and everything, blood poured from the wound, soaking his arm as he held it.

I heard a sigh and Magdolin shuddered. I looked over and her eyes were cracked open. *Her eyes.*

Instantly she dropped her sword. Her eyes widened at the sight of lapel. I couldn't read a single emotion in her wide eyed gaze. It was like she was neutral. Her body language. Her stare. Her lips. Her stance. It was all neutral.

"Your Majesty I'll be on my way, please forgive me, I wish to be pardoned." He said, folding his hands together and spoke in a pleading voice.

"Leave!" She said as she stepped back from both Lapel and I. I just glared at Lapel as he ran out into the tree line towards the trail back.

I snickered as he ran off into the trees. He ran like a scared rabbit.

I turned quickly to look back at Magdolin. Her face quickly faded to a face of horrification and she collapsed to her knees sobbing. Fisting the grass in her hands. "...Alexander." She almost silently sobbed.

I sat in front of her and quickly pulled her to me. I held the top of her mushroom and around her back as she started to break down in waves of tears. "I'm right here... I have you." I whispered as I did my best to bring her some form of comfort

She just shook, almost violently as she wept. It broke my heart. This couldn't be from Lapel showing up. Something happened in her dream.

She pushed away from me after a few moments and looked up at me. Her tear streaked face made me want to solve whatever was going on, faster. "Y-you.. N-need to leave.. Get a ..f-f-far away from me.. A-as possible." she said loudly in a broken voice. Her words caught on her exasperated breaths every few syllables.

I think what she said hurt me even more than seeing her cry. "I can't leave you, what are you talking about?" I said, grabbing her hands and rubbing the tops of her hands as she shook her head.

She swallowed her tears hard before she spoke again. "He's going ... t-to kill ..you A-Alexander. I can't l-let that happen to you." She said just as loud as last time but she was getting control of her breathing now. "Please" she gasped

I froze at her requests, I couldn't. I can't.

"Magdolin, I made a promise to you. And that was to get you out of this wretched awful kingdom. I'm not breaking my promise." I said quietly as held her hands tighter.

She shook her head again. "Alexander, you don't understand! He-" she started to yell back with more tears pouring from her eyes.

"I don't care, I'm not listening. I'm here to help you. I don't care what that includes or requires, I'll protect you. I won't let them take you Mags. You're my best friend." I said in a calming voice as I clamped one of my hands over her mouth before she could argue back. "I will get you to safety." I said even quieter as I gazed into those deep purple amethyst eyes.

She didn't fight back against me as I spoke. She just stared up at me as my hand cradled the back of her neck and my other was over her mouth. She wasn't crying anymore so that was one good thing.

She gently pulled my hand from her mouth and I let her. But I went wide eyed as her arms wrapped around my neck. I wrapped my arms around her back and held her flush against me. She was so soft and delicate, yet her hold on me was tight. I closed my eyes and let myself melt into the warm embrace.

"I owe you my life." She whispered into my hair.

"You owe me nothing." I said quietly as my hands rubbed her back.

We stayed like that. Four minutes and thirty two whole minutes of pure bliss for me. And I was glad she calmed down. By the time she pulled away the only sign she'd been crying was the glassines to her beautiful eyes.

I stood up and offered her a hand which she gratefully took.

"Why was lapel here?" she asked, leaning on my shoulder as she stood up.

"It's Lapel, what do you think he was here for?" I said sarcastically. I could tell that didn't help at all as she just frowned. "It's fine though. He's gone now. You should get back to bed Mags, it's still very late." I said, taking her by her own shoulder and leading her back to the wagon. I picked her up by her waist and set her down in the hay and blankets. I looked up at the sky and the moon was just past the center of the sky. I laid down in the hay as well and I heard Magdolin's breathing shallow down and become more separated as she fell asleep.

I sat up and looked at her, her eyes weren't wide open and she looked as if she was sleeping normally. I smiled and reached up over her and grabbed a bag. It had small sponge cylinders in it and I wound my hair around them in thick bundles. This way it wasn't curly in the morning, they would lay flatter when I did this. As I put all the rollers in my hair I layed down in the hay and quickly fell asleep under the stars. I rested, assured we wouldn't be bothered because of what had just happened.

·• ⋖⋛⋬⋗ •·

Birds chirped as the sun arose over the horizon, casting shadows of the trees, over the clearing. I sat up, rubbing my eyes and looked around. Magdolin was curled up with a blanket, still asleep in the hay, as I jumped out of the wagon. I stretched my arms out and yawned as deer ran through the woods and a few rabbits jumped around in the clearing, then scattered as they noticed my presence.

I put on my shirt and threw on my vest and belts. I pulled out my journal and began flipping through the pages. I sat down next to the horses and I began writing on the first blank page.

This girl she's a bit odd but she has the most amazing personality I think I've ever witnessed! She's beautiful, and polite. I love how she messes with me and teases me occasionally. I like that she's opening up to me as well. Charlie was obviously indicating towards me making a move towards her when she handed me that ring. I doubt I'll ever really do it because she's royalty, and she's against mixing colours. And she'd never be interested in a poison mushroom. We're known as nothing more than scum, something to be discarded. The only reason she tolerates me is because I'm getting her free from her constraints as queen. I'm glad I can give her that though. It's the very least I would do for her, at this standing point I wouldn't doubt that I'd do anything for her. Most of me wants to hold and protect her, I want to be with her. She's all I could ever want. I need her but she doesn't need me. And I'm not sure how to tell her without scaring her off, so I'm doing what's best and keeping my trap shut. But deep inside I know that I love that girl.

I went into deep thought as I filled the entire page with a fine delicate cursive writing style. I felt myself smile as I finished the last few words. I shut the book and went to slide my journal back in my satchel and saw the small black box that Charlie gave me. I pulled it out and slid my journal back in. I looked at the delicate ring. The metal wrapping around the gorgeous white stone. Small swirls and dots mixing were around the circular part of the ring.

I snapped the box shut and shoved it back in my satchel as I heard Magdolin start to stir awake. I stood up quickly and grabbed some horse food for the horses so it looked like I was doing something.

"Good Morning Mags." I said, walking around the cart as she sat up stretching. Her hair was all a tangled mess with some hay sticking out of it. I couldn't help but snicker quietly to myself.

"Laughing at me isn't a good way to wake me, Alexander," She said, smiling as she wiped her face off and rubbed her eyes. "But good morning to you as well." She added, crawling out of the wagon.

I laughed as she tiredly wobbled to her feet, I started to pull the loose hay pieces from her hair and tossing them to the ground as she fully woke up.

I grabbed a brush out from the side of the wagon I had for myself. I gently tugged at her hair and she shot me a dirty look before I started brushing her hair for her.

"Oh Alexander, I can brush my hair. You don't have to brush my hair, I can do that" She said, turning to look at me fully.

"Oh nonsense, it's my pleasure. Now tell me. How'd you sleep the rest of the night?" I asked as I turned her around again and began brushing her hair again. It was soft, oh so very soft. I could brush it all day long.

"It was alright, no more dreams." She said quietly as she stood still for me to brush her hair.

"That's good, but in your own good news I'm hoping to make it to the next safe house tonight. So no more dangers like lapel hopefully." I said with a small smirk.

I kept brushing her hair for a few more moments even after it was fully brushed and then I put it in a loose fishtail braid. I still remember when my mother had taught me how to do different braids

Chapter 15. Magdolin Poni

I threw on my colour cap, stepped into the treeline, and changed into my pink dress. I walked back to the cart as I plastered on my light pink lipstick. I crawled up on the wagon and sat on the bench as the wagon jerked and took off.

We rode out of the rutted path and the wagon got back on the dirt road. We rode back through the town we were in yesterday. The festival from yesterday was gone and picked up. Kids ran through the streets, laughing and giggling with each other. I smiled as the kids ran by the wagon, smiling at the horses. One boy yelled at Alexander and asked him to stop.

"Hey mister! Can we see the horsies!" The little boy yelled out. He couldn't have been more than five. He had his front teeth out and talked with a whistle to his voice.

I looked at Alexander smiling gently, "Can we please stop for the little ones?" I asked in a pleading voice.

"We need to keep a move on Mags." He said quietly and continued the wagon. I frowned but then took the reins from his hand and pulled them, the wagon yanked and Alexander frowned down at me. I smiled as I heard the kids cheer happily.

I smiled up at Alexander and he rolled his eyes with a sigh. The kids surrounded the horses, petting them and crawling on their backs. I awed as they did so, I jumped off the wagon as a little girl was trying to get up on Hope. I picked up the little girl. She looked about three.

"There you go sweetie," I said as I looked up at her face. I froze slightly, as she was the girl from my dream. The girl with a pink mushroom and blonde hair. I looked up at her wide eyed, I could see a bruise poking out of the neck of her dress. She looked down at me with a confused look on her little face.

I stepped back, shocked. I felt myself bump into someone and flipped around to see Alexander.

"Is everything okay?" He asked, grabbing my shoulders to steady me.

"That girl, she was in my dream." I said, looking up at Alexander as I started to slightly hyperventilate.

"No, calm down it surely can't be. Plus what is a small little girl going to do?" He said comfortingly, smiling. I shook my head and looked back at the girl. He was right. What could she even do? I took a deep breath

"You're right." I sighed, taking a few steps forward but then a loud crash abruptly made everyone fall silent.

"ADELINE!" A familiar male's voice screeched out across the street. It made Alexander and I both jump. I looked around and noticed that the little girl looked horrified. She was wide eyed and slightly hunched over. "When I call your name, you answer! DO YOU GOT ME ADELINE?!" The voice said again as a very familiar mushroom walked around the side of the wagon. Lapel trudged around the wagon, stomping his feet as he moved the kids out of the way and grabbed the girl off the horse.

"I'm sorry Papa, I'm sorry!" The little girl said as Lapel grabbed her by her little dress and yanked her down to the ground.

"SORRY DON'T CUT IT, YOU AREN'T SUPPOSED TO BE OUT HERE!" He screamed. I felt my blood boil as he yelled at the girl. She had done nothing wrong.

I looked up at Alexander whose jaw was agape in shock and anger. His hands clenched at his sides in anger. I felt like I could practically feel the anger seething off of him.

"Lapel!" I said with a strong voice as I stomped my foot to the ground. Lapel looked up at Alexander and I with a glare.

He looked as if he hadn't slept, possibly drunk. His face dropped as he recognized us. His jaw was still agape and the small girl was wiping tears off her face. I walked over and felt Alexander grab my shoulder but I yanked away from his grasp and approached the two.

"Where's her mother?" I said to Lapel glaring as he looked at me shocked, he glared at me and I scowled right back at him.

"Mommy?" The girl chimed in, getting upset and started crying more.

"She doesn't have a mother! She left me with her! She didn't want her!" Lapel yelled at me, I glared at him and then looked down at the girl as he let go of her. I reached down, wiped her tears off, and picked her up. She gratefully accepted it and held around my neck.

This poor girl, she looked so broken. This was so wrong, I can't leave her with Lapel.

"Well I guess that would explain why you aren't married, Lapel. An only father and no wife at all, you have no charm, only pride, and let me just say I don't think that this girl's mother didn't want her. I think she didn't want you." I said, scowling at Lapel. He had no right being a father, especially to a little girl. The kids around us started to leave from the awkward fight that happened before them.

"And what the hell are you indicating towards?" He said, glaring at me, practically frothing at the mouth.

"You aren't a proper parental figure Lapel, you shouldn't be left alone with a child, especially after that show you just put on in front of the other children." I said calmly as I rubbed the girl's back while I held her.

"Oh, and what? Are you saying your little, light in the loafers husband to a better father than me?" He said, pointing at Alexander accusingly.

"I do think so, and I think that would be the best option." I said, getting more furious by the second and I felt Alexander over my shoulder now. I could feel the anger coming off of all three of us.

"FINE! See if I care! Take this little leech and get her as far away from me as you can," Lapel said, throwing his arms up and stomping off. I huffed at his ignorance and held the girl close to me.

"She's coming with us now." I said, looking up at Alexander with a stern face and voice.

He just took a deep breath and put on a fake smile as his eyes showed anger. "I was going to suggest that anyway darling "He said, clearly furious at Lapel as he watched him storm into his house, slamming the door behind him.

Alexander rested his hand on my lower back as he guided me towards the cart. I held Adeline close to myself and made sure to be careful with her.

We both took our seat on the wagon, Alexander's face was red with anger. "I am not a homosexual," He growled, mumbling in anger as the horses took off. I set my hand over his and rubbed the top of his hand with my thumb.

My other arm resided around the little girl and she sat in my lap. Alexander seemed to cool down as he took my hand into his loosely. It was nice, holding his hand, comforting when the air was so tight.

"Where am I going?" The girl said, looking at Alexander as she held the skirt of her dress in her little fists. She looked… scared.

I took note of how her hair was matted and her dress had some tears on the seams and small rips and stains on it. She clearly wasn't taken care of and it shattered my heart. "You're coming to a better place with us," Alexander said, letting go of my hand and patting the girl's legs.

"You're going to stay with us for now ok." I added to Alexander's statement. She looked in between us both and started to cry.

"Oh, oh no no, baby it's okay." I said, cupping her face and hugging her. I looked over at Alexander for help. He looked nervous as well as he attached the reins to the small post of the wagon so the horses could lead themselves.

"No, Papa… He's gonna come… g-get me.. .and I'll get punished!" She said, heaving in air as she cried. I stroked her hair trying to calm her down.

"No it's okay. He isn't going to, we won't let him. Okay? I promise." Alexander said as he wiped off her tears.

"It's going to be okay baby doll, we will take care of you now, a-and we don't yell. It'll be much better." I said smiling, trying to make her feel better as I pulled her back to look at her face. She just looked at us as she stopped crying and caught her breath back to normal.

"Do you mean it?" She said, wiping her tears with the sleeve of her dirty little white undershirt.

"Yes, dear." Alexander said as I nodded my head. She smiled and laughed as her cries turned to hiccups and giggles. I smiled and laughed with her. I heard Alexander join in on the laughter. I laughed so hard I felt a few tears run down my cheeks, the laughter died down as a few more moments passed.

"Oh my, are you hungry?" I asked, looking down at her.

She nodded her head "..if that's okay," She said quietly.

"Of course it's okay, just ask and we'll do our best." Alexander said.

I set her on the bench and crawled into the back of the cart and dug through the hay. I opened a basket that had some water and bread, I knew it wasn't much but we'd be back at a safe house tonight so I'm sure we could prepare stuff there. I crawled back up to the front and sat in between her and Alexander and handed her the flask of water and the small loaf of bread.

Her eyes almost sparkled as she saw the bread and fresh water. She took the bread, tearing off small pieces and putting them in her mouth, chewing them fast.

"Oh, slow down there Missy, You've got all the time in the world to eat" I said with my arm around her. She still ate fast. I frowned. She must've been starving. As she finished about half the loaf, she crawled across my lap and stood in between me and Alexander. She ripped off a piece of the loaf and pushed it in Alexander's face.

"Oh no you can have it kid." He said, smiling.

"No, take it," She said insistently.

Alexander sighed and laughed as he took the small piece of bread in his mouth. She ripped off another piece and pushed it toward me. I politely took it and chewed it. She giggled and then ate the last few bites of the bread. She crossed her legs and sat in between me and Alexander. She reached and grabbed the flask and took a big gulp from it. She handed it back to me and she squirmed around and settled in a position where her head was on Alexander's leg and she curled into a fetal position using the loose fabric of my dress to cover herself like a blanket.

I smiled and awed, I looked up at Alexander, smiling. He was smiling back at me, she fell asleep there and snored quietly. "Awe" Alexander said as he took the reins in his hands again.

·• ⋖⟨⟩⋗ •··

A few hours later we arrived at the next safe house. This safe house was two stories and white, it was pretty and simple. I picked up the little girl and she gently woke up. She rubbed her eyes and woke up fully as Alexander opened the door for us.

"Well, good morning princess." I said teasingly as I looked around the house. This house looked a bit cleaner than the other houses. I started to think of things I could use to get her looking better. Alexander was in the kitchen, preparing some food to take out to the fire he had burning outside in the back yard clearing.

I took her and placed her on Alexander's back. She clung to him and wrapped her arms and legs around him.

"Hey!" He said laughing and turning.

"Hold her for a few minutes, I'm gonna go get some things for her." I said, smiling and running out of the house to the wagon. I grabbed the left-over fabric I had from my dress and came back in with it and soap.

"Bath Time!" I said, running over and snatching her off Alexander's back. She giggled and laughed as I held her against me. Alexander turned around from the counter smiling.

"I want you to be very careful back there Mags. The current is pretty strong." He said with a stern, but playful face.

"I know," I said, smiling.

"What are you gonna change her into? Your dresses won't fit her." He said, cringing a bit as we hit a stump in this mission.

"Well, I um… I'm not sure." I said, looking at her. It was silent for a few moments.

"…Well little lady, you're one lucky gal, I'll tell you." Alexander said, smirking and taking his vest off. "Most women would marvel if they got my shirt." He said, ripping off his shirt and throwing it at her. She broke out in giggles and laughter as she pulled it out of her face.

I watched as he put the vest back on. He then turned to look at me and I looked away abruptly. I felt my face flush with embarrassment as he caught me gawking at him. He wasn't built like somebody professional, but he was toned. Toned like you'd expect out of any mushroom who could live off the wilderness if he wanted too. He was *hot*.

I had to change the subject NOW. I pulled up Adeline and bounced her slightly as she giggled. "It's bath time. Say thank you to Alexander for, oohh, so kindly giving you his women marveling shirt." I said in a dramatic tone as I opened the backdoor.

"Thank you!!" She said, waving her hand as I walked out to the river side that was on the side of the property. I set her down and held her hand as we walked the small hike. I had my dress and Alexander's shirt in my other hand.

As we reached the river side I helped Adeline down and set her on a log as I took off her little shoes. They had little buckles and white socks underneath. Her feet looked bruised and scratched, and her face twinged as I took her shoes off.

"I know it hurts honey but we'll get you feeling better, I promise." I said calmly as I started helping her take her small dress off. I then took off my own dress and grabbed her, lowering us both into the water. The water wasn't an awful temperature and was slightly tolerable. I felt her grab around my neck and felt a shiver go up her spine. "Are you cold? " I asked teasingly as she nodded her head yes.

I smiled "Hold your breath!" I said as I dunked us both under the water. I came back up and she was giggling and shivering slightly. I laughed and grabbed the soap as we sat in the shallow water that reached just over my chest as I sat in the river stone. The water came to her shoulders as she stood. She splashed and threw the water around us as I ran my fingers through her tangled hair. I ran soap through it hoping to get more of them out but it didn't seem to work very well, I was afraid I'd have to cut her matted hair.

I washed out her hair as best as I could and washed her body off. She had cuts and bruises all over her and it made me curious and sad.

"So Adeline, what do you like to do?" I asked curiously as I started to wash my own hair and she splashed and kicked in the water.

"Uhm... I like playing and running," she said, stammering, trying to find the words. I smiled and wrung out my hair as I stood up out of the water.

"Well we can do lots of that Adeline." I said, sliding on my purple dress. I slid Alexander's shirt over her head and it draped over her like a cape. I picked up our dirty dresses and her shoes and socks. "Here, get on my back." I said, sitting on my knees as she crawled onto my back.

She was heavy and it made me stumble a bit at first as I stood up but I made my way up the embankment and started towards the house. Adeline would hold strands of my hair and move them around as I made my way up to the house.

I heard Alexander in the back yard and went around the side of the house. "Allie- zander!" Adeline called out as I set her down in the soft grass so she wouldn't hurt her feet while walking. She ran over to him as he was sitting on the ground next to a fire cooking something over it.

"Hey there Adel." He said, letting her sit down in his lap. I smiled as I set the dresses down on a log, they needed to be washed later. Alexander was wearing a white shirt now with his usual vest overtop.

"Well you look fancy." I said, sitting down next to the two of them as Adeline mumbled to herself and played with two rocks she had found.

"Why thank you. It was my fathers. Although I'm sure you preferred just the vest." He said, fooling with the collar.

"Oh hush," I said, looking down at Adeline to avoid his gaze.

Adeline's hair was still in a matted bunch up by her shoulders. I cringed knowing I'd done as much as I knew to fix it.

"Do you think you could help me with her hair?" I asked curiously, I had no idea what to do with it. It was a matted mess that fell at her shoulders in absolute dreads.

Alexander looked at her hair and shrugged. "It looks like a challenge I'm willing to accept," He said, standing up and walking around the house.

Adeline ran circles around the small area around the fire as Alexander set her out of his lap.

"Be careful, Addie," I said pointing at her.

"You be careful *Maggie*." She said, giggling and continued running. I smiled and watched her until she tripped over the edge of her shirt.

She hit the ground with a small "oof" and then got right back up and continued running around.

Alexander made his way back with a small bag, he sat back down next to me and waved Adeline over. She sat down in front of him and he pulled out a brush from the bag.

He started carefully moving the brush through her hair, untangling it slowly. Adeline flinched and gently sobbed as it pulled at her hair.

"It's okay, if we don't do this how will you have princess hair?" Alexander said, trying to lighten the mood. She snuffed her nose as her sobs turned to small whines and she flapped her hands around as he got the mats free from her hair.

"Are you a little bird, are you gonna fly off and away?" I said pinching her cheek and she giggled. As Alexander finally got her hair back to being straight and long. It reached down her back about halfway down her spine.

It was a pretty yellow blonde, a few streaks of white streaked her hair as well. It complimented the light speckled freckles across her face. She was adorable.

"Now you really do have princess hair." He said as he set her back on her feet and she took off running back around.

I smiled as she was looking better and healthier already.

Alexander pulled the iron skillet off of the fire and set it down on the grass. He grabbed three plates and dished out the fish he had prepared for the three of us.

"Come here, Adel." He said, setting her plate down next to him as she ran over and collapsed onto him.

"Fishy?" She said as she leaned against Alexander and poked at it with the fork.

"Is that alright with you, Missy?" He said back, smiling as he ate his.

"I love fish!" She said as she picked it up with her hands and ate it.

I smiled as the two were bonding and he had his arm around her. I ate my fish and took our plates inside, from the kitchen window I saw Alexander and Adeline running around the fire. It warmed my heart and brought a weird feeling upon me. I quickly shuddered it off and walked back outside where Adeline was now holding her hands up to Alexander to be picked up.

"I think she's tired," He said as he picked her up.

"I've got to run down the river again and wash our dresses, let's just put her to sleep" I said as I opened the door for them while they walked inside. I opened the door to one of the small bedrooms on the second floor.

The bed was clearly a small child's bed. He lifted the blanket and dusted it off a little bit before he sat her down and I covered her up with it. "Sweet dreams, Addie," I said, hugging her as she sat, smiling against the pillow.

"No, you can't leave me alone!" She said with a worried face.

"But Addie I- " I said until Alexander cut me off

"I'll stay with her" He said, laying on the edge of the bed and she giggled. I smiled and closed the blinds in the window and planted a small kiss on Adeline's forehead. Alexander smiled at the scene as Adeline squirmed down and pulled the blanket up. Alexander smirked up at me.

"I don't get tucked in either?" He said jokingly. I rolled my eyes and reached for another blanket off of the shelf. "Oh no, I'm not serious" He said, whispering and waving his hand.

"Well then sweet dreams you little sleeping beauty" I said whispering as I put my hands on my hips. He was still smirking at me and he rolled over as Adeline was asleep. I leaned over him and planted a small kiss on his cheek. I felt his muscles in his face tense up into a smile. "Goodnight" I said as I left the room leaving the door slightly ajar.

As I walked down the stairs and out the door into the backyard I felt that weird feeling in my chest again. Like it was hard to breathe or something, and my face felt hot. I brushed it off and picked up the dresses, making my way down to the riverside. I couldn't get the thought out of my head though, this feeling was weird and wrong. I couldn't let it continue. I slid my boots off and my tights and left them on the large log. I took my dress first, dipping it in the water and scrubbing the stains out with a bar of soap. I dunked it back in the water and then found a branch and hung it there for now. The sun was almost completely set over the horizon and casted a beautiful array of orange pinks and red, then faded to a dark blue and purple night sky.

I walked around in the ankle-deep water for a few more minutes and then out onto a sandbar. The water was cool but not an unbearable temperature. The night air dropped to about seventy five degrees around me. I smiled and let out a sigh, I cupped my hand and knelt down to the water and sipped it gently from my hands. I stood back up and walked over to the more shallow water grabbing Adeline's dress and started washing it, dirt seeped out of the small dress and I was extremely careful not to tear it any more than it already was. Once it was as clean as I could get it, I hung it up as well on the branch. I was about to slip on my boots when I heard footsteps.

My head darted side to side cautiously as I backed up into the water again. My fear died down as I saw Alexander walking down the embankment. He had some sort of wooden box.

"Alexander, you scared me!" I said as he came closer laughing. "And where's Adeline?" I said as he sat the box down on the log.

"She's dead asleep, don't worry" He said, taking off his shirt and laying it next to the log, his shoes followed as well.

"What are you doing?" I said, getting that feeling in my chest again.

"Oh, my manners, sorry. Would you like to join me Mags?" he said, smiling and turning on what I now recognized as a radio.

"Join what?" I asked curiously.

"Dance with me, come on!" he said, holding his hand out as swing music started to pour out of the radio.

"Oh, Alexander I'll fall out here," I said as he took my hand and drug me out into the sandbar.

"I won't let you fall. Trust me" He said, holding both my hands and spinning us around in the water, dancing to the music. I smiled and laughed as the water splashed around us as we danced and spun to the music. The soft sand of the sand bar shifted as we danced on it. I laughed and shouted as we danced. It was nice to finally be able to dance without being dolled up in some huge ball gown. Or forced to do it the proper way. Dancing in the shallow water, just having fun, was a whole new experience. Alexander had his hand resting on my waist and his other hand held my own as we danced kicking our feet.

As the song reached the end and started to slow down I laughed as I caught my breath. I stumbled around a bit and Alexander steadied me so I wouldn't fall back into the water.

"Oh my lords, that was exhilarating," I said happily as I laughed.

"Isn't it though?" He breathed, laughing as well.

Without warning Alexander let go of me and fell back into the deeper part of the water. He disappeared for a few moments and I started to get worried. I knelt down at the end of the sand bar to see if I could see him perchance.

"Alexander, this isn't funny" I said, brushing my hand over the water. It had no effect. It was too dark around to see anything. The sun had fully set and the stars filled the sky. All of the sudden a hand grabbed mine and pulled me down into the deep part. I gasped as I fell under the water. My feet couldn't reach the ground and I kicked and squirmed as I felt arms pull me up to the surface.

"I got you, stop kicking" Alexander said, laughing as he held me up.

"That was uncalled for mister!" I said, coughing as I caught my breath.

"Oh you're fine. Stop being dramatic" he said as he slightly let go of me.

"No! No no no, I can't swim. Don't let go of me!" I said, grasping onto his shoulders.

"Are you serious?" He said with a bit of surprise in his voice.

"Well it wasn't necessary for me to know so they never taught me in the palace" I said, wiping water out of my eyes.

"Okay well you need to know it out here. Look, all you do is cup your hands and gently push at the water and kick your feet, GENTLY" he said showing me how to do it, still not letting me go.

"Alexander, I can't do this. It's like teaching an old dog new tricks" I said, trying to do it but to no avail."

And who said you can't teach old dogs new tricks" He said, smiling as he let go of me.

I gasped as my head fell under the water. I kicked my legs and pushed at the water with my hands. I felt my head peak over the water as I caught my breath. "Alexander! I said don't let go of me!" I said angrily as he laughed.

"Well I think you don't need it. See, you're swimming fine on your own now." He said, pointing at me as I noticed he still wasn't holding me.

"Huh, so it isn't that hard " I said, a little bit shocked.

"Nope!" He said, swimming on his back around the deep part, avoiding the current underneath.

I focused on keeping the strokes I was swimming in even and with just the right amount of force to not let myself fall back under. I looked over at Alexander who was just floating on his back in the middle of the water. I swam over to him and pushed him down under the water, interrupting his relaxation.

"Hey!" he shouted as he came back up. I laughed until he grabbed me and threw me up out of the water. I fell back down with a splash and went back under water. Instead of coming right back up I held my breath and drug him under water as well. I pushed down on his head and came back up to the surface and gasped for air. His hands grabbed onto my sides as he came back up for air.

"Oh you're just trying to kill me now aren't you" He said, laughing and huffing for air.

"Maybe" I said, laughing. I looked down at him, the moonlight defined the loose wet curls on his head. His smile sparkled and it consumed me. I couldn't tear away from just admiring him. The water that made his face shine and his smile brighter than the sun. He was so handsome like that and it felt like he was pulling me closer to him at that moment.it felt like the world slowed as his face inched toward my own. We just floated their staring into each other's eyes, *sinful.*

I was oh so rudely interrupted by a force pulling me underneath the water. It yanked us both under the surface, I kicked and tried to swim up to no avail. I started to panic not knowing what was going on.

Chapter 16. Alexander Malencoy

I felt us both get dragged under the water by the current. I felt Magdolin squirming, flailing her arms around, trying to get back up. I was trying to get us both to the surface but it was a huge struggle. I wrapped my arms around her and swam as hard as I could upwards. I was able to get us both to the surface and I swam us back over to the sand bar. We both hacked and coughed up water and gasped in large amounts of air.

Magdolin was limp and I held her up to my chest as she caught her breath. Her chest rose and fell rapidly as she dug her hands into the sand and sat up.

"Are you alright?" I yelped in a rushed, worried voice. I used my hand to brush her soaking wet hair out of her face as she was still coughing a little bit.

"I told you that was a bad idea, " she said, pointing at me as her head was still down. I laughed as I brought myself to my feet. I reached down and pulled her up as well.

"Oh, it needed to happen, you need to know how to swim," I said as I whipped her off her feet and carried her out of the water. She didn't even try to let me put her down, it made me smile and I felt my heart warm a bit.

Her breath started to steady back down as I set her down on the shore. I grabbed the radio and the dresses that were halfway dry. She picked up her boots and my shoes and trudged up the hill behind me.

We made our way to the house. The fire was dying out now and the animals all were awake making their nightly symphony. I hung the dresses out on the porch and left the radio on the counter in the kitchen. We were both dripping wet and Magdolin looked exhausted and tired.

"I'm gonna go get my black dress from the wagon" she said, rubbing her eyes.

"No, no it's fine, you don't have to go back outside, I've got stuff inside you can wear " I said, walking carefully back towards the master bedroom of the house. I pulled out two extra shirts I had and a pair of slacks. "Here Mags" I said, handing her one of the shirts. "It should be big enough to fit you like a dress" I said as she examined the tan shirt, shrugging her shoulders.

"Thank you, this will be fine for me tonight. " she said taking it happily. I walked back out to the front porch and changed out my soaked clothes with the dry ones. I walked back inside as Magodlin set her soaked dress over the ledge of the porch.

She sighed as she went back into the house. My eyes followed her every movement, the way she looked in my shirt was jaw dropping. The shirt dropped to her mid thigh and flowed with her step. Her legs were long and dainty, and her hair was still damp and fell down her back. I watched her closely in awe at how gorgeous she was. I wasn't watching in a disrespectful way, but an admiring way. I'm sure as a princess she had gotten so much admiration she'd be sick of it by now but I couldn't for a second dare that I'd never stop admiring her. Her beauty cascaded to everything around her and she just lightened up a dark room with no effort. She was nice and kind and everything any male could ever dream for. I would do anything for her and I will never doubt that. It's going to kill me whenever I have to leave her on the island. Some other guy will try to take her from me, what male wouldn't try that though? I wouldn't blame them.

A sense of jealousy ran over me as I thought about another mushroom taking advantage of her. I hated when Lapel had tried, and on top of that he fought me. I wanted Magdolin, I wanted her all to myself. I craved her, I wanted to hold her and be close to her. I wanted to talk to her and just be able to interact with her more. I wanted to do special things with her, but I couldn't. My time with her is limited and I can't let myself get any more attached to her.

I opened the door to her room in the house, it was a small room but bigger than the one Adeline was in. She crawled into the bed and squirmed for a moment. I smiled as I walked towards the door "Goodnight Mags,"

"Goodnight Alexander" she said in reply as I shut her door. I walked down the hall and into the master bedroom, I collapsed down onto the bed. I peered over at the picture of my parents that sat on the bedside table, this had been my childhood home before we left.

My parents weren't exactly happy with my occupation or situation. They wanted me to be a carpenter or something useful like that. But no one would have ever bought anything I made simply because I'm a poison mushroom. And with this job I get to travel and meet some interesting people, like Magdolin. But Magolin was different from all my other travellers. She is special to me, way more than my other people. I sat up and realised my hair was still soaking wet and I hadn't put my curlers in.

I walked down stairs and I quickly rolled my hair into the rollers and trudged back up the stairs. Dragging my feet along and throwing myself down onto the bed again. As my thoughts carried on I drifted to sleep laying sprawled out on the bed. I slept like a rock snoring as the hours passed on.

·•·◁═╞▷·•·

The next morning I woke up to Adeline jumping up on me. "Wake up!" she yelled happily as she giggled. I huffed as her weight came down on me as I was sleeping.

"Oh goodness, good morning Adel " I said sitting up as she proceeded to jump up and down on the bed. I looked around and saw Magdolin, back in her purple dress, sitting on the edge of the bed as Adeline jumped and fell on the bed giggling. She looked up at me and started laughing.

"You put curlers in your hair?" she said, covering her smile as she laughed.

"Yes, of course I do, how do you think I stay this fabulous? " I said in reply as I acted like I flipped my hair dramatically. Adeline bursted out in a cackle and Magdolin rolled her eyes. I stood up from the bed stretching and yawning. "C'mon you two, I'll make you breakfast" I said, smiling as I took the curlers out of my hair and left them on the dresser.

"Oh actually I already did, I read a little bit closer in one of the cook books downstairs. So I promise it's not …toxic like the last time" Magdolin said nervously as she smiled.

"Oh really, well I'm sure it's amazing then" I said as Adeline clung onto my leg, smiling up at me. "And what are you doing Missy?" I said, putting my hands on my hips looking down at her.

"Ride! Ride!" she said, holding onto my leg tighter. I laughed and walked out of the room and down the stairs with Adeline clinging onto my legs. The smell of cooked ham and eggs filled around the halls as I walked down the stairs.

"Wow, Mags that smell is fantastic!" I said, looking over at her while I took careful steps down the stairs with Adeline on my leg.

"Thank you," she said, smiling widely at me.

As I entered the kitchen Adeline jumped up and hopped up in one of the chairs that Magdolin had stacked books up in so she could reach the table. On the counter there were two cast iron skillets sitting on some hot pads. One had eggs in it and the other had ham slabs fried and crisped perfectly.

"It looks even better than it smells" I said smiling as I got down three dishes for us.

"Thank you, how much do you want Addie?" she said, smiling at both me and Adeline.

"All! I want all of it!" she said, jumping up and down in her seat.

"Okay silly" she said, dishing a portion of eggs and half a slab of ham for her and setting it down with a fork. I got my plate and so did Magdolin and we sat down together at the table.

All of the food was cooked perfectly and tasted amazing. "Magdolin, you did quite the exquisite job on this." I said in a playful upright tone, like a fancy old duke. She laughed and finished her plate and collected the plates, setting them in the sink. I stood next to her at the sink and peered out the window. The sun was shining but I saw dark clouds in the distance.

"Awe what!" I said running out onto the front porch, it was humid and the horses seemed timid. I ran over to them and made sure there they were tied up well, the wind was picking up slightly making the leaves in the trees blow and sway. Magdolin was on the porch with Adeline as they grabbed the clothes down from the ledge that were there last night.

I was annoyed it was going to storm today, I had been wanting to make it to the next safe house. If it were still just Magdolin and I, I would attempt to make the trip in the storm but I wasn't going to make that girl go through it. She's already been through enough with her now old father. "I think we're gonna have to wait on taking off today Mags" I said as I grabbed some stuff out of the cart.

"I agree. " She said, coming out to the cart and grabbing a box that had the leftover fabric from Charlie and the black and gold dress I loaned her. I went and grabbed a few more things from the wagon as the clouds started to roll in.

I walked inside about to break a sweat, Magdolin was organizing some of the things in the living room area and I looked around, Adeline wasn't here.

"Adel?" I yelled out. I then heard giggles coming from out in the front yard. I ran outside grabbing her off the ground where she was playing with a few small rocks in the grass. I darted back into the house as soon as the rain started pouring down outside. Adeline giggled as I was holding her and shut and locked the door. "You need to stay inside Adel, it's gonna storm for a while obviously" I said calmly as she ran over to Magdolin.

"Alexander is right Addie, you need to stay in here, with us. Storms are dangerous." She said, walking over to a box we'd just brought in. She pulled out the leftover pink and white fabric and a needle and thread. "Now do you want to watch me make you a new dress!" Magdolin said as Adeline jumped and nodded her head. I could tell some sort of essence under Magdolin's calm talking. Like she was scared.

Magdolin sat down on the ground of the living room laying down the fabric and cutting out pieces. Adeline watched picking up the pieces of fabric she'd cut and spun them around laughing. I smiled and walked around the house making sure there were no leaks in the house still, which there was none. I was happy to see the old house was still holding up well. After that I walked back into the living room area and lit a few candles. The clouds covered the sky outside so it was getting dark inside as well, and I didn't want Magdolin to strain her eyes as she cut along the fabric.

"So Alexander, is this your old home?" Magdolin cut into the silence as I lit the candles.

"Yes, how'd you know?" I said curiously.

"The pictures, you were cute as a child" she said laughing and Adeline joined her laughter as Magdolin stood up with the different cuts of fabric and sat on the couch. She started to thread the needle with thread.

"Thank you, Mags." I said, sitting on the other couch as Adeline wrapped fabric around herself like a long fancy dress.

"Silly girl." Magdolin said as Adeline tripped over the long piece of scrap fabric. She just giggled and stood up, still playing with it. I decided being in the house for the rest of the day would be a good bonding moment, maybe *I could even make a move.* I thought to myself as I stood up and walked over to Magdolin and sat down next to her.

"So how does sewing work?" I asked, leaning over beside her, watching her small movements. I ran my hands along her shoulders, gently massaging her shoulders. They were tense, confirming my thought she was scared. "You don't have to be scared, it's just a small storm you know" I whispered down in her ear.

I felt a small shiver go up her spine and I had to hide a small smile. "Thank you... I've just never been somewhere outside the palace in a storm" she said quietly, probably not to fret Adeline.

"This house has endured much worse than this Mags." I said with a sigh as she returned to her sewing.

Her slim pale fingers worked the fabric and needle delicately and smoothly. Making the seams perfectly, "I don't know much, Alexander, Natalia taught me a little bit of it" She said softly returning to the previous conversation, not looking away from the needle and thread. I felt that feeling in my chest again, my admiration for her. She was beautiful when she focused, never any less than other times though.

"You seem to know quite a bit," I said smiling.

"If you say so." She said, turning and smiling gently.

The candlelight danced in her purple eyes. The warm glow on her face made her skin even more beautiful. Her lips were beautiful and delicate. I wanted to kiss her, I wouldn't dare try but I wanted to. The setting was perfect, the rain pounding on the house and the light thunder adding to it. Everything right now seemed perfect, wishing on everything that it would stay like this. My heart fluttered and I felt butterflies course through my body. I wanted to hold her so badly, to just touch her face. She was so sweet and I wanted her.

Just as I thought nothing could ruin this, something did. I heard two voices outside of the house, and both of us jumped. I looked at her and she set the dress she was sewing down on the ground and grabbed Adeline. I rushed them up the stairs and up into the master bedroom. Adeline looked very confused. I was looking around, frantic about what I should do. It could be travellers looking for a place from the rain that was pouring down. Or maybe just some lost people.

Magdolin was biting at her nails, I grabbed her hand and pulled it from her mouth. "What's go- " Adeline spoke out before Magdolin shushed her.

A loud pounding came from down the stairs, they were at the door. I froze for a few moments and heard Magdolin start to breathe hard. I shushed them both and motioned for them to stay as I closed the door of the bedroom and ran down the stairs. I opened up the front door with a smile but it quickly faded.

Chapter 17. Magdolin Poni

I sat upstairs holding Adeline on the bed in my arms. I waited patiently as I heard voices downstairs. I heard Alexander's tone slightly drop to one of annoyance. There was a female as well, she spoke with a very loud and snarky voice. And another, a male's voice. It sounded familiar to me for some reason. It sounded so eerily familiar to me but I couldn't put my finger on it, it was going to drive me crazy. I looked down at Adeline and motioned for her to stay quiet and stay put. She nodded her head as I set her down on the bed, I looked around the room and a little doll was sitting on the dresser. I crept over, being quiet so they wouldn't hear my footsteps, and I grabbed the doll and handed it to Adeline. She took it, smiling as she sat on the bed with it. I gently opened the door and closed it back quietly as I stepped over ever so quietly to the ledge of the stairs.

I saw two people. A girl, she was a black mushroom with red spots and she had short black hair. She had a white blouse on and a red skirt. She wore her corset on the outside of her blouse and skirt. I gritted my teeth slightly and raised my eyebrow and disgust. *What a brawd*, I thought to myself. She had such an annoying voice and the way she stood just irked me. And the way she spoke to Alexander infuriated me. And then next to her was a male, his mushroom was green.

A sense of nostalgia or deja vu maybe? Flew over me as I looked at him. He was so familiar to me. I leaned farther over the edge or the wall to see closer, I felt my foot knock something down and I felt my heart drop. A little candle holder knocked over and fell down a step. I froze for a moment until I saw the two people flip around to look up at the noise.

I flung myself away to where they couldn't see me behind the wall. "I knew you had someone here!" the female spoke out.

"Hope, it's none of your business" Alexander said in a stern tone.

"No, I wanna see what guy you're hauling around now, after all no female would ever want you of all mushrooms to take them across the kingdom" Hope spoke with a sassy tone and followed with a loud cackle as I heard her footsteps trail up the stairs.

"Darling don't" the male's voice spoke, there it was again, that feeling that I know that voice.

I looked around frantically, I could go back in the room but then they'd find Adeline. If this was someone who could do us harm I didn't want her in its way. I stayed frozen against the wall as the footsteps grew louder and came closer. It felt like my heart was going to beat out of my chest, then I saw a small boot appear from around the corner. Followed by the wave of her red skirt that had a slit in it going up her thigh. I could see fishnets underneath, *wow she really is a whore*. I snapped back out as the girl was now in full view of me. Her hair fell to her shoulders and she had a beauty mark on her left cheek. She was a little bit taller than me but not by much, she stood with a frown and her hands on her hips and her face quickly changed. It went from a frown to a wide eyed look of surprise and she started to laugh.

"Oh Alexander what have you got yourself into now!" She said, laughing at me. I had a weird feeling in my gut at that moment.

I had a feeling of offence and disgust as I looked at her. I stood up more straight and a look of sternness as she laughed. "That's no way to act to someone you just met" I said in a quiet but strong voice as I crossed my arms.

"Sorry I don't bow down to you like others *Madam*" She said in a snarky tone. I hated the way she spoke to me and it filled me with rage. I wanted to slap her so badly, but I resisted

"Dear, please come down stairs" The male spoke again in a worried tone.

"Okay," Hope said, grabbing my wrist and yanking me down the stairs with her.

"You're gonna let me go now!" I spoke in an angry tone as she brought me down the stairs.

"Oh come on you crybaby" She said as we reached the bottom of the stairs. I looked up slightly scared as I saw Alexander's cringing face as he held his arm. I felt ashamed for being there. I looked over at the male as Hope still held my wrists.

"Magdolin?" I heard the male say, I looked over at him as he spoke.

It hit me like a brick wall as I saw his face finally. "Raymond?" I said, breaking a small smile as I realised it was him. Raymond used to be the knight who stood guard outside my door. We used to have long conversations and he'd let me sneak out. We sometimes would go on adventures around the castle. But then he ran away, never to be seen again. I understood why he ran away but it still hurt knowing he abandoned me.

We both let out a laugh as Hope let go of my wrist. Alexander looked at us with a raised eyebrow. I ran over to Raymond and both embraced each other. I laughed as we pulled away. "You got out too" he said as we both laughed.

"Yes, of course I did, you left me" I said, punching his shoulder.

"I know I'm so sorry. I wish I could've taken you with me, but I see you found your way" he said with a soft tone.

"So you two know each other." Alexander interrupted, we turned to look at him and Hope both standing, arms crossed.

"He was the *princess's* guard when he was in the palace" Hope spoke out again, rolling her eyes.

"Oh dear, it's all in the past, now we're just old friends" Raymond said, putting his arm around my shoulder and shaking me as I laughed.

"Oh-kay well, yes old friends- " Alexander said before I cut him off.

"How do you two know each other?" I asked curiously as Alexander yanked off Raymond's hand. Part of me was curious why Alexander was getting so upset. I knew I was upset because of the hope's attitude towards me.

"Ex fiance" Hope said, planting her foot on the ground glaring at me.

"Fiance?" I said, surprised, looking at Alexander.

"You didn't tell your little princess girlfriend?" Hope said, walking over to me and shoving me away from Raymond.

"Girlfriend?" Alexander and I said, rolling our eyes.

"Whatever" She said, sitting down on the couch, crossing her legs. She infuriated me without even trying. A part of me was also upset that Alexander hadn't told me about Hope. I understand why he didn't though, I'm not that close to him to know everything. It just stung a little bit that he wouldn't have told me. I pushed down my anger and tried to paste on a smile as she sat down on the couch.

How disrespectful to just come into another's house and invite yourself onto the couch. I thought to myself, this female was nothing good in my eyes.

"So are you two seeing each other?" I said, turning to Raymond with a smile. He lifted his left hand showing a gold wedding band.

"We're married," Hope said, adding to it. The tension was so thick in the air you could choke. Alexander was visibly mad, Hope was lounging on the couch with a barbed look on her face. Raymond had a nervous smile as hope glared at him and she motioned him over. I walked over to Alexander who had an annoyed face still.

"Why are they here? " I whispered.

"Why didn't you tell me you had a boyfriend before he ran away from you?" Alexander said with an angry and annoyed tone, I looked at him with a confused and hurt expression.

"What are speaking about Alexander? " I said, furrowing my brows together. He rolled his eyes before speaking

"Forget about it" He said, snarling as he collapsed down on one of the chairs.

"Speaking of people seeing each other, what's up with you two? " Hope said, smirking and raising an eyebrow.

"Nothing, absolutely nothing " Alexander said, leaning his forehead against his hand. I felt my heart sink a little bit, I knew he was just speaking the truth. But something felt wrong when he said nothing, it felt like it hurt me in a way.

"Hmm well I would've thought you'd jump at the idea of having a princess as your escapee. You're the type to use your *surroundings*" Hope said, smirking. Alexander glared at her, thunder sounded loud around the house and lightning struck. The storm was clearly getting worse and the awkward silence was going to kill me.

"So what brings you two here in the first place?" I said, interrupting the silence.

"Well, we have been staying in the town you guys just passed through. We saw my dear *old friend* Alexander fighting a pink mushroom. And let me just say Magdolin, that pink mushroom facade you play is pretty convincing. I thought you were really pink" Hope said, snickering.

I hated how she made me look like a mockery, I hated her. "Oh, that's just lovely" I said, snarling a smile at her. She had a mean smirk back at me but quickly jumped.

She jumped a bit and flipped her head to look behind the couch. "Oh my god! You have a kid Alexander?" She said, laughing. *Oh no* I thought. She lifted up Adeline, who was still in Alexander's shirt from the night prior. "Awe I'll have to admit, she's halfway cute" She said, holding her up like a baby doll.

Alexander stood up snatching Adeline away and sat back down with her in his lap. "She's not mine," Alexander said coldly. Hope looked at me, raising an eyebrow.

"I.. I adopted her " I said, crossing my arms.

"Ah I see, fake mom and a wannabe dad, and unwanted kid" Hope said. Pointing at Alexander, Adeline, and I. I felt my blood boil again, I wanted to hit her so bad. I stood up angrily.

"Would you like to say that again because I will listen" I said fuming.

"Oh I will. Your kind will never be proper parents, you're a spoiled, rotten princess who expects everything to be handed to you" Hope said, standing up as well.

"I would appreciate it if you left right now" I said snarling. Raymond stood up nervously and Alexander stayed sitting down holding Adeline in his lap.

"No thank-" Hope started to say before Raymond cut her off.

"Ok, we all need to calm down, this is excessive " he said, putting a hand on both of our shoulders.

"You get your hands off of her " Hope said, shoving Raymond back.

"Don't shove him like that, he's your husband!" I said, glaring at Hope.

"Oh but why should you care Magdolin, it's not like he left you in the palace or anything?" Alexander said, setting Adeline in the chair and joining in on the yelling.

I noted that he called me Magdolin, not Mags. That hurt as well, about as much as him being angry at me. "Alexander, you don't know what all happened back then," I said in a quiet tone while holding the end of my skirt.

"Oh but I do, why don't I tell him? " Hope said, smirking at me with a cruel glare in her eye.

"Go ahead because I'd love to know, " Alexander said, nodding his head. I saw Adeline run up the stairs still holding her doll. I wanted to go with her, I wanted out of this situation.

"I can assure you anything that happened is all in the past dear we've discussed this!" Raymond said, laughing nervously.

"Oh shut up, those two were basically lovers. They took each other's first kiss. They'd sneak out together. Who knows what else? That's all Ray had told me." Hope said, looking at Alexander.

"Honey, we were kids and that's all we did I can assure you" Raymond said, putting his arm around her.

"Oh don't *Honey* me" She said, rolling her eyes.

Alexander looked even more upset and turned to look at me. I felt ashamed, I wished a pit would just swallow me whole. "We were kids, and I was lonely," I said, looking up at Alexander.

"Oh please, how old were you, they wouldn't let a kid be the princess's guard" Alexander said with a snarl.

"I was sixteen, it was almost four years ago!" I said, throwing my arms out.

"You weren't a kid then!" He said with a sigh. I overheard Hope's snickering, I looked at her, glaring.

"Is this what you came here for? To cause a problem? Because you did and you need to leave now " I said, glaring and pointing at the door and then up at Raymond. "Y- you need to go too " I said with a slight quiver in my voice.

"Oh I'm not leaving till I feel like it. " She said, crossing her arms and stamping her foot.

"Oh but you are, I'm done with this" I said pulling out my dagger, she smirked pulling out a long needle like dagger from her thigh garter. I saw Raymond and Alexander both dart and pull us back as I was about to lunge at her. Alexander held me back and Ray pushed her away from us. "You Ninny! Come and fight me like a real mushroom!" I shouted as Raymond took her out the door. As the door closed the rain still pattered down on the house violently.

It fell silent for a moment, I was still breathing hard from my outburst of rage. Pure anger still coursed through my veins, I thought I was going to vomit. Why would someone come somewhere to intentionally cause a problem? Alexander let go of me as their footsteps ran off and the sounds of a horse were heard trotting away. I stood there for a moment with my dagger in hand, I heard Alexander walk away towards the back of the house. I just stood there in my thoughts for a moment, completely lost for a moment. "Maggie" heard Adeline's quiet voice come from the staircase.

"Oh Honey" I said, putting my dagger back in its holder and rushing up a few of the steps and sitting next to her on the stairs, "I'm sorry you heard that" I said, hugging her.

"Are the yelling people gone?" She asked quietly.

"Yes, and I promise you that won't happen again" I said, rubbing her back. She nodded her head and started to go down the stairs. I didn't stop her, still clutching the doll. She went back towards where Alexander was. I stood up as well, I was going to finish the dress for Adeline so she wasn't in Alexander's shirt anymore.

I walked over towards the boxes we had brought in from the cart and pulled out the black and gold dress. I was going to take the gold trim from it and use it on Adeline's dress. I pulled it out and shook it a few times to get it unfolded, a piece of paper fell from it. I then remembered back at the first safe house about the pictures that fell out of the trunk. I picked up the picture and it was a picture of Hope and Alexander. Hope had the black and gold dress on and Alexander was in a matching gold and black suit. They were both so happy looking with big smiles and holding each other's hands. It made me feel weird,

I didn't like it at all. I felt my eyes well with tears and I didn't know why. My fists clenched the picture tightly as tears streamed down my cheeks, I threw the picture to the side.

I stood up leaving the dress there, I stomped up the stairs and into the bedroom I had stayed in. tears still fled my eyes and fury flooded through my entire body as I clung onto the pillow on the bed and screamed into it. I was so upset I didn't even know what emotions I was feeling. I just curled up into a ball and held onto the pillow. My nails digging into it, my vision was doubled from the tears.

I heard the soft patter of footsteps coming up the stairs, I wiped my face off and set the pillow down. Adeline pushed open the door with a worried look on her little face. "Hi Addie" I said, putting on a smile as she walked in the room.

"Maggie, are you my mom?" She asked softly as she stood in front of me as I sat on the bed. My eyes widened as I looked at her, I picked her up and pulled her towards me on the bed.

"Can I be your mom?" I asked with a shaky voice as I held her.

"I'd like a momma," She said, hugging around my neck.

"I'll be your mom, Honey" I said, rubbing her back with my thumb as I fought back my tears once again.

"Can we go downstairs?" She said, pulling back from my hug. I nodded my head as she led the way down the stairs, she picked up her doll off the couch where she left it and sat on the living room floor with it. Alexander walked in and sat on the floor with her, pulling her hair in a playful way and she'd laugh. I stood watching the two of them, I felt like I shouldn't interfere after the yelling. Alexander had a smile on his face and I didn't want to change that. I started to walk back towards the stairs until Adeline spoke out "Momma?" She said as I turned to look at her.

"Momma?" Alexander said, raising an eyebrow. His smile slightly faded. I felt another wave of guilt as I walked over to her and she pulled at my skirt and I sat down with them both.

"Yes Addie?" I said quietly with a frown. She just stayed playing with the doll. The air was still tight between me and Alexander, I could feel his gaze on me at certain moments but I didn't dare to look up. I didn't want to start another fight, especially in front of Adeline.

Everything that had happened kept replaying through my mind, why did it bother me so much? Hope bothered me the most, parts of me wondered what had happened between her and Alexander. But I didn't dare ask right now. And why did he have me in her dress? Why would he want to put me in something of hers? It felt degrading to think about. It tore me up the more and more I thought about it.

After about ten minutes of her playing, she stood up and hobbled back towards the stairs and up them. The storm outside still raged on, with the occasional clap of thunder and flash of lightning. I looked over at Alexander who was looking at his hands as he sat with his legs crossed. The silence once again was killing me. "...I'm sorry for earlier, I should've told you prior" I said quietly as I looked down at my legs. It was quiet for a few more moments before I heard his voice again.

"It's ok, I should've told you about her " he said in a still slightly angered voice. I looked up at him not looking away this time.

I couldn't really see his face from how his hair fell in it when he had his head down. I slowly lifted my hand up and moved his hair back from his face and he brushed away my hand from his face. "Just why didn't you fore-warn me there may be someone like him out here?" he said looking up at me with an angry look on his face.

"Alexander he did nothing to you" I said calmly but with a stern face.

"He was way too touchy Magdolin, he's a married male, and you're an old lover of his" he said standing up.

"Lover is a strong term, and he barely touched my shoulder" I said standing up.

"Oh come on, it's been less than three years since then. Magdolin, are you kidding me" he said, looking down at me. He kept calling me Magdolin and it felt like he was just pushing a knife deeper into my chest.

"Why do you even care, and why didn't you tell me about Hope if you're so mad about Raymond!" I said, throwing my arms out.

"You're important to me Magdolin! You're my friend. And I'm not proud about what I did with Hope. She was a mistake and I'm trying to forget her! Okay?" He said, shouting. I could see now that he had been crying, his eyes were glassy and his eyelids looked puffy.

"W-well it's not ok Alexander to be mad at me whenever you did the same, and tell me why you had me wearing one of her dresses" I said, picking up the picture of Hope and Alexander.

"Where did you find this?" he said, getting even more upset and snatching the picture. "I want you to know that all of this is not worth fighting over, this is insolent and I don't want to see that Raymond guy again! Not in my safe houses" Alexander said. A few tears ran down his cheeks as he tore the picture up into a bunch of pieces and dropped to the floor. I nodded my head as he stepped closer to me "...Don't worry your pretty little head about it, everything's gonna be fine. Okay? We're just gonna forget about this" He said, cupping my face in his hands as he was still crying and then he let go of me and he stepped outside onto the porch, leaving me alone in the living room. I was confused about what I was feeling and what he was feeling.

I cared about Alexander and I didn't know how to deal with this situation at all. He is my best friend and I need to fix this. After a few minutes I stepped out onto the porch and saw Alexander sitting there on the edge of the porch just a few inches from the sheet of pouring down rain that was everywhere around us. I shut the door behind me and approached him, I could hear him audibly crying now and my heart shattered. I fell down on my knees next to him and his hand covered his face quickly wiping off tears as he noticed my presence. I grabbed his hands away and wrapped my arms around him, joining him crying.

"I'm so sorry Alexander. I didn't mean for any of this to happen" I said, sobbing loudly. His arms wrapped around me tightly, we both cried and held each other close. The rain poured all around and a few drops would blow and hit me.

"I'm so sorry Mags, I was so rude for no reason. I can't be mad because of the past" He said as his hands dug at my back seeking some sort of comfort.

I held him tight trying to give him that sense of comfort. He just cried into my shoulder as we sat on the damp porch. I stroked the back of his head, his hair was poofed back up and curly now from the humidity and steam off the rain. I stopped crying myself just to try and make him feel a little better. I kept rubbing the back of his head and pressed my lips against the side of his head giving him a firm kiss. "I know that means *nothing* to you but it means something to me," I said laughing a tiny bit as he stopped crying and looked at me.

"No no, It means a lot, I'm sorry I said you were nothing to me." he said, holding me.

"It's okay we're done with the apologies" I said as he let go of me. I stood back up and helped him to his feet. I opened the door and led him back inside. Adeline came down the stairs holding the doll and stood at our feet wanting to be held.

"Allie-zander, I'm hungry" she said as Alexander picked her up.

"Okay Adel" he said, walking into the kitchen. He had a smile on his face now even though his eyes were still glassy.

As they walked into the kitchen I felt my eyes tear up again. I was so lucky for what I had here. Nothing could be better, even with the flaws. I had Adeline and now she's asking me to be her mom, and I have Alexander, my best friend. It felt like we were a family, I knew we weren't one, but I think this is the closest I'll get to the fairy tales I had read with my mother when I was a child. I stood next to Alexander and looked down, I felt all my emotions melt off as I saw something on his shoes.

"Alexander, what's on your shoes?" I asked, sitting down on my knees looking at his shoes. There were green vines growing up the sides of them, almost like the shoes had been left outside in the elements for months.

"Huh that's weird" he said looking down as well. I pulled off the vines and they were almost embedded into the shoes leather. I examined them in my hand as Alexander got down a pan and set Adeline down on the counter. I then looked in the living room and right there where Alexander had been standing were the roots of the vines. It appeared like they had sprouted from the ground there, but that's impossible. Maybe it was a phenomenon. I just brushed it off and picked up the small vines and threw them outside.

Chapter 18. Adeline Sanchez

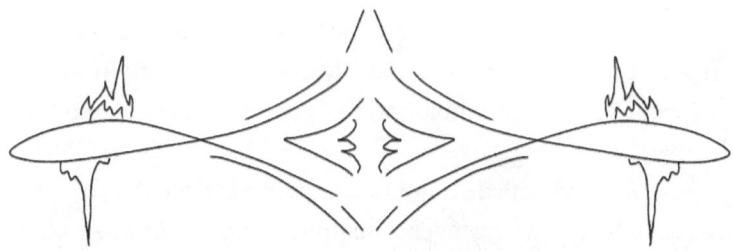

Alexander set me down on the counter top as he got out a bowl and ran water in it from the canteen. I put my hand down in it splashing with the pirates and mermaids inside the pan, creating waves that they jumped across. "Get your hands out of there!" he said, picking me up and making me soar up high off the ground.

"Wow!" I yelled, kicking my feet, as he set me down on the ground. I ran over to Momma at lightning speed and she picked me up and held me.

"Are you causing trouble?" She said, I was so offended. I couldn't believe it, this was such betrayal from my momma.

"No momma! I was playing with the waves!" I said backing up my alibi. "When did the momma thing start?" Alexander said, looking at me and momma.

"Earlier today, I don't mind it," She said, kissing me on the cheek. I laughed at the tickle of her lips on my cheek.

"How sweet" Alexander said, turning and focusing back on the food stuff he was making. I squirmed in momma's arms until she sat me down on the ground. I ran across the house and onto the couch, grabbing my doll, my best friend. Even though I only met her today I knew she was there for me.

Me and her went on an adventure up the treacherous stairs, climbing cliffs and mountains to reach the top. I looked over the edge at the dangerous slope we just conquered. "Adeline!" I heard Alexander yell out from miles away down the slope. I knew it was gonna be a dangerous way down the mountain but I went for it. I slid down the dangerous mountain top, hitting all the bumps on the way down, and holding my doll by her arm. I wasn't gonna lose her while going down the mountain side.

I reached the bottom and stood on the soft touch of the carpet. I looked back up at the slope I had successfully climbed and retreated from. It stood no chance for me and my dolly. I ran back in the kitchen at high speeds and my momma grabbed me. She put me up on my seat that she made into a big girl seat. The seat had a few big thick books on it so I'd be able to reach the huge table. "Dinner time Addie" She said, putting a napkin around my neck, I happily accepted it unlike other kids would've. I was a good girl and I think momma appreciated it.

Alexander set down a plate with mashed potatoes and green stuff. "What's that?" I asked, poking the long green things that looked like utter poison.

"Good stuff. You're gonna eat it," Alexander said, laughing. "Okay," I said, smiling and I put my hand in the mashed potatoes and squeezed it in my fist. I had to make sure they were thoroughly mashed properly.

"Adeline!" Momma said, taking my hand up as I tried to lick the potatoes off my hand. What the heck! They give me food and don't let me eat it! This is crazy!

She wiped my hand off with a napkin and got a spoon and then hand fed it to me. "I'm a big girl" I said with my mouth full as she got another spoonful ready.

"Big girls don't eat with their hands" she said, raising her eyebrows as she put another bite in my mouth. This was outrageous! I am three! I can eat on my own.

Alexander sat next to me and snickered, I looked up at him and curled my nose up at him. "Oh don't give me a stink face" he said, pinching my nose. I laughed and momma wiped my face again with the napkin.

"Don't laugh with food in your mouth, Addie. You need to have manners" She said, laughing.

"Oh she's little, let her have fun" Alexander said, backing me up. I nodded my head agreeing with him as Mom rolled her eyes. Once the potatoes were gone, mom picked up the long green things, I stared in disgust. I shook my head as she got it closer to my mouth.

"Open up, Addie," she said, raising her eyebrows again.

"Nu uh," I said, backing up against Alexander, he'd surely help me.

"You think I'm gonna help you?" He asked, looking down at me. I shook my head yes hoping he'd take the nasty green thing away. "Okay I'll help, " he said. I felt like I beat the game. I just beat momma and I don't have to eat gross stuff.

Just as I felt victorious I was broken back down again. Alexander grabbed my sides and betrayed me. He started tickling me and I bursted out laughing grabbing my sides and momma took this as an opportunity. She put the nasty gross slimy thing in my mouth. "Now chew that" she said, holding my jaw shut with her hand. I cringed as I slowly chewed it. It was gross and I kicked my feet as I did. Alexander laughed while he looked at me suffering to eat it. The betrayal I felt was unfathomable. How could he do that to me? "That's called asparagus" Mom said as I swallowed it with a gag.

"I don't like it," I said, putting my hand over my mouth.

"Well it looks like you have one more on your plate" Alexander said, snickering. I looked up at him angry.

How could he betray me TWICE?! This male is crazy to think he can get away from me. I have sailed the great bath river and I have climbed the stair mountain many times. And I defeated the ultimate boss, papa. I escaped him and that was my greatest achievement. And right now I was losing to asparagus. "Come on Adeline, it's just one more and it'll be over with" Momma said in a pleading voice. I shook my head no again, I wasn't going to torture myself. Alexander's fingers dug at my neck, tickling me again. I squirmed trying to fight off his attack but to no avail. I held back laughter but it beat me as I cackled loudly. Momma put the other asparagus in my mouth. I tried to spit it out but Alexander put his hand over my mouth. This really was true betrayal, Alexander was my other best friend and he has done this to me now. This was blasphemy.

"See that wasn't that bad" Mom said, wiping my face off as I swallowed the last bite.

"Never again Allie-zander" I said, glaring at him and smacking his leg.

"Oh now we have a miss attitude," he said, raising an eyebrow. I shook my head no and jumped out of my chair. They both watched as I ran off into the living room. They didn't follow me as I jumped on the couch with my dolly. I heard them talking in there but ignored them as I played with my friend.

Chapter 19. Alexander Malencoy

After everything that had gone down I felt awful for the things I said and did. I wished I could take it back. I could tell that Magdolin was still hurt from our fight and I hurt from it as well. My heart ached, not the same as hers but I wished I could just make us both forget about it. I wanted to be able to see her smile at me again. I wanted her to be close to me, and my mind won't stop racing. There's no way she'd ever agree to marry me after this. I really showed how big of a piece of garbage I am. And I don't want her to be burdened by being with me. I'll just end up hurting her some way or another. And I don't deserve someone like her. She's perfect, even with her past.

I have an overwhelming hatred for that Raymond guy, he just used her then abandoned her in the palace. Who would do that to her, surely he knew she wanted to leave. Part of me knew that they had to be soulmates. The way they just clicked so fast and jumped into each other's arms, reuniting. And I know that Hope is just using the poor guy for everything he's got. And I was harsh with Magdolin saying I wasn't going to let him around again. I needed to talk to her but not now with Adeline here.

I helped Magdolin feed Adeline as she was being stubborn about eating. As Adeline jumped up from the table and ran off to the living room I looked up at magdolin. "Mags I just want you to know, I really, I really am sorry for everything that I said and did. I didn't mean that about Raymond, if you want to see him before we leave town you can-" I said before she cut me off.

"No, I don't want to see Raymond, it upsets you and I don't want to see Hope ever again. She's a witch" She said with a look of understanding as her hand found its way resting on top of mine.

"Yeah she's a cruel one" I said, letting out a sigh and a small smile.

She just smiled and rubbed my hand with her thumb, it stayed quiet for a few moments before she cut in again. "Can I ask what happened between the two of you?"

I let out a sigh and nodded my head before speaking. "Hope put on a mask when I first met her. I thought she was the one after a few months of knowing her and decided to propose to her. But after being engaged for a month or two she started to act differently, she was mean and harsh. She didn't have that niceness that she used to trick me. I lost that smile I had around her, so I broke it off. She ran off screaming that she'd ruin anything that I tried to do and she's lived up to it so far. She'll find me ever so often and just screw things up for me. One time she used an axe on the wagon wheels and it halted my trip. I had a boy that needed to get out fast and it stopped the trip for a day. Another time she slipped a tab in my drink at a tavern and I fell unconscious. Not very fun, Mags" I said with a sigh thinking back on all those events. There were more but I didn't want to bore her with those.

"I'm so sorry, that happened to you. Slipping a drink is the doing of a mad mushroom." she said, moving her hand to intertwine with my own. Her hand was soft and warm as my own enveloped its small form. I noted that her nails no longer had that nice perfect almond shape to them, they had a less manicured look to them.

"It's okay Mags, I've found a new reason to smile." I said, squeezing her hand lightly. I watched as a smile spread across her face.

"Really?" she asked as she scooted to the edge of her seat. I felt a warm sense wrap around my body as she scooted closer. Was this really happening?

"Yeah" I mumbled as I nodded my head looking into her deep lilac eyes. The way they caught the candles around the house made my mind cascade into different scenarios and thoughts. I thought my heart was going to explode as she sat close to me and held my hand. My thoughts raced more and more. Should I lean in and kiss her? Should I stay put? Should I let go of her?

A huge flash ran through the house lighting things up momentarily and not a moment later a loud bang of thunder sounded throughout the whole woods. Magdolin jumped as well as me at the large commotion of the lightning. It fell silent for a few moments after until the sound of a high pitched whine and footsteps clambered towards us. Adeline was crying and jumped up towards Magdolin "It's okay, calm down Addie" She said, stroking her hair calmingly. Addie stayed crying and held onto Magdolin as she cradled her.

"Ok guys I think it's time for someone to go beddie bye" I said standing up teasing Adeline.

"I think you're right, the storm won't hurt you." Magdolin said, standing up still holding her.

"No no no, it's a big storm" Adeline said, not wanting to go to bed. I pulled out my pocket watch and looked at it.

"Tsk tsk tsk, that's not what my watch says, Adel, it says it's bedtime" I said, smirking as I showed her the clock that pointed to nine. She whined as she laid against Magdolin again. She smiled and then walked up the stairs with her and laid her down on her bed.

Magdolin tucked the blanket up around Adeline and rubbed some tears off her face. "It's gonna be okay, Babydoll" She said, giving her a peck on the forehead.

"No no, you can't leave me alone " Adeline whined, holding onto Magdolin's hair.

"Okay fine I'll stay here" She said, smiling. I smirked as Magdolin laid down on one side of the bed beside Adeline.

"You guys can't leave me out of this" I said smirking as I jumped beside Adeline. She giggled as I did so and Magdolin gave a soft smile up at me. I smiled as Adeline murmured to herself for a few more moments before she squirmed and got comfortable in her bed. Eventually her breath shallowed and steadied. I sat up slowly and got out of the bed. I looked down at the two, it looked like Magdolin had fallen asleep as well. I looked at myself in the mirror on the dresser. The green glow coming off my mushroom illuminated my face and shoulders. I gently creaked open the door and slipped out of the room. I was walking down the hall as I felt someone grab me around the neck, I stepped back, steadying myself as Magdolin jumped on my back.

"Were you just going to leave me there?" She whispered as I felt her warm breath on my neck.

"I thought you were asleep" I said quietly as I held her up on my back. My hands rested on the crook of her thigh and calves so she wouldn't fall

"Fair," She said, laughing as I walked down the stairs. I set her down on the couch and she picked up the small dress she had been working on for Adeline.

"So am I gonna have my shirt back soon?" I asked teasingly.

"Hopefully," She said, snickering as she rethreaded her needle.

"So why isn't Adeline wearing her shoes around anymore?" I asked as I noticed the small shoes next to Magdolin's boots.

"Oh they don't fit her, I was going to try and figure something out for the poor girl" She said as she put in another seam on the dress.

I frowned at the thought she had been wearing shoes too small, then it hit me. "I actually may have something for her," I said, standing up off the floor.

"Really?" She said, surprised, I guess it did sound weird. An unmarried male with no kids has a toddler girl's shoes.

"Well not me, but my little sister may have left clothes here. Like how my dad left shirts here" I said as Magdolin looked up at me and paused her sewing.

"You have a sister?" She asked, smiling. "What else have you not told me?" She said, laughing as she put more thread on the needle.

"Ah, not that much, but that doll you had given her was my sister's," I said, smiling as I thought back to my sister.

"What happened to her?" Magdolin asked as she leaned against the arms of the couch while she finished the last seam on the dress.

I smiled as I sat on the ground looking up at her. "Well Bethany and I grew up together. She was only a few years younger than me. But whenever I was about fourteen she got poisoned. Our neighbours were the type to believe poison mushrooms were dangerous. But at ten years old she'd take a hand out anywhere, and the mother of their household gave her something bad. She ended up getting sick and we lost her after a few days." I said, trying to remain a strong composure. I looked up at Magdolin again, who was looking intently at me.

112

"I'm so sorry Alexander. People are so cruel, "she said, frowning.

"No, no it's ok Mags,really" I said, trying to not get upset about it.

It was a hard subject but Magdolin deserved to know after all. "Bethany was my best friend growing up and no one else could replace her, but when she started to get sick it felt like my life was crumbling. I was in that awkward stage of transitioning from a kid to a teenager but I had my sister. Until I didn't, when she was gone my mother started to fall apart and my father's anger would blow over easily after her death. It wasn't very good to grow up in that environment but I'm still here." I said, trying to brush it off. I had to look like it didn't bother me even if it did. My sister's death truly made my life shatter.

Magdolin crawled off the couch and down in front of me on her knees. "Alexander, that's not something you can just brush off," She said, holding my hands lightly. It was clear she saw right through my act but I tried to keep it up a bit longer.

"No, Mags, really it's okay. People are just always going to hate poison mushrooms. There's literal books written on how to avoid us" I said, trying to laugh it off.

"Alexander, I'm being serious. I'm so sorry that happened to you and you didn't deserve that. Nevertheless, Hope following it up" She said, basically grabbing my attention physically. I just looked at her blankly as the candles in the room burned out. How did she make me feel this way? Like I couldn't look away from her, but I also want to sink away from the moment.

"Alexander, you're important to me, I want you to know that anything that's said about your type of mushroom isn't true. You're just like the rest of us and those monsters that ruined you guys should be locked up. And put through the same torture you've experienced!" She said, getting frustrated clearly as she looked up at me. I just smiled at her before speaking again.

"That's sweet of you Mags but I wouldn't wish this, even on them. And I think it's cute you'd even think something like that for me" I said, smiling as I felt a lump in my throat. I choked it back down though, I'd cried too much in one day.

"Plus it's been ten years, I think I'll be okay" I said laughing as I stood up. Magdolin stood up and looked at me blankly for a few moments.

"Ten?" I looked back down at her

"Yeah, actually no, eleven years" I said, giving it a second thought.

"You're twenty five?!" She said, surprised.

"Yep, I'm old, " I said laughing.

Magdolin looked surprised with her mouth opened slightly. "How old did you think I was?" I asked as I stretched out and looked at a picture on the wall.

"I thought, at the most, you were twenty two" She said as she looked at some of the books on the shelf.

"Ah, I wish. Are you just saying I look ridiculously amazing for twenty five, or are you wanting me to just be closer to nineteen for ya?" I said teasingly, smirking at her. She just laughed and rolled her eyes

"Oh please, wouldn't you like that?" She said, smirking as well. She picked up a book off the shelf and examined it. I peered over her shoulder and the book's title said *How To Avoid the Poisonous.*

I rolled my eyes and let out a sigh as she flipped through the book. It was a book that my father had got so he could find something else to rant about. She'd scoff every so often as she skimmed the pages. "Listen to this, if you surround thys house in a thin layer of copper. It shall keep away any poisonous fiends. What the hell?" She said, shaking her head.

"Yep, here let me see that I'll show you some more interesting things" I said, taking the book from her and flipping around till I found the page. I cleared my throat dramatically and arched my back like a professor. "Ahem, if thou art to come across a poison mushroom, avoid eye contact. Their eyes can send off magnetic waves to blind thou. Number two, don't let them touch you. Their skin makes poisonous spores that will make thine skin melt away, only leaving bone. The poison mushroom is nothing but a monster that will steal your kids, eat your spouses, and kill your families. Keep your household clean of any threat from them." I said, ending it with a dramatic clap of me closing the book.

Magdolin just scoffed "How can they make up such lies?" She said angrily.

"Eh, it's happened for years, and look at this on the back" I said, pointing to the back of the book. It had the king's crest implanted on it, meaning the king signed on it being authorised.

"Are you serious?" She exclaimed, snatching the book and looking at the crest before flipping through to the publishers.

"That wouldn't have been your father because the book's too old. Maybe one of your grandfather's" I said, laughing as she continued to look through the book.

"This is outrageous that the royal family would even consider signing something like this. It's ridiculous, some of these don't even make sense. Their tongues glow due to their radioactive blood lords, who would believe that " She said scoffing, but I just snickered.

"That one's true, actually. But it's not radioactive, it's the bioluminescence in my mushroom. It spreads down to our tongues, "I said, blowing out the candle on the bookshelf and sticking my tongue out. My tongue glowed the same green as my gills in the dark. She stared surprised for a moment before speaking.

"That is actually very interesting, do your hands glow too? I know your mushroom does but does anything else?" she asked, now very intrigued as she picked my hand up and examined it in the dark. My hand did not glow at all, it was normal.

"Uh, yeah, there's other parts" I said, nervously laughing as she looked at my hand and mushroom.

"Can I see?" She said smiling.

"No! Oh sorry, no" I said, catching myself from embarrassment. She shrugged her shoulders and let my hand down.

"Hm, okay" She said, putting the book back on the shelf and stretching her arms out. "It's getting quite late, I think I'm going to head to bed" She said, smiling back at me as she headed up the stairs.

"Okay Mags, I'll look for some shoes for her in the morning. Goodnight" I said, smiling as I stood in the living room.

"Good night Alexander," She said, going up to her room. I felt that swelling in my heart again. I think I figured out what it is for sure.

I loved this female. I loved her so much. Even though I was so cruel to her she still was able to brush it off and forgive me. She was perfect, perfect in every way to me. I couldn't ask for anything more, but I know I can't have her. I scaled the stairs and went into my bedroom. I collapsed down onto the bed and pulled out my journal. I jotted down another page worth of what I felt about Magdolin.

I wish I could explain to her how I felt, and how I saw her. I wish that on all my dreams and hopes that I could just have her, she's all I want now. I'd give up everything for her, just so it would be us. Her, Adeline, and I, alone, and happy. I wish she would see me the same way, see me as her equal. See me as her partner, see me as a lover. I love her, I love her so much. And I think I'd do anything for her to just say those words to me, even if she didn't really mean it.

I finished writing the page and laid the journal next to me on the bed. I laid on my back staring at the ceiling. Slumber hit me like a wall as I laid there, I hadn't done much today though. I guess it was just mentally tiring with what all happened. Worst comes to worse we will wake up with kingdom guards at our door, and that's if Hope turned us into the authorities. I doubt she did though, the guard tower wouldn't be open during the raging storm that was going over us.

I fell asleep quickly as my thoughts slowed down. I fell asleep on top of the covers because of the warm climate caused by the storm.

Chapter 20. Magdolin Poni

I stayed awake a little while longer listening to the rain pound on the roof. I rolled in the bed trying to get comfortable and fall asleep but it was to no avail. I just stayed there looking out the window. I saw the horses laying under a tree, asleep as the rain poured. I heard footsteps in the hall and perked up as Adeline came into my room. "Momma," She said quietly in the dark.

"Yes Addie?" I said calmly as I pulled her up on my lap in the bed.

"You weren't supposed to leave me," She said as she clung onto my hair.

"I'm sorry babydoll, I got lost on the way back up to your room. I needed to go get water" I said, stroking her hair as she fell back asleep in my arms.

As she fell asleep I was still wide awake, thinking. This poor girl was going to grow up with only a mother figure, and that was me. I couldn't be half of a mother, nevertheless a father figure. I understood that I needed to get a husband, and the sooner the better. I couldn't wait around to find my soulmate, this girl needs a dad.

But I don't want to go back to Lapel. He was abusive to her and she doesn't need that again. I wondered about the two men my father had arranged for me. Sure, I had never met them but back at the palace she'd have all of the things she needed handed to her. Even if that would mean giving up my own freedom, it would save her from having any struggle in life. And I could probably figure out some way to help

Alexander, and maybe even all poison mushrooms. If I could just speak to my father I'm sure I could convince him.

I can't let myself jump to conclusions though, I'm sure I can find a husband on my own. One that's committed and suitable to be a father, it didn't matter if he was a good husband. I just want Adeline to be happy, and I was ready to take the downfall. Surely it wouldn't be that hard, I am the princess of course. I'd just have to work my way around rebuking the crown at the wedding.

When a prince or princess gets married, they are automatically crowned king or queen along with their bride or groom. Even if the old king and queen were alive.

The more I thought about it, I fell more tired and began to drift off. I fell asleep within a matter of minutes as my eyes got heavy.

The next morning I woke up as Adeline crawled off of me. I gently rolled up on the bed wiping the hair out of my face. I crawled out of bed and stretched. It was still fairly early, the rain was starting to slow down, and the sun was starting to shine over the horizon. Adeline ran over to Alexander's door giggling as she pushed it open. "Shhh" I whispered as I threw her up on the bed. She crawled over beside Alexander and nuzzled up next to him. He rolled over and hugged her close to his chest without even opening his eyes. I smiled and sat down on the edge of the bed. I laid down with my back to Alexander's back, I saw his journal about a foot away from me. I heard him fall back asleep holding Adeline and my curiosity got the best of me. I grabbed the book swiftly with a smirk on my face. I opened it up to a page talking about Adeline. It spoke of how she was a cute thing but didn't know the arrangements that would be made with her one he left me on the island. He also admitted I'd be a good mother whether or not I was raised in a palace. That raised my confidence by a whole carton.

I flipped to another page more in the front. This one talked like it was before he knew me. It read off.

I have a new request for an escapee, this one is from the palace. Maybe this one knows the royal family. Maybe this one can tell me what all is going on with the royal family. Why are taxes so high? Why our towns aren't getting funded? Why haven't we seen the princess in years? I wish things could go back to how they were when I was young. At least then I'd have something to look forward to.

Reading the small clip broke my heart. The way he sounded was sad and his writing sounded dull. I snapped the journal shut as I felt him squirm some, I tossed the journal back to where it was. Adeline giggled as Alexander sat up. I smiled and sat up with him, I brushed the bouncy curls out of his face. He held Adeline and wiped the sleep out of his eyes. He looked over at me and I smiled seeing his hair bouncy and curly. "Oh that's lovely, I didn't put curlers in last night" He said, sounding annoyed.

"I like it," I said, smiling and touching his hair.

"Well you can, I won't," He said, laughing. I shrugged my shoulders and poked at Adeline. She jumped and squealed, giggling. I then started tickling her and she jumped in Alexander's lap cackling. She kicked her feet as Alexander suspended her in the air as I tickled her abdomen.

As her legs flailed around she accidentally kicked Alexander in the groin. "Oof" He said, letting go of Adeline and she fell down on the bed beside me. Adeline looked confused for a moment, I put my hand over my mouth, trying to not laugh. "Are you okay?" I said, giggling slightly as I picked up Adeline.

"No! She just kicked me, "he said, rolling on his back.

"I'll get her out of here then, drama queen" I said, giggling as I patted his shoulder. I took Adeline out of the room and closed the door. I headed down the stairs and set her on the floor. "Now don't go upstairs you got me, Little Missy?" I said in a serious but playful tone.

"Okay Momma," She said, giggling. I stood up and went into the kitchen, flipping through a cookbook.

I found oats in the book and I remembered when Natalia had made it once as a brunch for us. I landed on that for what I was going to make this morning. I got out the ingredients and started to prepare it. Adeline wandered in the kitchen and stood under my feet as I cooked. I heard footsteps upstairs as Alexander got up and was moving around. I finished cooking the oats and dished it out into bowls as I heard

Alexander's footsteps coming down the stairs. He brought down a small pair of black shoes, they had a little velcro strap over the top as well. In his other hands was a skirt and a blouse with socks. "Oh you found some things for her?" I asked, smiling.

"Yeah I did even though she's a stink" He said, pinching Adeline's nose and she bit at him.

"Stop that Addie" I said, setting down her bowl and Alexander's too. I gave them spoons and joined them at the table.

"So are we going to head off again today?" I asked, and I finished my bowl.

"That's what I'm wishing for as long as the rain stays gone. Who knows, we may have to run back here" He said, standing up and taking our bowls. Adeline was still eating, she was struggling to use her spoon. She held it in her fist tightly and would miss her mouth.

"Oh, hold on babydoll," I said, wiping her face and taking the spoon from her. I got a bite on the spoon and started hand feeding her. As I fed her I felt Alexander's gaze on me. I looked up at him and cocked my head. "May I help you sir?" I said teasingly as he shook his head.

"Oh no, no it's just, you know how to be a mom with little to no experience" He said, resting his hand on his chin as he leaned against the counter.

"Thank you, and I'm just trying to do my best even though I'm not" I said smiling as I got the last bite from the bowl and put it in Adeline's mouth. I stood up to put the bowl in the sink and helped Adeline down from her seat.

She went to run off and play but Alexander caught her in his hands. "Okay stink, your momma has made a, beautiful! Dress for you! So before anything else you're gonna try it on. And I got you some new shoes" He said, picking her up and taking her to the living room. I smiled at the scene, they looked like best friends as Adeline kicked her feet and laughed. Alexander dropped her down onto the couch and turned to face me. "I'll leave the little brat to you. I'm gonna go get the cart and horses ready to go" He said, giving a playful glare at Adeline before grabbing a few of the boxes on the way out to the cart.

I turned to face Adeline who was looking at the dress I'd made for her. "Ok Addie, let's do this, " I said as I took off Alexander's shirt and started to help her into her little dress. She squirmed as I fought it on her. It fit her a little bit loose but good enough. I was proud of my handy work and she looked cute in it. I slid on the socks and shoes Alexander gave her. Again, they were a bit big but it was better than her shoes being too small.

"Look how pretty you look," I said as Adeline spun around in the dress. I smiled as she giggled and shook her head. "Well Missy, we've got to get going, so find your dolly " I said, tapping her nose as I stood up.

"Where are we going?" she asked, sounding worried as we went up the stairs.

"We're going somewhere even better than this place" I said, smiling as I went into my room. I heard her run off to her room as I started to change into my pink dress.

As I finished getting changed I slid on my colour cap and looked at myself in the mirror. I looked at my face closely, my skin wasn't like porcelain anymore. It had a duller look to it and my hair isn't silky to the touch. *It seems I've lost my beauty,* I thought, looking at myself. I still had the same body structure, the empire cut of the dress made it fall perfectly over my hips so I didn't have to wear a corset. But what's a good body if you have an ugly face? "Lord, I am looking rough" I murmured to myself as I kept eye contact with the mirror.

"Hm, I don't agree" Alexander's voice interrupted me and it made me jump.

"How long have you been there?" I asked, nervously smiling.

"Long enough" He said, walking over behind me. "But what I can say is that when I see you, all I see is a beautiful, strong, independent female, who is quite literally the best mother ever to a kid she met just a few days ago" He said, moving my face to look at myself in the mirror. My eyes peered at him in the mirror though. "I also see a drop dead gorgeous princess, who has the most striking features that could catch anyone's gaze from a mile away. I mean, come on, you have bright beautiful blonde hair. And I have never in my entire life seen anyone with purple eyes. And you have the body of an angel. You could make any male, possibly female, fall in love with you without even trying.

I mean look at Lapel for example, he didn't even know you and was willing to fight over you" He said picking my hair up and he put it into a braid. I felt my face get a little bit hot as he finished braiding my hair. I turned to look at him as I realised something.

"You fought for me too," I said, looking up at him.

"Well, what can I say, you're kind of like my job right now. You think I'd let Lapel just steal you? No, you're my responsibility" He said, smirking as he turned towards the door.

"Your shirt's downstairs on the couch" I said, smiling as he yelled back up.

"Thank you!"

I sat there for a few more moments just lost in thought. I wanted someone, good with kids, a caring person, and most of all someone who can take care of Adeline if something happened to me. My mind started to race and I felt butterflies in my stomach. What if the male I was looking for was right here? What if it is Alexander? Would he want to marry me? What am I thinking? Am I crazy? He'd never want to marry me. I'm too much trouble, I'd get him slaughtered and no one would even turn to see because he's a poison mushroom. I need to just keep my mouth shut and my mind open to anyone else. Anyone else that's acceptable to be more specific.

I stood up and readied myself, as I walked I carried my purple dress and went downstairs to where Alexander stood with Adeline in his arms. "Are you ready to go my lady? " he said teasingly as he held the door for me.

"Well why thank you my good sir " I said smiling as I grabbed the skirt and blouse off the couch for Adeline. She needed an extra change of clothes of course. Alexander closed and locked the door and we made our way out to the cart.

"So Miss Adel you have a choice to make" Alexander said as I folded up my dress and Adeline's clothes and I set them down in the box with Alexander's shirts and the black dress. Adeline's face lit up as she waited for the rest of his statement. "You can ride up front or you can go back in the back of the cart and play with your dolly," he said, bouncing her in his arms.

"Back back!" she shouted happily.

"Okay" he said laughing as he gently tossed her into the air and she landed in the hay of the cart giggling. I smiled as I jumped up into the front of the cart. I got situated on the bench and Alexander jumped in taking the leads of the horses.

"So what are we going to go through today?" I asked, smiling as the horses took off.

"Eh not much, I intend to get to the next safe house but we will just have to see how that goes" he said with a sigh as he leaned back against the bench.

"Well I think we can make it, I'm sure" I said smiling and he smiled back at me.

"You're so optimistic, I love it. But I hope you're right, I don't want Adeline to have to sleep outside" he said peering back at her in the back of the cart.

Chapter 21. Alexander Malencoy

I'm starting to realise my time with Magdolin is running short, the closer we get to the island the more antsy I get to tell her how I feel. Even if I've only known her for a little more than a week, I know I love her. As we travelled for a few more days we went through many small towns and we stayed in a few different safe houses throughout the days.

I felt awful for Adeline, she'd get annoyed and bored of being in the cart all the time. Today she was upfront and I was letting her take the reins of the horses and she led them. But of course she got bored and jumped in the back, rummaging through boxes. "I feel bad for the girl, I know she's dying to get out" I said, frowning. Magdolin was leaning against me half asleep.

"I know, she'll be free of the cart soon" She said, leaning more into my shoulder, closing her eyes. She hadn't slept well last night because of Adeline. She didn't want to sleep. Magdolin didn't want to sleep knowing Adeline was still up so she stayed up. And her reminding me that soon they'd be at their new home made my mind run more.

"Well this next town were coming up to have a pretty cool park she could stop at. We've got time to spare today" I said trying to suggest something, mostly to try and slow down time even though it wouldn't be by that much.

"Yeah that sounds nice, she'll like that" She said murmuring, starting to fall asleep against my shoulder. It made me smile as she fell asleep against me. I didn't want her to leave me but I didn't get to make that choice.

I drove the horses for about another two hours. Going up and around hills and that's when we came across the town. I saw the peak of the huge manor on the hill. I loved this town, it was gorgeous and on a mountain side. I nudged Magdolin to wake up so she could see the sight. She groaned quietly as she sat up stretching her neck. "Look Mags" I said, almost whispering as she woke up. Adeline saw it then too, she jumped up towards the front of the cart.

"Wow!" Adeline said, looking at the manor in the mountain.

"Oh my gosh that's gorgeous" Magdolin said as she wiped the sleep from her eyes.

"I know, it's been standing for over three hundred years," I said, adding to the manor's magnificence.

"I think it almost surpasses the palace," Magdolin said, smiling as she woke up fully. As we entered the town the streets were paved nicely and smooth. The horses basically didn't pull any weight with how perfect the terrain was. Most of the people that walked on the street were gold mushrooms or navy. They're very highly ranked mushrooms, right below purple.

"Is this Alemania?" Magdolin asked, looking up at the mountains still.

"Yep, the Alemania. Ya know they say mythical creatures live in the woods here, and a witch who lives in the manor" I said, smirking, trying to scare Adeline.

"Monsters!" She said, looking at me.

"Yeah and they eat little girls' toes while they sleep" I said, twirling my fingers in Adeline's face.

"Oh Alexander stop," Magdolin said, pushing my hand down. I rolled my eyes and returned them back to the road.

"Do you want to go to the park, Adel?" I asked as we came to the turn.

"Yes!" She shouted out excitedly, jumping in the hay in the back of the cart. "Okay" I said, turning on the road towards the park.

Once we pulled up, Adeline was in awe at the huge play park. It was a large wooden play place that was shaped like a castle. "Go crazy, Adel" I said, parking the cart by the side of the road. She jumped out of the cart and jumped up to the play castle. She climbed up it and was running around the turns and stairs in the wooden structure.

"Should I go up there to make sure she's okay?" Magdolin asked.

"No, she'll be fine. It's a nice town and she needs to have fun, don't be a prison mom" I said, nudging her shoulder a little bit.

"I- I am not being a prison mom. I just don't want her getting hurt, "she said, watching her closely from the cart. She was able to stay still for probably another thirty seconds before jumping up. "I can't leave her over there alone. I want to keep an eye on her" Magdolin said, jumping out of the cart.

"Oh Mags" I said, sighing as I got out of the cart too. I tied the horses to a post so they wouldn't wander and I followed Magdolin over to the play area.

The sand that they had laid out on the ground moved under my feet as I stood next to Magdolin as she watched Adeline. I stood for about five minutes before I got tired of it. I sat down on the ground on my back, the sand felt nice. "Alexander, stand up right now" Magdolin said, looking down at me embarrassed.

"What? No one else is here right now. And who cares what rich snobs think of us." I said laying on the ground.

"I care, now stand up please" She said, holding out her hand to help me up.

"Hm fine" I said, pulling her down on the ground as well with a smirk plastered across my face. She gasped as I did so and I laughed as I pinned her down into the sand.

"Alexander!" she said as I jumped up and ran. She stood up, brushed her dress off, and ran at me. As she neared me I threw my arms around her waist and lifted her in the air, spinning her in a few circles before I set her down.

She stumbled trying to find her balance, I laughed as I held her shoulders to steady her. "Alexander Malencoy, you are the biggest pain I think I have" She said as she brushed her hair back down in the braid.

"Oh but I'm not" I said, smirking as I let go of her. Adeline was laughing and giggling as she went down a slide which caught our attention. She'd been out on the playground for about twenty minutes, part of me wondered when she'd get tuckered out. Magdolin sat down on a log bench that had been placed on the edge of the park. I decided I was gonna look around the town a little bit. I hadn't gone through Alemania in a few years. "I'll be back in a minute Mags" I said as she nodded her head and turned her head back towards Adeline.

I walked off the park and looked around the street. Not many people were outside right now, but the people that were gave me dirty looks. Which I understood why, but sometimes I wished that I'd get some slack from it. I walked around the circle fountain in the middle of main street. In the fountain were hundreds of pennies and nickels rested. Kids liked to do that to make a wish, but I knew some dad's pocket was hurting.

I walked past the fountain and looked in all the stores that were placed around main street. Lots of little boutiques, and a barber. Other little food stores and surpluses were here too. It was like a little stripmall almost. As I walked down the street I came across a flyer on a post.

"The Baron Marquee invites all thout would wish to attend. To the Marquee Manor, to attend thee ball of excellence. Those whom may attend must be dressed their finest. Come to be enjoyable, and to be entertained. All are welcome to come. Arrive at the manor at six pm and be prepared to leave by midnight. On the Eighth of September"

I snatched the flyer and examined it closer. This would be perfect to try and propose to Magdolin. It would quite literally be the best place. She was a princess and this is a laid back ball. She'd be in her normal setting. I'm sure I could find an area where we'd be alone. And if she said no we're only a day away from the island. I could just get Adeline tired and we could get a room at the manor and set her down for bed. It wouldn't be that hard to do. I've just got to ask Magdolin to go with me now, and it was tomorrow.

I folded the paper and put it in my satchel. I started my way back down main street. I reached the park again and Magdolin was still on the bench. I walked up behind her and grabbed her shoulders. She jumped and flipped around quickly. She let out a sigh "Alexander, that's not funny," She said, smiling and turning to face Adeline.

Adeline was crawling out of the playplace. "Allie-zander, where'd you go!" She yelled as she ran over to us.

"None of your business, Missy! Are you almost done playing?" I asked, picking her up and throwing her gently in the air before catching her again.

"I'm done, if you're ready to go" She said, laughing. I gave Magdolin a hand to help her up to her feet, and we made our way back to the cart. I stepped up into the cart as Adeline crawled to the back in the hay and Magdolin sat next to me on the bench.

The horses took off back down the road at a steady trot. "So you like Almania?" I asked, breaking the ever so quiet silence.

"It's quite divine, and I adore there architecture" Magdolin said, smiling up at me. Once again I was lost in those gorgeous purple eyes.

"Great..." I breathed, just looking at her. I was still thinking of how I would propose to her.

I'd be down on one day, shed be in a beautiful fine dress and for once people would congratulate me, not look at me in disgust.

But I couldn't be thinking about that now. I still have to ask her to even go. Never the less I wouldn't not get shade for it. She may not agree after all. "What are you gawking at?" She said with a sly smirk creeping across her face.

"Oh shut your trap, you've got that lipstick on again. It just caught my attention" I said, rolling my eyes and looking back towards the road. I still felt her gaze on me and I side eyed her as she was still smiling at me.

"I don't have lipstick on" She said, snickering under her breath as she sat back on the bench.

I felt myself tense up slightly as she said that, I'd been caught. I let out a sigh as I put my feet up on the front guard rail. Adeline crawled up to the front of the bed of the cart and started pulling at Magdolin's hair. "Ouch, Addie, what is it?" She said, looking back at her.

"I wanna see your hair," She said, pulling at her braid.

"Fine." Magdolin said, pulling her hair up and Adeline took it out of the braid and started trying to braid it again.

She put tiny braids in Magdolin's hair, but they were wonky. I didn't expect any better from a little girl, but Magdolin stayed content as Adeline went on. I smiled and turned back towards the, now dirt, road.

After a few more hours of patiently sitting in the cart, we arrived at the next safe house. This house was nothing spectacular, just a small log cabin and about two acres of land. I pulled the cart to the side of the house and tied the horses up as Magdolin collected Adeline and took her to the front of the house. I came up to the door and unlocked it for them. I came inside and fell down on the couch in the kitchen and living room mix. "Mags, you two are gonna have the bedroom, I'll be out here" I said, leaning up, my back ached from being on the road as always. I guess all the years of it was catching up to me from how it was hurting now.

"You can have the bed Alexander. I can tell something's bothering you" She said as she set Adeline on the ground and she took off running around the small cabin.

"No Mags, you and Adeline can have it. I refuse" I said standing up and walking to the cabinet area, seeing what there was.

"Alexander don't be stubborn please, is it your shoulders that bothering you?" She asked, following me around the small room.

"No Mags, trust me I'm fine" I said, pulling out some pasta, surely this would do.

"You really won't let me try to help" Magdolin said, frowning.

"No, you can help, just don't give up the bed. That's your's ma'am" I said, handing her a glass jar full of tomatoes. She gave me a look, which made me grin down at her.

She frowned and set them down on the counter as I got down a pan and poured water into it. I then lit the fire in the small wood powered stove and put the pan on top of it. "So, I heard about this thing happening tomorrow night, and I wandered if possibly, maybe, by chance, You'd give me the honour of attending it with me" I said nervously as I leaned against the counter.

She looked at me, cocking her head slightly. "The island?" She asked with curiosity in her tone.

"No no, I mean we only have a day's trip before you're there… but there's this thing happening at the manor and I was wondering if you'd like to go" I asked, looking back at her.

"What is it?" She asked, smiling as she leaned her elbow on the counter next to me.

"It's this ball thing, and I know that I'm not the mushroom that's made for things like that. But I'd really like to take you to this. Only because it's something like where you came from and I thought it'd be nice for you to go before you're on the island, and won't be able to anymore." I said, looking down at her.

She cracked a small smile before it faded. "I would love to Alexander, but I won't let Adeline stay somewhere alone" She said, looking down at her hands.

I paused for a moment before speaking again. "Well, about that, the manor has rooms for purchase there. If we put her down for bed in one of the rooms, we'd be right there in the manor with her, and if it makes you feel better I'll come and check on her every once and a while when we're there. I just want you to have fun" I said, grabbing her hands. Her smile returned on her face.

"You'd actually do that?" she said, raising an eyebrow.

"Of course I would, as long as you could grant me the pleasure of you going with me" I said, smiling and squeezing her hands.

"Okay then, I will go with you" She said, smiling and I felt a rush of adrenaline run through me.

"Great! Wonderful, I can't wait" I said smiling, I couldn't really control it. It just spread it across my face.

Magdolin was smiling as well. "Alexander?" She said, smirking and snickering.

"Yes?" I said smiling as I stepped a little bit closer to her.

"The water" She said, laughing and pointing. I turned and looked abruptly. The water was boiling over. I sighed and turned down the heat and set the pasta down in the boiling water.

It was getting quite annoying whenever it seemed that something may happen, but it doesn't because something else interrupted. I turned and smiled back at Magdolin as I cleaned up the spilt water. Adeline came running into the kitchen then, holding a cat. "Momma! Momma!" She yelled out, laughing. The cat looked sick and was missing an eye.

"Oh no" I said, grabbing the cat up from Adeline.

"What's wrong, why can't she keep it?!" Magdolin said as Adeline looked confused. I looked at the cat closer before rushing to the door with it.

"Mags I know you love cats and animals in general, but that one probably has fleas. And who knows what else. You don't want Adeline catching that do you?" I said, setting the cat outside and closing the door. Magdolin frowned and Adeline started to tear up. "Adel no don't cry, here wait how about this?" I said, picking her up and going to the stove to stir the noodles. "Whenever I drop you and your momma off at your permanent house. I will make sure you have as many cats as you want. Just not that one okay stink?" I said trying to calm her down and she wiped her eyes smiling. I smiled and sat her down next to Magdolin who still had her arms crossed and looked up at me looking disappointed.

"Oh don't give me that look, I will get you guys a cat I promise you that. Just don't guilt me into taking that one please. I don't want to drag it along if it's ill or diseased." I said, looking at her as I drained the water from the pan. I knew that if she kept up this disappointed act I'd cave in sooner or later. Magdolin had this way to get to my soft spot in my shattered heart.

"Fine," She said, rolling her eyes and cracking a smile.

"Wow, I've never seen you do that" I said, smiling as I put the tomatoes in the pan and added some dehydrated beef in to make a sauce.

"Seen what?" She asked, raising an eyebrow.

"Roll your eyes, you're getting some spunk to you. I'm sure your parents wouldn't like that." I said, smirking as I stirred the pan.

"You're right, they'd hate it" She said, smiling.

I loved her smile, the way it stretched across her face. She had small dimples that indent her cheeks when she smiled. Her eyes felt like they sparkled too. I wished I could see her smile more than I did. It seemed like she was always smiling but when she smiled at me it was different. And when she wasn't smiling it felt like the whole room was let down. It felt like her energy and feeling affected everyone. At least I felt that way.

I got down three plates and dished out the pasta on the plates then poured the sauce over top of it. Magdolin set Adeline up in one of the chairs and I set the plates.

The entire time we sat there I couldn't get my mind off of what could happen tomorrow. If she says no it'll be very awkward afterwards. But if I don't do it I'll never know. I have to ask no matter what. What if Adeline messes something up though? What if she won't go to sleep? What if she's not tired at six? Most of the time she goes to bed at nine. This is going to be ruined. I just knew it.

"Are you not hungry?" Adeline spoke out as she finished her plate, shoving the last fistfull of spaghetti in her mouth.

"He's just taking his time babydoll. And I wish you'd have manners." Magodlin said, wiping Adeline's face with a napkin and she stood up taking their plates to the sink. "Is everything alright though, Alexander?" She added, facing me as I finished my food quickly.

"Yes I'm fine, I was just thinking that's all" I said, smiling and putting my plate in the sink. Magdolin once again crossed her arms and looked up at me with a firm face. "I'm being serious! I promise!" I said grabbing her shoulders and turning her around towards the living room area.

"I'd prefer you talk to me. " She said, looking back at me.

"Well there's nothing to talk about. I don't know what you think is wrong, Mags." I said, shaking my head as Adeline came in clutching her doll.

"I'm tired!" She announced proudly. I smirked at Magdolin as she sighed.

"I think that's your goodnight call" I said as she took Adeline back to the bedroom.

As they left the room I let out a sigh and hunched forward. My back was still killing me from the cart. I bent backward and cracked my back around. I sat down on the couch with a groan and sank down into the couch. I looked up at the ceiling and closed my eyes, which halted the burning sensation in them. I laid back for a few minutes, almost falling asleep before I was interrupted by small, almost silent footsteps.

I sat up and Magdolin stood before me with her arms crossed. "Hm... I don't think Adeline will appreciate you not being with her" I said, smirking playfully and crossing my arms like her.

"Well she meant it when she said she was tired. I don't think she'll be waking up soon. And that means I'm gonna help you now" she said with a cocky voice. I blinked a few times before smiling and setting back further on the couch.

"Well, be my guest! And I think I might be taking back the brat statement. I heard some attitude in that statement." I said, snickering as I folded my arms behind my head.

"Well, only because you won't tell me what's wrong. Please just let me help," She said, sitting down next to me on the couch. I looked down at her with the same smirk playing across my face. It dropped though as I saw the sincerity in her eyes, it made my heart melt sort of. Like I needed to tell her, like she longed for the answer.

"Mags really there's nothing you can do about it" I said trying to laugh it off but she still kept the same sincere look.

"Please, Alexander." She said, looking up at me with those big purple eyes.

"Mags it's just my back, it's nothing serious it's just the cart hurts it" I said, pasting on a small smile.

"Well why didn't you just say that? " she said, giving me a small smile.

"Well there's nothing you can really do Mags!" I said laughing. "Yes I can, come here!" She said, pulling me down over her lap. I felt my face light up like a bonfire as my face pressed against one of the small pillows on the couch. My whole body tensed and I felt butterflies in my stomach as her small hands ran across my back. She pressed her palms into the back of my shoulder blades and continued down my spine.

As she reached the midpoint of my lower back and pressed in gently. I groaned and squirmed slightly as she hit that spot. That's where it had been bothering me. "Found it" she said snickering to herself as she pressed her hands around that area more, massaging it. My back would tense and arch as she made the muscles release from their tensed state.

She worked on massaging my back for a few more minutes and afterwards it was sore but felt relieved. Like a load had been taken off my shoulders. "Thank you Mags" I said sitting up on the couch groaning.

"Does your back feel any better?" she asked, running her hand up and down my back. I loved how she was trying to help, and it did help but it for sure didn't cure it.

"Yeah Mags, I feel way better," I said standing up from the couch and stretching my back. "Now, you better get back in there to your Adeline, she'll get mad if you leave her alone" I said, putting on a smirk as I looked back at her. She rolled her eyes as she stood up.

"Goodnight Alexander," she said, smiling at me.

"Goodnight Mags" I said, smiling back at her and she moved closer and wrapped her arms around me. I was shocked as she embraced me so suddenly. I accepted it gratefully and hugged her back.

"Momma" I heard Adeline's voice come from the other room. I let out a sigh as I let go of Magdolin and she walked off towards the bedroom.

I watched as she disappeared into the bedroom, how could a female just do that. Be so perfect in everything she does, I mean clearly not everything. Everyone makes mistakes but she seems to make very few, I don't care what others say. Some people may say I'm blinded, but I don't care if I am. I know I'm going to marry that girl.

I laid back down on the couch and rested my head back on the pillow. My thoughts were full of her, she's all I could think about. She's so beautiful without even trying, and she's an amazing mom to a kid she met just days ago. How could any male ask for more, she's all any male would need. She's all I need, and want. The more I thought of her my thoughts drifted away and spaced out, as I fell peacefully asleep.

Chapter 22. Magdolin Poni

I laid back down on the bed with Adeline and she fell back asleep clinging onto her doll. I laid there alone to my thoughts, they ran wild thinking about tomorrow. What was going to wear? My pink dress should surely be good enough. But for Alexander I don't think I would have anything, and he wouldn't exactly fit in. I know the invite said everyone is allowed, but I'm not sure they'd let him in. I know one of the palace balls wouldn't have let him in. Maybe if I made him a colour cap it would work, but if the lights were dim the fluorescence in his eyes and gills would glow. *I don't know a lot about living out of a palace but I've gotta figure this out*, I thought as I fell asleep nuzzled up next to Adeline.

The next morning I woke up to the sun shining in on us, the warm beams casting over me. I rolled over and sat up, my hair was all tangled and stood up. Adeline stirred awake as well and stretched her arms and back around while whining. "Good morning sleeping beauty " I said, smiling and picking her up. I brushed back my hair a little bit and walked out to the living and dining area. Alexander was still dead asleep on the couch and set Adeline down. "Go grab Alexander a blankie." I whispered into her ear. She nodded her head and ran off to the bedroom and came back with the blanket off the bed. I picked it up from her and threw it out to unfold it. As I went to put it over, Alexander Adeline crawled up on his chest. It was a cute scene as she closed her eyes and Alexander instinctively wrapped his arms around her. I smiled and laid the blanket over them both.

I looked around the kitchen area, there wasn't much in it but I'm sure I can find something to make. I rummaged around the kitchen for a few minutes but couldn't find anything, I shrugged it off and assumed Alexander had something in mind. I walked towards the back of the house again and saw the other door across from the bedroom. I slowly opened the door and saw a small room. It was more like a closet with the shelves lining around the walls and boxes down on the floor. I pulled one of the boxes from the wall and out into the hallway. Dust and cobwebs fell to the ground as I opened the box up.

Tons of pictures were in the box filling it to the brim. A happy little couple and two kids. The more I looked at the faded black and white pictures I recognized Alexander as being one of the little kids. He looked so happy in the pictures, holding onto his little sister's hand playing and dancing in the pictures. Their parents also looked happy watching them. There were also pictures of Alexander and his friends, a small bunch of kids one of them being Alexander and who I believe was Charlie. The other kids were all low ranked mushrooms, that's probably why they were allowed around Alexander. That's a horrible thing to think I know but it is the sad truth of it all.

I smiled as I looked through the pictures, he looked so happy. I wish I could see that childlike smile on him that I'm seeing in these pictures. I put the box back in the closet and looked up on the shelves, there were some clothes piled in there. I chose to leave them alone, surely Alexander wouldn't want me in his things. I shouldn't have even been in the pictures, but my curiosity is too big for me.

I closed the closet back and walked back to the main room and Alexander and Adeline were both still asleep. They looked so peaceful in slumber together, one day Alexander is going to make an amazing father. His wife in the future will be very happy with him. I hope I can find someone like him. Someone sweet and kind to me and Adeline, I doubt I find that though. It's time to stop listening to that dream. Today is my last day in equilibrium and after tonight I will have a new life.

That was odd to think about, after today it would just be me and Adeline. I'm much happier to think I have Adeline though, at first I was going to be purely alone. I wonder what kind of people live on the island, I'm assuming a lot of them are poison mushrooms. Maybe there will be another purple mushroom that ran away there, you never know until you see. It would be amazing if I could find another purple there and be a happy family. It would be like a safe haven away from the kingdom.

The only problem with me getting a husband would be fighting back royal status. Whenever I am to wed me and my husband shall be crowned king and queen then as we are announced married. It would be difficult to find my way around that, but I'm sure I'd find a way. As for Alexander, I'm sure he'd find someone else to help escape the kingdom. I'm sure he'd find someone else to help, like he always does. He's always going to be a helpful person, and someone dependable. At least he'd always feel like that to me, even if I never see him again after today.

I turned to look at them and then crawled over beside the couch where they both laid asleep still. I was really going to miss Alexander, he was a great friend to me. I laid my head against the couch cushion next to the two of them. I felt Alexander's arm wrap around my shoulder and I felt his hand on my face. "Well good morning Mags" he said in a soft sleepy voice and his thumb gently rubbed my cheek.

That feeling was back in my chest again, and my cheeks felt hot. "Good morning Alexander," I said sitting up and Adeline then started to stir awake. I smiled and picked her up off Alexander and set her on the ground as she rubbed her eyes. Alexander got up as well, stretching his arms out. I found it oddly amusing how he'd scowl his face when he stretched.

"I'm hungry, " Adeline announced while playing with fists full of my hair.

"Ouch ouch Adeline no hair pulling" I said trying to move with her hands to not get my hair pulled more. Alexander then pulled her small hands free from my hair.

"Well Adel I was gonna go into town and get you guys something for breakfast. That's if you're okay with fancy food?" he said, tapping her nose.

"Fancy food!" she said excitedly.

"Yes Adel " he said, slipping on his shoes.

"Oh Alexander, I could make something, we don't need to spend your money" I said interrupting the two.

"Boo" Adeline states while sticking her tongue out.

137

"No Mags i insist, it'll be my treat" he said standing up and resting his hand on my shoulder.

I looked over at Adeline who was sticking out her lip in a begging face. "Fine if you insist, Alexander," I said with a sigh and broke a small smile.

"Yay!" Adeline cheered out jumping up and down.

"I want to make the most out of our last day together... I mean like us three together. Cause ya know it'll just be you and Adeline after today." he said with a little bit of a stammer in his voice. I smiled a bit more as he stuttered his words, it was cute.

"So, what do you want to miss Adele?" he said, interrupting and picking up adeline. He bounced her in the air as he spoke and she cackled to herself. My chest got that warm feeling at the cute sight.

"Flappy-jacks!" she yelled out happily.

"Then I know exactly where to go girls!" Alexander said happily as he opened the front door leading outside. I followed them both outside and out towards the cart. "Mags, do you think you'd like to take a horse instead, I'll let you ride hope." he said, setting Adeline down while he unhooked the cart.

"Why don't we just take the wagon?" I asked curiously.

"Well it's just easier to be on horseback when we aren't going far, and I thought it'd be fun for you," he said, grabbing the halters and a few saddle bags out of the cart.

"Oh, well I suppose I can try," I said, shrugging my shoulders.

"Lovely!" he said, leading Hope over beside me. "You know I'm just now realizing who you named this poor horse after." I said, smirking up at him.

"Eh I see it wasn't a good idea now" he said shrugging. He picked me up by my waist and set me up on Hope's back.

"I do prefer this Hope a lot more though" I said, brushing the soft but rough hair of the horse.

"Howsey!" Adeline said laughing as Alexander held her to his chest as he got on his horse.

"Yeah horsey! Hold on Miss Adel " he said, grabbing the reins of his horse.

"So we lead them with these ropes?" I asked curiously.

"Yep and nudge her with your feet, gently! She's touchy Mags" he said moving his horse beside me. "Ok, I think I can" I said doing as he said. Hope jerked forward and took off on the dirt path. Alexander rode beside me on his horse with Adeline in front of him. "So, I've forgotten what you told me the other horse's name was?" I said as the horses trotted down the road and towards town.

"Oh this is Serenity, she's a good girl, she's just antsy sometimes," he said, patting the side of the horse. Adeline was playing with the small intricate braids in serenity's hair that Alexander had put there.

"Serenity is a beautiful name, I like it" I said smiling as I looked back at the path ahead. The road rutted with gravel and the trees that lined the road were a beautiful green and some of the leaves had already begun shifting to a vibrant orange and red.

After about twenty minutes we arrived in town and Alexander stopped his horse next to a small building that looked like a cottage. "I know it looks rough but I can assure you that it's amazing here" he said, getting off his horse and taking both the reins of Hope and Serenity, and tying them to a post.

"Oh I'm sure it's lovely Alexander," I said as I looked at the building. There were a few tables outside and it had a patio area.

"Well let's get inside" Alexander said, helping me down off the horse. I grabbed Adeline off serenity and held her as Alexander led the way in the small restaurant. The door creaked open and the dining area was mostly empty. There were small tables scattered around the moderately sized dining area. A few people sat around some of the tables and two waitresses were walking about between them. One of the waitresses spotted us up at the entrance and gave us a wide eyed look before rushing up to the front.

"Just the three of us" Alexander said with his normal charming smile and positive demeanour. The waitress had a look of annoyance as she brushed past us and held the door open.

"I can't serve you. I'm sorry, we don't serve to anything ranked below a brown." She said, ushering us outside.

"What? This is outrageous are you kidding me? I used to come here all the time " Alexander said, crossing his arms as we stepped outside.

"The two ladies can come inside but you sir can sit on our patio area, we have new owners." The mushroom said, closing the door as we stood outside.

"But ma'am he's with me, this is my husband," I said as I held Adeline in my arms and tried to keep a calm composure.

"Well miss that's a sinful thing for you, and I believe a pink mushroom could do much better in search for a male to wed. Now I can sit you outside or you can leave" The lady spoke in an assertive but rushed tone.

"Well then well just lea- " I said with a hint of annoyance from the female's words but Alexander's hand came to rest on my shoulder.

"We'll sit outside please," Alexander interrupted me with a sigh as well.

"Very well follow me," the lady said, setting down a few menus on a table.

"I'll be right back with you folks" she said going back inside the building.

"This is an outrage, why must people be like that?" I said as I sat down angrily.

"Mags please it's alright, I'm used to it by now" Alexander said sitting down as well.

Adeline crawled up in her chair as well looking up over the table. "Why do we have to sit outside?" she asked, looking at the menu.

"Because people don't like the colour of my cap Adel" Alexander said leaning back on the chair.

"Well mommy is lying about her colour why isn't she in-" Adeline spoke aloud before Alexander put his hand over her mouth.

"Shh," Alexander said, putting his other hand to his mouth, shushing her.

"We can't say that out loud babydoll!" I whisper shouted at her.

"Sorry.." she said quietly.

"It's okay just hush hush okay?" Alexander said with a soft smile on his face. He peered over each shoulder just to see in case anyone had heard Adeline. He turned his head back down to the menu. "Okay girls, well I know Miss Adeline wants pancakes, what do you want Mags?" he asked, sitting down his menu.

"I'll just get eggs I think" I said, setting down my menu as soon as the waitress came back outside. She spat out a few bland questions about what we wanted and took our orders. As she wrote it down and left to go back inside.

"Where's my pancakes?" Adeline asked with her fork ready to dig into some.

"Patience, they have to make it for you, you little snot " Alexander said, settling into the chair he sat in. I sat upright in my seat the proper way as I was taught when I was young.

After a few moments the waitress returned with two plates and a bowl. She set the plates down in front of me and Adeline and the bowl in front of Alexander before marching back off inside.

She hadn't even said a word to us, this was simply awful treatment. They had given Adeline her pancakes and I got my eggs but Alexander was given some sort of stew and not what he'd ordered. That made my blood boil over seeing they'd just given him rock bottom. "I'm going in there and speaking to the owner, this is horrendous service" I said standing up from the table. I was fuming over what they were pulling here.

"No Mags really it's fine, it could be worse," he said, grabbing my wrist and pulling me back down in my seat.

"No alexander-" I growled

before he cut me off. "Please Mags, Adeline is enjoying this." he said with an almost pleading face. I looked over at Adeline who was happily using her hands to pull apart the pancakes and dip them in the syrup. Even though I was furious I knew I should let Adeline enjoy this before she can't anymore.

"Fine.. but we're switching" I said, snatching his bowl and he grabbed the bowl as well.

"No mags stop that, you aren't gonna eat that nasty stuff," Alexander said, pulling the bowl back. I pulled his hand off the bowl with a smirk.

"No sir, I've had princess treatment my whole life. Now it's your turn to have something nice, Alexander," I said, pushing the plate of fancy eggs and toast over to him.

I watched a small smile spread across his face, I smiled as well with him as he accepted the small gesture. I looked down at the brown mess of a soup they called edible, surely it didn't taste that bad. I picked the bowl up and raised it to my lips as I took a small sip of it. It tasted like beef broth mainly and some mixed veggies possibly, but it was edible and slightly tolerable. As we all ate I sucked down the stew and Alexander and adeline finished their plates. I stacked the plates up and the waitress returned and just stood there silent. I set up properly and crossed my arms, I couldn't stand this ladies' attitude.

"Here you go ma'am" Alexander said, handing the lady a few bills out of his pocket. "Oh it will be more than that for this, I wasn't even supposed to serve you!" she spoke boldly putting the cash in her apron.

I stood up picking up Adeline, I was about to boil over on this mushroom. "No this is outrageous, you won't be seeing us again!" I said, grabbing Alexander's wrist and pulling him up from the table. I trudged out of the area and out to the horses. The lady came walking out behind us.

"Hey! I'm being serious, I expect more!" she yelled furiously. I halted in my step and put Adeline in Alexander's arms. He gave me a confused look before I turned around and calmly approached the waitress.

"I order you to take your lousy… no good, medium wage paid ass back in that restaurant right now. Or this won't be pretty." I hissed as I glared straight through her. She just looked at me with a look of disgust but then it faltered. I'm assuming she'd seen the purple hue of my eyes now that she was this close to me.

"I-..i um," she started to stammer before I took my chance. I quickly grabbed the cash out of the front pocket of her apron that Alexander had handed to her. She gasped and then yelled some curse as I took off in the opposite direction towards the horse. Alexander took off next to me as he realized what I'd done.

"I don't care who you are! I'm not scared of you!" she yelled out as I jumped up on Hope's back and Alexander and Adeline got on serenity. "I hope you have a good day ma'am" I yelled back with a hoarseness to my voice. I flipped her the middle finger which I could see her jaw drop. Alexander let out a small laugh.

I kicked the sides of Hope, which was a mistake. Hope took off galloping as I held onto her halter, I heard Alexander laugh as he took off on serenity quickly catching up to me. "Pull back on the halter" he yelled out over Adeline's giggles. I did as he said and hope came to a stop as I laughed looking back at the restaurant that was hidden from the distance.

"Again!" Adeline yelled out as Alexander came to a stop next to me.

"I don't think your momma can handle that, you wild child. There's a market I think your momma could handle though. What do you say Mags?" he said looking over at me.

"I think we could do that" I said smiling as Adeline looked eagerly up at me as if she was begging to go to the market.

"Great!" he said, taking off towards town on his horse. I rode next to them as we rode into town. It was a smaller market than last time and was just set on the sides of the road.

"I wanna go there" Adeline announced pointing at a stand down the aisle. I looked around the stands and saw a few jewellery and clothing stands, the stands Adeline wanted to go to were toy stands of course. Alexander stopped the horses towards the end of the aisle and tied them to a post. "I wanna go to toys! Toys!" she shouted jumping up and down.

"Do you want to go with her?" I asked, looking up at Alexander.

"Will you be alright on your own? You know what happened last time." he said, holding Adeline's hand.

"Yes I'm sure now you two don't go getting in trouble," I said, brushing past them and in towards the market. I walked over to the clothing stand I was originally looking at, there were fancy dresses and other things set up all around it. A green embroidered waistcoat hung up on one side of the stand. It had fancy beads and swirled designs all over it. The buttons on it were gold and went all the way up and down the front. I knew that Alexander would look spectacular in it, and he needed something to wear tonight. I walked around to the front of the stand and there was a male standing behind the small counter.

"What can I help you with today my lady?" the older mushroom asked with a smile. He was a red mushroom, clearly a merchant and has the natural skills to sell things. I could tell from the warm smile and friendly introduction that he might be a scammer. Many people act friendly at vendors, at least my mother had told me that.

"Yes hello, I was curious about that waistcoat over there" I said pointing at the side.

"Ah a fine choice madam. It's hand crafted and made with the finest of silk this side of the kingdom!" he said, grabbing it down and showing off its flashy beads and thread in the sunlight.

"Yes it is lovely, would you possibly want to trade for it?" I asked looking at the vest, I knew it'd fit Alexander and look amazing on him.

"Why, of course, depending on what you have. But can I just say I do have other waistcoats in other colours, I'm assuming this is for your husband. And I have one in pink." he said smiling as he rested his elbows on the counter. When the mushroom smiled his mustache went up as well.

"Oh no this one's gorgeous, he'll love it and it is for my husband", I said smiling back friendly.

"Oh I see, he doesn't like matching his mushroom colour, I can't blame him. Red on red would get boring for me, but i'll set this vest back here and come back with something to trade madam. He said pulling the waist coat back and smiling. I nodded my head and walked away from the vendor stand. I looked around and saw Alexander and Adeline at the toy stand, I knew I had to hurry up. I ran up to Hope and looked in the saddle bags, there wasn't much besides a few small pouches of coins. I went around to the other bag and a smile spread across my face. There sat folded up was the black and gold dress, I pulled it out and walked back down to the stand. I saw a sage mushroom talking to the old male now.

"And how much would you want for that?" the sage mushroom asked, pointing at the waistcoat I reserved.

"Oh no sir, I have a lady holding that for her husband." the vendor spoke, shaking his head.

"Well I'm a male I have the right over her!" he said getting visibly angry.

I walked down next to the counter as well, not looking at the mushroom who was fuming. "Well right here's the nice lady who will be taking it off my hands" the old red said laughing. His laugh was loud and hearty, but in a good way.

"Oh come on, look lady I need that tonight and you're not gonna get in the way of that!" the sage mushroom spoke in a demanding tone. He pointed at me accusingly like I'd stolen something from him. I flashed a glare up at him, staying calm.

"I wouldn't speak to her that way sir, she is ranked higher than you," the old mushroom said smiling. The sage mushroom shut his mouth then before trudging off somewhere else.

"Thank you," I said quietly as I set the dress up on the counter.

"My my, what a neat dress!" the mushroom spoke, picking it up and examining it closely. "Mhm, oh very nice lace. Oh and the zipper is in excellent condition, ah even better! These necklines are very popular right now." he said smiling as he looked over.

"So do you want it?" I asked nervously, I needed it to be a yes.

"Hm...I think we have a deal!" he said, handing me the waistcoat over the counter.

"Oh thank you! Really this is just what I needed!" I said, folding the waist coat and holding it close to me.

"Of course madam, it's my pleasure." he said, hanging the dress up on a hanger and placing it up on one of the vendor walls.

I took a glance down at the counter and saw a few containers of what looked like paint. "What are these?" I asked curiously pointing at the bottles.

"Age defying spot cover ups! They're like magic I swear, how do you think I keep my mushroom looking young? Whenever your mushroom starts losing colour those are safe to use on your noggin." he said talking with his hands exasperatedly.

"So it's paint for your mushroom cap?" I said picking up a jar of the white one.

"Yes mam!" he said, nodding his head.

"Could I possibly take one of these too?" I asked, looking up at him.

"Hmm... sure you're a nice young lady, can I know your name before you leave?" he said, nodding his head.

"Oh thank you sir, and it's Mary," I said, holding the jar in my hand and the waistcoat in the other.

"Mary, that's a lovely name. Well have a good day and take care." he said smiling and stepping back from the counter.

"You as well!" I said, stepping away and going back up to Hope and putting the two items back in the saddle bags. I walked back down in the vendor area and seen Alexander and Adeline walking back to the horses. I walked back down to them and Adeline had a frown on her face and Alexander looked like he was about to burst out in laughter.

"What did you two do?" I said putting my hands on my hips.

"Allie-zander told them to not make my dollie clothes!" she said pointing at Alexander and running up to me.

I picked her up and held her on my hip. "Aw Alexander being mean?" I said, looking at Alexander teasingly.

"No! The stand didn't have doll clothes and she wanted me to order them to make her some" he said laughing as we walked back to the horses.

"Well did you find anything at least? " he asked, helping me up on my horse and then getting on his own with Adeline.

"I actually did," I said, leading the way back to the safe house.

"Oh what is it?" he asked, hurrying his horse up to catch up with me. "Well, are you gonna tell me what you got?" he asked anxiously.

"Yeah what'd you get momma? " Adeline added.

"You'll see later " I said, smirking.

"Fine," he said with a sigh.

After about a thirty minute ride back to the safe house, Adeline was already complaining that she was hungry again. "Oh come on babydoll are you really hungry again?" I asked getting off my horse. Alexander set Adeline down and then got down himself.

"It's okay Mags there, granola and some other stuff she can have so she won't starve." he said jokingly as Adeline ran inside the house.

"Yeah she's starving alright," I said, rolling my eyes.

"Well, are you gonna tell me now?" he said, coming up around behind me.

"Well ask politely," I said, smiling back up at him as he took the halter from me and tied the horses up.

"Well in that case can I pretty please see whatever it is?" he said leaning up against hope.

"Yes you may" I said, reaching in the saddle bag and pulling out the waistcoat.

"Oh Mags you didn't have to get that," he said looking at the vest.

"Oh but I wanted too Alexander, and I got this for tonight," I said, getting out the white mushroom paint.

"Mags this is so sweet of you, thank you" he said feeling the vest in his hands. The look on his face was priceless. "I haven't been given anything in years..." he murmured under his breath. I felt my chest do the warm thing and my stomach jumped.

"Well I wanted too Alexander, you're my best friend and it's the least I could do," I said, holding the jar of paint in my hands.

"This means more than you could imagine Magdolin" he said raising his eyes from the waistcoat to me, the smile that was present on his face was so genuine compared to any other time I'd seen it.

I felt his arms wrap around me and his hand held onto my shoulder, holding me close to him. The warm feeling in my chest flourished and spread out across my whole body. I hugged him back tightly, my arms embraced around his back. The light smell of his cologne filled my nose, it was a musky but sweet smelling scent and wasn't overpowering. His hair gently brushed across my face. It was soft and silky, I wanted to play with it and just feel it. I wanted to just be closer to him, not physically. But emotionally I wanted to be closer, I didn't want to stop being held by him. I felt safe here. It's going to really hurt once I'm alone with Adeline and he's gone. It was going to hurt worse after tonight surely.

I then felt a small tug on my dress, I looked down and a small dove was pulling on my dress. "A dove?" I said quietly. Alexander pulled away and looked down at the dove as well, he knelt down and gently rubbed its head. It was only a baby dove and its bright white feathers made it look so innocent and perfect. "There's the mother," I said, putting my hand on Alexander's shoulder. The mother dove was waddling nearby, her flock following behind her.

Alexander then ushered the little dove over to its mother and they went on their merry way into the woods. "Those were quite adorable weren't they" he said standing up.

"They were doves, a sign of love" I murmured to myself.

"What..." Alexander said, I felt my heart stop noticing I spoke out loud.

"Momma! I need help!" Adeline yelled as she stood on the front porch holding a bag.

"What is a baby doll?" I said walking to her with a sigh, grateful for her interruption. She held up the small bag full of nuts and raisins. I opened the bag for her and she smiled happily as she took it back and ran inside.

"What a stink" Alexander said, coming up behind me again.

"Isn't that right, what time is it?" I asked walking back up into the house.

"Quarter till two, no wonder stink was hungry" Alexander said laughing as we went inside.

"True!" I said shutting the door. It was getting closer to six and we needed to be out of here by five if we wanted to be there on time.

Adeline was sitting on the couch munching on the granola and nuts. "Hurry up Addie, we have to get you cleaned up" I said ruffling her hair.

"If I'm going to be playing the part of a florist mushroom, I think I have an idea Mags." Alexander said, walking back to the closet I was in this morning.

"Clothing wise?" I asked, sitting down on the couch with Adeline.

"How'd you know?" he said in a loud curious voice.

"I was poking around this morning, show me what you have in mind," I said snickering to myself.

After a minute or two Alexander came out into the living room area and he had on a full white outfit. The shirt fit him perfectly and had a frill in the collar, it had cuffs on the sleeves at the end to show his arm form in the closeness of the fabric. The white pants fit him perfectly as well falling to his ankles and not too baggy on his legs. Even his brown leather shoes matched as good as gold with the rest of the clothes. "You look amazing!" I said smiling as I stood and I grabbed the waistcoat and helped him put it on.

I buttoned it up from the bottom up and my hands met his as I reached the middle. I smiled and pulled my hands back and looked at him. "You truly do look dazzling, Alexander," I said smiling.

"Yeah you look awesome!" Adeline said, yelling out loud.

"Thank you girls," he said, smiling down at me.

"Do you want to see if this paint is gonna work?" I asked curiously, holding up the jar.

"Why not," he laughed, shrugging his shoulders. I sat down on the couch and Alexander sat on the ground in front of me. I used two of my fingers to dig out a lump of the white paint and spread it across the black on Alexander's cap. "That feels weird," Alexander said, leaning back against my legs.

"Oh you're fine you baby" I said with a smile spreading across my face. I worked around the green spots on his cap and covered all of the black with the white. The paint went on smooth and dried pretty fast. "Okay Alexander all done." I said, smiling as he stood up. He stood up and straightened out his clothes. I couldn't tear my eyes away from him, he was so handsome in that outfit. He looked sophisticated and well put together, he was truly eye candy. "Your eye catching Alexander," I admitted, picking up Adeline as she was done eating.

"Thank you Mags, you are quite the eye-catching lady yourself." he said with a smirk playing on his face. I felt the butterflies in my stomach as he said that. I hid it from my expression, only showing a smile as I set Adeline down on the counter top in the kitchen. I dipped a rag in the bucket of water Alexander had brought in earlier. "No reply okay" he said teasingly as he leaned against the countertop next to me and Adeline.

"Oh hush," I said, wiping Adeline's face off with the rag.

"Oh are you blushing?" he said, getting teasingly close to my face.

"Oh no I am not you old charmer." I said, shoving his face back as he snickered to himself. I finished washing off Adeline's arms and little legs and picked her up.

"Well I'm ready to go when you are *m'lady.*" Alexander spoke with a smirk and bowed as he stepped back and away. I set Adeline down on the ground, smiling at how playful Alexander was being.

Adeline ran off somewhere in the house and I looked in the mirror pulling out my lipstick and started getting ready myself.

Chapter 23. Alexander Malencoy

I had a big grin as I stepped outside onto the porch, I couldn't believe I was actually getting this opportunity. Adeline ran outside as well slamming the door behind her as she skipped onto the dirt path. "And where do you think you're going, Missy?" I said following her at a stroll.

"It's top secret!" she said, looking up at me. "Mhm, I don't think your momma would want you running off without her." I said putting my hands on my hips.

"Well that's why you're going with me," she said, pulling at my pant leg. I followed her as she went down the small dirt path behind the house.

She skipped along the path, her small boots clicking on the rocks that scattered over them dirt. "So adel where are we going?" I asked following at a slow stroll behind her.

"I dunno, I just like the tweets" she said looking up as we walked.

"Oh I see, I'm sure you'll like where you and your momma are going then," I said smiling. Magdolin and Adeline will be truly happy on the island.

After a few moments of walking farther down the wooded path I looked down at adeline. What if she didnt want me as her dad? Did she ever even consider asking me to be her dad, as she had asked Magdolin?

"Can I ask you a very important question? It's gotta stay top secret though, no telling your momma." I said stopping her in her tracks and kneeling down to her height.

"What is it Allie-zander?" she asked, turning and looking at me. She had her doll in her hand, it reminded me of how my sister used to carry it everywhere.

"Well Miss Adel... I was just wondering if you'd want me to be your... well your father" I said pausing to think if this was even a good idea to ask. She looked at me wide eyed for a moment before a high pitched squeal left her mouth. Her mouth formed into a frown and she started crying. "Oh no Adel no I'm sorry, it's okay if you don't want me too. I didn't mean to upset you!" I said, holding her shoulder as she cried. I wiped her tears with my other hand trying to calm her down.

"I don't want you to turn into papa, he was nice before. I don't want the same to happen to you Allie-zander" she said, gasping as she cried. It was sad how lapel had affected poor Adeline so much.

"...I won't be like your papa I promise, I'll stay this exact way I promise you. I'll be the best father I could be to you, I want to be that Adel." I said, wiping her tears as she calmed down. She choked on her air as she wiped her own tears off with the back of her hand.

"Why do you wanna be my dada?" she said, looking up at me with glassy eyes.

"Well besides you being the most amazing and pretty little snot for any girl your age, I happen to really like your momma. I love your mother more than anything, and I'm gonna ask her tonight if she feels the same." I said reaching in the pocket of my trousers and pulling out the small black box.

I handed the box to Adeline and she used both hands to carefully open the box. The stone on the ring shone all around on the leaves as the sun had caught it in its rays. "It's really pretty, I think momma will say yes." Adeline said smiling as she closed the box and the last of her tears dried up.

"And that's okay with you?" I asked, smiling as she handed the box back to me.

"Yeah! I want you as my dada!" she said with an excited smile as she snuffed her nose and dried her face off on her dress. I smiled as I slid the box back in my pocket and stood up. I picked her up happily and hugged her.

"Thank you Adel, and remember you can't tell your momma." I said as I set her down. She gave me two thumbs up and she started running off back to the house laughing.

I smiled, I smiled for real which didn't happen that often. If tonight went right I'd have everything I could ever ask for and when we get to the island it will be perfect. Just Magdolin, Adeline and me, alone as a family. I just have to do perfect tonight no matter what. But what if Magdolin's perception on mixing ranks is still the same. I'm at the very bottom of the rank scale and she's at the very top. And I'm sure she still has some feelings for that Raymond guy.

But wait, he's a sage mushroom. So she did have feelings for another rank beforehand. Maybe that's why she had felt so pushed away from the thought of trying it again. I have to see because if i never try i'll never know and I think there are feelings there, somewhere at least. I thought to myself as I strolled slowly besides Adeline ran.

I walked back down the path catching up to Adeline and as we stepped up on the porch again, Magdolin opened the door. The way she stepped out onto the porch was beautiful. Her dress swayed with her legs and the wind, her hair had a half pulled back style and parts of it framed her face wonderfully. The tint of the light pink lipstick on her lips made her look gorgeous, like I could just kiss her so easily. I want to kiss her badly, to just feel her lips on mine would be like passing to heaven. I knew I needed to marry this female, no matter what.

"You look gorgeous Mags" I said, star struck by how she looked. Even if it was the dress I'd seen her in for the past week it still was jaw dropping. It just fell above her foot and had a loose skirt, keeping her modest but it lined on her hips perfectly. It outlined her natural beauty and I was obsessed with her.

"Thank you Alexander," she said with that smile that I loved so much. Her smile could fill an entire room, and in my situation my whole world.

"Yeah! Pretty momma!" Adeline cheered, holding her arms up to Magdolin.

Magdolin picked up Adeline almost effortlessly, everything she did was admired without cause or reason.

"Well, are you ready to go madam?" I said bowing playfully before her and offering her my hand.

"Of course my good sir." she said, taking my hand as she stepped off the porch down the two steps leading off of it.

"Well then may it be my pleasure to escort you miss." I said smiling as I swept her off her feet. Adeline was still in her arms as I picked her up and set her up on Hope's back. She laughed as I'd caught her off guard and pulled her off the ground. Her laughter was like the sweetest symphony to me, I savored it every time I got to hear it.

I grabbed Adeline from her and I crawled onto Serenity with Adeline. I loved Magdolin but part of me didn't want her riding with Adeline just yet. Adeline did squirm around a lot when on the horses. "Well may our journey across the town begin madam" I said with a snotty attitude as I adjusted the ruffle collar on my shirt to act uptight. She laughed again and I smiled at her before taking the lead with serenity.

The slow trot of the horses in sync made a glorious beat with the birds and animals in the trees. "So Mr. Malencoy, what name are you planning on going by here?" Magdolin's voice cut through the animals symphony, but with the beautiful twinge of her voice I didn't mind. She was right, I wouldn't have to be Alexander tonight. I could be anyone, as long as I remained a good cover up as a gardener.

"Hm well to make it easy on you I'll be Alexander Potts. And I'm your escort to the ball because your late husband passed over a year ago. How does that sound?" I said looking over at her. The way her eyes looked at me was so pure, she had big beautiful doe eyes and the purple hue of her irises just drugged me in my hair.

"Oh you don't want to be my husband in our little cover stories anymore?" she said teasingly as she acted offended.

"Oh please, no, I just want you to have the best time you can. And even if I am acting as a gardening mushroom you still get a lot of trouble for posing as my wife." I said, coming back to her statement.

"Oh I see, well thank you for looking out for us both Alexander." she said smiling and looked back up at the dirt road.

Was she really upset she wasn't posing as my wife? No she wouldn't be, she isn't that petty, she's understanding. I'd love her anyway though, she was perfect to me at least.

For another forty five minutes, actually forty minutes and thirty two seconds, we rode on the horses at a steady pace. We arrived at the manor and many people were already feeding inside the main doors. Everyone was dressed in their nicest clothes and most of them outdressed us easily. "Well, we're here madam Mary," I said, hopping off Serenity with Adeline and tying the horses to one of the many designated places for horses.

Magdolin took my arm and I held my arm up properly for her to do so. I held Adeline's hand in my free hand and we walked up towards the entrance. The manor was huge and the sound of the orchestra inside was spewing out of every opening in the manor. There were many obviously rich folks around us as we got near the front entrance. I started to get nervous as we got in the line, only a few people away from checking into the room.

I felt myself starting to breathe harder, I wasn't good with speaking to people that I knew would turn me away normally. I felt Magdolin squeeze my arm gently and I looked down to see her giving me a calm smile back. Seeing her trying to be comforting towards me warmed my heart. I was Alexander Potts tonight so I guess there really wasn't much to worry about. I steadied my breath as we stepped up to the desk of the rooms to buy.

"Hiya! Welcome to the manor folks, now are you wanting two rooms? One for the girls, and one for you sir?" a male on the other side of the desk said with a cheeky smile.

"Oh no one room is fine." I said, forcing on my normal smile I'd give to anyone else. I saw the male's smile falter slightly at the thought of us three having one room. "Oh no you've got the wrong thought, i'm just escorting her here tonight. I'll be taking my leave as soon as she's done with me!" I said with a charming laugh which surely would get me a pass.

"Oh haha! I see, well I hope you have some fun while you're here sir." the male said, laughing with me. I set the money down for the room and he handed me the key to our room.

I turned smiling at Magdolin who was now holding a sleepy Adeline in her arms. "Well madam mary, we've made it through the guards," I whispered in a teasing tone. She snickered slightly at the comment, staying quiet to not wake up Adeline as she fell asleep in her arms. The carpet in the manor had intricate designs embroidered into the fine fibers of the fabric. The designs in the walls were perfect as well. The way the arches reached over and between the walls was something I'd never seen before. We reached the room and I opened it for Magdolin. The room was kept nicely and had expensive velvet and beautiful paintings hung all around the bedroom.

Magdolin set Adeline down on the bed and covered her with the silk sheet and velvet comforter. She pressed a kiss on Adeline's forehead before standing up. "I'll be right back babydoll" she murmured before walking over to me and taking my arm once more.

I liked how she held my arm with both of her hands, it made me feel special. I had that privilege to get that. I opened the door to the room and stepped out into the hall. As soon as I took a few steps down the hall I felt a firm grip on my shoulder. It was one of the workers at the manor, he had a frightened look on his face. "Can I help you sir?" I asked turning around, I felt Magdolin's hands hold onto me a little bit tighter as I turned to look at the male.

"Yes sir, I need you both to follow me. Someone would like to talk to you if you'd like to stay here." he said with an urgent tone to his voice.

Shit they surely have found out who I am, or worse Magdolin! I looked down at magdolin with a worried expression. She just gave me a calming smile and pulled on my arm as the male started walking. We followed behind him, leaving some distance between us and the mushroom. My mind raced with some of the worse outcomes this could be. *They're going to behead me. I just know it! And poor Magdolin will be put in that arranged marriage!* The male led us away from the ballroom and towards the east wing of the manor. My mind wouldn't stop running wild as I thought of the horrible things they would do to us. Magdolin seemed to not be as worried though.

The worker stopped at an older looking rotten door. It was a smaller door and had multiple locks up and down the sides of it and a few chains in front as well. It had an eerie feel to it and got cold as soon as we were within a few feet of it. The worker started to unlock the multiple locks with a large key ring with bunches of keys.

I looked down at Magdolin as she let go of my arm, she had a more scared look now that we were at a door. I decided to take her hand in mine, I held her hand lightly in my hand to try and keep her calm as she had done for me. She held my hand tight as the male cracked the door open, the door had to be at least three inches thick. The mushroom had to use all his strength to even open the door.

Inside the area where the door sealed away was a small circle shaped room. As we stepped inside we saw that it wasn't a room, it was a stairwell. The sketchy looking stairs scaled up the sides of the wall about one hundred and twenty five feet. I felt a chill go down my spine as the smell of mildew and sounds of something dripping from the stairs and hitting the stone ground. "Sir, can you please at least tell us where we're going?" Magdolin spoke out as the male started going up the stairs. He paused his steps turning around.

"I can assure you that this will be quick, hopefully." he said, turning around and walking up the stairs. I squeezed her hand lightly and mouthed "it'll be okay," I whispered. I knew I was horrified but I needed her to be calm.

We followed the male up the stairs, it took quite a few minutes to reach the top of the stairs and there again was a locked door. This one had very few locks though. The male knocked on the door and the sound of someone could be heard on the other side. No footsteps were audible though, it sent another chill down my spine. Something loomed in the air that almost felt draining, I could feel Magdolin chill as well. Something was definitely wrong. "Are these the ones you want? " the male said, knocking on the door again. He had a more stern look, almost angry. But the nervousness was still very present.

"Yes..." a voice said from the other side of the door. It had a low pitched voice and I couldn't exactly decipher if it was a male or female. The voice had an odd sound with its voice as well, Almost like it echoed and repeated itself and had a cover over it. Magdolin held my hand even tighter as the voice cut through the air. The male turned to us with a fierce mean look and he brushed past us to go back down the stairs.

I looked at him and tried to decipher if we should follow him or stay but I was interrupted. The sound of the locks getting unlocked erupted around the circular stairwell. I turned to look wide eyed, Magdolin still held my hand tight.

The door creaked open slowly revealing a dark room, unlike the other door you couldn't see in it at all. "Come in please'" the voice echoed inside the room. Magdolin let go of my hand before taking the first few steps into the room. I followed her inside, I knew I should have gone in first but it seemed Magdolin had more courage than me.

"Who are you?" I said in an assertive voice trying to sound strong.

"Well, I can be your best friend if you'd like Alexander" the voice said ending it with a child-like laugh, it sounded almost demented.

The door slammed shut and I could hear the locks being rolled back into place. The only light that shown in the room was the luminescence from my gills and eyes. "How do you know his name?" Magdolin said, flipping around and running into me. I grabbed her by her shoulders to steady her. I could feel her panicking and breathing fast, I held her close to me trying to keep her calm.

"Oh I know your name is Magdolin, or princess to be more accurate," the voice said. It sounded like whoever it was walking around us, circling us like prey. Was this a child? Who is this? I held Magdolin protective against my chest, whoever this was wasn't someone who needed their hands on her. Especially because they knew who she was. "Oh haha my apologies, I forget you poor creatures can't see in the lower end scale of light" the voice said snapping its fingers.

With the sound of its snap echoing through the large room, hundreds of candles lit around the room. Large tapestries hung around the huge room and things that hung from the ceiling surrounded the room. Lots of baskets full of bread and other baked goods, some were rotting. Bundles of glass jars and jugs of water sat around and rocks. It looked like a nick nack collectors dream room. Vines grew all around the sides of the walls with various flowers and fruits sprouting from them, some had thorns as well. As I looked around the room I was startled when I saw a female standing just a few feet away from us.

She was odd looking, wide eyed and her eyes had multiple pastel colours mixed within her irises. She had an eerie smile and her hair was messy. She had tight brown curly hair like how my own was naturally. Her mushroom was also something I'd never seen before in my whole entire life. It had water essence molecules floating around it like a mycolgian mushroom and four pyromanian mushrooms formed around her main cap which had two main colours. Black and white both flowed throughout her mushroom. Then the rags she wore as a dress of some sorts. She looked as if she hadn't seen the sun in years but she had a darker skin tone. She was very tall and had a proud looking stance. Magdolin audibly let out a small scream as she seen her standing in the corner ominously.

"Oh sorry, don't be scared. Don't tell me they didn't tell you about me?" she said laughing to herself. Magdolin gently pulled away from my hold as she looked curiously at the female.

"Who are you?" Magdolin said with an extremely shaken expression.

"Oh they didn't! How lovely, ahaha. Oh where are my manners! I look like a train wreck" she said, snapping her fingers again. This time a swirl of colours ran around her and her rags and matted hair was transformed into a long dress that dragged the floor and a vest style overcoat. Her hair was long and luscious black curls, truly showing how dirty it was prior.

Chapter 24. Amasa Tessa

"Oh stop gawking, I can do a lot more" I said smiling at the two as they looked utterly confused.

"What a train wreck!?" Magdolin said, confused. I also took note Alexander looked more frustrated than confused. "Oh I forgot you guys don't have trains yet, I'd much rather be stuck in the mycolgia kingdom." I said, prancing over to a tapestry on my wall. This specific tapestry was what I wanted to tell these two.

"You're the witch, the one in the folk tales aren't you?" Alexander said. I laughed and turned to face them again.

"Oh my my the things they say about me are crazy, I guess it's better than being killed like my ancestors. But no darlin' I'm not a witch" I said skipping over between them.

"Then who are you, and how do you know who we are!" Magdolin said, crossing her arms.

"Oh dearie I know much more than just that, and I was just about to tell you that. And just a bit of a spoiler, I am none-other than a princess myself!" I said, holding my hands up as I expected an applaud. "Oh no applause, well my plants can for me" I said, making some vines clap together for me. "Oh thank you thank you" I said bowing playfully. As I looked back up at those two they had their jaws dropped.

"You are a witch!" Alexander said, stepping back and throwing his arm out to 'protect' Magdolin.

"Oh hush no I'm not, you can do that too," I said pointing at him.

"No she's just a mad mushroom, what are you supposedly a princess of?" Magdolin said glaringly. I laughed at her to myself, before drifting over beside her. I rested my hands on her shoulders and I reached down and pulled out her dragger from her boot. "Hey!" she shouted as I held the dagger.

"Now I'm just showing you something, calm down." I said, forming molten rock over her feet so she couldn't jump at me. I smiled as Alexander ran to her side. She yelled as I formed the rock, mostly in shock. "Up here princess I'm gonna do a trick for ya." I said as I extended the dagger out into its full length. She looked at me shell shocked for a moment.

"How'd you do that, only purple can!" she said confused and almost scared.

"Well darlin' if we look at it on paper I'm your half sister, Amasa Tessa" I said smiling as I retracted the knife down and handed it to her as moved the stone, uncovering her feet.

"You're what! You have a sister!?" Alexander said, looking at Magdolin.

"I don't, what are you speaking about!?" Magdolin said, looking at me.

"Oh yeah we are! Same momma." I said laughing as they both looked distressed. It was funny seeing them so shaken.

"Oh take those dumb disguises off around me." I said using my vines to pull off Magdolins cap and I used a pod of water to wash off the paint off of Alexander's head.

"Hey!" They both yelled in unison.

"How… How are you, my sister" Magdolin said.

"And how am I supposedly able to do that!" Alexander said, pointing at the vine that held Magdolin's cap.

"Ah well yes, to answer both of those questions I may as well tell you the entire story. Would you like to hear?" I asked, smiling as I sat down on my chair.

"Sure…" Magdolin said cautiously. I noticed Alexander had a little bit of a disappointed face and I knew exactly why.

"Oh dear don't worry, it won't take long! I'll leave plenty of time for you to do your little thing." I said, smirking at Alexander as I used my vines to move over a small couch over behind them and knocked them down into the seat. I formed some rocks in front of them as well, making a small table between us, and then sprouted some tea leaves on a plant on the table. I grabbed some tea cups and brought over three pods of water and filled the cups. I dropped a few tea leaves in each cup before looking up at the two of them.

"Sorry I just don't get visitors much at all, the last I had was three years ago and it was just a kingdom guard with another threat. Oh and the daily manor worker but they just bug me." I said sitting up and taking a sip of my tea.

"Can you please just tell us the story you're wanting to tell?" Alexander said, crossing his arms and leaning back in the seat.

"Ah yes my bad, this story actually began with the poison mushrooms." I said pointing at one of the many tapestries on the wall. This particular one had a poison mushroom as a queen. "The poison mushroom was not always the poison mushroom. They were originally royals. They were the rulers on Equilibrium, at least back when it was equal," I said snickering.

"What? No. again as I said she's crazy," Magdolin said shaking her head. Alexander was looking more intently now as he looked at the tapestries.

"I know they didn't tell you this Magdolin, but I need you to trust me and shut up as I speak." I said, rolling my eyes as I looked up at the wall again. "The purples were nothing but mere soldiers for the upper class royals, like kings and dukes. The purples were excellent soldiers, they had natural talents and magic with their weapons. They also had dreams every new moon to help and predict the future attacks. Whenever they moved the ranks around to sages as army men they sucked." I said flashing a smirk at Magdolin. "But back to the story. The poison mushrooms held great power that's why they were the rulers. They had powers to control plants" I said, pulling up a flower plant in a pot next to me. "And you dear Alexander can as well, you are a direct ancestor of these exact mushrooms that ruled." I said, turning to look at them. Magdolin had an annoyed look, but Alexander looked highly intrigued.

"If this is true then why was I never taught it, I mean I am the princess." Magdolin said, giving me a glare.

"I'm getting there. One day the Pyromania kingdom sent a threat of waging war over Equilibrium and they had to fight. But the king was unable to assist in the battle. He had fallen ill of a sickness and his wife was burdened with taking care of her infant. The purples then took it into their own hands to lead the troops of mainly sages into war. But to no mushroom's surprise they lost without their king. The few purples that survived returned to the palace and seen their king was better and healed. The king set out to seek revenge for his lost people and won the battle single handedly! The poison mushrooms were very powerful back then clearly." I said turning to make sure they were still paying attention.

"But if that's all true, why don't I have these so-called plant powers?" Alexander said, raising an eyebrow.

"I'm getting there," I said calmly.

"And again none of this aligns with what I've been taught" Magdolin said with a snotty head turn.

"Please have patience, back to the story… again. Whenever the king returned he found the purples in his throne. He was heartbroken because his wife had fled the kingdom and left their baby at the hands of the purples. The king was in such despair he let his guard down and he was slaughtered by another purple from behind. Their baby was one of your ancestors, Alexander, but the story continues from the queen's perspective. She fled to the outskirts of the kingdom as the newly found royals sent out a warrant for any so-called poison mushroom to be killed. They made up false books and claims about their sick and cruel nature and it drove all the poison mushrooms away and to an island. This is the very island you take escapees to Alexander," I said pointing at a map.

"But how come everyone just forgot that the poison mushrooms were royals? And how come I wasn't slaughtered as a child whenever I lived in the kingdom?" he said, not fully believing me.

"Well this was hundreds of years before you were born so you merely get half of what the old time poison mushrooms got. And for now no one remembered it was because the new purple king and queen ordered for any town member to remember this in the future, and would be killed. So they all vowed to not lead this onto their children. All except the purples, each coronation of the king and queen in private the new king and queen are told the story I'm telling you now. But I know more than what they would know because of one reason. They don't know that the direct bloodline of poison mushrooms from the royalty still exists. And it exists in Alexander here, they would look at him and think he's just any old poison mushroom" I said sipping my tea.

"But how do you know that I'm not just some other poison mushroom, how do you know I'm of descent from them" he said looking back up at the tapestries.

"I'll get to that," I said, looking at Magdolin. She was looking at her hands as if she did something.

"Magdolin?" I asked, raising a brow smiling.

"My ancestors were monsters! How could they do such things? And I swear at this point everyday I learn something horrible we've done." she said as Alexander comforted her by resting a hand on her shoulder.

"Greed and revenge takes you far places dear" I said resituating myself in my seat.

"But back to the queen that fled, she escaped to the island and hid away there. Soon a kind sage mushroom made it to the island one day in a panic. In his arms was the baby of the king and queen. The sage mushroom had been ordered to kill the baby but didn't have the heart. So he brought the child to the island and left it to grow with a family of other poison mushrooms. They didn't return the baby to the queen because they believed she'd gone mad. Specifically because she had fallen in love again after her husband had passed. But the reason they called her mad was because she was in love with the prince of Mycolgia. He'd come to the island to visit her in secret, their relationship as a whole was sinful. I mean mixing colours was bad enough, but entire separate kingdoms would surely get you killed. But anyways they continued seeing each other and soon the queen fell pregnant with the prince's child. At first they were mortified and the prince came clean to his father and told him the truth on his mysterious trips above land. His father was understanding gratefully and allowed it. Once the baby was born the two got married and lived happily while they lived, the baby girl grew to be a powerful and beautiful young mushroom. Everyone in the Mycologia kingdom adored her mix of water and plant power. Some even called her the daughter of mother nature herself because of how she thrived from her powers." I said pointing at a different tapestry which depicted the image of my grandmother.

"Her name was Evelyn, she was my grandmother." I turned to look at the two Magdolin still looked upset at the thought of her ancestors doing such things.

"But what happened to the king and queen's baby, the poison mushroom?" he asked as he held Magdolin's hand.

"Well give me a break, my voice can't go on forever. And be a real male and hold a girl's hand how it should properly be held" I said smirking and making a vine intertwine their fingers together. I snickered as I watched Alexander's face gain a tint of red across his cheeks.

I took another sip of my tea before diving back into the story. "Well Alexander the infant poison mushroom grew up not even knowing that he was royalty and because of that he never found out of his powers. And there was never a word spoken about Evelyn on land, she was simply something that resided underwater in the Mycolgia kingdom. Until word got out to the Pyromania kingdom. And something about them, is they've always been the same. They're violent destroyers who choose to live engulfed in fire and flame. At the time my grandmother Evelyn was coming of age around nineteen the king of pyromania requested an arranged marriage between her and his son. Obviously the king of Mycologia denied the request because bringing a completely healthy and thriving kingdom and mixing it with a disastrous and crumbling kingdom would bring them both down. But little did they know that the prince of Pyromania that requested the marriage wasn't going to just give up. He was mesmerised by the stories of the girl that could create water and plants and her unending beauty. He needed her as his wife, so one day he broke into the Mycolgia kingdom and kidnaped the princess. The kingdom of Mycolgia was in panic as their daughter had been kidnapped. The prince kept the daughter of water and plants for himself locked away in the palace of Pyromania. He didn't tell anyone and kept her for himself against her own will. Hah I guess the apple doesn't fall far from the tree. I'm stuck in a palace of sorts too" I said snickering to myself.

"This is a manor." Magdolin corrected me.

"Oh hush, but anyways after years passed something happened. The prince of pyromania was found slaughtered and after about twenty years of her disappearance my grandmother was found dead as well. The question loomed over who had done it but then the truth came out once the monster himself came forward, my father." I said pointing at a tapestry which depicted a male mushroom. He had not only the power to create plants and water but the destruction abilities of fire and molten stone.

"Why would he kill his parents!?" Alexander said, sitting up in his seat.

"He was a monster! He wanted to be freed from the castle and he did so once he was old enough. He was on the run fighting and creating chaos in the Pyromania kingdom, until he discovered the other kingdoms. He escaped to Equilibrium, he hid out there for hundreds of years. With the mycolgian blood running throughout him he could live for far longer than any normal mushroom, as goes for me. But finally once he got ballsy enough to do so, he broke into the palace only to see a new type of mushroom ruling that he had not learned about, that meant he didn't have all of the powers. So one night when the king was gone for the day he got his way with the queen. Your mother!" I said pointing at Magdolin who looked mortified.

"W-well that's not true at all I don't remember that!" she said, getting visibly angry.

"Well it was before you, whenever your mother conceived the child, me. They immediately hid me away here, she didn't have the heart to kill her own child. I was taken care of by maids in the manor and when I turned about five I was locked in here. And for my father, he was found and killed for his crimes and disgusting acts. And a few years after our mother gave birth to me, the little bundle of joy princess Magdolin was born." I said looking down at my cup of tea that was half empty in my hands. I took a sip of my tea waiting for any questions. "No questions? Ok " I said standing up.

"No I have many, why aren't you the ruler of Equilibrium? Or any of the other kingdoms, why are you locked up?!" Magdolin said, standing up and following me around the room as I walked to a counter.

"Well they thought I was dangerous, which I could be. But I am not interested in ruling. I just want to be free, I have more powers than anyone ever. It's sad that the only thing I have to ask for is to be free." I said looking down at my hands.

"But if you're so powerful why haven't you just broken out of this manor," Alexander said standing a few feet back.

"Well I would and trust me I've tried, but they made a pact. Until the kingdom has returned to its glory, a kingdom that could sustain being in a world with me. So basically until the kingdom is back in the hands of the poison mushrooms, I'm trapped here." I said looking at them.

"That doesn't even make sense." Alexander said folding his arms together

"Magic ties it is a thing," Magdolin said, glancing at Alexander. "My parents would never give up their crown though, and they definitely won't listen to me after I've escaped," she added, hugging her arms tightly. That's normally a sign of guilt or anxiety. I smiled and let out a small laugh.

"Oh but dear there's many ways, I'll let you figure it out though. Even a poison mushroom just being fed into the current royal family would be enough for me to escape," said, shrugging my shoulders. They both watched me as I gathered a few things and I dropped it into a small cast iron bowl, I flicked a small flame into it and the items lit ablaze. The fire was multi coloured and an image appealed above it. "Oh look there's your mommy and daddy Maggie" I said looking at her as she got on her knees to see the picture more clearly.

"Where are they going, there in a castle carriage?" she said inspecting the image.

"I don't know, I can only see them," I said, shrugging my shoulders. I looked over at Alexander now that Magdolin was distracted. I pulled him away and towards another area of the room.

"Hey!" he said angrily.

"Don't hey me, I need a word. I know what you're planning tonight and I need it to happen ok. Even you just landing a kiss is what I need. Now I know she's your Juliet, your amore, your soulmate, your mi vida. I need you to make that happen tonight though ok!?" I said in a whispering rushed tone so Magdolin couldn't hear.

"I can't promise anything, and I only understood one of those things you just said, " he said nonchalantly.

"Oh how lovely. Oh! I almost forgot." I said pulling over a small pot in between us.

"What is that for?" he said, raising an eyebrow.

"C'mon, make a plant," I said excitedly.

He just looked at me blankly. "I cant" he said blandly as he stood like an idiot. How could he just be so negative about this, he's literally a king in disguise.

"Ok let me help, so you've never had anything odd happen with plants around you at all?" I said looking at him.

"No, I'm starting to see the crazy in you though," he said as Magdolin came up behind him.

"You have thought, do you not remember after hope and Raymond came over? That night the small vines came from nowhere" she said, looking up at him. I smiled in glee, this was something.

"So what were you feeling at that moment Alexander? What made you do that!" I asked slightly, jumping in my spot excitedly.

"I wasn't feeling anything!" he said, crossing his arms.

"Yes you were, you were upset" Magdolin said, cutting him off.

"Aha! Perfect. Of course emotions are the key for you my friend" I said happily as I just found the key.

"I'm not your friend," Alexander added on. To try and trigger his feelings I went up behind him and pinched his back. "Stop that!" he said, flipping around annoyed.

"No, I need you to just try and focus your emotions and feelings down to your fingertips okay? Magdolin it's just like how we channel our blood to our dagger. So try and help him " I said, folding my hands together. Magdolin gave a small nod before guiding his hand out towards the flower pot.

I smirked and started circling them doing small things to irritate Alexander like pulling his hair or just poking at him. None of it seemed to work and I felt myself getting agitated. "Feeling any major surge of emotions, like anger?" I said, grabbing one of my large books off the shelf. "No," he replied as Magdolin walked over to me.

"Is this where you've learned everything about the past?" she asked, looking at the towering bookcase filled with ancient books.

"Yes indeed little sis" I said tapping her nose and walking back over to where Alexander stood. I definitely didn't think of Magdolin as my sister even though she had the same mother as me. She had taken everything from me in a way, I should've been a princess even though I wouldn't want to be. I just wished I had loving parents like she did, and I don't understand why she ran away. I turned back to focus on the mission though. I took note of the ring box in his pocket and decided to use it as leverage. "So make sure you're focusing on those vines dude" I said snickering as I went up behind him and I grabbed at the ring box.

Instantly his face flinched and he grabbed my wrist with his left hand, glaring at me. I smiled and laughed as a vine shot up from the pot, it grew over the size of me and reached the rafters of my room. "Aha! Wonderful. Such a fine specimen of vine. I've never seen one so healthy!" I said running to the plant that had struck out of the pot, it was truly amazing.

"I just did that.." Alexander said breath taken as he looked at his hand.

"Ah! Even look at the thorns! It truly is based around your emotions!" I said laughing hysterically. I could rip my eyes away from how powerful this plant was. I assume it was because all of the years of his magic being pent up and not being used. He truly radiates potential, I'm sure he could just break the pact and free me but I can't play that card. I have to play this smart and patiently, like any logical person would do.

"You... you have magic" Magdolin said walking over beside Alexander.

"I- ...magic hand, what!?" Alexander said as he started to breathe fast and out of breath.

"Oh now darlin' stop freaking out! It's completely normal, natural even, you're born with it!" I said smiling. I saw my words were not doing much and he was still panicked as much as she was confused. I decided from here on it was out of my hands and I had to let nature take its course.

"Well there's not much else I can do for you two, I'll be happy to show you your leave!" I said smiling as I clasped my hands together.

"What! No, I have so many questions, "Alexander blurted out.

"Tsk tsk tsk nope, you will learn eventually I promise you. But now you two need to have fun. That's what they say, right?" I said pushing them both towards the door. But before I could even open the door I stepped back and realised they didn't have their caps or anything, and what is Magdolin wearing?! Simply not good enough for these balls.

"Oh I can't send you both out like this," I said, snapping my fingers. A bright light flashed around Magdolin putting a colour cap on her mushroom to make it pink again. As for her dress it transformed into a floor length gown with silk fabric and lots of lace forming around the bodice. Her hair was then formed into tight curls framing her face and fastening part of it back with a hair clip. "Oh how gorgeous," 'I said, smiling at her, now I looked at Alexander. "Now for you, I think we can do a bit better " I said, snapping my fingers once more.

His dull white undershirt was ultimately updated to a more vibrant, new looking shirt. It had a ruffled neck with a light green tie around the neck as well. His vest stayed the same because I knew Magdolin single handedly picked it out. The pants were cinched up to fit him better too. I changed his low ankle leather shoes to a grand pair of knee high brown leather boots. His mushroom was also topped off with the white paint he wore prior. "Ah there you go now, you both look like you fit in here now." I said, folding my hands together as I unlocked the door with some vines for them.

They both just looked at me blankly for a moment before I jutted in again. "Oh please now go out there, and do what you came here to do. Forget I even exist please. Ahaha," I said, pushing them out and slamming the door.

As soon as the door shut I locked it and rushed over to the small fire I had burning earlier and put it out. I knew if this didn't play out right tonight I'd never be freed.

Chapter 25. Magdolin poni

As soon as we were back in the stairwell I looked up at Alexander, still in shock over what had just happened. Why would she do that, just pull us out of nowhere and drop a bombshell on us. "Alexander, are you alright?" I said, taking his hand in my own. I liked how my hand felt in his, it felt natural. His hands were rough but had a softness to them that I adored.

"Yes I'm alright Mags, I'm just a bit shell shocked" he said shaking his head before seeing a small smile form on his face. When he looked over at me his smile lit up the whole stairwell. "Let's go to the ball, we might as well not waste any more time." he said, shrugging his shoulders and leading the way down the stairs.

As we reached the bottom of the stairs the worker that had led us here was standing there. "Are you folks alright?" he asked almost automatically.

"Yes thank you sir" Alexander said reassuring him as we left the stairwell. As we stepped back into the nice carpeted floors of the manor I felt a sense of relief wash over me. I took Alexander's arm as the worker stayed back locking the door back with the tons of locks on it.

I've learned from tonight so far that my family are traitors to their kingdom and that Alexander should be king. Also mixing colours has never been against the law, it's to prevent others from gaining power like how they hid away Amasa. I also learned how toned Alexander was. I knew he was very strong but he looked sort of skinny to me. But now that I was actually holding onto his arm and being so close to him I can feel he's got muscle, but he's just got a thick layer of skin. I guess you could say he really does have thick skin. I love the way it feels to hold his arms though, I think I just like being close to him.

I allowed my head to fall onto his shoulder as we walked down the corridors. I didn't notice any change in his stature as I did so, so I stayed like that. I found myself smiling over it, this was something I hadn't felt in a long time. Do I love Alexander? I think I do, but I doubt he feels the same for me. I'm sure now that he's learned that he's supposed to be king he'll just drop me at the island and go take back the throne that is rightfully his. And I won't blame him for it at all. Who knows I might return if I hear word he's king.

I'm sure though that I do love Alexander, I truly am in love with this male. Even if it's impossible for him to be my soulmate, I'll love him for what he's done for me.

As we entered the ballroom of the manor the sound of the symphony on stage playing was magnificent. The ladies' huge hooped dresses prance in the dance floor with their escorts or husbands. The smell of freshly baked goods loomed in the air as well, this was much different than the balls back at the palace. They were much more mellow and calm than the upbeat music that was being played here. I felt a smile spread across my face as I took in the atmosphere.

Alexander led me into the ballroom and down towards the main hoard of people. "I've never been to something like this, " he whispered as we walked back towards one of the corners of the huge grand ballroom.

"And for someone's first time, you look like you fit in," I said, smiling at him. He did fit in perfectly, everyone must have thought he was a successful florist. I wasn't sure how to think of how myself looked and was curious to what others thought. A housewife? Maybe a model? I'm not sure.

A few finely dressed mushrooms walked over to us. There was a pink mushroom couple, a navy mushroom and a red. "Hello there!" the red mushroom said with a big smile. Her dress puffed out in many different tiers, and her makeup was done professionally. The navy mushroom had his hand tightly around her waist.

"Hello! And who am I having the pleasure of meeting?" I said, giving a curtsy and bowing my head.

"Oh the people at this ball always have the best manners, I'm Esmeralda Patay." she said curtsying as well.

"It's a pleasure to meet you, and your escort I'm presuming?" I said looking up at the navy mushroom. His hand was now resting on the small of her back.

"Oh yes, this is my servant. He's just here as my escort. I'm assuming this is your florist? Do you pose as a muse for artists?" she asked, looking me up and down.

"Yes actually! You got it right on the dot" I said, smiling and nodding my head. Little did she know she just gave me the best cover up story.

I turned to look at the other pink mushrooms that stood with us as well. "What line of pink mushrooms do you fall from dear" the female said with a stern face.

"Im Mary, daughter of James Porter. I blurted out trying to make it sound natural. She raised an eyebrow as she looked at me and Alexander both.

"Hm, I've never heard of you. So you're a model for artists?" she said, opening her fan and fanning herself.

"Yes and this is my personal florist" I said, presenting my hand open to Alexander.

"Humph, well i'd be hoping you aren't doing sinful things based on the way you both pranced in here." the husband spoke out in a snobby tone. I felt my heart cinch a little bit, maybe this was a bad idea. In my peripheral vision I could see Esmeralda roll her eyes.

"Well I can assure you sir we wouldn't participate in such things. See my friend Mary here is widowed and simply needed an escort, so I kindly offered." Alexander said with a charming smile. The male didn't seem so impressed and he and his wife walked off.

"Old geezers can't let lose I guess," Esmerelda said with a laugh as she waved her hand in her face.

"Hah well we should let you folks have some fun yourself, tata friends!" she said, waving as they walked away.

I looked up at Alexander who let out a sigh as he looked at me. Out of the corner of my eye I saw something that seemed out of place. There was a sage mushroom standing alone to the side and she was in a dress of her own. Her dress wasn't elegant, it was more of a dull tone and more peasant looking. I took note that all of the other sage mushrooms were men and they were guards around the edge of the ballroom. The female gave me a sense of familiarity that I couldn't quite put my finger on.

"Alexander, does the mushroom look familiar to you?" I said pointing nonchalantly at the sage mushroom. He turned to look at her himself, after a few moments he looked over at me with a nervous face.

"That's Amarilla, the one who almost caught us, remember?" he said nervously as he turned his back to her.

"Oh Amarilla! She was so sweet!" I said excitedly. She wasn't the nicest because she gave a tip of where we were but she didn't turn us in. and I knew there is something in her that's good.

"Sweet!? Mags- I mean Mary, are you crazy? We need to avoid her at all costs ok?" he said trying to get me to walk with him towards another area of the ballroom.

"No Alexander, she looks lonely, we should go talk to her." I said standing my ground as Alexander tried to pull me off.

"Mary, I can't let you do that, you don't know if she'll turn you in!" he said sternly and in a pleading tone.

"Well alexander you've done your job and you've got me away from home, and I've had the most amazing time. So if I did get caught I don't think I'd mind, and it wouldn't be your fault. Your job was never to protect me." I said with a soft smile trying to reassure him.

"I know it's just, I want to protect you, I don't want to see you get taken away," he said in a soft tone as he took my hand into his own. I felt my chest get tight as he did so, I liked the feeling of him wanting to protect me. I'm also very proud of how he's taken finding out about his history and being able to act completely normal still.

I squeezed his hand gently. "Look Alexander, I understand you don't want me to go but I am, so if you want to come with me you can. Okay?" I said, shaking my head. He sighed and rolled his eyes.

"You lead the way," he mumbled, I smiled and took his arm as we walked over to Amarilla. I made sure not to just flat out and blatantly show myself to her because we were in disguises. I went up behind her and gently tapped her shoulder. She flipped her head over her shoulder and gave me a nasty glare.

"Can I help you miss?" she said, turning around fully to face us. Her arms were crossed tightly over her chest.

"Hi Amarilla," I said excitedly.

"How do you know my name?" she said raising an eyebrow and looking closer at us

After a few moments of looking at us her eyes went wide and her arms loosened slightly in shock I think. "Why are you here?!" she hissed as she recognized us.

"Just having fun I suppose," I said with a nervous smile at her reaction.

"It was dumb of you to bring her here," she said looking over at Alexander.

"I was just trying to be nice, something you clearly don't know much about," he said, putting his hands on his hips.

"Oh I do actually, I'm here for charity right now." she said, flipping her hair away as she turned her head cockily.

"That's the dumbest thing I've heard, you're standing here doing nothing," he huffed with an attitude.

"Shut up ok, it's hard to try and make it by as a sage mushroom, no one wants a female knight." she hissed glaring at Alexander. I could basically feel the pressure around us, the tension was high and thin.

"Well, anyways what are you doing here Amarilla?" I asked curiously with a soft smile. She rolled her eyes as she crossed her arms back.

"Well if you must know, August over there was actually able to guard here tonight." she said pointing over at a guard in full armour. From looking at him I could recognize him. The guards stood around the whole ballroom in pairs of two. Augustus was slumped over slightly and tired looking compared to the guard next to him.

"So these aren't actually knights for the manor? Are they just freelance guards?" I asked her curiously.

"Exactly, and the only thing they could find for me ironically was an 'in disguise guard'. And now I'm here, even though I'm not really in disguise, or fit in" she said with a sigh. "I wish I could just be a real guard," she murmured to herself.

"Well I believe you'd make a great guard, just wait I promise things will turn around eventually, it always does," I said with a calm smile. Amarilla flashed me a small smile before quickly shaking it away.

She cleared her throat before saying "well miss, I believe you should go and enjoy yourself before someone gets suspicious,'" she said, turning her head and facing another direction. I smiled before turning back to a bored looking Alexander.

"Come on." I said as I took his arm and walked about the ballroom.

"So where are we going?" he asked as we walked about the ballroom.

"Hm anywhere I guess, I've never been to a ball like this," I said, shrugging my shoulders.

"Well I think I'd be honoured if you'd give me the honour of a dance," he said in a playfully royal voice.

"And I'd be delighted to have a dance with you" I said, taking his hand as he held it out to me. We started to walk out towards the dance floor. We got to the very edge where people were dancing and I started to put my arm around Alexander's neck and intertwine my fingers with his when we were interrupted.

The music came to a halt for a few minutes, we separated looking at each other to see if the other knew what was happening. After a few moments of silence some of the people around us whispered.

Esmerelda and Malakai spotted us and walked over to us. "Do you know what's going on?" Malakai said, holding onto Esmeralda. I was definitely getting the feeling that they weren't just a boss and servant.

"We don't have any idea either" Alexander said with a frown. I could tell Esmerelda was getting nervous, I was too as well. I looked over at the symphonic band and they were just sitting there, something was off.

"Maybe the band is just taking a break from playing" I said, resting my hand on Esmerelda's shoulder.

As soon as I finished my sentence a male walked out in front of the band. His voice was loud as it rang through the silent ballroom, it made me jump slightly and Alexander's arm snaked around my shoulder. I leaned into his embrace as he did so, it was comforting. This feeling felt like a warm blanket wrapping over my body. "Ladies and gentlemen! I am Barron Marquee, the owner of this manor." he said with a loud grand voice that echoed throughout the room. I couldn't believe this was the mushroom that enslaved Amasa. I'm sure he was paid off but still he was a sick male. "And may I just say it is an honour to have you all here tonight but it is a bigger honour for me to announce that we have very special guests here tonight!" he said again holding his hands out, as if trying to project his voice more. Gasps and light chatter was heard among the people until he spoke again. "Now I know everyone here is important in some way but let me introduce you... to the great..." he paused as trumpets blared out in an intervieled tune. My face fell pale as I recognized the tune. "..our mighty and grand majesties, king and queen Poni!" he said, talking over the trumpets as my parents came out from a pair of closed doors.

I felt as if I might faint at that moment. They had never came to anything like this before. "It is an honour to have them here tonight folks! This is the first time any royal has attended a public event in over a hundred years!" the male's voice said again loudly as my parents took their seats in two thrones set up in a balcony about fifty feet up from the ballroom floor.

The trumpets' tune came to an end as they set down in the thrones set for them. I looked up at Alexander with my face pale and frozen. He himself looked extremely jumpy and nervous as he looked up at the king and queen in the balcony area. His nervousness quickly faded to a stern and angry look.

I knew what he had against my parents but I couldn't let him get overworked. I quickly found his hand and intertwined my fingers with his and squeezed his hand quite tight. His hand held my own with a tight hold as well. I looked down at myself and started panicking, if they recognized me not only would I be taken back but they would look at me like I was a monster. I was lying about my identity and I was wearing a gown they would have never approved of. A thin sheet of sweat covered my face and neck in a cold sweat.

Esmerelda tapped my shoulder with her fan and handed it to me. "It can be nerve racking seeing the king and queen for the first time" she whispered in my ear.

"Yeah you can say that" I whispered back nervously. I quickly fanned myself trying to remain calm but I couldn't help but pick up a nervous pant. Was my corset too tight? Was it because I was holding Alexander's hand? My parents being here? It was all, but mainly my parents. I felt like the entire world was on my shoulders and any wrong move right now would make me drop it. The male kept speaking but I didn't hear a word of it, it just became a blur in the jumbled mess in my head at the moment.

Just as soon as he spoke he stopped. As I started to hear things around me I could hear the music and sounds of people's laughter. "Mary? ...is she okay dear? Mary?" I heard a few voices as I blinked a few times and closed the fan back instinctively. I looked and saw Alexander looking down at me, his pupils were dilated and he looked very scared. Esmerelda was looking at me as well with a worried look, Malakay was right behind her as well. I felt two hands on my back and realised Alexander and Malakai were holding me up from falling.

"Oh my goodness i'm so sorry, pardon me I felt light headed for some reason," I said handing Esmerelda her fan back.

"Well are you okay now dearie? If your corset is too tight I can go and help you fix it" she said with a smile on her face but a caring tone.

"No I can assure you I'm fine, thank you for the offer, we will probably see our way out about right now right Alexander?" I said, waving my hand trying to maintain a smile and turning to look at Alexander.

All he did was nod his head with a small frown on his face. "Oh you can't leave yet dear! You two haven't even danced!" she said, grabbing my wrists and pulling me out on the dance floor.

"No Esmerelda I really shouldn't, I should be getting going, I have a daughter." I said trying to find an excuse as she shoved me out on the dance floor with her. She gave me a few spins before I met up with Alexander by bumping into him.

I turned to see Malakai taking Esmerelda into his hold and they smirked at us both. I looked up at Alexander and he had a very nervous look. I just let my instincts take over and I took his hand and wrapped my other arm around his neck. We had no other choice as the people swirled around us, I knew the dance but it was clear Alexander didn't. "Just flow along with me it'll be ok I promise, just try and keep a low profile." I whispered, putting his hand on my waist as I started moving to the steps of the dance.

Alexander nodded and started to do his best to move along with me and watch the other people. "I'm so sorry, I would've never brought you here if I knew they were gonna be here." he whispered as we came to a part in the dance where he came down low and near my face.

"No Alexander it's alright, as soon as this is over we will leave, I'm not risking you getting hurt in any way," I whispered to him as he spun me. My dress flowed out as he spun me around, it felt magical being there but I couldn't let it sink in with the underwhelming pressure of my parents watching.

"I don't care about me, I care about you right now. I can't let them take you back, I had so much planned for tonight. I'm sorry I can't give you it now," he whispered with a frown as he lifted me in the air and spun around, matching the pace of the other men.

"I had something I wanted to tell you as well, but I agree now is not the time." I said with a sigh.

"Just tell me please, I can assure you I can't run away because I'd have to stop dancing," he said with a small laugh at the end of his sentence. A swoop of violin and cellos crashing rang through the symphony, I spun Alexander around to the beat, as did the other dancers.

"I don't want to scare you off, Alexander, you're my best friend," I whispered pausing to make sure I wanted to say this. As the music paced up as it was getting close to the end of its music we continued through the dance moves and steps.

"You can tell me Mags, you may as well," he whispered.

I looked up at him as the song started to slow for the last time. His eyes gleamed, that beautiful colour of green basically shined. I felt my hold on him grow tighter as I opened my mouth. I tried searching for some unique way to say it but it just blurted out before I could even think. "...I love you Alexander." I said aloud as the music came to an end.

Everyone around us froze in place, not to me confessing but to the end of the song, as you should do at the end of a dance. Alexander looked down at me shocked and wide eyed. I just stayed quiet and looked down knowing I shouldn't have said anything.

I felt his hand rest against my chin and guided me to look up at his smiling face. I felt my face flush a shade of red as I saw his own face plastered with a hint of blush. "...I love you too Mags.." he whispered as everyone started to walk to the side of the dance floor.

I felt my heart light ablaze and something inside of me jumping making me let out a small laugh and I grabbed Alexander's face eagerly and pulled him down to me. His lips were warm and soft on my own, it felt like the world had just shifted as his arms wrapped around me pulling me into his embrace. His lips were sweet like sugar, he kissed softly and carefully. His hands wrapped around me and stayed on the top and small of my back. My hands resided on the sides of his face, as the kiss went on. A feeling fled around us and inside of me, a feeling that this was right and what I should have done. I knew I had done the right thing. A powerful force of wind blew around us forcing people back into one another physically.

I pulled away to look around us. Specks of colour, purple and green, floated around us like an ominous mist, swirling in delicate yet beautiful swirls and designs around us both. I didn't care who was looking right now, the only thing that mattered right now was Alexander. As I looked up at him meeting his eyes I noticed his normal green eyes had a swirl of purple within them, but before I could talk he spoke. "Oh Mags, why's there green in your eyes?" he said, cupping my face.

"There soulmates!" Esmerelda yelled out excitedly.

"This proves colours can mix!" Malakai added on pointing at the king.

As I looked at Alexander I felt my heart sink as I noticed the white was gone of his mushroom. I saw by his facial changes that mine was gone as well, I felt my mushroom and sure enough my colour cap was gone, nowhere in sight to be seen. It went silent for a few moments as I just looked up at Alexander, he was smiling, and I felt one grow on me as well. For some reason I didn't care about being caught, I was content. I knew Alexander was the one I was meant to be with, and I knew nothing could change that.

"Magdolin Vivienne Poni..." I heard my father's voice ring out in anger throughout the ballroom. Alexander looked up at my father in anger.

"It's not polite to use a ladies full name without permission," Alexander yelled back. My father's face showed pure anger, but I didn't care. I wasn't scared for the first time in forever, I felt like my parents words or cares didn't matter. My mother however sat still with a stone cold face, stern.

"And just who do you think you are young one" my father hissed back as he used his magic to form into his suit of armour as he stood on the ledge of the balcony. I hadn't learned how to do that just yet, it was complicated and required a lot of focus.

"Oh well wouldn't you like to know" Alexander growled back. This infuriated my father, he took the jump off of the balcony hitting the ground sending a shockwave through the ground of the manor as his boots made contact with the marble floors. Some of the ladies in huge dresses toppled over like dominoes.

"You are going to eat every word that just left your mouth boy." My dad screamed in anger. I drew my dagger out and forced it out into its sword length, but Alexander pushed me behind him.

"Alexander let me help!" I said pulling at his arm.

"...no Magdolin," he said coldly. My father was basically frothing at the mouth with anger.

"Go now Mags!" he said loudly as he shot a few vines up from the ground beside him.

"This is my fight as much as it is yours!" I yelled, stepping in front of him and pointing my swords directly at my father. My father lunged at us planning to attack but Alexander was able to deflect his attempt with a vine.

As the fight wrung out I went in to hit my father but he deflected my sword with his own. "Magdolin what has possessed you my child?!" he hissed as his sword clashed against my own. My father was much stronger than me and I definitely wasn't fighting at my best with this huge dress on.

Chapter 26. Amasa Tessa

I sat quietly in my own thoughts, my fears having come true as I heard the royal trumpets being rang. I watched from another vision fire I made. It was all falling apart, Alexander hadn't proposed and that's what I needed. I couldn't interact or do anything to warn them of what to come.and i sure as hell didn't want to make another worker go grab them again. I watched my mother through the fire mainly, her face staying cold and angry looking. Oh how I wish I could just destroy her, she's the reason I feel this pain and longing in my heart. I turned my attention back to Alexander and Magdolin in my fire and was shocked to see they had figured it out, they were soulmates.

I felt a rushing sensation in my body and the walls in my tower shook. I felt a surge of power in my body, it hurt so bad but felt so good.

I laughed as I bursted the door to my room open, sending the giant door falling down the stairwell. "Aha! Freedom! It feels so good!" I yelled as I could finally leave my room. I broke the next door with rock bursting through the locks.

I ran as fast as I could down the hall long, intricate halls. My magic writhed through my body like an immense fire.

I threw vines and stones up on the walls of the manor. If I was going to be scarred for the rest of my life by this place, I was leaving my mark as well.

I forced rock against a pair of large double doors as I entered the ballroom with a bang. I sent vines climbing up the walls and rock over parts of the floor, I couldn't control my magic. I felt the powers in me had grown magnificently, and this was only half of the power. Whenever the poison mushroom was back in the throne I'd be completely free of my restraints.

The king looked at me with horror in his eyes. He had Alexander in his hands, Alexander had a bloody nose as well as a black eye, he looked at me with a smile as I entered. The queen watched from the balcony wide eyed as I broke into the ballroom. The crowd looked shocked and all intrigued. "Hey step daddy, hi mommy, long time no see. Oh you should put my soon to be brother in law down." I said with a smirk and cackling.

I sent pods of water flying at the king lifting him off the ground and encasing him in stone up to his shoulders. "That's enough with you for now" I said, giving Alexander a hand up. "And you shouldn't be using your powers like that, you don't even know how to control them!" I said looking around as he stood up.

"Where's Magdolin!?" I asked urgently.

"She went to go get Adeline." he said, steading himself.

"Come on we can't leave her alone" I hissed at his stupidity for letting her go on her own. How could he let her just run off alone in this situation?

I looked up at the balcony and just as I expected the queen was gone. I ran down the hallway, Alexander was a few feet ahead of me. I'd never run like this, I was never able to, having been locked up in a room. As we rounded the last corner Alexander faltered before running again.

Magdolin was just standing frozen staring at something that she blocked from my view. As I got closer I was able to see. There stood the queen cradling a sleeping Adeline. "So you can't even talk to your mother without bringing along this abomination and this idiotic lover of yours. You'd never even look in the way of the suitors we offered you, and you chose this male. He's nothing but trouble Magdolin, he is the mushroom of destruction, it's only because you're royal, your lips didn't melt off when you kissed him." the queen spoke directly to Magdolin, acting as if we didn't exist besides her. Her cruel words made me want to jump at her, but she was holding the child so I couldn't. Any child has a right to live and I don't know if this crazy old lady has made a threat.

"Mother, just hand me Adeline and we will go our separate ways. You'll never see any of us again. I can promise you that." Magdolin spoke, holding her hands out for Adeline.

"Is that what you call this flea-brained child, Adeline? What kind of name is that? And your coming home Magdolin, this kingdom needs a queen. And this child needs to just be thrown in an orphanage, I'm disgusted to even hold it," the queen said, turning away from Magdolin's open arms and holding Adeline away from her.

Magdolin stayed still for a moment and silent, I couldn't even hear her breathing. "...I'll return to the palace on one condition," she mumbled barely audibly.

The queen snarled her nose up before speaking "I will be open to your requests." she said in an uptight voice.

"Alexander and Amasa will be free to do whatever they please as long as it doesn't involve me, you, or father. Adeline will be put in the best place she could possibly be put in. and I will not be forced into a marriage." she said in a low voice as she looked up at her mother.

mother snarled up her nose at the idea. I looked over at Alexander who was looking at Magdolin with pleading eyes, it was clear he didn't want that at all.

"Magdolin you c-!" he said but was cut off by the queen once more.

"Fine, this arrangement will be fine," she said with a scoff. Magdolin's shoulders slightly relaxed as her mother held Adeline out to Magdolin.

Magdolin held Adeline close to her and as she turned around to face me and Alexander she was sobbing, tears stained her cheeks as she kissed Adeline's head. "Mags.." Alexander said embracing her, he was crying himself as he held onto Magdolin. She pulled away though and gave Adeline to him. She gave him a quick kiss on the cheek before she gave me a small nod and turned to mother again.

Her mother held her arms out to Magdolin and she slowly approached her and fell into her embrace. It was pitiful to see a female so broken down she collapses in her pain inflectors arms.

They stood there for a few moments before mother looked up at Alexander and I. "It's so sad that that can't be the arrangement though, we had something else in mind." mother spoke with a twisted smile on her face. I watched her fist swing up and hit magdolin on the top of her mushroom.

She went limp and her mother held her up. Mushrooms had sensitive areas on their cap and even the strongest of mushrooms wouldn't be able to not pass out if hit there.

I flipped around noticing she said we. There stood the king and he hit Alexander and I on our mushrooms. Everything went black.

Chapter 27. Adeline Sanchez

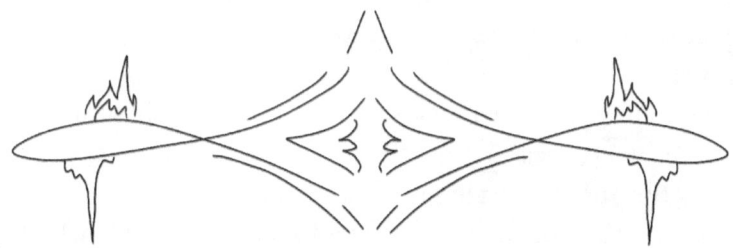

I woke up with the weight of a cow on me. I squirmed and cried waterfalls as I saw momma on the ground and she looked dead. Alexander was dead too, and this weird looking lady was laying across the hall dead too. I cried louder and tried to escape from Alexander's grip around me. "Why is there a child Delilah?" I heard an old mushroom say. I felt his big hands pull me out of Alexander's hold and I kicked trying to get down.

"Well Magdolin said it was her daughter." the old lady said. The old lady and male didn't have mushrooms, they had big spiky metal things on their heads. They were weird looking nonetheless.

"What did you do to my momma!" I said fighting against the old mushroom's hands, I needed to escape and help momma.

"Oh calm down, Magdolin's fine and she's not your momma. Let me make that clear young lady" the Delilah lady said with an attitude.

"I don't think your papa would like that attitude," I said, still kicking my feet.

"Good thing he's dead you brat! She's a feral hector, look at her!" the lady said, walking over to us and just let momma hit the ground.

"Oh Delilah, she's just a child, how old are you?" the old male said, holding me on his hip.

"I'm not telling you anything," I said, pushing against him.

"Her name's Adeline, that's all I know. She's getting dropped off at an orphanage on the way back to the palace." the lady said.

A few big scary looking guards walked in and grabbed momma first carrying her like a sleeping queen towards the exit where we came in earlier. One knight grabbed Alexander roughly and pulled him over their shoulder. "Momma! Allie-zander!" I yelled out as they took him.

"Be careful with that one, there's a special handcuff for that one in the carriage." the lady said pointing at the weird lady on the ground. A few guards had to pick her up because she was really tall, but she was really pretty.

"Alexander? That's that male's name?" the old mushroom asked me.

"I don't trust you!" I yelled loudly as he turned and we started following the guards carrying momma and alexander.

"Listen little girl, you're too young to recognize me but I am your king. You will answer me!" he said with a threatening tone.

"Then whose that" I said pointing at the mean old lady.

"I am the queen you brat" she hissed as I pointed at her.

"But momma called you her momma" I said, still looking at the lady.

"We are Magdolin's parents, now tell me is that male's name Alexander?" the king said, looking down at me as we walked out of the big huge castle.

"...you're my grandma?" I said looking at the old mushroom.

"Oh she's dumb too, how lovely," the old lady said with a laugh.

"Momma didn't say I had grandmas!" I said looking at the old king. He sighed and looked at the knights as they put momma and alexander in the back of the old looking carriage. The big lady was put in last and she was tied up and had huge handcuffs around her whole hands. Momma and Alexander only had rope around their arms.

"Shouldn't we put the male in handcuffs too, he had magic." the queen said looking up at the king.

"He barely knew how to control it, he's not that big of a threat. We do need to get Magdolin's dagger though" he said, stepping up into the carriage. He reached into momma's boot and took her magic knife.

"Leave that alone! That's mommas!" I said, reaching for the knife.

"Stop that," the old male said, holding it away from me.

"Oh and lock the child back there, I don't want to deal with her in our carriage." the old lady said.

"I'm not going to lock the child back here!" he yelled back at her.

"Hector I'm telling you too" she replied back in an angry tone. He looked at me with a sad tone.

"I'm sorry kid" he said, setting me down in between momma and alexander and he tied a rope around my stomach and tied it to the side of the carriage wall.

I crawled over to momma and moved her curls out of her face, she was still dead looking. The knights closed the carriage doors and it was really dark. It was still night time but I felt like the sun was waking up.

The old male and lady were walking around the carriage to get in the fancy one pulled by two white horses. "What if Magdolin is pregnant with that monster's child?" the lady said with her voice growing farther away.

"Well then we will have to find another tower to stick the abomination in," the old male said. Those people were mean and I couldn't believe them, betraying their own daughter like that. They are liars too! And if momma has a baby I want a little sister, I won't let them take it away. And they cannot force me in an orphanage, I remember old papa using that as a threat against me.

I tried shaking momma awake but she wouldn't budge, she was still asleep. I tried waking Alexander and he wouldn't wake up either. I started crying, it was scary being alone in that dark carriage. I felt the entire carriage jerk and I slid back as the carriage went forward. I could hear the horses foot stomps take off in a run like how Alexander's horses did.

The rope around me tightened as I slid back too, which only hurt worse. I cried more as I was in agony from the tight rope. I fumbled with the knot but it was tied too tight for me to figure out.

I heard a groan come from the other side of the carriage, so I turned around to look. Through teary eyes I could see the big lady with a funny mushroom sitting up. "...what happened?" she said in a low growl as she sat up. Her handcuffs didn't allow her to sit up all of the way. She just sat hunched over. She looked up and around the carriage. "..Adeline? Why are you here" she mumbled.

"How do you know my name?" I asked through tears.

"...I'm a friend of your mommas, why are you in here? Did they hurt you? Do you know where we are?" the lady asked, looking at me nervously.

"I'm okay, the old mushroom kept me from the old lady" I said as the weird lady looked at me. Her eyes were very pretty, they had a bunch of colours.

"Ok kiddo that's great, we've gotta get your parents up though," she said trying to pull at the handcuffs.

"Allie-zander asked momma to marry him!" I said excitedly. I looked at mommas hand and she didn't have Alexander's ring.

"Oh not yet kiddo, he just... I don't know, he just kissed her. They aren't married yet." the lady said as she paused as she spoke.

"Oh" I said with a frown.

Alexand clearly was just too scared to do it, what a wimp. I crawled over to him and moved his hair from his face.. He was bleeding! "What happened to allie-zander!" I said looking at the weird lady.

"Well that old male beat him up," she said, trying to pull at her handcuffs.

"Why didn't you help him!?" I said breath taken, momma or this lady didn't help Alexander.

"I did my best, kid, can you try and get out of that rope?" the lady said ignoring my question.

"I already tried," I said, sitting my butt on the ground.

"Great enthusiasm kid," the lady said, rolling her eyes.

"I know," I said, crossing my arms contently.

We sat there like that for an eternity, I sat there dreading it. All of a sudden Alexander then sat up and fought against his restraints. "Allie-zander!" I said happily. He looked up and his eyes were going the wrong way. The weird lady bursted out in laughter hunching over from how much she was laughing.

"What's going on, why's everything blurred?" he said, panicking as he blinked a bunch. His eyes fell back into place eventually. It was pretty funny seeing Alexander cross eyed like that.

"..oh god...that was hilarious" the lady said as she stopped crying.

"Was I cross eyed!? What happened! Magdolin!" he said looking around frantically. "Adeline!? You're here?" he said looking at me.

Chapter 28. Alexander Malencoy

"I don't know grandma put me in here" Adeline said, shrugging her shoulders.

"Grandma?" I said looking at her.

"Adeline can you try and get Alexander out of his ropes?" Amasa said, trying to pick her handcuffs. Adeline crawled over to me and was trying to fumble around with the knots in the ropes that bound my hands behind my back.

"Wait, where's Magdolins dagger?" Amasa asked.

"Oh the old lady took it" Adeline chimed in. "got it!" she said as she undid the bindings on my arms. I sighed as I worked my wrists around and got the ropes undone.

"Thank you Adel" I said untieing the rope around her waist.

I seen Magdolin still passed out on the ground of the carriage, the sun was starting to come up now. I crawled over to her and rolled her over on her back. "Mags come one wake up" I said cupping her face and moving it to the side as I checked for her pulse. She was breathing still and I felt relieved. She wasn't waking up though, I looked around and there was nothing I could use to try and wake her up.

"Alexander just give her time to wake up, we all got hit pretty hard," Amasa said in an annoyed tone.

"Are you kidding me? no!" I said, picking Magdolin up and untying her ropes from her arms. I could hear Amasa audibly sigh as I held Magdolin's unconscious body.

I looked at Amasa confused on why she didn't just break free from them with her powers. "Why don't you just break out of those?" I said, raising an eyebrow.

"Because they're magic bound, I can't," she said, tugging at them more and more. She was gonna end up hurting herself if she kept it up. I brought up a vine and did my best to work it around inside of the handcuffs locks. After about a minute of fumbling around with it I got it unlocked. Amasa looked at me surprised. "How could you do that but not overthrow the king?" Amasa said, flexing her wrists around.

"I don't know, it's a lot to deal with" I said looking back down at Magdolin in my arms. The sunlight peered through the slots of the prison carriage.

"Well there's no point in staying here longer, we'll just be getting further into the castle's perimeters. We need to escape Alexander, especially since you're so eager to get her up." Amasa said, cutting through the silence again.

"We can't just leave while Magdolins still knocked out," I said, looking up at Amasa like she was dumb.

"Well good thing your little princess is up then." she said, throwing a pod of water at Magdolin. Magdolin shot up gasping as she wiped the water from her face.

"Amasa! Don't do that," said scolding her as I brushed wet hair from Magdolin's face.

"Momma!" Adeline yelled, hugging Magdolin. She coughed and sat up rubbing her head.

"Where are we?" she mumbled, rubbing Adeline's back.

"Why are you asking me this is the first time I've ever been out of the manor" Amasa said snarky as she stood up.

"How nice" Magdolin said with a sigh as she rolled off my lap and to her feet. I took her hands and helped her stand up.

"Okay i'm gonna stop the carriage with rock, I'll take the kid and you get miss princess Alexander." Amasa said, picking Adeline up and holding her against her chest.

"Wait, we don't even know where we are." Magdolin said, pausing us in our tracks.

"We will figure that out Mags but we need to get you out of here right now" I said trying to pick her up but wasn't able to easily because of her dress.

"Oh you're kidding me" she hissed as she tore at the fabric with her hands. She left the top layers of the dress on the ground of the carriage. She had on her stockings, chemise, and corset still, which made her much easier to pick up. I held her at my side and gave Amasa a small nod signalling I was ready.

The cart came to a halt and Amasa shot the doors of the carriage open then a vine and I jumped out of the carriage with Magdolin. The two guards that were driving the carriage were already jumping off and running around.

I shot a vine up from the ground to stop one of them but it ended up side shooting and hitting the carriage. Amasa shot rock up from the ground forming it around the two guards and instructed me to watch them.

"Come on! You need to control those vines better, I know you can do it!" Amasa said, rounding the cart with Adeline.

"I'm sorry I'm just not used to it" I seethed, watching the two guards who fought at the solid rock around them even though they had no chance of escaping.

"How do horses work!?" Amasa called out. I sighed knowing she was trying to get the horses freed from the carriage. I ran around to where she was and began untying the horses from the heavy carriage. I set Magdolin up on one of the horses and took Adeline from Amasa.

"Get up on that horse with magdolin, I know where we are now. I have a safe house across town," I said, pushing Amasa towards magdolins horse.

Magdolin held out her hand helping Amasa up on her horse. "We're gonna have to run mags, are you gonna be okay?" I asked, looking back at her with a worried face. These were kingdom horses, I'm sure they would go a lot faster than Hope or Serenity. She nodded her head and kicked the horses hard causing her horse to take off.

I followed after her, the safe house was a good distance away but I'm sure we'd make it there before anyone would notice the prison carriage was abandoned. Adeline was giggling as the horses galloped as fast as they could. The loud sounds of finely crafted horseshoes rang all around us.

I looked over at Magdolin, she was holding the horse's hair and leaned forward. She looked like she'd done this for years, Amasa was latched around her waist holding on tight with a nervous look. I smiled and turned back to the road holding Adeline and the horse's hair at the same time.

Within an hour we arrived back at the safe house. This was a safe house with a fireplace and one bedroom. Sure it had a beautiful view over the lake but one bedroom wasn't ideal for four people. It would have to do. "Let's put the horses around back" I yelled out to Magdolin as I went around the house. I got Adeline off the horse and then got off myself.

I walked over to Magdolin's horse and grabbed Magdolin off her horse, hugging her tightly. "I'm so sorry Mags, that was way too close" I said, holding her against me tight.

"It's okay Alexander," she said, holding me back.

"How sentimental, so much for manners when you don't help the other lady down," Amasa said, interrupting the moment.

"I help you down!" Adeline said, holding her tiny arms up as if she'd helped the huge lady off the horse.

"Oh no kiddo, it's fine I can get off myself," Amasa said crawling off the huge clydesdale. I looked back down at Magdolin's smiling face and it just made me smile brightly. I wanted to just stay like this, holding her close.

"Do you wanna go inside kid" Amasa said down to Adeline. Adeline nodded her head jumping up and down as always. I rolled my eyes and gently let Magdolin go from my embrace. I led the way from around the house and unlocked the door. As I opened the door I seen the ashes in the fireplace and the small pillow me and Magdolin had left there when we first came through this town.

Adeline ran inside laughing, Amasa formed a small tree in the fireplace and lit it with her fire powers. I looked down at myself, the crisp white shirt I wore was now stained with dirt and blood.

I felt Magdolin's hand reach up to my cheek and she brushed the dry blood from my nose. "You just got all torn up" she said with a frown.

"I think I could say the same for you Mags" I said brushing loose stays of her messy hair out of her face. "Well I think I look great in my chemise" she said with a playful smirk playing on her face.

"I never said I didn't like it," I said with a smile. She did look utterly beautiful in it, it was just a shame she has nothing else not to wear.

"What is this place?" Amasa asked, looking around the house.

"It's one of my safe houses, I thought that was obvious since you know everything." I said annoyed. I knew Amasa needed to be here but I really just wanted time to go to Magdolin. I wanted to propose once I got the chance.

"Well no duh, I'm saying where did you get them. I know you have them placed around the kingdom" she said, rolling her eyes. I really wanted to punch her, but I knew that was wrong. She's going to my sister-in law, and she's a female sadly.

"Well they were my homes from when my parents lived in the kingdom, and then the rest came from relatives that have left too." I said walking more into the house.

"Interesting," she mumbled, looking around the house.

Chapter 29. Amasa tessa

I need to find out what to do. I can't just sit here and rot away hiding in the house, I need to get Alexander on that throne. I need to be completely free to do whatever I want, and I can't do that right now. "So what's your guys plan to do now, we can't just sit here forever." I said looking over at them. It seemed like they were almost too scared to make the next move.

"I'm not sure" Magdolin admitted picking up Adeline. I rolled my eyes and walked over to Alexander.

"I need you to propose to her tonight ok, or else the plan I have is not going to work." I whispered in a stern tone.

"What's your plan?" he asked, looking back at me with a glare.

"Just do what I say and you'll see, it worked last time." I hissed back at his questioning.

"It worked only halfway, and this is my future you're toying with now." he said, crossing his arms over his chest.

"That was out of my hands, but I believe that I'm the person to trust in this situation," I said, glaring at him.

"Hm, well I don't, I'm gonna do what I want." he said in a cocky tone. I knew deep down he was going to propose if nothing else interfered.

"Oh well, I'm going outside" I said loudly, walking outside leaving those three inside. I'd prefer to leave them alone, maybe then he'd get the opportunity to talk to her.

I walked out to a tree in the yard, it was a small tree. Pitiful to be more exact, it was small with few limbs. I put my hands down into the dirt around the base and focused my energy. I'd never been able to work with trees or already grown plants.

The tree grew under my touch, blooming flowers that grew into apples as I watched them. I retracted my hands from the soft dirt and stared at the tree in awe. "Wow, that's new" I said, bringing over a pod of water from the lake and watering the tree. "I wonder what else I could do" I said, running over behind the house to the lake. I snapped my fingers and my dress was swapped to a swim dress.

I jumped into the lake taking big strides to stay afloat. I'd never swam before but I'd read many books on it. I came out towards the inner side of the lake. I shot up big streams of water from the lake forming different shapes and designs. I formed a cylinder of water under me and shot it up into the air, I went up in the air with the cylinder. It shot me up about twenty feet into the air. I didn't intend to make it so big and yelled as I came back down and hit the water on my back. I groaned as I came back to the surface. Despite the pain I kept throwing water pods and sparks into the air practicing them.

"Wow! How do you do that?!" I heard a small voice say on the shore of the lake. I flipped around and Adeline was standing on the edge of the water.

"Does your mom know you're out here?" I said moving the water around me and pushing myself to the shore.

"Uhm no," she said, looking as guilty as a jailbreaker. I smiled as I looked down at her.

"You're just a sneak, aren't you?" I said laughing. It was surprising how sneaky she was, she could get out of the house without being noticed.

"Can I go swim?" she asked while pointing out at the lake. I thought about it for a moment. Sure Alexander and Magdolin might be mad but who am I to even care.

"Sure kiddo, you have a cool auntie after all," I said, snapping my fingers and I gave her a little swim dress. She looked cute in it, the dress was pink with white sparkles all over it. She was in awe as she giggled and looked up at me. "You like it?" I asked, looking down at her.

"Yes!" she said excitedly. She ran down to the shore and was almost in the water before she stopped. She looked back at me fumbling with her little hands.

"What's the matter?" I asked, walking down beside her.

"I don't know how to swim," she said, looking up at me. I frowned, I should've known she didn't know how to swim, she's too young.

"Well good thing I can help, I'm not teaching you but I'll help you out little missy." I said leading the water up the side of the shore and to my feet. I picked her up and walked down into the lake again. The water wasn't very warm but it wasn't cold either, it was lukewarm. It was cold enough to make Adeline kick her feet though.

I formed the water around her little waist and I let go of her. She kicked her feet around for a few moments and then just floated, she looked up at me laughing. "Fun?" I asked, smiling at her. She started splashing the water's surface all around her.

"Yeah!" she shouted happily.

After a few more moments of me trying to get a hold of swimming myself, and keeping the water flowing around Adeline, I heard a loud mean voice. "Amasa! What's wrong with you!? She can't swim!" Magdolin's voice rang out across the lake's surface.

"Dont worry I've got her under control" I said calmly. I picked Adeline up out of the water with the water flowing around her as she giggled and kicked. Alexander stood behind magdolin with his arms crossed, Magdolin herself was almost fuming.

"Why did you not ask me permission!? Where's her dress at now!?" Magdolin said, trudging down to the shore of the lake.

"Oh calm down, she's fine," I said moving the water around her to the shore next to her momma before setting her down.

"You still should have asked permission Amasa, she's my daughter!" she said, picking up Adeline.

"And I'm her aunt technically!" I said swimming on my back.

"Oh please, barely." Alexander scoffed. I threw a pod of water at him, drenching him from head to toe.

"Maybe that'll get some of those stains out of the shirt for you" I said looking over at them. Alexander's hair poofed up into a soaking wet frizz as the water set in his hair. "Oh my gosh! You have curly hair!" I said laughing and kicking at the water.

"Oh hardy har har, shut up" he said rolling his eyes.

Adeline was practically trying to crawl out of her mom's arms and back to the lake. "Stop it baby, you need to get dried off." Magdolin said fighting against her as she held her.

"I wanna swim!" Adeline said as she started crying. Magdolin looked tired as Adeline cried in her arms, bouncing her slightly trying to get her to stop crying.

"Oh stop it please, I don't wanna see you cry. Shh shh," she said looking back at Alexander. Alexander looked dumbfounded for a moment before he tried reaching out for Adeline. I snickered to myself before I shot up a vine and wrapped it around Alexander's ankle. I drug him into the lake by it, he clawed at the ground and yelled as I drug him in.

"Amasa really?" Magdolin said, annoyed as she set Adeline back down on the ground.

"Oh he's fine" I said as Alexander gasped and came back to the surface about twenty feet from shore. Adeline slowly hobbled back down into the water and I made sure to keep water flowing around her as she kicked out towards Alexander.

I thought it was absolutely hilarious whenever I humiliated Alexander, I'm not sure why but it is exhilarating. Magdolin sat down on the shore with her feet down in the water with a sigh. "I don't want her to get burnt, I heard that's bad for you," Magdolin added with a frown.

"She's fine Magdolin and if you're so scared, here." I said, snapping my fingers. Adeline's little swim dress earned itself long sleeves and a sun bonnet on her mushroom.

"That's better, thank you." Magdolin said, crossing her legs. I looked over at Alexander who was holding Adeline up in the water now. I guess he didn't trust my abilities to keep her safe but who am I to care. I also do not understand why Alexander doesn't just propose to Magdolin already, it's the one thing that's holding me back. If the chance of a kingdom guard were to stumble across us it would be horrendous.

I decided I needed to make this move on faster. I flowed the water up the shore and around Magdolin, she gasped as the water followed around her and drug her down in the water. "Amasa!" she yelled as I pulled her out into the deep part.

"I thought you knew how to swim?" I said curiously as I let her go. She clawed at the water trying to stay afloat, she could keep her head above water but only enough to breath. Alexander gasped and started to panic on what to do as he held Adeline. I smirked before I shot a stream up behind Adeline and it cascaded her up in the air a few feet. I moved the water around and pushed myself forward to catch Adeline.

Alexander sighed before he dived forward to help Magdolin. It was quite a cutely disgusting sight to see, the two of them with their arms intertwined with each other. Magdolin gasped as she caught her breath. I looked down at Adeline who was holding onto my shoulder.

"I'm done swimming," Adeline announced to me. I smiled and nodded to her. I snapped my fingers and changed her and myself back into our dresses as I stepped back onto the shore.

"Where are you two going!?" Alexander yelled out as he helped Magdolin to swim.

"Oh hush I was just gonna go somewhere else, Adeline's tired of swimming." I said with a shrug. Before I could totally leave I shot up another cylinder of water underneath Alexander, flipping him up about nine feet in the air. Adeline cackled as he came down and hit the water. I set her down and took her tiny hand into mine as I made my way up to the house.

I let Adeline loose in the small house, and I myself began poking around at anything I could find. The house only had a few closets and then the main room with a kitchen and living area. One of the closets was just empty with a few brooms. The other closet had lots of books. I closed it back fast, the last thing I wanted to see was more books.

I heard the door to the house slam shut, I walked back out to the main area with a smirk hoping to see a ring on a thinger. Of course I didn't see one though, I let out an aggravated sigh. Magdolin and Alexander stood with an annoyed look on their faces. "Look at those party poopers, can't keep up with us, can they Adeline?" I said teasingly down to Adeline.

Magdolin rolled her eyes as she wrung out her hair. Alexander sighed before sitting on the edge of the fireplace. Adeline ran over to her momma grabbing at her soaked chemise. "Adeline you need to stay with me from now on!" she said, patting her head but not picking her up to prevent her from getting wet as well.

"Oh auntie Amasa can't hurt a fly!" I said leaning on the counter of the kitchen.

"You could take down a kingdom if you wanted to, don't lie to the kid." Alexander huffed under his breath.

"You could be my friend! But it seems you don't want anything to do with that hm?" I said, trying to antagonise him.

"Leave him alone Amasa, it's not our fault you got stuck with us." Magdolin queued sarcastically. I paused folding my hands together, I didn't like that attitude at all, I needed to bring the mood up somehow.

"Well Mags, that's not a kind way to speak to your sister is it?" I asked with a smirk.

"I barely consider you family" she said with a mean glare. It's clear none but the child trusted me still.

"Ouch sis, that burns. I forgive you though," I said with a shrug as I walked over besides her and Adeline. "My, you're still in your undergarments. Has no one taught you manners?" I said teasingly as I looked at Magdolin. She was slightly hunched over and in her undergarment dress and corset. Alexander looked rough as well, the light red stains on his white shirt and pants from his blood.

"Well this just can't be done, for either of you." I said, snapping my fingers. With a flash of colours that swirled around them both, Magdolin's hair was dried and brushed falling down her lower back. Her dress was a light purple with a black tulle overlay that reached her ankles, and a roman neckline on the bodice. Alexander's stained white pants and shirt were just tied up and changed to black, with a freshly pressed look to them. They both looked at themselves as Magdolin picked up Adeline.

"Momma looks pretty with dark colours," Adeline said pointing at the black tulle which accentuated the purple underneath.

"Yes she does" Alexander added while resting his face in his hand. He had a dumb smile spread across his face, it made me want to barf.

"Thank you." Magdolin said with a soft smile and a sigh. She looked back up at me with her eyebrows furrowed together. "How do you do the clothing thing, it's not really part of your quota" she said while propping Adeline up on her hip.

"Actually it's very interesting! Back at the manor those books held little spells as well, one being clothing and fabrics. It's all very fast moving and fast acting magic. You quickly form the cotton plants and then weave it with vines and such things. It moves so fast that's why you only see flashes of colour." I said trying to explain it to an understanding point.

"So I can form more than vines?" Alexander asked, standing up.

"No duh, you've seen me make plenty more, you just need practice" I said turning back to Magdolin. He let out a hearty sigh as a response.

"I'm going outside" he said as he headed back towards the door.

"I don't understand men" I said looking down at Magdolin. She rolled her eyes before setting Adeline down.

"He's nothing but sweet Amasa, I wish you'd treat him better," she said sitting down on the ledge of the fireplace.

"Oh please, you've only known him for a few weeks. I'm just saying I don't understand it. Explain it to me." I said sitting down next to her. I knew what love was, I'd just never experienced it. Personally I didn't want to either, having soft feelings for someone felt gross and unnecessary. I needed them to *love* each other though, so I had to play into this.

She looked up at me with her brows furrowed. "Im being serious Maggie, tell me the secrets to this whole love thing!" I said resting my chin in my palms, attempting to sound interested.

Adeline came over and sat in between us looking up at her mom. "Yeah momma!" Adeline said, pulling on her arm. Magdolin sighed and looked down at her feet.

"I'm not sure how it works, Amasa, it just does. When I first met Alexander I was a bit shocked because of the whole poison mushroom scare, but after that we became good friends. And then later that friendship slowly morphed into feelings, I pushed them down saying it was wrong and how I'd get myself hurt like the last time I saw someone with another colour. But I couldn't keep them down, his charm, his kindness. Anything he did felt like a direct punch to my gut, like I needed to fall for him. And trust me I fell hard, like I face planted in stone. He is anything I could ask for, and I don't think anything could change my mind that I love him. Even if it came out that my people ruined his entire life, he seems to not be bothered and still cares for me." she said with a small frown that slowly turned to a smile as she spoke.

The whole declaration of love she just declared made my stomach churn. I hated the way love sounded, it sounded like being tied down and staked.

"That is so adorable, I could just cry. You need to go find him now and tell him how you feel, you haven't been able to!" I said urgently as I rested a hand on her shoulder.

She just looked at me confused. "Yeah momma! You need to go explain how you feel to allie-zander!" Adeline said standing up, throwing her hands up.

"I'm sure he already knows that, so I told him I loved him." she said, looking at me and the child both.

"And that's all you said? Do you want Alexander? Because you have to go earn him if you want him sis!" I said pushing her slightly and Adeline cheered.

"I- ... okay" she said standing up and going outside. I sighed but she opened the door again.

"You two stay inside, especially Adeline." she said before closing the door back and her footsteps trailed off the porch. I snickered lightly to myself. I always loved how I could poke and prod my way to get things, it's how I usually got what I wanted back at the manor. I'd just bug the workers till they snapped at me.

Adeline grunted as she instructed us to stay inside, she looked up at me as if I had something to do. "What are you looking at?" I said with my hands on my hips.

Chapter 30. Alexander Malencoy

I was out in the woods off the path of the house in a small clearing practicing with my plant magic. Some plants would shoot up in the wrong direction or be the wrong colour, it was like I couldn't control them. I was getting more aggravated by the moment. I looked around at all the flowers and plants in the clearing, it had its beauty but was not correct.

I groaned and sat down on the ground against a tree. I felt lost without any guidance on these newfound powers. "Alexander?" I heard Magdolin's voice call out through the woods. I felt a pang of relief as I stood up and cracked my back.

"Right here Mags," I said walking out onto the path where she was wandering about. She turned to look at me with a smile on her face. I smiled back at her as she approached me.

"Alexander, I think we need to talk," she said as she was right in front of me.

"Ah ah ah" I said, stopping her and I did my best to sprout up a flower. It was a pretty flower but it was missing a petal and some of the colours flushed around it. "Darnit" I growled, annoyed. She picked the flower still and looked at it closely.

"It's beautiful," she said, smiling brightly. She then looked into the small clearing I had been practicing in, all of the deformed plants and miss coloured flowers stuck out. She walked around them looking at them closely.

"I know there not the best but I'm still learning, I guess," I said nervously as I followed behind her.

"My Alexander what are you talking about, I've never seen anyone that could do something as amazing as this." she said, looking back at me with the flower still in her hand.

Something about seeing her with a flower that I had created made my heart flourish. "It's not as amazing as you," I said quietly as I pushed a flower behind her ear. Her soft smile made my heart jump as she looked up at me. I am so lucky to even have met her.

"...so I came out here to talk to you, away from those two." she said with a sweet tone to her voice. It was like candy, a sweet honey that coated her voice, it is something I crave dearly.

"Well I'm all ears Mags" I said leaning up against a tree. She smiled again before leaning up against the tree with me.

"...well I was wanting to finally talk about what happened on the dance floor." she said, moving her arms up and motioning a dance move before awkwardly laughing and stopping.

"I know, it was nice wasnt it?" I said, nudging her shoulder slightly. She looked so perfect in her dress, even her just near me made it even better.

"It was lovely, I agree, but I just wanted to tell you... I love you doesn't even cover half of how I feel about you." she said, reaching out and holding my hand gently.

I wanted to just grab her and hold her forever. "I feel the exact same for you my dear." I said, pressing a kiss on the top of her hand. I loved watching her as I did that. Her cheeks would flush slightly with a light tint of red.

"No I really mean it Alexander, I love you with all of my heart. You rescued me and protected me." she said, holding my other hand as well.

"Well you saved my sorry butt a few times as well. I'll always love you Magdolin, and you have no reason to try and explain it." I said, squeezing her hands lightly. She laughed quietly and looked down avoiding eye contact. I grabbed her chin and made her look up at me. "I'd like to explain how much I love you if that's okay?" I said looking down into her eyes. The normal purple colour had a tiny hint of green still, I loved it. She gave me a small nod allowing me too. I felt my heart swell as I composed myself.

"Well…it's not really explaining, more like a declaration" I said, taking a deep breath. It honestly felt like my heart was going to beat out of my chest but I kept a cool face.

I closed my eyes as I reached into my pocket and pulled out the small black box. It felt like the world was shaking, this could easily make me or break me. I fell down on one knee and cracked the small box open. I watched her eyes widen and one of her hands crawled over her mouth. "Magdolin Poni, this is very out of nowhere considering I met you for the first time a few weeks ago. But I know that I love you dearly and that I always will, no matter what, through thick and thin. It would be my greatest honour if you gave me the gift of your hand in marriage…" I said while holding a hand over my heart and one holding the box up.

I felt my heart pounding in my ears as I awaited her answer. She stood there frozen for a moment looking at me. I felt like I was going to pass out, I wish she'd just answer.

She dropped down on her knees in front of me with both of her hands over her mouth. I moved to where I was on both of my knees as well and set the ring down on the grass beside us. "You don't have to say yes Mags, I just wanted to see I guess." I said quietly as I put my hands in my lap.

She shook her head and put her hands down on her lap as well, I could see two lines of tears streaming down her face. "Wow, why are you crying?" I said, cupping her face and wiping her salty tears with my thumbs.

She started laughing as I did so, she kept crying though. I was confused on what this was, was it yes? Was it not?

"No," she mumbled through laughter.

"Oh it's not? That's fine! That's okay" I said a little bit in a hurt tone but quickly hiding it.

"No!" she said putting her hands over mine on her cheeks, still laughing.

"Yes!?" I asked excitedly, sitting up slightly in place.

She nodded her head smiling as she looked up at me. I felt a stinging sensation go through my entire body as she nodded her head. It felt like I was going to melt.

I wrapped my arms around her and held her tightly against me, I didn't want to let her go, ever. I just held her there rocking her side to side before pulling away to look at her face. I was eternally grateful for this, I'm grateful for anything I ever have or do with her. "Thank you" I said laughing with her.

"No thank you Alexander," she said smiling. She grabbed the sides of my face, her thumbs brushing over the stubble on my jawline. I smiled as I looked into her eyes, her gaze was soft but intent. She pulled my face down to hers and kissed me.

Her lips were so soft I couldn't get enough of them. I moved my hand to the back of her head. The way my hand rested on the curve on the back of her neck just felt natural. Her lips would form a smile as she kissed me, it made my heart skip a beat. She was sweet, sweeter than desert. Her hair ravelled around my fingers as she pulled away from the kiss. I couldn't do anything besides just smile at her, she was so beautiful. It was like looking over a mountain at sunset. Nothing could compare to her, ever.

"Before I even realised I loved you, I wanted you." she murmured under her breath. It made my whole body feel all warm and soft, like I was at home with her.

Soft and fast crunching of leaves and sticks interrupted us as always. Adeline rounded around the tree in the entrance to the clearing. "Adeline, I told you to stay inside with Amasa," Magdolin said in an annoyed tone.

"You wanted her" I said teasingly as we were still on the ground. Amasa then came into the clearing out of breath.

"I tried to keep her inside... oh god... why is she so fast?" she said out of breath as she leaned on the tree.

I just looked back at Magdolin and sighed. Adeline ran over and sat down next to Magdolin, and then she went wide eyed as she saw the ring.

"You're married now!" she yelled out with a wide mouthed grin, spreading ear to ear. Her smile was cute, a few teeth missing in the front made it cuter.

"No, not married babydoll, just engaged I guess." Magdolin said, patting Adeline's mushroom.

"There's levels to being married!?" Amasa asked loudly.

"Not levels, stages, I would have thought you'd know that miss know-it-all." I said, rolling my eyes.

"Well that's just dumb!" she said in a panicked tone.

"And why does it matter to you?" I asked as I picked up the ring box. I slid the ring out of its prison, I took Magdolin's hand and gave the ring its new home. It fitted around her hand and tightened on its own, almost like magic.

"How did it do that?" Amasa asked, looking closer.

"It's beautiful Alexander," Magdolin said, looking down at her hand.

"Thank you, Charlie gave it to me to give to you," I said, squeezing her hand.

"Who is this Charlie!? What sorcery is she using to get a ring to do that" Amasa said urgently.

"Do you mind Amasa?" Magdolin asked as she stood up. I stood up as well next to her with my arm around her shoulder.

"Is Allie-zander my dada now?" Adeling asked, pulling on Magdolin's dress. Magdolin looked up at me for any faults in my expression.

"Well I'd love to be if that's what you're wondering." I whispered to Magdolin. Her smile spread across her face again as I spoke. She looked back down to Adeline before picking her up.

"Yes he is." she said, holding her on her hip.

"Yay!" Adeline shouted out, hugging Magdolin.

"How sickeningly cute!" Amasa announced standing a few feet from us. I rolled my eyes as I picked Adeline off of Magdolin.

"I'm going to the house you weirdos" Amasa added as she walked off towards the house. I sighed as she left and looked at Magdolin.

"So what now?" I asked her as I held Adeline up to my chest. She looked off to the side before shrugging her shoulders. "Anything you want, I'm happy as long as I'm with you." she said brushing some hair out of my face, I had forgotten my hair had bounced back up into curls.

"Well we can't really stay here, we should just get a move on as always." I said, mocking her and shrugging my shoulders. She snickered and took my free arm.

"That sounds like us doesn't it?" she said, leading me out of the clearing and back towards the house.

Her footsteps were light and peppy. My heart still beat out of my chest, I couldn't believe she actually accepted the proposal. She's come a long way from the rule stricken princess she was. She's still a princess to me though, she's more than a princess actually.

Her boots clicked on the boards of the porch as we went back in the house. I set Adeline down as I opened the door for the three of us. Amasa was sitting on the living area floor forming little formations with rock and plants. "Whatcha makin'" Adeline asked, hopping down onto the ground next to Amasa.

She jumped as Adeline had shocked her. "I didn't hear you guys walk in" she hissed under her breath.

"Can you make me a dolly?" Adeline asked, leaning on Amasa's arm. She had a grossed out look as the kid was laying on her, but her gaze on Adleine softened.

"Adeline you have a dolly." Magdolin said, holding her hand out to the doll in Adeline's clutch.

"It's fine," Amasa said with a sigh before forming a small doll. It had a pink dress and a pink mushroom, it looked like Adeline. Adeline's face lit up as she grabbed the doll and giggled loudly as she ran off in the house with her two dolls.

I laughed watching her skip off, it was a funny sight. "So what are you two doing now?" Amasa asked, standing up with an annoyed tone.

"Well we could have discussed that but someone had to go outside." Magdolin said, crossing her arms.

"Well that's not my fault I never agreed to babysit for the two of you did I?" Amasa replied putting her hands together. She was clearly getting agitated and annoyed for some reason. I was getting annoyed as well.

"Well we didn't agree for you to come along with us." I replied with a frown.

"Excuse me? I have helped you both out tremendously. Now how about we all three act like adults." she said, turning her attention to me.

The way her voice rattled was bone-chilling. It sounded electronic and repeated like an old radio. "Well what do you suggest?" Magdolin said with a sigh.

"I suggest you both be smart, go get married and then you'll both be crowned king and queen. It would fix everything for mushrooms like me! Once that witch of a queen and evil king are out of there, I could do whatever I want." she said excitely in a convincing tone.

Magdolin curled her nose up at the idea. I understood why she did, the idea of Amasa with complete freedom wasn't good.

"What would you do with said freedom and who said I wanted to be a king." I said leaning on Magdolin.

"Nothing bad I promise, but if I can't get freedom I'll forever be on the run and so will you two. And they'll never stop hunting you down, they won't stop till they have us. It would be in the best interest for your daughter and me!" she said with big promising eyes. She'd also motion things out with her hands and arms.

"So had this been your plan this whole time? Just so you can be free, only looking out for yourself? How do I know you won't try to overthrow this kingdom? It's bad enough as it is Amasa." Magdolin said, grabbing onto Amasa's shoulders and shaking her slightly.

"No no I swear I wouldn't, I just want to be free to do as I want. I'd stay under your watch if it's what you require. But the only way for peace would be if you take the throne, I swear. I know you don't fully understand Maggie, I know you're only sixteen," Amasa said, grabbing Magdolin's shoulders as well.

I rolled my eyes, is she really this crazy? "I'm nineteen Amasa, and I do know. It's just I don't really want to see mom or dad, nevertheless showing up to take their places." Mags said, pulling away from Amasa's grasp.

I moved my arm around her shoulder to try and offer a form of comfort to her but she just pulled away. She buried her face in her hands, hair fell around her hands and face. "B-but if you don't, nothing will ever be right! Magdolin please make the right decision, you have to do what's right, fix what our ancestors have done!" Amasa said crowding in around magdolin again.

"Give her space." I said, pulling Amasa away from Magdolin.

"No! Don't you want to be free too, they'll hunt you more than they ever had now that they know your affiliation with her. Also, I'm the only one who can help you, show you how to harness your power. But we can't show our true power unless you're the king!" she said, pointing at me and yelling.

"You need to stop! This is our choice and she doesn't need to be pressured into anything for you or my sake!" I said holding her back from Magdolin. It wasn't much help that she was larger than me, and she was strong.

"You're the male, why don't you just make the choice!?" Amasa yelled, yanking away from me. I was jaw dropped she'd say something like that. It is an accustomed thing but in this situation I believe that Magdolin would know better.

"Yes… yes she's right Alexander, you choose!" Magdolin said quietly. She walked over and grabbed my hands as she spoke.

"Magdolin I'm not choosing for you." I said, holding her hands back. I couldn't choose our future alone. I wanted us both to be happy wherever we were, even if we were hiding. I didn't want Amasa there necessarily, but in a palace I wouldn't have to put up with her all the time. There was no way I was making the call though. "Please Alexander I'm fine with anything I just want to be with you," she said with tears forming in her eyes.

I hated seeing her cry, it nearly brought me to tears thinking about her crying. "Mags no I can't, you're the educated one I want you to make the call. I'm fine with being a king, or a hideaway like I've always been. I'll work with anything you wish." I said cupping her cheek lightly in my hand.

She looked up at me with a frown and a tear ran down her cheek. I swiped the small tear with my thumb and gave her a soft smile. Amasa stood a few feet away with an anxious look on her face. Magdolin paused and just looked up at me. She stayed like that for a few moments before speaking.

"...Alexander I think we need to fix things" she said quietly and turned her vision down to the ground. A new feeling fled throughout my body, it was scary to think about. A mix of fear and unsettlingness, mixed with happiness and bliss. I was overly happy that Magdolin and I had found settling ground. But at the same time the outcomes of her parents may be bad.

"Alright Mags, if that's what you wish." I said brushing her hair back and letting my hand fall from her face.

"Are you sure though, I don't want anything to happen to you. Are you sure you can handle this?" she asked, looking up at me with sorrowful eyes.

"Yes mags, as long as you're by my side as my queen I'll be happy. No matter the threat or consequence, I'll do my best by you and Adeline," I said softly.

I meant everything I said, Magdolin was the life I wanted even if I had to take care of an entire kingdom along with her. This would also fix things for my kind, make us be accepted. The only problem would be getting the kingdom to accept me. I'm sure they'll be 'overjoyed' their princess is back but not her newly found to-be-husband, me.

"Thank you Alexander," she said, wrapping her arms around me. I gratefully embraced her back tightly, I loved her being close to me. "I promise it'll all work out, I will make sure of it." she said, clawing at the back of my shirt.

"Oh shh I know, don't worry Mags." I said, running my hand over her mushroom.

Amasa shouted happily jumping up and down laughing. "Yes yes, you guys are making the best decision. Oh I'm so proud of you two!" she said, still cackling happily.

"Don't think you're going to just do whatever, you will be staying with us no matter what. I don't trust you Amasa. Magdolin said, squeezing me a little bit before letting me go.

"Okay okay I know, it's just what now?" Amasa asked, stepping back with her fists balled up in excitement.

"Well I'll have to do some digging to find a preacher I can pay off. I'm sure Charlie can find me someone. I said smiling down at Magdolin.

She smiled back at me, I wanted to kiss her but Amasa was right there. "Oh this is wonderful, oh, oh my goodness I'm going to shout it for the world to hear once I can!" Amasa yelled happily.

"When shall you depart for this magical Charlie figure?" Amasa asked slightly crouched over as she tried to contain her own excitement.

"Morning would be best, I'd wish to join you as well," Magdolin said, squeezing my hands.

I paused and looked down at her before shaking my head. "No Mags, I need you to stay here and watch these two. Plus everything's going to be extremely guarded around here. I'm sure,I'll be lucky if I get through" I said, squeezing her hands back.

"Not without my help you won't, ill disguise you before you leave. Although I'd like to meet this magic charlie, I'll stay as well." Amasa added, planting her hand on the small table in the corner of the room.

Magdolins smile faded into a frown. "Alexander, I don't want you just going in there and getting captured alone." she said with a stern and worried tone to her normally soft voice.

"Well it's better me just getting taken than you so it's settled I'm going." I said with an upbeat tone trying to change the mood.

"Alexa-" she stuttered before I cut her off.

"Nope, Alexander going alone!" I said picking her up and setting her over my shoulder.

"Alexander!" she yelled in shock and laughed. She was lighter than I would've thought. I held her firmly over my shoulder as she kicked her feet a little bit. "It's getting dark Mags you better go check on your Adeline!" I said walking towards the bedroom where Adeline was.

"Put me down!" she yelled still laughing as I balanced her carefully on the blade of my shoulder.

"No!" I said in a whiny tone. As I opened the door to the bedroom I was greeted by the sight of Adeline on the bed playing with her dolls.

"Momma!" she yelled while cackling as she saw me holding Magdolin over my shoulder.

"Save her Adeline!" I said laughing and throwing Magdolin down on the bed next to Adeline. Magdolin laughed and giggled covering her mouth as I set her down.

"You're full of giggles momma" Adeline said crawling over to Magdolin's side as she laid on her back still laughing.

"You wanna see her laugh more?" I said teasingly as I held Magdolin down on the beds quilt cover. She looked beautiful on the bed like this. Her hair was sprawled out around her and she was red-faced from laughing.

"Yeah!" Adeline yelled out, clapping her tiny hands together.

I smirked as she said yes and looked back down at Magdolin. I started tickling Magdolin's sides as she bursted out in loud laughter. I started chuckling to myself as she kicked her feet. It was amazing to see her laughing and smiling uncontrollably, I loved it so much. Adeline laughed as she joined in tickling her momma's neck. Magdolin shrieked with laughter as we both tickled her.

"Ah! Stop...stop hahaha no no no stop!" Magdolin yelled loudly as she squirmed and kicked her feet.

"What is this form of torture?" Amasa's voice rang through the room with true confusion.

"Tickle torture" I muttered smiling as I kept tickling Magdolin.

"Yeah! Tickle torture!" Adeline said cackling.

"Oh don't think you're getting out of this little lady" I said, letting Magdolin go from my ticklings grasp.

She gasped as she sat up slightly. I turned to look at Adeline and began tickling her, her little laugh was big and loud. She kicked her legs around and rolled around on the bed.

"Stop! Stop dadda!" Adeline screamed out as she kicked around. I paused momentarily and looked at her and then at Magdolin who was just as shocked as me.

"Oh you" I said, picking Adeline up and hugging her tightly.

"How utterly sickening, it's hard to not adore for you isn't it?" Amasa murmured to Magdolin. I ignored her and just hugged Adeline, I couldn't believe she actually thought of me as her father. It was an odd feeling but I liked it.

Chapter 31. Magdolin Poni

I smiled as Alexander embraced Adeline's small little body, also rolling my eyes at Amasa's comment. "Okay it's getting late you two, it's someone's bedtime." I said, pulling Adeline away from Alexander's hold.

I yawned a bit as I tucked Adeline in the bed under the cosy handsewn quilt. "I think you're tired yourself Mags," Alexander said teasingly.

"Oh I couldn't go to bed yet." I said, waving my hand.

"What! No, I can't sleep without you momma!" Adeline yelled out sitting back up in the bed. I sighed, I forgot that Adeline refused to go to bed without me.

"Momma's gonna stay, don't worry kiddo." Amasa said, shoving me down next to adeline.

I grunted as she did so but didn't fight back due to Adeline crawling next to me. Adeline squirmed around in my arms, getting comfortable as Alexander closed the blinds for us. "Well goodnight you two," he murmured, brushing hair out of Adeline's face.

Her eyes were closed as she tried to fall asleep. Alexander snickered to himself as Adeline drifted off to sleep within seconds.

"What are you two going to do?" I asked Alexander as he kissed Adeline on the forehead gently. Part of me really didn't want to leave those two alone, but Adeline wouldn't go to bed without me. Nevertheless, I was tired.

"Not much Mags, I'm gonna go clean up some and then go to bed," he said smiling. I gave him a small nod and smiled back up at him.

I felt his hand envelope the side of my face, I closed my eyes instinctively as I felt his lips close with mine. I kissed him back gently and then he pulled away a moment later. His kisses were like candy, and his lips were cracked yet soft and heavenly. "Goodnight princess" he mumbled as his lips parted from mine.

"I thought I've told you not to call me that," I whispered as he stood up and started to head for the door.

"It's with a different context now." he said, flashing a smile and closing the door behind him.

I smiled to myself at his words, I felt that flourishing feeling in my chest. It was such a nice feeling to know that he loved me back now. It felt almost as good as when I realised my feelings were love. Adeline also was clearly happy with the situation, and happy with Alexander as her father.

It's just not going to stay the same as Adeline or I had thought. We are going to be in the castle from now on. I hope she will like it there, I'll make sure she'll have all my attention. I'll make sure she won't grow up like me, I thought to myself as I held Adeline close to me.

I felt my eyelids grow heavier and my thoughts slowed. And just as soon as it began I was asleep.

Later in the night I awoke to the feeling of the weight shifting on the queen size mattress. I forced my eyes open slightly, but only cracked them due to how sleepy I was. Alexander had laid down across from Adeline and I. It was much darker now, I was glad he was finally going to bed.

I drifted back to a calm sleep. It was a good feeling to know I had my new family here with me, my daughter Adeline, my soon to be husband Alexander, and hey even if I don't fully know her my sister Amasa is here. Maybe by some miracle chance my parents will accept us and won't despise us in the palace.

The sun's rays shown through the blinds in the window and down onto us hours later. I squirmed and rolled over as I began to wake up.

Adeline woke up as well and crawled in my lap. I groaned and stood up from the bed holding her.

Alexander was still asleep sprawled out on the bed, I was glad he was choosing to stay asleep. I gently opened and closed the door as I left the room. Amasa was standing in the kitchen, multiple vines were springing from the ground doing various things. "What are you doing!?" I whispered. Adeline's half asleep body still resided in my arms.

"Um making breakfast," she said back in a normal tone of voice. I motioned my thinger up to my mouth to tell her to be quieter. "Oh, is your little lover boy asleep?" she asked in a whisper. I nodded my head yes in an annoyed tone with a snarled look on my face.

"How cute." she mumbled sarcastically as she used vines to pull a bread pan out of the small stone oven she had formed in the empty spot in the counter. It was smart of her to use her vines but it seemed lazy as well.

Her powers were very interesting, especially for someone like me who only can dream of things and weapon abilities. "What you're able to do is interesting Amasa," I admitted moving towards her and watching her hand movements. The way her fingers moved motioned certain vines to do specific things.

"I know it's impressive" she said with a smirk playing on her lips as she spoke. I rolled my eyes, I knew she ate up the compliments.

"So, Amasa, did you know mother at all?" I asked her in a quiet voice, I didn't want to upset her. Her smile fell a little bit but never fully faltered.

"Well I remember when I was around four years old, mother visited me once. She just looked at me, like I was some sort of monster. She asked my nannies if my other mushrooms could be removed, she was furious when they said no. I ran to her and hugged her, or at least I tried. I didn't understand anything, I didn't understand she didn't want me, I thought I was still in the castle then. She just shoved me away from her, it hurt. That's why I was always kind of jealous of you, I wished I was you. I wanted mom to love me." she said, getting quieter as she spoke. She looked down as she motioned the vines to set down the bread pan and threw a pod of water at the fire in the stone oven.

The smell of eggs and fresh bread moved through the house. Mother had never been fair to me, but never at the level she showed Amasa. "If it makes you feel any better, mother was never a mother to me. She rarely spoke to me once I was past my adolescence." I said, holding Adeline closer to me.

"Why would she have done that, you were her perfect child?" Amasa said, raising her eyebrow at me.

"Well, she's just not a good mother I suppose, she clearly didn't want to be a mom. I remember how she despised even having to put me to bed," I said, pasting on a smile looking up at Amasa.

"Well, make sure not to repeat it," she said, booping Adeline on the head with a vine. I snickered as Adeline flashed a smug snarl up at Amasa.

"I won't," I said quietly, looking down at my daughter in my arms.

I turned around as I heard the door to the small bedroom shut with force. Alexander stumbled out groggily towards us. He set his elbows on the counter and rested his chin in his hands. He still looked exhausted, as if he hadn't even slept. "Alexander? What has happened to you dear?" I asked, setting Adeline down. I moved aside the loose curls in front of his face and felt his forehead with the back of my hand to see if he was hot. He felt fine, not over temperature or anything.

"He's just tired from our lesson last night, show her what you learned Alex." Amasa interrupted, with a smirk. I didn't really like her calling him Alex but I'm sure I will get used to it.

Alexander groaned and stood up but still slightly hunched over. He motioned his hand up and a small vine rose through the cracks of the wooden floorboards. He then waved his hand and the thin vine did as well, he had a goofy tiered smile on as he did so as well.

He looked pitiful like that, it would never change the way I saw him though. "It's barely anything but he did good for only a few hours of practice. At least he has some-what of control now" Amasa said in an ecstatic way.

"He clearly didn't get enough sleep, Amasa." I said, frowning at her.

"Well that may be true but he will get used to it, controlling his magic will naturally drain his energy. He has to start somewhere as what the greatest mushrooms say," she said with a cocky smirk and planting her hands on her hips. I rolled my eyes and turned back to Alexander. He was more awake now, he still had big eyebags though.

An indistinct silence ran through the room for a few moments. "Well... Alexander, are you ready to go talk to the magical charlie figure?" Amasa said, folding her hands together excitedly.

"Absolutely not! He's exhausted" I said, putting my foot down to the idea. Amasa's face fell to an annoyed look.

"But Magdolin we need to get a move on before the kingdom finds us" Amasa said angrily.

"We will do that okay but he needs to rest!" I said, crossing my arms.

Alexander's hands found their way on my shoulder. "I'm alright to go mags, I just need a second is all" he said with a groggy voice. I frowned again but looked down at my feet where Adeline was pulling at my dress.

"Well that solves it! He's going!" Amasa said, snapping her fingers. With a swirl of colour and a flash, Alexander was given an orange colour cap. His black outfit was changed into brown slacks and a loose humble white tunic.

"Thanks" he mumbled under his breath. I was disappointed he was just letting her push him around like that after making him stay up late.

"You don't have to go, Alexander," I said, urging him to stay as I picked up a fussy Adeline off the floor.

"It's fine, just stay here with these two and I'll be back sooner than you know." he said cupping the side of my face. His hand was warm as he pressed a messy kiss on my forehead.

"I'll go instead" I said as he let go of my face.

"Absolutely not," he said, shaking his head.

"Hah nice joke, they catch you immediately no matter the disguise." Amasa added resting her elbow on my mushroom.

"Just stay here, I'll be back soon, I promise," Alexander said, grabbing my hand and squeezing it lightly. I hesitated before I let out a sigh.

"...Fine, just be careful please," I said looking up at him. I watched his tired eyes form a smile and he looked down at Adeline in my arms.

"Now you gotta stay and protect these two missy," he said, crouching down to Adeline's level.

"Bye bye Allie-zander," Adeline mumbled, waving her hand. Alexander nodded and headed towards the front door.

Part of me wanted to stop him and not let him go, at least not alone. But I know that's not an option, this needs to happen, at least maybe not now? As the door shut behind him I felt myself settle down slightly. The sound of horses' feet galloping down the road soothed me in a way, I trust him I know he can do this.

Chapter 32. Alexander Malencoy

Everything seemed dull right now, the morning birds chirping in the woods sounded annoying. Amasa forced me to work until I could get a single vine to do exactly what I motioned it to do. It exhausted me beyond a normal extent, I could barely crawl out of bed. My eyelids still feel heavy. Not only the lack of sleep, but using my powers drained me as well.

As I entered town I kept my head down to avoid any suspicion. Kingdom guards were placed at every single street without fail. I dropped my horse's speed to avoid any direct suspicion and made my way towards Charlie's back door to her shop. It felt like every guard was eyeing me down and that I'd be captured at any second.

Trying to fit in with the crowd around me I dropped myself off the horse and onto the street next to me. I swiftly pulled the horse into the alley with me and tied it to a pipe that was coming out of the side of the building next to us.

"What are you doing sir?" a strong voice demanded from behind me. I froze, completely encaged my fear and tiredness. I was an orange mushroom right now, I could just lie as I always did.

"Going to my sister's shop my good sir," I said lying through my teeth as I turned to face the guard. I kept a charming smile despite the tiredness of my entire body that ached for rest. As I saw the face of the guard I felt my heart drop suddenly. It was Raymond. He was going to turn me in for sure, probably just to impress Hope as well. Then he'd steal Magdolin! No that's too far Amasa would protect her, hopefully at least.

Raymond's face fell to a look of confusion and then went slightly pale. "You can't be here, you better have her on the escape island," he whispered in a harsh tone. The way he spoke to me infuriated me, who was he to tell me what to do.

"She's safe." I hissed back. I was too exhausted to deal with this joker.

"I'm being serious you peasant, if she's not safe i'll kill you." Raymond proclaimed pointing his finger at me. The way he could sound intimidating under his breath was uneaseing. He infuriated me with what he was saying. He acted all nice around Magdolin and now he's going to be cruel with me? The only reason he's a guard anyways is because of the accident, I'm sure they've enlisted every sage mushroom around. He abandoned Magdolin anyways, he's worse than me in every way.

"Like you have a whole lot of room to talk, you abandoned her. At least I'm not going to do that," I hissed, shoving him back from me.

"You better watch your back, the only reason I'm not reporting you is because of her. I care about her and I'm telling you don't screw anything else up you idiot." he said, backing away and back out towards the street.

He irked me so badly, I wanted him gone. Looking at it now I don't feel bad he's stuck with hope, they're clearly meant for each other.

I turned to go back to the door and slowly opened it. The whole shop looked abandoned. *Shit is she gone?* I wondered to myself as I quickly but quietly stepped inside. I looked around the small shop. All the glass ornaments still hung from the ceiling and her glass blowing tools were still in the workspace, but no sign of Charlie. "Charlie?" I whispered as to not gain much attention outside. I flipped around as I heard the sound of a glass object falling. Charlie stood holding a hammer over her shoulder in a defensive way. I sighed and let out a small laugh of relief. "Oh Charlie thank god, I need your h-" I said as she cut me off.

"You've got a lot of nerve showing up here. You could get me killed for being in affiliation with you." she said pointing the hammer at me.

"I'm in disguise Charlie, and I need your help please I know you can help," I said pushing the hammer to the side. I took note of how she wasn't in pants like normal. She had on a white tiered skirt that reached the tops of her ankle boots.

"No absolutely not, I've helped you your whole life. Whatever it is, no!" she said, shaking her head.

I was shocked she was acting like this, she'd never treated me like a monster like the others. She was supposed to be more like my sister. "... Charlie, what's going on? Why are you acting like this?" I said, stepping back to give her room.

"I had guards raid my shop! And then they shamed me for not being feminine... they almost claimed me of being a witch. I'm not risking anything again." she said angrily. She looked anxious and jumpy like she was scared to even move.

"Listen Charlie, I can fix all of this if you just do this one favour for me. I promise you that it will fix everything and you won't have to hide like this anymore." I said motioning around the store and then back to her dishevelled form.

She just glared at me for a few moments still holding the hammer in her fists tightly. She sighed before letting her guard down slightly. Her shoulders fell and the hammer fell down to rest beside her. "What is it you're wanting?" she asked through a glare. "And why do you look horrible?" she added crossing her arms.

I let out a sigh of relief, glad she'd hear me out now. "Well it's a very long story but basically what happened is I did what you said and asked Magdolin to marry me. And I was going to ask for you to find someone to marry us underground kind of," I said with pleading eyes as I looked at Charlie. She looked disappointed and raised an eyebrow.

"Really? No! The only thing you need to focus on is getting her out of the kingdom Alexander! Not marrying her!" she said, shaking her head.

"No no no listen Charlie we have a plan, once we are married we will be crowned king and queen and then we can change the kingdom, me and Magdolin will fix it!" I said folding my hands together in a pleading way.

"What if it doesn't work Alexander! It could end up worse!" she said, throwing out her arm.

"It won't, I promise! You just have to trust me." I said, trying to calm her down as I reached out for her.

"No Alexander …just no," she said, getting quieter. She crossed her arms and hugged herself. I can tell that something happened to her more than just guards raiding the shop. This has all affected her on a different level, but there's nothing more I can do. Surely I can figure something else out for me and Magdolin.

"I'll leave you be then Charlie. If you need me you know where to find me." I said with a frown and made my way towards the small back door. As I turned the handle I felt her grab the back of my shirt.

"I'll do what I can Alexander, I may have connections to find someone but I'm not making any promises." she said as I turned to face her. I felt an overwhelming amount of joy coursing through my body as she spoke. I kept on a small smile though, to not show how much this really meant to me.

"Thank you, Charlie," I said excitedly. She shook her head and cracked a small smile.

"You better get back to her, I don't wanna keep her waiting." Charlie said, ushering me out of the door. I nodded my head and ran out towards my horse where I left it. "And get some sleep you look like you need it." she yelled out at me from the back door of the shop. I threw a thumbs up at her as I took off on the horse. I forced the horse to take off in a sprint down the road and out of town. It did catch some of the guards' attention but I didn't care as long as I got back home.

I made the trip within five minutes, a new record for me I assume, which is great for my lack of energy. As I got off my horse and tied it off to the post by the side of the house I could tell no one was outside. That was a good thing, it's best for us to remain inside and away from any lurking eyes.

I drug my feet across the dirt of the path up to the house. I opened the door and Adeline automatically jumped up from where they had been playing a card game. Amasa had a handful of cards which she threw down in anger as Magdolin sat down her last card. That's when the exhaustion really hit me like a wall. Everything felt heavy, like a ton of bricks got laid on top of me. Adeline clawed at my leg whining to be picked up. She felt heavy as I picked her up even though she couldn't weigh more than thirty pounds.

"How'd it go?" Amasa said annoyed as she had just lost her game.

"Are you alright Alexander." Magdolin said in an urgent tone. I sat down against the wall and ground with a groan, Adeline crawled off my lap as I sat down.

"I got it sorted out," I said with a sigh as I rested my eyes shut.

"You did not answer my question," Magdolin said in a soft voice. I heard her footsteps move over beside me and scoot down the side of the wall next to me.

"I'm fine Mags, Charlie said she'd try to work something out." I said, opening my eyes slightly as she rested her head on my shoulder. I leaned my head against hers and sighed. It was a calming moment in the whirlwind of thoughts that were weighing down my whole body. My eyelids fluttered shut as my thoughts dulled down.

Chapter 33. Amasa Tessa

Watching alexander fall asleep on Magdolin made me want to gag, how could they be so utterly disgusting with each other. It might just be a love thing. The little one then did her small waddle over to me. "May I help you?" I said poking at her and speaking in a teasing tone. She laughed as I poked at her side. She was cute. I'll give her that, especially just for a pink mushroom.

I turned my attention back up to the other two. This Charlie girl they spoke of must be important. I've never read about her so she must be a new inspiration for all around. "So what is to happen now?" I asked Magdolin.

"We will wait, and we shall wait patiently Amasa. There is no rush at all," she responded blankly and gave me a cruel look.

"Well don't be upset with me, I'm just curious! And there's totally no rush whatsoever ever." I said in my defence even though it wasn't true.

"No, you're just wanting to get this over with," she said, calling me out on my untruthfulness.

"Well tell me you don't want this over without lying. We're trapped in this trashy house and can't leave. I feel like I'm back in my tower," I said in my defence. She just looked at me blankly.

"No I am fine with this, I'd be happy with anything as long as I have these two. It might be easier for yourself if you just try and enjoy it," she said sternly before looking back at Alexander.

I scoffed and walked out onto the porch. How could I enjoy this, being stuck with the three most cheery and annoying people. I think the little girl is the most tolerable out of all of them. As for a fact I could since she followed me. I flipped around and she was trying to be sneaky and follow me. "You're gonna get in trouble in the future for sure," I said, fighting off a smile.

She trailed up to me and just giggled as I talked. I didn't understand what was so funny I wasn't doing anything. "How can I do that with my voice?" she asked, grabbing at my dress.

"What do you mean?" I asked, looking down at her.

"You have a pretty voice, it sounds like a jester's," she said laughing.

I knew my voice was different but I never realised I sounded like a clown. "I'm not a jester little girl, I'm a powerful being," I said, proclaiming my identity. I wasn't going to be degraded by a three year old.

"I think you're silly," she said laughing. I couldn't believe the absurdity of this snot nosed little brat, I'm the most powerful mushroom around. "You should have a witch-stick if you're so powerful! I used to read about them." she added, acting like she had a wand.

"A wand? No thank you that's not my style kiddo," I said looking at the cuticles of my nails.

But then again maybe a wand would make it easier to harness my powers. I'm good at focusing it around myself but after those two are married I may not be able to handle it all. "Mabey a staff would be better for me?" I mumbled to myself.

"Yeah! A witch staff!" Adeline yelled out jumping up and down.

"I'm not a witch you brat" I said looking down at the ground.

There was a small patch of dirt in the yard of luscious grass. I closed my eyes and held my hand out. I focused my energy to form a grand stick with all sorts of glowing designs etched throughout it. The glowing lines and curves filled with stone, water, and vines. I opened my eyes as it fell from the air, I caught it and examined it. I've created many things before but something like this that could harness magic has never been made before. This could also make me keep my head straight and not make me go power crazy like my father.

"Wow! Can I see? "Adeline said, reaching for the staff. I picked her up by the back of her dress.

"Oh no! Sorry kid but you can't touch this. Your mom might kill me," I said, holding her in the crook of my elbow and side. I opened the door of the house and set Adeline down.

"Don't hold her like that Amasa! She's a kid!" Magdolin hissed at me.

"What is that!?" Alexander said wide eyed.

"Well it's nice to know you're awake now" I said, rolling my eyes.

"You didn't answer me," he said standing up. He was still clearly tired but was trying to just push it down.

"It's a magic stick!" Adeline cried out running to Alexander and Magdolin picked her up though.

"What is it?" Alexander said more confused now that she had added that detail.

"No it's a staff, and honestly it's to protect you all." I said leaning the staff against a wall.

"Mhm well i'm sure that it won't, keep that away from Adeline." Alexander responded looking at the staff.

"How did you make it?" he asked dumbly.

Clearly I didn't want to explain it to him, he can't even harness his own powers. "I don't know, I just did okay?" I said with a small scoff. I didn't want to have to explain this to any of them. I didn't want to be stuck here with these losers, I just wanted to be free and alone.

Throughout the rest of the day it consisted of Alexander failing trying to stay awake and Magdolin attempting to help him. I was stuck with the little one.

"Auntie Amasa what are we doing now?" Adeline asked, looking up at me.

"You really think of me as your aunt? By god I'm not even related to you by blood kid, but I'm not sure what we're doing. It is getting late so I presume that tomorrow will instill our future. Also about it getting late means it's your bedtime is it not?" I said looking down at the small child as we stood on the front deck of the house together. She just frowned at me as I told her it was her night night time.

"I'm not tired, auntie Amasa" she said clamouring at my legs. She'd always grab the fabric of my dress as if she was trying to climb me.

"Are you wanting to be held? Why do you try to climb me?" I said, reaching down and picking her up.

She nodded her head up and down, kicking her feet rhythmically with her head. "I don't understand children like you, so needy, but I presume I would've been the same way if I wasn't always alone back then." I said, holding her a little bit closer to me.

This girl was like me in a way, she didn't fit in with Magdolin or Alexander. But Alexander and Magdolin didn't really fit in with the kingdom's standards either, they were different colours. All different ranks, I'm a different rank from them all. It's all about the ranks.

Adeline buried her small head in my shoulder and closed her eyes. It felt like my heart skipped a beat, why am I acting like this? I'm not maternal whatsoever, I just guess I feel sympathetic for this child. She'll be like me in the palace, an outcast compared to the rest of the palace men. She's only a pink baby, she just doesn't understand she's around some of the most powerful mushrooms right now.

Her breath slowed down and she held my hair in her small fists. I can tell she was almost at least four but she acted younger, and she was much smaller than she should be. These are all signs of abuse prior to whenever Magdolin or Alexander found her, it's all a shame. She really is like me, I hope one day it will all be over for all outcasts like ourselves.

It's all up to those two now. I thought to myself as I looked in through the small circle window of the house at Alexander and Magdolin.

Chapter 34. Magdolin Poni

I picked up the plates that sat on the small ledge of a counter and put them in the underneath cabinet space. "You don't need to do that Mags I can," Alexander said with a small yawn as he walked beside me.

"Oh really I'm sure you could do that right now with how tired you are. I think you're about to time out for the day, are you not?" I said teasingly as I stood back up beside him. He just gave me a small smirk and rolled his eyes. "Don't roll your eyes at me, mister" I said playfully, pointing a finger at him. He just grabbed my hand and pulled me close to him. I gratefully fell into his embrace and wrapped my arms around his waist. I liked how he held my shoulder and the top of my mushroom at the same time with both of his hands. The way my hands brushed over each other when I hugged him. He is warm when I hug him and it makes me feel good to even be near him, especially to be this close to him.

I nestled my face next to his chest and collar bone and he gently rubbed my shoulder with his thumb. His chin rested on top of my mushroom, I loved how he felt comfortable to do that with me. His heartbeat was slow and calm and his lungs rose and fell gently. He let out a deep sigh and leaned back against the counter and wall still holding me tight. "I'm so glad you were able to tell me you loved me on that dance floor, you know that right princess?" he said, squeezing me gently in his arms.

"I am too Alexander, I don't regret much from that night. Besides you losing all of your things, your horses, your journal. I'm so sorry about those things, they can't be replaced..." I said with a frown.

He pulled my face back and gave me a frown back. "That stuff doesn't matter anymore, you were the prize I got at the price of those things. And it's a price I'd be willing to pay over and over again." he said with a soft sleepy smile.

It felt like my heart was melting as he spoke, I'd been wanting to hear those words from him. "I love you Alexander," I said, holding back some tears. I didn't want to cry, I wasn't sad whatsoever. I was happy, very happy, overjoyed. Right here in front of me was going to be my husband, this kind caring male. He's just been misunderstood his whole life, he's truly a gem that's been done wrong before.

"I love you more princess" he said in a soft voice looking down at me. His statement wasn't true, I clearly loved him more. I'd have to just give him this one though, he looked too cute tiered like this. I wanted to kiss him again, I wasn't sure if I should or not. Maybe he wouldn't like that again this soon.

"You make me feel like I'm in a love song, written by the most creative poets. My soul jumps within itself when I even think about you. There's not one cell in my body that makes me think you aren't the love of my life, my dear." I said brushing some curls from his face with my palm. His eyes were tired and soft as he had a smile plastered across his face.

He pulled my face to his by the back of my neck. His lips pressed to mine again, meeting in a beautiful unison. My eyes automatically shut as if I'd done this forever. I held his face in my cupped hands. The small stubble that always seemed to be on his cheeks pricked at the palms of my hands. His lips were still as soft as ever, he was a very respectful kisser. He didn't push into anything and was just simple and nice with it. This could be due to his tiredness but I adored it about him.

As he let me go again and looked back down at me I couldn't help but laugh and look down at my feet. My shoes were right between his own and his arms remained around my back not letting me go.

His head pressed against my own. I closed my eyes again as I leaned my forehead to his. I belonged here, no part of my mind thought I didn't. I needed to be here with him, forever and always.

A cracking sound interrupted the moment. I jumped slightly in shock. It sounded like trees cracking and bending. "Amasa and Adeline are out there," Alexander stated as he darted out towards the door. I felt my heart skip a beat as I followed him. He flung the door open and Amasa was standing there. She held Adeline's sleeping body across her chest and she had a panicked look.

The cracking sound was coming from in front of us in the woods. "What is that!?" Amasa whispered in a nervous tone. I threw my thinger over my mouth to shush her. Alexander stood in front of us with his arms out preventing us from coming forward.

A high pitched wail erupted from the wooded area. Alexander took a step back and I covered my ears from it. Adeline started to cry as the sound pierced all of our ears. Amasa held Adeline tight trying to calm her down.

It was the same scream from the creature inside the kingdom, from the first night I met Alexander. There's no way it could be the same creature though, maybe the same breed but not the same animal. I reached down for my dagger but it wasn't there. I forgot they took my dagger at the manor. There was nothing I could do, I am useless right now.

The huge long haired monstrosity crawled out of the woods screaming its horrific tune. The nasty smell of its oily hair filled the air. Alexander looked back at me wide eyed as if I had the answer. I just looked at him blankly, I had no idea of what to do. I knew that the animal was blind but had excellent hearing but that is it, and he knew that too.

I looked at Amasa who was also freaking out in her own way. She was our only way of defence, Alexander was beyond exhausted and didn't know how to use his powers. I took Adeline from her arms and pointed at the creature. She just looked at me nervously and her face went pale. I didn't understand why she went pale at first until I felt something wrap around my torso.

It was wet and slimy, the scent made me want to gag. I just held Adeline close to me to make sure I didn't drop her. Whatever it was yanked me hard, a squeak of pain and shock left my throat as I was pulled off the porch. Alexander yelled as I took off. As my head steadied and my hair fell from my face so I could see I was met by the sight of being suspended almost fifteen feet off the ground. Held by the tongue of the wretched beast above its disgusting fowl mouth. I kicked my feet and let out a yell as I realised the situation I was in. I held Adeline tight as she kept crying. I wanted to comfort her but I was crying myself.

On the back of the creature was a long gash, healed but recently tore. This was the same creature as before, has it been hunting me? A feeling of dread ran over me as I felt its tongue loosen around my waist, causing me to slip a little.

I couldn't do anything, nothing but fear consumed me. On top of it all, Adeline got drug into this. It would be fine if only I was eaten, but Adeline has a whole life ahead of her.

Amasa still looked frozen on the porch steps, but not looking at me or the beast. It seemed Alexander was gone as well. I just closed my eyes and accepted whatever was to come. There was no point in trying to scream and fight a mindless monster without any sort of defence or weapon.

"I'm sorry, Adeline," I murmured into her ear. This was my fault, I attacked the monster back then and now it's my time to pay. I think I'm happy with what I've had though, even if it's been merely a few weeks I've had the best hours in them. If I were to die from this I would die happy. It was poor Adeline who was paying, I should've just left her with Amasa. Alexander, Adeline, Charlie, even Amasa all mean so much to me. They've helped me and cared for me, they didn't turn from me and chose to assist me.

Something started happening though. The tongue that held me up in the air went limp. I felt my hair blow around me as I fell towards the ground. I clenched my eyes shut and held onto Adeline as if it would cost me my life.

Right before I hit the ground I felt something stop my fall. I uncurled from the ball I'd formed around Adeline, I was sitting in a pile of curled up vines with little flowers on it. Adeline held onto me shaking slightly, I held her tight and brought myself to my feet.

There stood Alexander, his hands were clenched and his arms were raised up as well. The green on his mushroom glowed brightly like an aura around him. Vines were entangled around the beast up-rooting from the ground.

"Alexander!" I yelled out. I was so scared for him, he couldn't keep up this fighting. He was tired and had almost no energy.

Amasa must have just now realised she should help. She jumped off the porch and up next to Alexander. She formed large rock spines and vines around the beast with her staff. With the entanglement of vines and stone around the creature it started to freak out. It tore from the vines and frantically ran back into the woods. Amasa let out a sigh and then a small laugh, she spun her staff around in a circle and planted it on the ground. She clearly was very flaunty with her abilities. "You did good, Alex, I'm surprised you had that in you!" she said, looking over her shoulder at Alexander.

Alexander's arms fell down to his sides and he fell backward, hitting the ground with a thud. "Alexander!" I yelled rushing over beside him. Adeline crawled out of my arms and onto the ground next to me.

"Well I should've expected that," Amasa added, looking down at Alexander.

I laid my ear to his chest and listened closely, he was alive and breathing. It was like he was just asleep, as if he just decided to take a nap. He was extremely exhausted though, so this probably took out everything he had in him. "Come on, let's get him inside Amasa" I said, trying to pick up his limp body with his arms.

He was very heavy and I couldn't really get him off the ground by a few inches. Amasa sighed and then used vines to pick him up off the ground. The way she'd maneuver the vines was elegant and smart. One would come up and another would retract back into the ground. Once inside the house she threw his body down onto the bed inside the single bedroom. "You couldn't have been more gentle with him?" I hissed in an angry whisper at her.

"Oh shush, he's perfectly fine. Just let him rest" she said without a care in the world about what just happened. Adeline crawled up on the bed besides Alexander and into his arms. She was clearly tired as well.

I sighed and walked beside both of them, placing a small kiss on their foreheads. Even if none of it was official, they were my family. "Come here, let them sleep," Amasa whispered. I listened to her and followed her out of the small room. The click of the door shutting brought a sense of relief through my body.

"I know you're worried about him but you need to just just trust him, this is all a part of the learning process I suppose," Amasa said sitting on the ground and crossing her legs.

"Learning process? Are you kidding me, this seems like torture for him!" I said, rubbing my eyes.

"Torture seems excessive to describe it by... I understand what you are saying though, you really care about him." she said with a pause.

I looked at her and crossed my arms. "Hah, so you think I'll believe you know how to care for someone?" I said sarcastically as I sat down beside her on my knees.

"Just because I'm not like you doesn't mean I don't have my own feelings," she said, placing a hand on her chest cockily. I rolled my eyes and looked at the empty fireplace.

A long silence screamed throughout the room. I felt Amasa look over at me a few times but she'd always quickly look away. "...what was mother like to you?" she asked in a quiet voice. Even when she tried to be quiet her voice was always clearly heard from how her voice sounded and doubled over each other.

"Mother wasn't the best, but she was better than my father so I'd always turn to her," I said with a small sigh.

"I think my dad was worse." she said with a small scoff as if she was joking.

"True, I think you win with the father issues," I said with a small smile. It was a weird feeling to think I had a half sister that I'd never known about till a few days ago.

"I'm sorry for all that happened to you Amasa, I don't think you deserved it" I said softly. I truly did feel awful for everything that my whole bloodline had done, to Amasa, the poison mushrooms, everyone really.

"I'm a freak, what would you expect them to do? It's not your fault Magdolin, really you are different from them and I'm glad you are but you can change what they've done." she said, talking with her hands as well.

"I will change it amasa I promise" I said with a small frown.

"You can try, I'll believe in you just as much as you believe in yourself," she said laying on her back and she formed a small bed out of vines and leaves. "Now I'm gonna get me some shuteye, m'lady. I'm sure your prince is awaiting you in your room with your little one!" she said, waving her hand around dramatically.

I rolled my eyes at her sarcastic attitude. "Goodnight Amasa," I said, hugging her as she had her eyes closed.

"What are you doing?" she said, opening her eyes and looking at me weirdly.

"Giving you something you've needed clearly," I said, hugging her tightly. She didn't fight against it or try to pull away, she just sat there. Her breath would hitch every few breaths, I took that as my cue to let her go after a few moments. "Sleep well Amasa" I said standing up and walking back to the bedroom.

"Thank you Maggie," she said quietly. Her voice was different this time, it sounded almost normal. I smiled and nodded to myself as I entered the bedroom quietly turning the door handle to not wake anyone up.

I crawled into the bed where Alexander and Adeline were both sprawled out on the bed. I laid next to Alexander, his arm wrapped around me pulling me close to him. I was truly happy with what I had right now. What more could I even ask for, I have the most important people around me.

Chapter 35. Alexander Malencoy

A cold splash flew over my body, I flung my head up forward and yelled. Amasa was giggling with Adeline in her arms, she had just thrown a pod of water at me. "What is wrong with you!?" I said waving my hands in the air.

"It's your wedding day! Wake up it is noon" Amasa said with a big smile spread across her face. I knew she was just excited to be freed, not the marriage.

"We're not getting a wedding, we're just going to get legally married, Amasa I thought you knew that." I said crawling out of the now soaked bed.

"Well about that, your not-so-magical Charlie friend arrived here and I spoke to her first! And I rearranged the plans based on what Adeline told me!" Amasa said loudly and excitedly.

"Oh that's just lovely, so Charlie's here?" I asked as I left the bedroom with Amasa and Adeline right behind me.

"Yes and she brought a weird church mushroom," she said with a happy tone of voice.

"Great, that's a priest," I said smiling. I looked around the empty house and there was no sign of anyone. "Where is everyone?" I added, looking at Amasa.

"Outside, actual Adeline, you're the wedding planner you get out there!" she said, setting Adeline down on the ground. Adeline giggled and ran out of the house, slamming the door behind herself.

"Magdolin's okay leaving the plans to Adeline?" I asked, rubbing my undereyes.

"Mhm, she has a very fairytale-like vision that I adore!" Amasa said snickering to herself.

Lovely I thought to myself. It didn't matter though, as long as I was marrying Magdolin I didn't care how it went down. She's the love of my life.

I opened the front door and walked outside, the sun beaming down on me as I stepped off the porch. The door clicked shut behind Amasa and we walked around the side of the house.

Along the lake said there was an old male, Charlie, and Magdolin all talking together. I started to walk towards them but Amasa stopped me as the priest made his way towards me instead. "I know you want to go speak to your bride but according to all of the books I've read on weddings, the groom isn't supposed to see the bride right away," Amasa said, grabbing my shoulder.

"Oh god, why do we have to go all out like this Amasa. I'd just like to marry my wife." I said, crossing my arms.

"Not wife quiet yet, son," the priest said, setting a hand on my other shoulder.

"I'll leave you two to do this!" Amasa said, giving us a thumbs up and going back around the house.

I didn't know what this guy was trying to tell me about but I didn't really care, I know my feelings for Magdolin. I don't need a priest to confirm them for me, my love for her is strong.

The priest wore a long black robe with some gold details along its seams. He had on a weird hat on his mushroom as well, I never fully understood some religious traditions.

"So I've heard your story from a few different perspectives, you're in a lot of trouble, boy. Luckily for you I think I'm on your side, I like your motives, and I like the choices you've made so far," the priest said, sitting down on the edge of the porch. He patted the board next to him to have me sit down beside him.

I sat down next to the old preacher with a small grunt. "So what do you think? Do you want to marry Miss Magdolin? She's a fine young lady." he said with a smile and holding his bible on his lap.

"Yes of course I want to marry Magdolin, it's all I'd ever want to do with her," I said looking down at my shoes.

"I know that's what you want to do but are you willing to risk your life for her?" the priest said, folding his hands over his bible.

"Yes, without question," I said, crossing my arms on my knees and leaning on them. I know I was making it obvious I was annoyed by all of this but it was all idiotic.

"I know that this is very irritating to you Alexander but it's all needed to be said okay?... with you agreeing to take Magdolin as your wife, you're also taking in Adeline Poni, is that understood?" he said flipping through his bible.

I nodded my head, I loved Adeline almost as much as I did Magdolin, she was like my daughter already. "You will protect and be by their side no matter what? Including illness, spiritual struggles, or any other kind of problem or situation?" he said searching down a page of verses.

"I will devote my entire life if it means protecting them." I said looking up at the preacher's face.

He nodded his head and looked down at the bible in his hand "proverbs eighteen twenty two, he who finds a wife finds a good thing and a favour within the lord. If you are to accept Magdolin and marry her, you shall be favoured by the lord, son." the preacher said with a wide smile.

"I will sir, I will be favoured by your lord because I'm going to marry her." I said with a smile. I liked the feeling I was doing the right thing, and I am doing the right thing absolutely.

"Aha see this is why I like your spirit son, you are smart and confident! Just don't let that pride get to you," the priest said excitedly. He clearly got a kick out of the outlawed and sinful marriage.

"I won't sir, I'll be the best husband I can," I said standing up and offering the preacher a hand. The old male took my hand and stood up laughing.

"Haha now where's that weird lady?" the preacher said as he started walking around the house. I liked this old geezer, he seemed like he was just out for an adventure.

"Amasa should be around the house," I said, leading him back around the house. Charlie came darting around the house and laughing and smiling.

"Alexander, I can't believe you're actually doing this!" she said with her hands out open. The priest continued around the house on his own as I stayed with Charlie.

"I told you I was gonna do it, now we're just here," I said, shrugging my shoulders.

"You didn't tell me you guys got a kid either, she's so cute. All morning she's been running around telling us how to put things up and how we were gonna do this for her momma," she said smiling.

She was clearly back to her old self now that she was out of that monitored town. "I'm glad you feel better Charlie, and I'm glad you like adeline. I'm also glad you're here, thank you for getting us a priest. Things are going to change today for the best, for everyone." I said, smiling ear to ear. Everyone I needed was right here with me.

"I'm glad you're doing this for the better, and because you and Magdolin are adorable. But you can't just run off to some palace and just forget me okay? Amasa should be over in a minute to get you 'suited'" she said with a softer, more calm smile.

"Of course I'm not gonna forget you, you'll be lucky if I don't force you to move your store to where it's in the palace corridors," I said, acting uptight and acting like I was adjusting my collar.

"No getting uptight either you brat" she said punching my shoulder.

"Fine, fine I'll try at least." I said, mocking her.

Amasa came prancing around the corner skipping happily. "Alexander Mr. Groom! It's your turn!" she yelled pointing her staff at me.

"Wow watch where you point that thing crazy lady," Charlie said, putting her hands up playfully.

"I'm the crazy one? Alexander lied to me and said you were magical, I think he's the crazy male," Amasa said, planting her staff on the ground.

"You said I'm magic?" Charlie said, looking at me with an eyebrow raised.

"No I did not... it's a long story-" I said as Amasa cut me off.

"Well anyways we've got plans, Alexander, what do you wish to wear. I was thinking of a plain black and green suit, who could go wrong with that," Amasa said, snapping her fingers. The familiar colours of

Amasa's magic swirled around me, forming new clothes around me. The suit was perfect and fit nicely.

"Thanks amasa" I said looking at myself. I straightened out the cuffs of the jacket of the suit.

"You look what Adeline would call handsome." Amasa said with a proud smile.

"Yeah I have to admit that the tall ladies magic really is something else isn't it." Charlie added nudging Amasa's side.

"Aha it is pretty impressive if I do say so myself" Amasa said with a sly snicker to herself.

I peered around the corner of the house, hoping to see Magdolin but she wasn't in sight. "Ah ah ah no sir, no spying and stalking for Magdolin." Charlie said, yanking me back by the collar of my shirt.

"I don't know why we are having to follow this traditional agenda, Magdolin and I wanted something small" I said with a sigh. I appreciate how much they all wanted to do with this but it was a lot. This day was already really rushed and going faster than I would've liked. I wish Magdolin and I could just take our time with things like this, but it is for the best. Plus it will just be us in the palace, no one bugging us. *Well not totally, I'll have responsibilities.* Oh god I almost forgot about that, I'm going to be the king.

I felt my heart start to beat fast and I was breathing out of pace. I felt sweaty and hot as I tried to control my heart rate. I grasped my chest as it got out of hand. I feel like I should be overjoyed, I was getting married after all. I'd be king as well, I'd be in charge. I should be happy, crying with happiness. I'm here panicking though, why am I freaking out.

"Alexander, are you alright?" Amasa's voice said faintly.

"...yeah yeah i'm fine, i'm just thinkin'," I said crossing my arms.

I looked back at the two of them and they were both shooting me with a worried look. I sighed and then forced on a small smile. "Do I look fine?" I asked nervously trying to avoid the other problems at hand. Charlie rolled her eyes and scoffed, Amasa nodded her head and gave a thumbs up.

"So are you ready son?" I heard the old preacher's voice say from behind me.

"Oh yes!" I said excitedly, flipping around to face the preacher. I wanted to just get this ceremony over with so I could call her my wife officially.

"Let's go then son" he said, holding his arm out to mine. I took his arm and walked beside him. He had a slight hobble in his step and walked slower than a normal older male.

"Don't be afraid child, the lord is watching over you right at this moment" he said as we approached a small rock platform that Amasa had clearly formed. I knew that the preacher could feel my arms shaking slightly and that's why he mentioned that. I wasn't fully listening to him and just nodded my head. The one thing that was on my mind was Magdolin. I wanted to just see her.

I stepped up onto the rock platform and helped the preacher up as well. "So what now?" I asked as he straightened out his robe and hat.

"We wait," he said with a big smile as he flipped through his bible. I looked down at my feet, my black leather shoes tied perfectly. I rocked back and forth from my heel to toe trying to remain calm. I knew the second Magdolin came out my heart would melt. I could just feel it within me how beautiful she'd be, somehow more beautiful than she already was.

After a few minutes which felt like hours Amasa and Charlie walked from around the house. Amasa wore her regular dress she always seemed to choose. Charlie wore an orange button up blouse that complimented her hair nicely and a pair of black slacks. I was glad she had gotten over whatever happened to her back in the village, she seemed free to herself again. Although Amasa stood proudly and confident I could tell a part of her was worried this wouldn't work to free her. I can't predict if her being completely free is the right decision but the only thing deciding that is me loving Magdolin. And I will always love Magdolin, ever since I laid my eyes on her. I knew I couldn't ever leave her alone again. I made the best decision by deciding to help her throughout the kingdom after I found out she was the princess. Now she's the princess of my heart, unlike before. I used to hate the royal bloodline, it's ironic that she's my soulmate. I'd never want to change that though, she's the only princess I'll ever love again.

Adeline came prancing out of the woods with a big smile. She clutched a small wicker basket in her hands from which she tossed small flowers. She had on a big poofy white and pink dress which was bigger than she was herself and drug behind her. I felt a small chuckle escape my throat as she messily threw the flowers in her path.

I felt my face get hot as my mind kept telling me Magdolin was about to come out. I found myself taking deep breaths and trying to contain my smile as Adeline reached Amasa and Amasa pulled her to the side. I looked down at my feet again trying to hold back my excitement, it felt like my heart was going to stop from how hard it was pounding in my chest. I heard a gasp come from Charlie but it felt like I was frozen. "Oh I know I told her to be more flashy but she's gorgeous in something simple," I overheard Amasa whisper to herself.

"You look so pretty momma" I heard Adeline say with a happy shriek to her voice.

I was frozen, I was scared to look up at her. I knew she'd be drop dead gorgeous but what if she changed her mind last minute? What if she decided this was a mistake? I couldn't bring myself to bring my head up at all. I heard the sound of fabric rustling and the clicks of heels across the stone platform. My eyes shut with force and it felt like I was holding my breath.

I felt small, delicate, gloved hands pull my hands apart from their folded state. She held my hands in her own, I could hear a small laugh coming from her as well. "Alexander, open your eyes." she said with the most cheerful tone I'd ever heard out of her before.

I did as she said to do and opened my eyes. I didn't dare look up though. I could see in my hands were her hands with white gloves with an ivory lace trim on the wrist. Below them was the white fabric of her dress in front of me. I could see small lace details and embroidery laced into the fabric. I wanted to look up and see her soft beautiful face but I was still horrified. "Do I have to move your eyes for you too dear?" she said sarcastically and cheerfully. I watched her hands move up to my face and pick it up slightly.

It felt like my heart stopped beating as my vision moved from our feet up to her face. She was smiling brightly with that intoxicating lipstick she wore occasionally. A smokey eye chill lined her eyes. I'd never seen her with makeup on, I loved it. Her hair was pushed back and waved over her exposed shoulders. Her dress was very simple and humble. With sleeves that wrapped around her chest and shoulders with little embroidery designs. A white veil of fabric was secured to the front of her mushroom. Not even the sheer of white fabric could hide her beauty.

My jaw fell slightly agape, just seeing her like this was an astonishment. She was more beautiful than I could've ever imagined. "...You look magnificent mags," I mumbled under my breath looking at her dumbly. I probably looked like a small boy in the sight of a goddess. She laughed under her breath and shook her head.

"My, these two are just meant to be together, I can see it in their eyes." the priest said, interrupting the moment. "May I begin?" he added. I nodded my head in sync with Magdolin as he moved Magdolin's hand in mine.

"In Genesis two twenty three it quotes 'husband and wife become one in the bond of marriage'. Marriage is something that is a gift from the lord and is something to be cherished. These two today wish to be joined in the holy matrimony of marriage. I am the one here who shall join them. I would make this speech much longer and go on for hours if I wanted but I will hurry this as you have all requested." the preacher said, looking up and down from his small bible.

I gently rubbed Magdolin's thin thingers and stared at her face as the preacher spoke. I may not care about all of the holy matrimony talk but I didn't mind it because I had my Magdolin. My perfect, sweet Magdolin.

I spaced out a lot of what the priest said as he rambled on talking. I held all my respects up to the preacher, but I just couldn't get my mind off of her. I was snapped out of my little transfection on her as the preacher said my name.

"Alexander Malencoy, do you hereby take Magdolin Poni as your lawfully wedded wife?" the male said, looking at me.

Without even a second to spare I answer smiling. "Yes, I do," I said looking back down at Magdolin.

"And do you Magdolin Poni take Alexander Malencoy as your lawfully wedded husband?" he asked, looking down at Magdolin. "I do," she said quietly while smiling.

"Lovely, now may I have the rings please?" he asked, looking up at Charlie. Charlie stood up and made her way up to the rock platform, but not stepping up on it to show respect. She pulled out the two boxes which contained the rings. "I made these especially for you two," she whispered as she bowed her head and handed them to us.

I looked at the ring box I was handed which held Magdolin's rings. The wedding band was gold with small carvings of flowers and two swords which pointed to three gems. The middle gem was green and the two besides it were a beautiful shade of lavender purple. The engagement ring was the same one I carried with me for weeks and proposed to Magdolin with, it still shone brightly. I reached out to hold Magdolin's left hand which she held out gracefully. I gently pulled off the small glove that covered her hand.

I took the small wedding band out of the box and slid it over her thin ring finger, and then followed it with the engagement ring. The rings were so beautiful on her. Even their beauty couldn't compare to her own though, they just complimented her.

She then took my left hand and slid my ring on my ring finger. It adjusted down to size on its own like the other rings had done for Magdolin. I smiled looking down at my ring. It had our initials engraved next to a green gem and a lavender gem. It was a simple ring and it's all I would've ever wanted.

"That precious isn't it, the rings are gorgeous. But I'll make this quick for you all. Miss Magdolin?" the preacher asked, looking at the bible and then at Magdolin.

"Yes?" she asked, looking at the old priest.

"Do you accept taking this male's last name and becoming Magdolin Malencoy? By doing this you will devote your life to this male and promise to be by his side for life, do you understand?" he said, looking at Magdolin with a stern look.

"I accept," she said, looking back up at me.

"And do you Alexander take Magdolin Malencoy as your wife. By this you will promise to always be understanding and cari-" he started to say before I cut him off.

"Yes I do, I accept" I said rushed. I was too excited, I just wanted this to be official now,I needed it to be.

"Okay well I see you're ready for this son." the preacher said with a small laugh. "You may kiss your bride," he said laughing as he snapped his little bible together.

I let out a gasp as I moved Magdolin's veil over her mushroom to reveal her face to me. My body was practically shaking as I looked down at her. Her smile was toxic, it filled my whole body with adrenaline and oxytocin.

I closed my eyes and crashed my lips down onto hers. I didn't want to be so aggressive with it but I was just so exhilarated I couldn't control myself at all. A small giggle escaped her lips as I pulled away from the kiss for a moment. I laughed a tiny bit myself before grabbing her and scooping her up by her waist. I kissed her again, my lips moving in rhythm with hers. Her lips were so sweet like honey, or a smooth sugary candy.

A sharp wind flew around us and a gasp and hardy laugh came from the preacher. Adelines thrilled shrieks of laughter yelled happily as she clapped her hands. I set her back down before pulling away from the kiss. As I opened my eyes I realised something major had changed.

I was now not only a married male and a king, but my mushroom was gone. Magdolins was also gone, instead a beautiful detailed tiara styled crown with purple encrusted gems around it sitting on her blonde hair. "Your mushroom," she mumbled looking up at me.

"Yours is gone too Mags" I said not caring. She smiled and shook her head.

"Not Mags anymore mister Malencoy, it misses Malencoy." she said, stepping closer to me and tapping my nose.

"Ah not just that misses Malencoy, you're a queen now." I said, tapping her nose in return.

"Momma, dada!" Adeline yelled happily jumping up on the rock and running up to us. A small tiara was sitting on top of her mushroom. I laughed and picked her up as she ran to us.

"Ah look at the little princess dear" I said, bouncing Adeline gently in my arms.

"We are the kings and queens now!" Adeline said happily shouting and giggling. She waved her arms around and kicked her feet as I held her. I couldn't help but just smile at everything at this moment, I felt happier than I'd ever been before.

I looked over at Charlie and Amasa. Charlie was holding Amasa firmly. Amasa looked close to passing out and was holding onto her staff tightly. "Amasa!" Magdolin said, rushing to her side.

I set Adeline down and followed Mags, picking up the tail of her dress as she ran. Amasa was breathing hard and her hair had glowing strands within it. Four depictions formed on her forearms. Fire, water, plants, and a sword, all began to indent into her skin, branding her in a way. She grunted as it all stopped. Her hair stopped glowing and she opened her eyes. "What was that!?" Charlie said, grabbing Amasa around her shoulder.

"Something good," Amasa said, looking over at me and Magdolin before letting out a quiet gruff laugh. "You guys look good in crowns," she added, laughing louder as she stood up on her own.

I rolled my eyes at her comment and sighed. "Are you alright Amasa?" Magdolin said, still not convinced.

"Yes I'm fine I can assure you, but now that this is done I'm sorry to ruin your honeymoon or whatever, but we need to get a move on. I'm sure the whole kingdom is in distress now that their king and queen have been de-crowned. We need to get you guys to the palace immediately." Amasa said, fixing out her sleeves on her dress again. Charlie nodded her head in agreement.

"I agree with your funny looking friend here, and when you get to that palace fix things for us all out past the palace walls my king and queen." the priest said, coming around us and in front of us.

"We will, I promise you all that. And Thank you sir," I said, nodding my head down at the priest.

"Thank you too Charlie," Magdolin added, hugging Charlie. Charlie hugged her back gratefully.

"It's no problem 'my queen' now I can say I've had the honour to hug a royal" Charlie said sarchasitcly bowing before us.

"Oh stop it Charlie, Adeline? Come here baby doll we've got to get going," Magdolin said, turning and waving adeline over off the rock platform.

We made our way around the house, Charlie and the priest left on their horses they rode here and made their way back towards town. "Are you both ready to go?" Amasa asked as she hoisted herself up on one of the horses.

"I believe so," Magdolin said, walking towards the horse where Amasa was. Amasa stuck her hand out stopping her.

"Ah ah ah, I want to ride the horse with my niece," she said, crossing her arms after securing her staff to the horse's saddle. Magdolin rolled her eyes. "Oh and that was a trick question, just because you roll up to the palace in crowns doesn't mean they will accept you as a king and queen. You must look the part too!" Amasa added before snapping her fingers.

Amasa herself was then in a tailcoat suit that was embroidered finely. She looked at me and then snapped her fingers again. A green flash ran around me and I was in a tailcoat suit as well. It was much nicer as well with a black velvet cape draping across me and grazing the ground.

She snapped her fingers again and Magdolin was put in a corseted square neckline dress. "Oh god I haven't had to wear a corset in ages." she grunted stabeling herself as she stood.

I brought my hand around her shoulder to help her stand straight and prevent her from falling. "Lovely! Let's get a move on then," Amasa said, picking Adeline up with a vine and setting her on the horse with herself.

I sighed and lifted Magdolin up on the horse we were going to ride on. "Thank you dear," she said smiling as she adjusted herself sideways on the horse.

"Of course," I said, pulling myself up on the horse. As I got adjusted I took the reins of the horse in one hand and held Magdolin loosely in my other arm.

"Alright, no time to waste!" Amasa said holding her own reigns with Adeline sitting in front of her. I watched her whip the reins of her horse and it took off in a trot.

"No time to waste!" Adeline yelled while throwing her hands up. I felt a laugh escape my throat and guided my horse to walk beside Amasa's horse.

After about an hour of riding the horses we arrived in a small town. As we started to pass by people, their stares didn't leave us. Guards still stood at every street like when I came to retrieve Charlie. I watched them all look at us and go wide eyed.

Magdolin kept her head high and eyes midway, just how she'd been trained as a child. I didn't let the 'king role' take over me and just rode as I had always done. The banter within the town had stopped and went silent. The only thing you could hear was the trotting or the two horses we rode.

The knights begin bowing their heads and bringing a fist over their hearts. I was shocked they'd do this, I would've supposed an uprising or overthrow. It seemed like the opposite was in store, I felt a smile spread across my face. "I think they're happy their princess has returned," I whispered into Magdolin's ear. She flashed me a small smile and shook her head.

As we made our way through the rest of the town I saw a familiar face, Raymond was there again. He was still on the street near Charlie's store, and standing next to him was Hope. Her face was of anger and shock. Raymond was also shocked. Part of me wanted to get off the horse and rub it in both of their faces, but I couldn't. I kept my head held high and kept my horse moving.

"How did you do this!?" Hope yelled as we passed by them. I ignored her and kept the horse moving. I heard the heels of her boots click against the brick road in a rushed movement. "Answer me right now Alexander!" she screamed, grabbing at my cape that I was wearing. I yanked the fabric from her hands and turned to look at her.

Raymond ran out in the street after her grabbing her and pulling her back to the side street. "Why are you all bowing to him, he's a poison mushroom! He's a monster!" she yelled angrily fighting against Raymond's hold as she saw everyone bowing their heads.

"That's your king now, don't speak such filth in his presence," a mushroom next to her said, shaming her. I had to contain my laughter, it was hilarious to see her getting humbled.

I turned my back to them and continued, I'd prefer to never have to deal with hope ever again. She can throw her petty little fit by herself or with her new male toy.

Chapter 36. Magdolin Malencoy

After hours of riding on the horses and going through many towns and dealing with some angry mushrooms occasionally, we ended up just a few miles outside of the palace city. The sun was setting and Adeline had already fallen asleep on Amasa. We entered a small village with small houses scattered around here and there.

"Did you have a safe house around here, it's going to be dark soon?" I said, looking at Alexander. He shook his head with a small frown, I sighed. I knew we needed to find a place to rest, Adeline would be fussy and we'd be at the palace in the night.

"What do you suggest dear?" Alexander asked with a small yawn. I thought for a few moments, watching all the small houses pass by. I'd feel horrible to ask some small family in a shack to let us stay there. As we got further into the small village I saw a bigger brick building, it was clearly a leader's house. A town leader maybe? Maybe just a rich mushroom.

"I think we should stop there, I'll go to the door," I said, taking the reins from Alexander.

"Are you sure about this?" he said, grabbing the horn of the saddle as I kicked the horse and jerked forward.

"I'm confident" I said as I pulled the horse up to the end of the road by the larger home. Amasa followed behind as I got off of my horse. I picked up the front of my dress and made my way up to the large wood door of the house. I looked back at Alexander and the others before knocking on the door.

After a few moments of patiently waiting a child came to the door. He was a small golden mushroom and just looked up at me wide eyed.

"H-hello little boy, are your parents home by chance?" I asked politely as I bent down to his height.

He just kept staring at me, flashing his sight up from my eyes to my crown every few seconds. "Are you a queen?" he asked cocking his head to the side.

"Well yes I am technically," I said with a smile. His jaw fell dramatically, I loved how unserious kids could be.

"Ma! Pa! There's a queen here!" the boy said yelling into the house. I laughed and stood back up, folding my hands together in front of me.

The sound of heavy footsteps came from across the house and towards the door. "Ryder if I catch you lyin' again I'm gonna make you clean out the hog pins." said a husky voice with a country twang to it.

Once the male came into frame behind ryder. He was a tall mushroom in a loose brown shirt and suspenders holding up his pants. A cigar stuck out of his mouth in between his teeth. "See I told you pa, it's a queen," ryder said, holding his hands out to point at me.

"Huh, well look at that. Whaddya need." he said rubbing the stubble on his face.

"Well my good sir, my sister, daughter, and husband need a place to stay tonight. I was hoping you could be gracious enough to spare us a place to stay?" I said politely and quietly.

He looked up from me and over at the horses where my family sat. "Well… is it true your husband's poison mushrooms your highness?" he said with a gruff sound to his voice. He dropped his cigar in an ashtray next to him and put his hands on his hips. Ryder still was just staring up at me.

"Yes he is but I can assure you that what you've been told is lies. He's the nicest male yo-," I started to say but the male cut me off again.

Ah ah ah no I know darlin' my family knows the truth, I'm assuming you've learned the actual truth?" he said, waving his hand to shush me.

"Yes I know now" I said with a slight nod of my head.

"Great, well I'm proud of you to be honest. I'm glad the throne is going back to who it belongs to. My name's Arthur, Ryder here will take your horses around the back for you guys to the stables," he said with a smile spreading across his face.

I let out a sigh as he agreed to let us stay. "Thank you so much sir, this really is great of you," I said, thanking him.

I turned and walked back down to Alexander and Amasa. "What did they say?" Amasa asked impatiently.

"We're staying here," I said, taking Adeline's limp sleeping body from her.

"Well I knew we'd be here anyways Amasa. Mags here has a charm to her," Alexander said, smirking down at me as he got off his horse. I rolled my eyes at his comment before I was interrupted.

"Wow! You're a tall lady!" I heard Ryder's voice yell out. I turned around to see him standing in front of Amasa.

"Whose kid is this?" Amasa asked, annoyed as she crossed her arms.

"How do you do that with your voice!?" he asked urgently. Alexander started laughing loudly as the young boy asked Amasa tons of questions.

The boy turned quickly as he heard Alexander's laughs, "are you the king!" he asked, rushing over beside me and Alexander.

"Yeah I am, who are you?" Alexander said, looking down at Ryder.

"I'm ryder! I'm six and a half!" he said, holding his hand out to shake Alexander's. Alexander paused for a moment and then shook the boy's hand.

"Pa told me to take your guys' horsies, go on inside," the boy said as he gathered the reins to the horses. I looked over at Alexander who was just staring at his hand.

"Are you alright Alexander?" I asked, putting my hand on his back.

"Yeah... it's just no one's ever offered to even shake my hand before while im openly a poison mushroom and... not in disguise," he said, letting his hand fall to his side.

I sighed and kissed his cheek while rubbing his back. "It's okay, that's going to change," I whispered to him. Adeline started to whine as I held her to my chest.

"Well you better get Miss Fussy to bed, I'm gonna go help that kid with the horses," Alexander said, kissing Adeline on her mushroom and jogging off to catch up with Ryder.

I shook my head and then walked up to the house holding Adeline. Amasa followed behind me and another child opened the door for us. This one was a smaller girl, close to Adeline's age. "Thank you, what's your name?" I asked, walking into the house.

"I'm Betty," the little girl said shyly.

Amasa walked in looking around suspiciously. "Are you sure we can trust these people, do you not think it's weird that gold mushrooms are farmers? They could be criminals of some sort." she whispered in my ear.

"Amasa calm down, we're gonna be fine" I said, slapping her with the back of my hand gently. She scoffed and rolled her eyes like an emotional teenager.

"Arthur, are you kidding me, we don't have enough rooms for them!" I heard a female's voice say impatiently.

"Martha, yes we do, they are staying here," Arthur's voice said sternly. I heard footsteps leaving the kitchen area and out to where Amasa and I were. It was the Martha lady. She was my height and wore a simple dress that fell to her ankles.

"Oh, hello your majesty," she said, bowing her head.

"I'm sorry we are a burden to you ma'am" I said quietly. She looked up and frowned at me. "Oh no your majesty your not I promise, I shouldn't have said that in there. I'm sorry you overheard," she mumbled her apology. It stayed quiet for a moment, a very awkward moment.

"Ma, I'm tired," Betty said, pulling at her mother's dress.

"Well um… queen Poni, Betty here has a bunk bed, could your little one stay in Betty's room?" she said, trying to make up for what she said.

I looked down at Adeline in my arms, she was half awake. "I think that would be perfect, and its Malencoy." I said, setting Adeline on the ground with a small smile.

She let out a small whine and looked up at me, I could tell she was about to have a fit. "You're going to go with Betty here, Adeline. Be a big girl about this babydoll," I said brushing her hair out of her face. She gave me a big puppy dog face and stuck her lip.

"You can come with me, I'll be your friend," Betty said, trying to hold Adeline's hand. Adeline held her doll's in her other hand as she walked off with Betty upstairs.

I was glad the girl wanted to make Adeline her friend but part of me feared Adeline was going to be too shy. She'd never really been shy before, but then again I've never seen her really interact with other kids around her age. She may also just be tired, I'm sure she'll be fine, that Betty looked nice.

Alexander and Ryder bursted into the house through the front door laughing. Everyone flung their head around to look at the two of them. I had to hold back my own smile, I liked seeing Alexander like that, he looked so happy. "Pa, these guys are funny!" Ryder said laughing and running to Arthur.

"That's great son," Arthur said looking at his son and then up at Alexander.

Amasa sat down on one of the couches by an old fireplace in the house. I gave her a look which clearly indicated to her to stop acting so impolite. "No she's fine, please you two have a seat too," Martha said, ushering us to sit down.

"Thank you," Alexander said, sitting down as well. He patted the spot beside him for me to sit as well. I sighed and then sat down next to him. Martha and Arthur sat down on the couch opposite to Alexander and I.

"So what's the deal with you guys, why are you farmers?" Amasa said, crossing her arms and legs.

"Amasa tessa you better act nicely," I said sitting up slightly looking over at her. I couldn't believe her audacity.

"Well it's a long story, but basically I didn't like this uptight prissy life like the other gold mushrooms. So I decided to do this line of work, my eldest son didnt like it though so he left," explained with a frown.

Amasa didn't seem very pleased with that answer. She took a breath and opened her mouth, about to probably go on a rant to the mushroom. "Ya know I could bombard you with endless questions too. You seem very interestin'," Arthur said, interrupting her. Amasa scoffed and leaned more into her seat, clearly not happy.

The silence was killing me. I hated the pressure in the room. "Well what happened with your eldest son if you don't mind me asking?" I asked, interrupting the silence.

Martha laughed to herself and looked at Arthur to talk. "Well my oldest, he was a brat, Antonio decided that he was too good for living on a farm. He didn't have anywhere to go so he just ended up living in the attic for years, but then his dream came true. Your father Hector Poni came to our door looking for a gold mushroom to suit his daughter," he said pointing at me.

I felt my face fall to confusion. *Could that be the arranged marriage that my dad wanted me to get into?*

"And then he rambled on about how Antonio was perfect for this because he was instilled with a work ethic from being raised on a farm, and he was a gold. The kid wasn't worth anything work-wise though, he just sat upstairs while we worked our butts off, "Arthur said shaking his head.

"Where is Antonio now that I've been gone from the palace?" I asked, raising an eyebrow.

"Well about that, he's still at your palace. While you were gone your parents started to discuss HIM being the new king even if you weren't the queen," he said with a hearty laugh ending it off.

I felt my jaw drop slightly, I couldn't believe it at all. *What about the other suitor my father picked? What happened to him?*

"That's just sad," Alexander said looking up from where Ryder was showing Alexander all of his small wooden toys.

"We know, this kingdom would have fallen apart if you guys wouldn't have returned," Martha said, setting a hand over her heart. She was right, if anything that I had changed or went differently, it would have caused all of these people to suffer. Even if I stayed in the castle Alexander and all poison mushrooms would still be in the dark. Amasa would still be trapped and I would be stuck with some lazy gold mushroom.

"I'm so glad I left the palace now," I murmured to myself.

Martha and Arthur laughed at my comment, Amasa rolled her eyes. "Hey I am too," Alexander said, resting his hand on my lower back.

That only encouraged them to laugh more, Ryder also had a child-like laugh that rang through the room. "So how did you two meet?" I just said nervously. I hadn't even meant for anyone to hear me.

"Oh arranged, but we got along well and were happy," Martha said, waving her hand.

"Oh that's sweet," I said smiling. It was amazing that even though they were arranged they still loved each other.

"How about you two? I'm curious to know?" Martha asked, leaning her face in her hand. "This old town doesnt have enough going on to keep me entertained."

"Well, my maid found me a male who would sneak me out of the kingdom, to escape from my responsibilities," I said looking down at my nail beds.

"I was that male! And then she just drug me in by my collar with her charm." Alexander said proudly interrupting me. I smiled at him, I loved it when he was bright and happy like this.

"Aw how adorable, well im glad thats worked out for you," Arthur said in a gravely county accent. I turned my head to watch Ryder show Alexander all of the toys that were in a box on the floor.

A loud bang came from upstairs with the noises of things rolling across the floor. "Oh that came from Betty's room," Martha said, standing up and heading up the stairs.

"Oh that girls always got somethin' to make a mess of," Arthur said with a groan as he stood up and followed his wife upstairs. I got up as well, worried if Adeline was hurt. I couldn't hear any crying, just a light pitter patter of feet on the floor above. Martha opened the door to the girls' bedroom and immediately sighed.

I came up beside her and peered into the room. Both girls were standing there with their hands behind their backs looking guilty as ever. I took note that Betty had given Adeline a nightgown to wear as well. That small fact made me smile until I saw a shelf on the ground. "Adeline what happened?" I said as I walked into the room and started picking up the miscellaneous things on the floor that had fallen off the wall.

"I thought you girls were going to bed?" Martha said, joining me and picking up items. Alexander's footsteps trailed up the stairs and into the room.

"We didn't mean to," both of the girls said in sequence with each other.

"Well that don't answer our question," Arthur said, picking up the shelf off the ground.

"Let me help," Alexander said, grabbing one end of the shelf and fixing it back up on the wall.

"Well we wanted to play with the dolls on the shelf and it fell down," Adeline said with guilt trembling in her little voice.

"It's quite alright queen Poni, stuff falls apart around here all the time. You two just need to go to bed now though, so gettin' there Betty," Arthur said pointing at the bed.

"Oh Malencoy actually, and yes I agree girls," I said leaning down and picking up Adeline.

Martha sat Betty up on the top bunk while I tucked Adeline down into her bed underneath. "Be good and stay in bed now, goodnight Adeline," I said, pressing a kiss on her mushroom.

I stood back up and left the girls room with the others and shut the door quietly. Arthur stood outside shaking his head. "I'm sorry Betty is normally always well behaved," Martha said with a sigh and shaking her head.

"Oh don't apologise, as long as Adeline is alright it's okay. And I think that your Betty is a delight, she's just an innocent girl," I said reassuring her. It was the truth that I believe the girls got along wonderfully.

"Well that's wonderful, we should probably let you two rest though. You have a long day of travel tomora' if I suppose correctly?" Arthur said, putting his hands down his front pockets.

I looked at Alexander and he nodded his head in agreement. "Yes we agree that would be nice." I said with a sincere smile.

"Okay great, we'll get you guys settled in then. Is your sister okay to stay in the attic by chance? I'm sorry we just don't have two guest rooms," Martha asked looking behind me.

I turned to see that Amasa had come up the stairs silently somehow. "Oh Amasa... is that alright with you?" I asked her. I gave her a stern look, she needed to say yes. I didn't need her to cause a problem.

She gave me a stink look and crossed her arms. "Fine," Amasa said with a growl in her voice.

"Alright then, Martha will show you two to the guest room. I'll take this one to the attic" Arthur said in his normal gruff tone.

Martha led Alexander and I to a guest room. The room was small and humble, but sweetly kept. "You folks are welcome to join us for breakfast if you like, I'll leave you two to be for now," Martha said politely.

"Oh thank you, really thank you. I'm so glad you're letting us stay," I said with utter seriousness.

"It's no problem, your majesty," Martha said, closing the door to the guest room, leaving me and Alexander to ourselves.

"Oh finally, silence," Alexander said, laying down on the bed.

"Oh, was Alexander getting tired of being around other people?" I asked, teasing him. I undid the laces on the back of my dress and slid off the bodice of my dress. Following it my skirt and petticoat were draped over a chair. I fumbled with the back of my corset, it was tied too tight for me to get it undone. The slight rustle of sheets could be heard as alexander got up from the bed

"Alexander to your rescue," Alexander whispered as he removed my hands from the ties.

"So dramatic for no reason... I love that about you," I said smiling. I moved my hands to the edge of the seat that I was standing behind. His hands pulled the ties of the corset, tightening it more before the ties loosened. I gasped as I was let free from the corsets hold on my waist.

"Aw, has the princess been out of her dress code for too long?" he said, sticking out his bottom lip making fun of me.

"Oh hush," I said, rolling my eyes. I slid the corset off over my head and was left in my chemise and drawers. I turned around and faced Alexander who had a sly smirk playing on his face. "What are you gawking at?" I said reaching up and undoing the clasp on his cape and let the cape fall to the floor. The detail of the jacket he wore underneath was incredible. It was thin black leather with tons of tiny flowers and vines engraved into it. "Amasa does great things with the clothing she can manifest," I mumbled with a small laugh.

"How do you think she made leather?" Alexander asked jokingly.

"A faux" I said as a joke.

He rolled his eyes dramatically. "That was the cheesiest thing I think I've ever heard you say," he said unbuttoning the jacket.

"I thought it was funny," I said, smirking and sitting down on the bed.

"I think you need to learn what humour is," Alexander said, pulling off his boots.

"Hmm, I think you actually like my humour," I said teasingly.

"No I love you, not your humour," he said walking over to where I was sitting on the bed.

"Scoot over ya dork" he said looking down at me as I sat still on the edge of the bed. I shook my head no, I felt like being a pain. "Okay be difficult," he said, shaking his head.

He picked me up off the bed and up to his chest.. Even if it was only for a few mere seconds his hands were wrapped around my back and rolled over me on the bed. I laughed as he flipped onto the bed on his back while laying me on his chest. His arms were still wrapped around me as I stopped laughing under my breath.

I smiled and rested my head on the top of his chest and just looked up at him. He grabbed the crown off of his head and looked at it. "Loot at that, how did that just appear," he said with a scoff. His crown was very interesting; it was a ring crown with spikes around it. On the inside was a mini poison mushroom cushion with guard wires over it.

"I'm not sure how it works, I think you look great with it though." I said, setting his crown on the other side of the bed.

"If you think mine is good, look at yours Mags," he said with a small laugh.

I pulled off the crown on my head and looked at its small details. It was gorgeous, all of the lavender stones glistening in the candlelight that lit the room. The gold on it as well made it more beautiful. Nothing could deny that it was extraordinary how a mushroom head could just transform into a crown. "It is interesting," I said with a sigh as I set my crown next to Alexander's.

I laid my face on his chest and let my eyes close. "Here princess sit up," Alexander said after a few minutes.

He pulled me up and set me beside him as he reached over and put the candle out with his thingers. He then rolled back over, faceing me now and pulled his arms around me. I moved my hands up to the sides of his face, my thingers running across the light stubble on his cheeks. I loved the little bit of stubble on his cheeks and chin. It resembles his personality, he seems rough and spikey but underneath he's so much more.

One of his hands ran through my hair and combed through it gently. I squirmed and got more comfortable, draping one of my legs over him.

His hand that had been tangled in my hair slid down my body. His hand lazily dragged down across my waist and hip then finally resting down on my thigh. His hand completely covered the side of my thigh with ease.

His hand grazed over the birth emblem I had etched into the top of my leg. "What's that?" he asked as his fingers traced the lines of the branding.

"Magic tat," I said jokingly as I looked up at his face, the moonlight from the window lit up the room enough for me to make out his facial features.

"Hm interesting," he said lazily looking into my eyes. He had a small smile and his eyes were half open. I brushed some of his hair from his face with the tips of my thingers. "I love you Mags," he whispered quietly. His breath was hot on my lips from how close he was to me.

"I love you too Alexander," I whispered. As I spoke I watched his lips slightly part, but he just stayed where he was. *Was he gonna kiss me or not?* I thought to myself curiously.

After a few more moments he crashed his lips down onto me. I closed my eyes instinctively and kissed him back. This wasn't like any other kiss I'd experienced though, it was longer and he didn't really pull away. His lips moved against mine in a sensual, fast paced way, I did the same as my hands moved around the back of his head. My thingers combing through his thick dark hair. It felt like static ran through my chest and entire body. My face lit up like fire, even hot to the touch.

His tongue gently pressed against my lips and as I opened my mouth to catch my breath he pressed his lips to my open mouth. I felt his tongue run against my own and I let out a small gasp. The kiss remained passionate with our tongues dancing together. I tilted my head to the side as we kept the pace of the kiss an even set. His hands gently moved to hold my head steady. I could've melted right there as I felt a building hunger form within me. I wanted him, so badly. I yearned for him, I ached to feel him explore me.

As we broke away from the kiss I caught my breath and Alexander wiped my bottom lip with his thumb. I looked up at his face. He looked so handsome like this, red in the face with moonlight lighting around us. "You look so beautiful Mags," he said in a husky sounding voice. Before I could respond he pressed another sloppy kiss down on my lips. When he pulled away this time he let out a small groan. My entire body felt like it was on fire and I needed relief.

"...We should probably get to sleep," Alexander mumbled. His hand slid back up to my hair.

I really didn't want to go asleep yet, it was the last thing I wanted to do. He was right though, we weren't in our own home, plus a day's travel tomorrow. "Agreed, goodnight I love you dear," I whispered quietly. It was best we stopped there anyways. The last thing I'd need was anything going further in someone else's house. I moved my hands around his head and held onto him tightly. He himself then squirmed against me to get comfortable. He hugged me around my waist and laid his face on my chest. That made my face go hot as well but I did my best to ignore it.

Eventually my mind settled and I could finally fall asleep.

The next morning the sounds of pots and pans clanging downstairs woke me up. The sun gazed across the floor through the window. Alexander seemed to not be affected by the noises. He was still clung onto me snoring. "Alexander dear," I said, dragging out the r in dear.

He still didn't want to wake up, he just groaned and held his eyes shut. "Come on, we gotta get up," I said, cupping his face and making him look up. He opened his eyes and frowned at me. I just smiled and sat up, crawling out of the bed.

Alexander stayed laying down in the bed as I got up. I hadn't even realised there was an attached lavatory in the room. I hadn't seen a lavatory since I was in the palace so I was shocked. I walked in and looked in the mirror, I washed my face in the porcelain sink. I wiped my face off on a towel beside the sink and hung it back up. "What is this?" Alexander asked in a tiered voice.

I jumped, not realising he'd gotten out of bed. "A lavatory?" I said, looking at him in the mirror.

"A what!?" he said confused.

"You get ready in here, not many people have them. We have them at the palace though," I said, running some water in my hand.

I reached up to wash Alexander's face off. "Nu-uh nope, I don't trust that. How does water stay clean in pipes like that, a creek is significantly cleaner," he said dodging my hand.

"Alexander Malencoy, are you being serious, it's clean now come one don't be a pain," I said with a sigh.

He was acting like a child. "Nope!" he said walking out of the small room.

I sighed and then washed my hands and left the bathroom. I slid on my corset and tried to tighten it myself, but I failed. "Do you need help?" Alexander asked as he finished buttoning up his jacket.

"Yes please" I said, handing the ties into his hands. He grabbed onto the ties and then pulled them, cinching the corset tight. I felt my breath hitch as I always did when I got my corset tied off. I Heard Alexander snicker to himself as he tied the corset. "What's funny?" I asked, catching my breath as I started to slip on my petticoat.

He then tied the little ribbons on the petite coat for me. I appreciated him doing that for me. He grabbed the skirt and slipped it over me and followed the bodice. He finished dressing me like his own little doll and picked up his cape. I fixed the cape around his chest and pinned it in place with the fasteners.

"Thank you princess," he said, smiling down at me.

"No, thank you dear," I said, grabbing his crown and my own. I set his crown on his head and fixed his hair all around it.

He took my crown and then set the golden crest on my head. "My beautiful queen..." he mumbled before pressing a kiss to my head.

Chapter 37. Natalia Sawyer

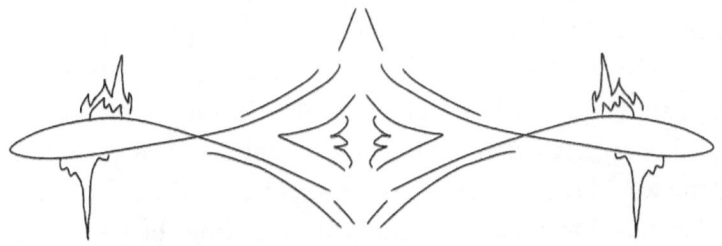

I walked quickly down the empty halls of the palace, on the detailed carpeted floors and carved walls. The queen... Well now Delilah Poni had requested something to drink. Ever since Magdolin left I'd become one of the many queen's assistants. I wasn't one of the favoured ones either, Delilah and Hector blamed me for Magdolin's disappearance. Even though I was the reason they could never prove it, therefore I went 'unpunished'.

I'm not sure what's happened to Magdolin, I was told she was seen with a poison mushroom at some manor party. I would have hoped she'd be smarter than that and not go somewhere like that with someone that dangerous.

Nothing has been the same since the crown has been re-owned. The kingdom has no current leader, no one is for sure what's happened. I hope it's the best situation possible, Magdolin got married. Even if she did get married I doubt she'd ever return, she's probably off at the island the butcher had told me about. I trust the butcher and his judgements, that's why I allowed him to get a hold of the con artist to get Magdolin out of here. Could she have possibly met back up with Raymond? I'm sure Hector would allow her to be married to Raymond, even if he did leave he was strong willed.

My thoughts were cut off as I reached Delilah's ward. I creaked open the door to the sight of all of the other hand maids surrounding her. I came forward and handed her a glass and poured her a glass of water from the jug.

"Oh you brat this water is room temperature, just leave!" Delilah hissed as she threw the glass of water at me. It soaked my entire bodice and face. I nodded my head and set the glass on a nightstand and made my way out. The other hand maids gave me a sny look, I knew they all hated me. It didn't help Delilah was being dramatic about having her mushroom back. She hated having it in her way, it was a dumb thing to be dramatic about. Everyone else has to deal with it every day.

As the large wooden door shut I let out a deep sigh. I started to make my way down to the eastern wing of the palace. I looked down at my boots as I walked down the halls. Ignoring the painted ceilings and stained glass windows. All of this pressure was just too much for me, I hated being hated even though I deserved it. Maybe I could get the butcher to hook me up with someone to get me out of the palace as well, or I could just run away. I didn't need an escape artist to get me out of here, I could just run.

I arrived at where I was wanting to be, Magdolin's old room. No guards guarded this room anymore due to her absence. No one else even bothered to come in here anymore. I opened the door and left it open behind me, I liked to feel like she was following me inside.

Everything was the same as she had left it, perfectly in place. I looked up at the painting of her on one of the walls. It was one of her professionally done one's to show her in her princess age. She was only fifteen in the picture. I felt tears fill my eyes as I kept looking about the room. All of those memories we had made together. She wasnt my owner, she was my friend, my best friend. I fell down to the ground, crouching over and crying into my hands. I couldn't believe I was really all alone now.

I looked back up at the painting as I tried to stop crying. I remember when she got that painting. I had just started being her hand maid, she hated her old hand maid. I didn't blame her, she was an old witch who was very old fashioned. So the king and queen chose me, someone her age and someone she could try and relate to. The day she got the painting done she was so annoyed she didn't want to sit still so I did my best to keep her entertained while she stood still. Later that week when the painting had the final details done and was hung on her wall we sat on her bed and made fun of the artist's work. He had gotten her face completely wrong, and put tons of makeup on her. We always said that the painter liked the younger age clearly because of how he drew her at fifteen years old.

Those days were fun and so simple, if it were my choice I would've kept it that way. That's not what Magdolin wanted though. Whenever she wasn't with me she was stuck to do whatever her parents said no matter what.

I heard footsteps coming into the room with me. I shot my head up with hopes of what I always dreamed of, looking up to see Magdolin. It wasn't of course, I sighed as I saw Antonio standing in the door frame. I stood up and wiped my tears from my face with my sleeve. "What the hell are you doing in here?" he said in a hateful tone.

"Just reminiscing," I said looking up at him. I hated him, he was such an entitled prick. When Hector found him he was some farm boy in rags. Now he just thinks he's diamonds because he is dressed in fine clothes and a cape.

"You don't deserve to reminisce on her, it's your fault she's not here and I think you know that. She was supposed to be my wife," he said walking closer to me. I just glared up at him. "What happened to you as well, you look a mess." He sneered looking at my soaked hair and bodice.

"Delilah apparently doesn't like water," I said sarcastically. He turned his nose up at that before grabbing me by my chin.

"Don't speak of your queen like that you peasant," he said, yanking me forward.

"She's not my queen, and I don't take orders from you," I said, pulling against his hold.

He fought against me and it ended up being a full on squabble of him trying to restrain me. He eventually got a hold of me and made me look back up at the painting of Magdoin. "You see that, that's the face of what I could've had. Do you see how beautiful she is? I could've had that if you weren't so stupid," he hissed down into my ear.

I grunted trying to pull away from his hold. It did no use, he had me fully pressed against him and he surprisingly had great strength in restraining me.

I felt the tears start to flood my eyes again as I listened to his words. "Oh good you're gonna cry, that's the only thing I want to see you do. I want to see you suffer, you brat," he whispered in my ear like a snake. He was a snake, and a pain, the biggest pain I ever felt. I didn't want to give him what he wanted, but I felt like I needed to cry, so badly.

I thought for just a split second, what would Magdolin want me to say... then it hit me. "You said she's beautiful in that picture right?" I said not showing any emotion.

"Of course I did," he said, oblivious to what I was about to say. It felt like I was about to explode in laughter as I formed the words in my throat.

"Well you must like little girls, the mushroom who painted that was specifically attracted to minors. She was fifteen in that picture," I said snickering. He fell silent for a few moments.

"I should kill you, you know that?'" he hissed as he kicked my feet out from under me. He grabbed me and shoved me against the footboard of Magdolin's old bed. I groaned as I hit the oak wood of it harshly. I sat up slightly, he grabbed my mushroom and shoved my face down into the quilt on Magdolin's large bed. "You are a selfish disgusting brat, you've been pampered for your kind and it clearly went to your head. Someone needs to put you in your place, luckily for you it won't be me," he said moving one hand to the small of my back. He pushed down with both hands. The details of the floral footboard stabbed into my hips and stomach. "You can just take this as a warning to leave this room alone from now on." he said putting down more force on me. I screamed and I felt the wood dig into my skin and bone. I couldn't tell if it broke my skin or not but it hurt like hell. Screaming did no good either due to my head being shoved into the quilt.

"What do you think your doing sir Antonio." I heard a voice say. I heard footsteps run across the floor and a crash. I felt Antonio's hand leave my body. I couldn't move too quickly, from the injuries I now had. I gasped and groaned as I pulled myself off of the footboard. It had not broken skin but was bruised, badly. I could feel all the muscles where all of the bruises were. I could feel my heart in my head as it started to get blurry. Pain writhed through my body, and I had to sit down on the chest at the end of Magdolin's bed. I grabbed at my stomach and hips applying pressure to bruises. I couldn't help the tears that fell from my eyes and the gasps that came naturally from the pain.

As I moved past some of the pain I was brought back to attention where Antonio was verbally fighting with Graham brown.

Graham was a nice mushroom, he was kind, and was the other suitor for Magdolin. I felt like she would like Graham, he was a pure white mushroom. He seemed to be the only one who didn't hate me. Nevertheless he didn't exactly like me, he just left me alone. "How could you do that to her, she's proven innocent!" Graham yelled at Antonio.

"I don't care! You are just as bad as her!" Antonio screamed as he started to storm out from the door. "W-wait, no you two leave! I'm not done grieving my lost wife," Antonio said, sounding like a spoiled brat and crossing his arms.

"You didn't know her, you have no one to grieve" I growled, still sobbing.

"Shh, he's not worth your breath," Graham said, gathering himself and walking beside me as I sat on the chest. I just looked up at him, I assumed I looked pitiful. He held his hand out to me to help me stand, I took his hand and attempted to stand. I fell back down pitifully on the chest. Gasping and grabbing my hips and stomach.

"See what you've done, Antonio, this is what you've done in your fit of anger!" Graham yelled, shaming Antonio. Antonio still stood at the door like an entitled brat. He pointed at the door, signalling us to leave again. Graham gritted his teeth at him before speaking. "Miss Natalia, there's no point in gifting this *brat* with our presence." Graham said, scooping me up in his arms.

I definitely did not fight against him carrying me, I couldn't even walk on my own. He made his way out into the hall and we were greeted by a servant running down the hall. I looked at the servant as he ran, Graham stopped walking as well. Antonio must've seen the confusion on our faces because he stepped outside of the room as well.

"The princess! The queen! She's returned!" the servant yelled out of breath as he approached us.

"What queen, the queen has been here?" Antonio said with a scoff.

"...queen Magdolin," the servant said, catching his breath from running.

I felt my heart jump in my chest and my eyes went wide. "M-m-Magdolin… queen," I said, fighting against Graham's hold on me.

I tried to run as I fell from his arms. After only a few steps I collapsed and began crying worse as I gritted my teeth.

"Natalia! Stop, we're going to go see her!" Graham said, helping me back up off the ground. He picked me back up off the ground and held me like a baby. Antonio had already started sprinting off down the hall towards the southern entrance to the palace, the main entrance.

Graham did his best to keep up with him with me in his arms. "We need to go faster!" I cried to Graham.

"I'm going as fast as I can, don't think you're going to miss her, okay." Graham said, trying to reassure me. The closer we got to the southern wing I cried more. My anticipation was killing me.

As we entered the entrance hall it was full. Hector and Delilah were standing together in the middle of the hall. Other servants and workers lined around the hall behind Hector and Delilah.

We were standing to the left of them all at the south wing entrance door. No Magdolin was in sight though. "That servant lied to us, I'll have his head," Antonio murmured to us.

"No… she has to be here," I said, holding back more tears as I bit my bottom lip.

"She is here, just not right here. She's been sighted outside the palace clearly." Graham whispered to us both. Everyone in the hall was silent. It felt like my heart was beating out of my chest as I waited patiently.

After ten minutes of feeling like I'd pass out from my heart beating so fast the sounds of footsteps were heard outside of the huge wooden doors. a voice was heard as well, a female, not Magdolin though.

"Oh no don't do that, I want to make a big entrance for us!" a voice said loudly but was dullened by the walls of the palace. It was more like five voices though, I could barely distinguish if it was a male or female from how they sounded. The sound of something clanking against the ground rang in the room before the doors that scaled to the thirty foot ceilings, flung open. Huge vines and stone grew against them keeping them open.

A maniacal laugh erupted from the centre of the door. As dust cleared an odd mushroom stood proudly holding a stick of some sort.

Her mushroom was something like i'd never seen before. "What ... the ... hell." Antonio whispered.

"Mom! Step daddio! How's it going! Can you believe it, I'm technically a princess of sorts but I prefer duchess more." the lady said laughing. The mushroom spun her staff proudly before slamming it to the ground. Even more vines spurred out from the spot she casted the staff. "Oh don't worry the palace will clean it up once it's renowned, who knows it may fit the decor!" she laughed proudly.

Hector and Delilah looked frozen in place as they watched the mushroom step forward. I was confused now Delilah had no other children to my knowledge.

More footsteps were heard. I gasped as I saw Magdolin, and I was more shocked as I saw a poison mushroom next to her. She also held a small pink mushroom in her arms. She looked at her parents coldly. She then set down the little girl on the ground, I could see a crown on her mushroom as well. None of this made sense to me, there was no way this was real.

"She got married," Antonio hissed to himself. He was right, she was married, but who was the odd mushroom, and who was the child?"

"So you've finally returned, with our crow-" Hector began to say before the poison mushroom spoke.

"Our crowns, truly, should be mine. I'm just not a selfish monster like you." he said with a hardness in his voice. Magdolin held his arms and just glared at her parents.

"Let me retry that. *Magdolin*, what do you intend to do with your new found leadership?" Hector said, trying to not lose his patients.

"I don't believe I'm the one you should be asking that question, I've learned what our bloodline has done to the poison mushroom father. I'm simply doing what's right and fixing what you have just carried on." she said coldly.

What is wrong with her, what is she saying!?

Maybe she's brainwashed by something, this poison mushroom has done something to her clearly. That monster probably kidnapped her and the little girl.

"Is she insane?" Graham whispered to us. I shrugged my shoulders as he still held me. We looked over at Antonio who looked pale.

"...my pa told me about this, I thought he was crazy…" he whispered looking at us.

"So?" I said looking at him with a raised eyebrow.

"She's telling the truth, he's supposed to be king," Antonio said, looking scared. I went wide eyed and looked back at Magdolin and her husband. I noticed the little girl had wandered over to us as well.

"Put me down!" I ordered graham. He didn't question it and set me down. The king and Magdolin continued talking but I had a new goal now. I sat on my hands and knees and waved the small girl over. She had her blonde hair in a small braid and wore a big dress. She saw me and waddled over to me.

"Hello" she whispered to me.

"Hello, what's your name?" I asked, looking at the little crown on her mushroom.

She looked at me suspiciously before answering. "Adeline," she mumbled, with her hand in her mouth. In her other hand was a two dolls.

"I like your dolls," I said pointing at them.

She smiled and swayed back and forth. "Who are you?" she said giggling to herself.

"I'm your mother's friend, Miss Natalia," I said smiling.

"You're my friend then, mommas friends are my friend" she said smiling and jumping up and down lightly.

"Get off the ground you idiot." Antonio hissed, kicking my back.

"Don't kick my friend!" Adeline said, trying to run past me to 'attack' Antonio. I grabbed her and pulled her over to me. Graham pulled me up off the ground and helped me stand up keeping his hands on my waist. I held the little Adeline girl against my chest.

"Father you're irrational and together me and Alexander are going to fix your mistakes!" I heard Magdolin yell in a cruel tone. I saw her pointing at her father assertively and he had his arms crossed.

"And after that? You will have a mixed child with a poison mushroom to carry on the crown it will be a disaster!" Delilah said, defending hector.

"That's what you think! When it's controlled mixing it isn't bad mother! For example Amasa creates amazing things all on her own and she doesn't do anything bad with it. Also Adeline is the princess right now... Adeline... where's Adeline..." Magdolin said looking at her husband seeing if he had her. I stepped forward knowing I needed to.

"Hey you can't walk," Graham said, holding me back.

"I have too," I said, forcing myself to step forward. "Magdolin!" I yelled out holding Adeline.

She looked over at me for a moment then went wide eyed. "Natalia?" she said as she ran over to me.

I started crying and laughing as she stood in front of me. Her husband then moved beside her. "This is Natalia?" he asked looking down at me.

Before I could respond Magdolin took Adeline from me and handed her to her husband and she wrapped her arms around me. I cried as I hugged her back tightly. I was standing very awkwardly from the pain that was in my hips and stomach but I didn't care anymore, I had Magdolin back.

"I missed you so much" I cried into her shoulder.

"I missed you too," she said, hugging me tightly.

"Natalia, step away from the queen. Return to your quarters," I heard Delilah say angrily.

"All servants and workers return to your quarters" Hector added. Magdolin let me go, not fully but just enough to look at me. She then turned and gave her father a stern look.

"Natalia is not going anywhere," she said firmly. Her father gave her a glare, piercing like a knife.

"Fine" he growled between his teeth.

I looked back at Magdolin smiling deeply, I could just cry. I knew I had to be strong for her though, I couldn't be a baby like that. I felt a pain run through my torso and I fell forward grabbing my stomach.

Chapter 38. Alexander Malencoy

Natalia, Magdolin's friend, fell forward, Magdolin pulled her closer and held her up. The two hunks that has been standing over by a door rushed over. The white mushroom grabbed Natalia from Magdolin and held her in his arms. The gold one approached Magdolin as the other male stepped back.

"Princess Magdolin, I am Antonio Williams. I see you're happily married but can I just ask you to reconsider your choice of husband. I can assure-" he said grabbing her hand and falling down on one knee.

I kicked him in the chest lightly, just enough to send him down on his back and cut off his little speech. "You're embarrassing yourself," I said looking down at him, with a small smirk. He just gave me a dirty look as he stood up and brushed himself off. "It's not very smart to egg on a king. I would have thought you'd known that from rotting in your parents' attic," I said turning to face away from Antonio. Magdolin did as well, although for Amasa you couldn't stay the same.

"Yeah no if you end up living in an attic I suggest reading into some things like history!" Amasa said trying to just be snarky.

The room fell silent for a few moments, it was very tense. Hector and Delilah both stared angrily at us. For once I didn't feel scared to face someone like them. I felt like I was the one in control, I was the one in control, I could have anything I want now. Hector crossed his arms after a few minutes of just standing there.

"What is it you want?" he grumbled angrily. I smirked at the thought we'd made him crack.

"I want my dagger returned to me immediately, and you will both publicly resign your authority to us." Magdolin said assertively. I was so proud that she was able to stand up to her parents for once, unlike how she used to act around them.

Hector snarled his nose and Delilah seemed depressed at the idea. "...fine, but you will have to come to us as your advisors. We don't trust you Magdolin, for obvious reasons. Why would we ever leave a kingdom in your hands alone?" Delilah said in her upright asshole voice. How could someone be so rude?

"I can assure you Magdolin is trustworthy, I entrust her with my life already. To add to it, how are you any more trustworthy than her? You've been lying to your people for decades carrying on centuries. I believe the kingdom will appreciate her much more than you once we spill your little secret you've kept from them." I said speaking before Magdolin could. The fury that burned within me was heart aching, I've hated them for so long and now even more. To learn what they've done to my kind, to Amasa entire family, and my wife? They will pay their penance somehow.

"And who says they would believe you two, they will say that Magdolin is just under your influence. They will never accept someone like you as king, Hector said in a cruel tone. I didn't let his words get to me, they couldn't hurt me any more.

I know I'm not a monster for sure now, Amasa proved it, I myself prove it more and more by the day. I think what mostly proved it was that someone was capable of loving me, and she was someone I loved dearly. "Do not speak to your king like that unless you wish to be banished off the face of this island." Magdolin said, stomping her foot. I ran my hand across her shoulder, shushing her.

"Well whenever the people who know the truth come out and speak as well they will all eventually accept it. Also for a tip of advice, they already are talking and spreading the word of what's going on." I said calmly. They had no right to know just how mad I was truly.

"What are you talking about the 'people who know the truth' no one outside of the royal family knows what actually happened." Delilah said with a grossed out face.

"Excuse me mommy but I know,"

Amasa said, sneaking around Delilah and snickering in her hair. Delilah jumped and grabbed her chest, horrified Amasa would even get that close to her.

"I am not your mother! You're an abomination!" she said, hissing at Amasa. Amasa just laughed and then returned to wandering around the huge hall.

"Nevertheless your little super star here knew as well." I said, laying my hand out notioning at Antonio who was still standing by Magdolin's friend and the white mushroom. He looked horrified as I pointed at him.

Hector quickly looked at him. "Is this true?" he gritted through his teeth.

"W-well your highness, I didn't have a choice to know what my father told me." Antonio stuttered while going pale.

"I would've had your head, not marrying my daughter if I knew that." Hector hissed, looking away from Antonio. Adeline who was in my left hand, cackled and pointed at him.

"Your child has no manners Magdolin." Delilah said looking at Adeline.

"I'm glad to see you see her as my child now, where is my dagger I believe I requested it? As for this little chat, I believe it is over." Magdolin said with a stern face.

Adeline squirmed in my arms wanting to be let down. I really didn't want to let her down due to the situation but I did anyway. She started to wander over to where Amasa was looking up at the mural on the ceiling. Maybe she won't get into trouble over there.

"This is not over, young lady," Delilah said, sounding defeated.

"Should I bring back the banishing threats? I'm the queen now I believe it's time for me to take *my* throne." Magdolin said in her stern voice. I hadn't really heard it until today, I liked her standing up for herself. She grabbed my arm and started to drag me up to a door which was behind her parents.

"Magdolin we've been trying to tell you that you're not ready yet!" Hector yelled as we brushed past him and opened the door.

The room was huge with candles that were hung on chandeliers that lit up the entire room. The walls were carved and more detailed than the rest of the palace, this was the throne room.

There towards the middle of the diamond shaped room were two grand chairs. Both were purple and white and by the way they were detailed you could tell which was the king and queens.

Magdolin held my hand tight as we approached them. "Magdolin please just rethink this, I don't think you can handle a kingdom. That's what we've been trying to tell you!" Delilah begged as they ran in the room.

As we reached the huge thrones and stood before them it was an odd feeling, I felt like I belonged here. I did belong here. The feeling of something having a lethal grasp on me surrounded me, *this was my place.*

Amasa walked into the room as well with Adeline in her arms, then followed the two men and Natalia.

"Your right mother, I can't handle a kingdom. We can though." Magdolin said looking up at me. I looked down at her and smiled, I knew it right now there was no doubt we couldn't handle this together.

"Yes we can." I said, fighting back the urge to just grab her and hug her. She smiled and nodded her head, she looked back at her parents and took a deep breath. She sat down in the shorter, smaller seat. The throne glowed a light purple, the room felt full of life like how when Amasa's magic was used.

I then took a seat in the king's throne, it glowed a green like what was on my mushroom. The colour from the seats drained their colour and the floors slowly changed from the plain white marble with purple accents to a grey and black marble. The entire room went black and then sparks of colour flashed from the candles in the air and then purple white and green accents dashed all around the room, bringing it to life with colour. It looked like lighting flittering across the walls. The small etchings of electric green and a dashing violet carved intricate into the black tile floors.

I was in awe as I watched what happened around me, Magdolin's jaw was dropped as well as she watched colours fly around her. It was beautiful watching all of it unravel and claiming the palace in our way. I'd never seen anything even close to this, it was brilliant and amazing.

After all of that took place Magdolin and I had our ceremony of being crowned queen and king with the public. They even had us do our wedding again, I wouldn't say I hated it though.

Most of all though, Hector and Delilah came forward themselves and told the truth about poison mushrooms. It took time for the people to accept me as their king but eventually they all came to soften up to me. I always did my best to be the best king, husband, and father I could. Magdolin always helped me no matter what was going on. Hell, even Hector started to soften up to me and accept me. I wish I could say the same for Delilah, she seemed to be the same prissy little female.

Adeline is five now and growing like a weed, she has her own room now too, even though she comes running into our room when she has a nightmare.

Amasa chose to stay in the palace as well, and ironically she stays up in the north tower. She's also seen a lot in the courtyard practising her powers. Adeline's really grown to like Amasa, really taking her in as her auntie.

For Natalia, she got hitched to mister pure white Graham. After mixing colours was proved to be okay many mushrooms got married and found their soulmates. Charlie herself is still a lone wolf, she opened up multiple shops around the kingdom after I gave recognition of her work.

Antonio got shipped back to his father's farm for his disrespect towards royalty.

As for Magdolin and I, we're doing great, eating for two actually. After months of trying for a baby we finally are going to be able to give Adeline a little sibling. Not that Adeline is already too much to handle but it will be amazing to have one of our own. Magdolin can't keep her head out of books for different baby names and such, Adeline's no help either. She'll be right beside her momma helping.

I made my way down the hall which was full of life. Plants grew beautifly on the pillars on the walls. Purple and white flowers were painted in significant ways up and down the halls. I came to the door of our room and pushed open the oak doors. Magdolin, Amasa, Natalia, and Adeline were all sitting on the edge of the bed looking up at the wall. "What are you four looking at?" I asked curiously.

Graham entered the room next to me. "Oh Natalia there you are." he said with a sigh and went to stand next to her. "Oh wow they did a good job on that" he added looking up at the same place in the wall the girls had been looking at.

I moved over beside the bed to where I could see what they all were gazing at.

On the wall was the painting that had taken the artist over six months to even sketch out. It was of Magdolin, Adeline, and I. Magdolin had a soft smile that was identical to hers, even in the painting you could feel her beauty. Adeline was in between us with that same grin she always had playing on her face, they didn't illustrate her missing teeth but it still was amazingly accurate. Plus her teeth were finally coming in, so maybe it would be accurate in a few months.

I looked like me in the painting, the artist had done a fantastic job no matter what teeth he messed up.

A small knock came from the door and then the servant let themselves in. "mail for king Malencoy." the young boy said with an envelope in his hand.

"Oh just put it with the rest of my mail, I'll mess with it later today," I said, shoeing the boy with a wave of my hand.

"Well your majesty this seemed urgent, a strange male came to me specifically and said to get it to you right away." the servant said nervously and held the envelope out.

"Oh well in that case I'll look at it now." I said with a small smile as I took the envelope from the boy.

There was nothing written on the outside of the envelope at all, just the wax seal that held it shut. It wasn't wax though it was a burnt substance like a small little patch of charcoal holding it closed. I broke the seal with my thinger and Magdolin had now wandered over beside me and was holding my arm as I opened it up. I slid out the yellow aged paper and unfolded it. Neat cursive covered the entire page basically, it looked… familiar to me. I started reading the letter from the top which was addressed to Alexander, not king Malencoy.

My heart sank as my eyes skimmed over the pages, how could this even be happening. I thought I sent troops of guards to the island?

"Alexander, what's the matter? You look pale" Magdolin asked grabbing my back to steady to me. "My mom," I said, starting to panic.

Alexander Peony Malencoy

Alexander in the start of our story was twenty five and a simple peasant male due to his ranking. But before all of that it was quite the opposite. As a child Alexander enjoyed exploring the woods with his little sister even though his parents despised it because of their dangerous neighbours. He had a few childhood friends but most were taken away from him for his safety. He had a deep hatred for the royal family all throughout his childhood. Most was just pure unbridled fury towards the Kings, he tried his best to respect the Queens but it was hard. He was just a child, what else was he supposed to believe? As he got older he slightly matured but never recovered from the underlying hatred.

One time when he was six all mushrooms were summoned to the palace for an announcement. Every once and a while the Kings and Queens would do this, and they enforce for all mushrooms to attend. His little child heart burned from anger as he watched the two rulers of the land step out. He didn't really understand why he didn't like them, it was mainly because of his father. It only got worse as he saw a bubbly little baby girl swaddled in a light purple blanket.

So forth from that day he kept his nose out of royal stuff and just left it alone. He'd listen to his father rant about royal stuff but he mainly just tried to ignore it and visit them as least as possible. Whenever the princess and him met again, it was a bit different. Nineteen years later she wanted out of the palace and to be freed. The first thought to run through his mind was. *I'm dead!*, which he rightfully had to think.

Magdolin Vivienne Poni

The princess and now queen of Equilibrium is now twenty one at the end of *this* story, and pregnant. But of course these pages are dedicated to backstories, sadly Magdolin's was quite... boring.

It was the same thing for her every day, day after day after day. She'd wake up, eight in the morning sharp and then get ready for the day. Unlike how she's teaching her children she would go to class from nine to five in the afternoon. Her classes ranged from archery and swordsmanship, to lady-likeness and then the primary education of course. After she turned twelve she got a new handmaid named Natalia who was just a year older than her and a new guard outside of her room. They all three became good friends and once they were older Magdolin and her guard became an item of sorts but he left one day. No one knew where he went, it was like he evaporated. This left Magdolin depressed and upset, she had to move on though. She couldn't let her parents know she had feelings for another rank. That's when things got interesting for our little princess. She struggled choking down the pill that she'd be forced into marrying someone else and on top of it she had just lost what she thought was her soul mate. (He clearly wasn't, as the

creator I hate him:) she only belongs with Alexander) Natalia did her best to keep her comforted but as the years passed, she couldn't stall anymore and the king and queen were forcing her to get married. That's when Natalia took the reigns and got Magdolin on her feet by getting her out of the palace

Fun fact: When Magdolin turned twenty one she ended up sloppy drunk after Natalia gave her a half glass of wine. She's a lightweight compared to Alexander who chugged at least three glasses of whiskey

Amasa Tessa (no she doesn't have a middle name)

You really think I'd spoil my favorite mysterious girl? Here's some art of her though, I won't starve you of that.

Adeline Delilah Malencoy / Sanchez

When Adeline was first born her mother fled almost instantly after giving birth. Some might say she left without reason, but she'd have other words concerning Lapel. She wanted to take the baby girl but in the end decided it would be a good punishment for her ex lover. So Adeline was left with her drunk of a father.

The barely five years they were stuck together Adeline was tortured. As soon as she could walk, lapel would force her to do work around the house that would normally be left to a spouse. Adeline always did as he said to avoid any type of punishment and took her advantages to leave the house. Even if a door was left ajar she would run into the streets to play with the neighbor kids. Even at the young age of two she did her running off game. It was worse when there was a festival or event in town for poor Adeline. Lapel would lock her in their house and not let her out as he went out for himself.

Lapel hated this and would do his best to stop her from running off because of the shame he'd get for running off his wife. He always looked for another woman he could claim to be the mother of Adeline just for the validation of his neighbors. He found his perfect opportunity when he came across a shorter, blonde haired pink mushroom in the plaza one day. She was basically an older version of Adeline and he couldn't let that slide away. But once her poisonous companion showed Lapel who was boss he backed off for a little while at least. Another occurrence happened which Lapel did not speak of. Then a day later Adeline snuck out of her house and into the street where kids were surrounding horses playing on them. And their forth Adeline found her new mother and then soon to be father.

Charlie Smith Diginton

Charlie grew up in a crowded household, she had nearly thirteen siblings and four of her cousins living with her and her parents. Since the family was so crowded it was hard for her poor parents to keep up with all the kids. Charlie being the youngest would usually sneak off with the two mysterious kids that lived in the woods near their house, they were her best friends until one disappeared. Charlie also learned Greek from her father growing up, and she and her father were best friends. He taught her the art of metal working as well, using certain metals would make sizable jewelry, which lured Charlie greatly. Her father also gave her the nickname smithy growing up and it stuck with her.

As she grew older the boy that lived in the woods would visit less frequently. When Charlie found out why she was grossed out. Her best friend Alexander had been seeing some snobby mushroom. Some rare rose breed, they were quite literally useless breeds of mushrooms too, right up next to pink mushrooms, they were just simple musses. She specifically hated her because she came to her door step and called her out for being a whore of sorts for hanging around 'her man'. Charlie instantly just turned her nose up though of course, I mean especially because she was only sixteen at the time and because she was grossed out partially at the thought of Alexander. It was sad that he and hope lasted so long to her, for four years anyone would be sick of it.

I mean listening to him ramble on one day about how great she was then talk about how she was the worst really got to Charlie. Plus on top of it, Alexander complained about how they weren't soulmates and one time asked Charlie if there was a way to change that. That infuriated Charlie.

She had to give it to him though, for someone as low ranking as him, it was surprising to even see him with someone. But besides that fact Charlie despised this "Hope" he was seeing. Not that she could say anything, Alexander hated the boys that she'd have her eyes set on.

Once she was seventeen she opened up a shop when an older woman had passed away. And by that time her friend Alexander had started doing his own little business, smuggling. She agreed to help him only because it was her best friend but it was too limits of course.

Hector and Delilah Poni

Hector was one of three sons, he was raised to high standard in the palace. He'd face his father's wrath if he ever was to disobey him or his mother. One of his brothers was slaughtered by an unknown enemy and his other brother ran away, leaving the crown to hector. At the young age of sixteen he was forced into a marriage with a young fifteen year old Delilah. She was a single child and raised on the very outskirts of the kingdom. Her parents tried to keep her hidden from others' eyes so she wouldn't be found for the kingdom's next choice for a Queen. It was to no use though, when the king fell old and ill he sent troops to find any trace of a purple mushroom left beside them for his son, safely they found Delilah in her small cottage by the bay side.

When she was forced back to the palace they were married within twelve hours. The culture shock for Delilah was atrocious. She wasn't allowed to see her parents, the only two people she had ever known. Hector took pity on her at first but then his parents started pressuring him more and more. Until the day his father passed when he was twenty.

Delilah always kept her head down and her mouth shut just to avoid anything. Her and Hector never even spoke unless they had too. Once Hector's father passed and it was just his old crippled mother, he gave Delilah a choice. She could return to her parents or she could stay, Hector didn't want to keep her more than she had to if she didn't want this life. Delilah took her chance and ran, but halfway through her journey she found out her parents had passed.

She returned to the palace and then fully accepted Hector as her husband. From then on they grew to love each other.

Hope Abriam Steelheart

Hope is a very bipolar woman. She's a year older than Alexander and grew up with her gypsy mother. She ran into Alexander one day in the forest. She froze dead silent in her tracks as she saw the scrawny looking teenage boy. At first she was in horror, she'd heard these awful things about poison mushrooms and now she was face to face with one. She thought about running and telling her mother but she knew she wasn't supposed to interrupt her mother when she was around whatever man she was with at the time. She was on the verge of fleeing before she realized the boy was crying. She cringed at first, he looked awful, bad skin and sobbing, looked like he hadn't eaten in days.

She slowly approached him and knelt down to him. He didn't even look like he'd hit puberty yet. She introduced herself and helped the boy out for the next few days while she was in that town. He was only fifteen and she was sixteen so when it came time for her mother to move on to the next boyfriend she gathered her things to leave. But Hope didn't want to go, so she ended up staying with Alexander.

As the years passed on she began becoming more unstable. Without her mother around she didn't have a role model and just did as she pleased. She made Alexander an accessory because of his rank and she abused that, she abused him. Once he had enough and quit to become a smuggler she tried reporting him but it didn't work and she ran off but didn't leave without causing trouble. Shed do anything to get in his way.

After she had her fun with toying with Alexander she followed in her mother's footsteps in a way. She did what she had to and became a traveling courtesan. Mainly for upper class gold mushrooms until one day she met Raymond. She saw him as a quick way to money and she seduced him, drawing him in with her looks. From then on she eloped him and now they're stuck like glue.